"Needed to talk to y... warehouse where I kee... of old projects and mothballed experiments."

"Go on," I managed to say. All I could think was *I would kill to get a look inside that warehouse.*

"Thought no one knew about it, but there was a break-in the other day. They took something."

"What did they take?" I asked.

"Prototype of the Codex."

"Prototype of the . . . wait, the *Redwood* Codex?"

"What's the Redwood Codex?" Summer asked.

"Part of the biological egg-printer," I told her, then asked Redwood, "Do you know who stole it?"

"I have my suspicions."

"Who?" I asked, but at that moment, I had a feeling I knew. "Oh, no."

"Yes. My old partner."

Robert Greaves. Former CEO, dog killer, and all-around asshole.

"Aw, what the hell? What is he planning for it?"

"Not sure, but I'll say this," Redwood said. "It's nothing good."

BAEN BOOKS
by DAN KOBOLDT

THE BUILD-A-DRAGON SEQUENCE
Domesticating Dragons
Deploying Dragons

DEPLOYING DRAGONS

DAN KOBOLDT

BAEN

DEPLOYING DRAGONS

A Baen Books Original

Baen Publishing Enterprises
P.O. Box 1403
Riverdale, NY 10471
www.baen.com

ISBN: 978-1-9821-9292-1

Cover art by Dave Seeley

First printing, September 2022
First mass market printing, September 2023

Distributed by Simon & Schuster
1230 Avenue of the Americas
New York, NY 10020

Library of Congress Control Number: 2022938976

Printed in the United States of America

10 9 8 7 6 5 4 3 2 1

DEPLOYING DRAGONS

CHAPTER ONE
The Missing

My first day back at Build-A-Dragon should have been a triumphant return.

Part of me wondered if it was a dream. Six weeks had passed since I'd left this building for the last time. My ID badge still worked to get me into the parking garage; I supposed that was something. Forget the grand return; if I'd had to park my Tesla in the guest lot I wasn't going in. Simple as that.

Going back felt weird. I'd gotten in earlier than usual— on purpose, because I didn't want to deal with any uncomfortable encounters—so I met no one as I walked into the sleek steel-and-glass building and took an elevator to the seventh floor. Design and Hatchery. On impulse, I took the shortcut through the hatchery proper, expecting that the cost might be dodging the ever-present egg carts and white-garbed workers. But no one was in there, and all but one of the hatching pods were empty. The sole occupant of the only active pod was a large egg with beige and black tones. Judging by the shape and size it was a Rover model. I wondered how many we'd keep selling of those now that dogs were coming back. I moved on, tugging open the pressure-heavy door to the design lab.

Anyone who walked into this part of the building couldn't help but notice the God Machine—the biological printer that produced viable dragon eggs was the only one of its kind. It was also massive. Minivan-sized, you might call it. The robotic arms hung still in the cool air of the lab, which wasn't all that unusual. Eggs printed quickly, and judging by the state of the hatchery, business had slowed. But I found no one sitting in the cubicle-workstations that were arrayed like honeycombs around the bio printer. The whole design lab was empty. Not a worker or a projection monitor in sight.

Something's wrong.

A strange masochistic part of me speculated that they were all hiding somewhere, waiting for me like it was a surprise party. That would have been awkward enough, but at least it would have offered some explanation for the ghost town feel. I probably needed to go find Evelyn to learn what the hell was going on, but I couldn't resist the urge to sit down at my old workstation. It was strange how familiar it all was—the softness of my chair cushion, the cool metallic surface of the desk, and the faint metallic smell from the warm air rushing out from the computer servers that surrounded the God Machine. They were called Switchblades, and a photo of them in a magazine years ago was what had brought me to this place. Raw computing power was a valuable commodity in genetic engineering. The human genome alone had more than three billion base pairs. The dragon genome wasn't that large, but it was far more exotic. Lizards and amphibians and all manner of creatures had contributed DNA sequences to it. The thought of being able to engineer dragons again brought a thrill to my stomach.

A new sound intruded over the steady hum of the machinery, a staccato of heeled shoes clacking on the tile floors. The frenetic energy of those footsteps made me smile.

Evelyn Chang entered every room like she was running late for a meeting. Which she probably was. She was a head shorter than me, petite but not frail. She looked younger than her thirty-nine years. She also wore a new power suit that fit her perfectly. As long as I'd known her, she'd found a way to exude an intimidating air of extreme competence. But she looked at me and smiled, and I found myself smiling back.

"Noah Parker," she said.

"Evelyn Chang."

"It's good to see you."

"It's good to be here." I cleared my throat and glanced around. "Where is everyone?"

"I didn't want to overwhelm you on your first day."

That's why it's a ghost town. I relaxed a little. "I can handle it, I promise."

"We have a lot to talk about."

"I know." I waved it off with a casual air. The tension was still draining away. Then I looked at her and saw how she'd pressed her lips together. Evelyn pressed her lips together in a certain way. I knew that look. "What is it?"

"When I announced that you would be promoted to

my old position, not everyone was pleased to hear the news," she said, seeming to choose her words carefully.

"Who was displeased?"

"O'Connell felt that he should be the new triple-D."

Director of Dragon Design, she meant. It was the coveted title here, and the one she'd dangled in front of me to get me to come back. I nodded, hardly surprised. Brian O'Connell had been the senior designer when I joined the design department. He was a brilliant programmer and had written the code for our biological printer. Sometimes I think the design work chafed at him, though. He wasn't happy that Wong and I cracked domestication together. Nor did he like it when I was tasked to design a replacement for his flying model, the Pterodactyl. Or Terrible-dactyl, as some had taken to calling it. O'Connell never gave me the time of day after that. I think he took it as a personal affront. "He was here the longest," I said. "You didn't want him for the role?"

"Brian is an excellent programmer," she said.

But not a leader, was the unspoken end of that sentence. "I hope you made the right call."

"You are the right choice, Noah Parker. I have no doubts."

I tried to counter the flood of pride by reminding myself that hiring back the corporate whistleblower had plenty of PR advantages, too. "Sorry it cost you a good designer."

"*Two* good designers."

"The Frogman quit, too?"

"He told me 'I go if he goes.'" She shrugged. "So he went."

Damn. I bit my lip. It shouldn't have surprised me, because O'Connell and the Frogman were tight. Even so, it grated just a little. And with the Frogman, we lost a lot of serious design expertise. He had a background in developmental genetics—in other words, how organisms developed before birth—and that knowledge had proven incredibly useful in designing some of our early models. "What about Korrapati?"

"She's taking some time off, given the recent events."

"I see." That was a bit disconcerting, but it didn't sound permanent. "Well, where's Wong?"

Andrew Wong worked in the cubicle next to mine, and he'd been my closest work friend when I'd been here before. He was a great sounding board, too. More than once, I'd thought about consulting him on what to do to prove my brother's mutation caused his disease—a necessary step to get him into gene therapy trials—but I hadn't wanted to put him at risk. He'd come here on a work visa that required a corporate sponsor. No one worked harder than he did.

"Wong is back in China," Evelyn said.

"Oh, hell." Until that moment, I hadn't realized how much I was looking forward to seeing the guy and his crooked grin. "Voluntarily?"

"He went home to visit family. His sister was getting married."

I exhaled. "You had me worried." The way she'd said *back in China* had made it sound like a more permanent thing. And something in her face made me concerned. "When does he get back?"

"We are not sure."

Uh-oh. This was starting to sound more like one of those immigration horror stories. It actually surprised me that he'd taken the chance to go back. He really wanted to stay in the U.S. as long as he could. "Is his family okay?"

"Yes, they are well. But he was not allowed to book a return flight."

I opened my mouth to say that we *needed* Wong, and demand to know what she was doing about it. That's what the old hotheaded Noah Parker might do. But I was the Director of Dragon Design now, so I should start acting like a leader. I forced myself to take a calming breath. "I would like to help however I can."

That was the last thing Evelyn expected me to say, based on the flicker of surprise that crossed her face. "That is very kind of you."

"So, what, did he have a problem renewing his visa?"

"His US visa is fine according to our contacts at the State Department."

"But you said he might not be allowed to come here."

"Correct."

I shook my head. "I'm confused."

"The US is not preventing Wong from coming here," Evelyn said. "China is preventing him from leaving."

"They can do that?"

"Yes."

"But *why* would they do that?"

She shrugged. "Any number of reasons. If he or any of his relatives were political dissidents, or involved in criminal activities, or criticized the government in public."

"You don't think that's it, though, do you?" I asked.

"No. I think it's not about Wong directly."

I felt like she was making me extract every bit of information by force, and I had to push down a wave of irritation. When she did this it was because she wanted to test me, or at the very least to teach me something important. *So what is the undercurrent here?* Wong was a really good guy, and he'd left his former laboratory in Shenzhen on good terms. And here Evelyn was saying she thought it wasn't about him at all.

"They want something," I said.

"Yes."

"Do we know what that is?"

"Not yet, but I have a call scheduled with them tonight."

"Would you like me on it?"

She pursed her lips, and I could tell she was playing out some kind of mental chess match in her head. "Yes, if you don't mind. I think your participation might throw them off a bit."

"Will they speak English?"

"If we ask them to."

"Good." First day back and I was already in over my head, but I knew in my bones that whatever we were going to do, we needed Wong.

CHAPTER TWO
The Negotiation

Evelyn had set the call for five P.M., the end of our workday and the start of China's. It was also *the next day* in Beijing, but I tried not to think about that. The globalization of time across the planet was a weird thing. It was hard to imagine how Wong could make trips back and forth while adjusting to the time difference.

I'd spent the day resurrecting my permissions on Build-A-Dragon's servers and clearing out the design queue. When I'd left the company, we had orders popping into the custom queue constantly. It signaled that the mainline models were selling well; only a fraction of our customers ponied up the extra expense for customization. Still, I liked the challenge of it, of taking a customer's often-ridiculous request and finding a way to make it work. Other than designing the occasional prototype, it was my only chance to do real engineering.

Fifteen minutes before the call, I forced myself to log out. By impulse, my feet took me to Evelyn's office down the hall from the design lab. It was empty inside except for the desk and chair; Evelyn must have already claimed the CEO's office upstairs. The nameplate outside had changed, too. Now it read NOAH PARKER, PHD on a framed placard with my title.

DIRECTOR OF DRAGON DESIGN.

Six months ago, this was a coveted position in biotech. Now it meant leader of a team of effectively one. The office was still nice, at least. I took the chair and savored the way the leather enveloped me. Not to diminish the chairs in our design lab, but they simply didn't compare. Something about the material. It had the same texture of the driver's seat in my Tesla, which made it Nappa leather. Pure luxury. Well, I wouldn't keep it long if I didn't start rebuilding the team. With that grim thought, I headed to the elevator.

The C-suite of the Build-A-Dragon Company naturally occupied the top floor of the company headquarters. I'd attended a few meetings in the executive boardroom but had never seen the CEO's office. Entering it was like storming a castle. First there were the outer doors, then a sort of antechamber with a small desk. If Greaves had had a secretary, he or she was no longer employed here. I skirted the desk and entered the inner sanctum, a spacious corner office that made mine look like a janitor's closet. Evelyn wasn't there, but she'd probably run in thirty seconds before the call. I admired her office while I waited.

The outer walls were glass floor-to-ceiling and offered a spectacular view of downtown Phoenix. The only thing that obscured them were Evelyn's plants—all carnivorous species—which seemed to be thriving in their sunny new home. I had a theory that each one represented some milestone she'd achieved in her career. I was curious to take inventory.

Sure enough, there was a new addition: a handsome ceramic pot decorated with Mandarin calligraphy—which I couldn't read—that held six or eight slender shoots, each one shaped like a chunky golf club. *Cobra lilies*. A fitting choice for her ascent to CEO of Build-A-Dragon. They even looked a little like dragon heads.

Evelyn hurried in juggling her tablet and a bunch of papers and saw me inspecting them. "What do you think?"

"About the office, the view, or the cobra lilies?"

She laughed. "All three."

"Nice, very nice, and I thought they were illegal."

"Buying and selling cobra lilies is illegal. Owning them is not."

That was a convenient loophole if I'd ever heard one. "Possession is nine-tenths of the law," I said.

"So it is."

"Speaking of which, what's our plan to repossess Wong?"

"There are two steps," she said. "First, we find out what they want, and second, we figure out a way to give it to them."

"What if they want something we don't have?" I knew Evelyn had contacts with the U.S. government, but if China wanted a prisoner released or something, that was beyond even her power.

"Let's hope it does not come to that."

"So, what do you want me to do? Sit here, stay quiet, try not to insult anyone?"

"I've been thinking about this, and I wonder if you should do the opposite."

"Really?"

"They are not expecting you on the call, so we will introduce you as Wong's immediate supervisor. Feel free to unleash your inner..." She trailed off.

"Ignorant white man?" I offered.

"Your words, not mine."

"Well, then." I grinned. "I can do that."

"I knew I could count on you." She was already opening a new projection monitor in midair to initiate the call.

The window didn't expand the way I expected for a video feed. It remained wide and narrow; even though I couldn't see what Evelyn could on her side, I knew it was audio only. "No video?"

"They prefer it that way."

"Who are we speaking to, anyway?"

"Someone at the Chinese Ministry of Foreign Affairs."

The call connected a moment later. I recognized the greeting of whoever answered on the other end, but the Mandarin between them and Evelyn that followed was so fast that I didn't catch a word. It reminded me that I was a long way from speaking the language with any kind of proficiency. There was a pause, and Evelyn made a flicking gesture to put her microphone on mute.

"We're being connected to someone high up," she whispered. "A deputy minister."

"Is that unexpected?"

I pulled up my tablet and ran a quick search. There were two possible names. Both were surprisingly high in the organizational chart of the Chinese government.

A man's voice spoke to us. Evelyn replied, and I recognized an extremely polite request to speak English. *Thank God.*

"Of course," he said.

"Minister, I'm here with Dr. Noah Parker, who is Wong's immediate supervisor," she said.

"Hello, Dr. Parker."

I fought the instinct to reply with the correct Mandarin response to an introduction. I even knew the polite version. Instead, I cleared my throat and kept my tone neutral. "Nice to meet you."

"We are familiar with your work on biological simulation."

A deputy minister knows about my work. Somehow that was both flattering and terrifying. "Oh. Wow."

"And your brother's gene therapy, of course. What a story."

So that could easily be a compliment or a threat. Evelyn's face didn't clue me in to which it was, but I remembered her advice. "I'm happy to say that he's doing well, thank you."

"And Dr. Chang, of course, we have watched your career with great interest."

I smiled in private amusement at the unintentional *Star Wars* reference. *Or was it intentional?*

"You are too kind, Minister," Evelyn said.

"What you have done at the Build-A-Dragon Company

over the past year is truly remarkable," he said. "I have a personal interest in dragons, as do many Chinese."

Evelyn's eyes narrowed like a hawk that had spotted a mouse. "Yes. It is unfortunate that ordinary citizens can't buy them."

Oh, beautifully played. China had an import ban on our dragons, which was a bummer because the market was huge. This guy worked in the ministry that had implemented the import ban, just as they'd implemented Wong's exit ban.

"Well, we must be cautious about foreign technology," he said.

"Our dragons are infertile by design," Evelyn said. "We have numerous safety studies, which I'd be happy to share."

"Perhaps if we understood more about the underlying technology..." the minister said.

"The dragon genome is public domain," Evelyn said.

He paused. "It's my understanding that the genome itself is more of a blueprint. Going from that to a living organism is more challenging."

"Of course," Evelyn said.

I admired how she limited herself to those two words, which themselves could carry more than one meaning. Now the conversational ball was in his court.

"Our laboratories in Shenzhen have managed to perfect much, but not all of the process."

But not all of it, because you don't have Simon Redwood. The Redwood Codex was the heart of our biological printer and a closely guarded secret. Also a possible fire hazard, based on its appearance. But the ugly jumble of wires and circuits somehow rendered our dragon eggs viable. It was why our company had succeeded where so many other would-be purveyors of synthetic organisms failed.

"It's difficult work," Evelyn said.

"Perhaps there are insights that you could offer, in the spirit of international cooperation."

Oh, hell no. They wanted to duplicate our confidential processes to produce their own organisms. This was what they wanted, and it was exactly what I'd worried about. Something we were unable to give.

"Unfortunately, some of the process is proprietary."

"I see."

Now *he* was using two words, and again they could carry multiple meanings. At least one of which was *You're not getting Wong back*. Evelyn sighed, which told me this was going about as poorly as I thought it was. There was no way we'd give out trade secrets, no matter how much we wanted Wong back. Which sucked. So many of my plans for dragon designs relied on him, on his dauntless work ethic. That gave me an idea. I should probably have cleared it with Evelyn first, but that wasn't what an overconfident white man would do.

I leaned forward. "However, since you do have an interest, it would be our pleasure to send you one of our dragons as a gift."

Evelyn smiled at me, which I took to mean that I hadn't overstepped.

The minister paused. "To me personally?"

"In the spirit of international cooperation," I said.

He was silent a moment while Evelyn and I waited on tenterhooks. "What kind of dragon?"

"A custom model, so it would be one of a kind. I'd design it myself."

"Could it be . . . black and red?"

"We can do that."

"I would appreciate that very much," he said.

I pumped a fist. It would take a couple of weeks to print the egg and get it to Beijing, but this was something.

Evelyn gave me a thumbs-up. "Well, I'm certain we've already taken enough of your time, Minister."

They said goodbye and the call ended. Evelyn leaned back in her chair and exhaled heavily.

"Well, that was interesting," I said.

"Good idea on sending him a gift."

I spread out my hands. "Dragon diplomacy."

She laughed. "Our version of panda diplomacy."

"Do you think it will be enough to get Wong back?"

Her brow furrowed. "Let's hope so."

CHAPTER THREE
The Promise

As much as I wanted to tackle the Chinese dragon design, it was already well past quitting time by the time I got back to the design lab. Well, *my* quitting time at least. It was the busy season at Summer's architecture firm, so I wouldn't get to see her until the weekend. I climbed into the Tesla and enjoyed the fact that it, too, kept me ensconced in Nappa leather.

"Good evening, Noah Parker," said the car.

"Hello, beautiful." I took a deep breath. "Let's go to Mom's house."

I let the autopilot take over. As we circled our way to the exit of the parking garage, I noticed how many spots were empty. Granted, it was later in the day than I usually left, but the wide-open spaces reminded me of the hatchery with its mostly dark pods. Maybe people at Build-A-Dragon had lost some of their dedication to the work or lost their work period. Either was possible given the bad publicity and sales outlook. I shook my head, determined to avoid negative thoughts.

Despite the apparent lull at Build-A-Dragon, traffic getting out of Scottsdale lived up to its reputation. Thus, it was pushing dinnertime by the time I reached my mom's house. I expected to park in my usual spot out front between the mailbox and the neighbor's driveway. I still laid claim to that spot, at least in my mind, even though I'd moved out years ago. Unfortunately, it was occupied by the time I got there. By a black Tesla Model 3 that was so new it practically sparkled.

"You've got to be kidding me."

There were no other options, so I had to turn around and park across the street like a relative from out of town. I armed the highest security setting as soon as I closed my door.

"Security system armed," said the car.

"Damn right." I crossed the street to get a look at the rival Tesla that had dared take my spot. There was a custom Arizona plate on the back. C-WRTHY.

"Oh, *hell* no," I muttered.

Sure enough, the front door opened to reveal the grinning mug of my younger brother, Connor.

"N-capacitated," he said in greeting.

"C-cucumber." I jerked a thumb over my shoulder. "Someone parked in my spot."

He put on a furrowed brow, as if confused. "It's almost like you've been entirely replaced with a new version."

"Don't worry, I keyed it up pretty good."

His composure broke. "Oh, man, don't even joke. It's a lease!"

I groaned. "Thought you weren't allowed to drive."

"My doctor signed off last week." He gestured at his

legs, and then it hit me. He was *standing* there, without a walker or even a cane, for the first time in . . . I couldn't remember how long. The gene therapy was working. If his doctor had really signed off, it meant he'd retained his nerve sensory abilities. He moved back to let me in.

I marched past him, muttering "Let's go, C-worthy."

"You like that, huh?"

"I almost threw up in *my* Tesla."

We walked into the too-warm interior—Mom liked to keep the temperature a firm three degrees above ambient—and the nostalgia flooded over me. The rooms, the furniture, even the smell of roast beef and mashed potatoes wafting in from the kitchen. No matter how irritating my brother could be, the food here was worth it.

"Hi, sweetie!" Mom came around the kitchen island and hugged me.

"Hey, Mom." I tried unsuccessfully to avoid a kiss on the mouth. Her breath smelled only faintly of wine, which I took for a good thing. She'd prepared the "Parker Special" which was a nod to our Irish roots—peas alongside the beef and potatoes. We squeezed around the little square table that occupied most of Mom's kitchen space.

"How was it today?" Mom asked.

"A little strange," I admitted. I was half-tempted to tell them about losing virtually the entire design team. It wasn't my fault, not directly at least, but it felt vaguely embarrassing. I settled for a vague truth. "Lots of people are out right now."

Mom raised her eyebrows. "I imagine so."

"What does that mean?"

"Well, given what came to light about the company and its CEO—"

"*Ex*-CEO," I said.

"Yes. Well, it probably has some people reevaluating whether they want to work for the company. Or buy its products."

"They're crucifying you on social media," Connor said.

I groaned. I'd avoided social media as best I could and this was why. "How bad is it?"

His phone appeared in his hand like a magic trick. "Well, *bad company* is still trending."

"Bad company?"

"Capital B-A-D company."

Build-A-Dragon Company. "Yikes." I hadn't given much thought to the acronym. Neither had the marketing department, by my guess.

"There's another hashtag coming up, though," Connor said.

"Yeah?" A small part of me hoped it was something positive, like *buy dragons* or *dragons forever*.

"Yep, it's BoycottBAD." He grimaced. "Whoops. I just boosted it."

"Dude!"

He shrugged. "I don't work for the company."

"You're driving a Tesla because of the company," I shot back.

"No one is saying this is your fault, honey," Mom said.

"Um, good, because none of it is. Greaves is responsible, and now he's out."

"Which is a good thing. It's just . . ."

"What?" I demanded, and my tone was too rough. I

could tell from the way she blinked, and how Connor raised his eyebrows. I took a calming breath and softened my voice. "What is it?"

"Well, it's surprising you're going back to work there," Mom said.

"Evelyn needs me," I said.

"You don't owe her anything."

I almost said that I *did* owe her something, that she gave me just enough free rein to achieve my secret goal when I'd joined the company. Beyond that, she'd offered me her old job, which was still a desirable posting in the biotech field no matter what social media said. And beyond *that*, I couldn't deny that Build-A-Dragon exerted a strange gravitational pull on me. I'd felt hollow when I was gone, and more complete when I went back. But it was hard to put all those things into words. Harder still to do so in a way that wouldn't leave me open to criticism. So I settled for "It's complicated."

"Well, I'm sure it will all blow over soon," Mom said.

Somehow I doubted that, but I let it go. "Yeah."

"As long as you're still going to be there, I wanted to ask you about something," Connor said.

Mom frowned at him. "Connor, now is not the time to—"

"Why not?"

"He's only been back one day."

"He said he's staying," Connor said.

"I'm also right here, and I can hear you," I said dryly.

Mom threw up her hands. "Well, you might as well go ahead." She got up to refill her wineglass.

"We joined a group," Connor said.

"A cult?" I whispered.

"It's an online support group for BICD2 families."

BICD2 was the symbol for the gene that caused Connor's muscle disease. The full name was bicaudal D cargo adaptor 2, so named because it had been discovered in Drosophila melanogaster, better known as the fruit fly. That's how important the gene was. It was found in every species from human to fruit fly.

"Oh."

"We joined last year, when things . . . weren't going so well."

Well, now I feel like a jerk. I hadn't known that, and I felt mildly guilty that they hadn't told me. If anything, Connor and Mom had worked extra hard to hide his decline from me. But I guess they had their reasons. "Did it help?"

"Yeah, some." He shrugged. "My symptoms were progressing, but I was still on the milder end of the spectrum. For some families, it's only the parents who join."

Because the child doesn't survive. It happened sometimes, especially with the patients who were born with new and severe mutations. Hell, maybe that's what Connor was planning for. Without the gene therapy, it might have happened. And they hadn't told me.

"Anyway, they follow all of the latest research on the gene."

"Really?" I did, too, but I'd come up in academia.

"Oh, yeah. They're all over it."

Ordinary people reading the latest research. I shook my head in amazement. "I had no idea."

"So when they heard about my variant, and how you proved it was causal, there was a lot of excitement."

"Oh, come on. You're pulling my leg now."

"I'm dead serious."

Finally, someone had read my work. Finally, someone *cared*. I mean, other than Connor and Mom and his doctors. I hadn't experienced this feeling in a while, not since I published my graduate thesis. "That's awesome."

"The thing is, I'm not the only person who had a maybe-diagnosis due to a variant of uncertain significance."

A VUS. They were a real problem in the current genetic testing paradigm. It wasn't anyone's fault, not really. The medical genetics community set stringent guidelines on what was required to classify a new genetic variant as disease-causing. The problem was that new mutations were cropping up all the time. New variants by definition haven't been studied yet, so it was difficult to get them over the bar. Even if the symptoms fit the known disease perfectly. If your variant was classified as a VUS, as Connor's had been, you didn't qualify for most gene therapy trials.

"How many are there?" I asked.

"In our support group alone, there are dozens. Some of them have messaged me, asking if you can help."

"With dragons?"

"They're the only synthetic organism that's close enough to humans."

Wow, they really are *following the research.* "We got lucky with your results. Like, really lucky." The test dragons themselves, the Condors, had escaped into the desert. I'd thought that was the end of the whole experiment. Then they showed up, for one day only, and I got the sample I needed. I hadn't seen them since. Part of it still felt like a dream.

"I know, and I told them that. But they're desperate, and they don't all have brothers like you."

That might be the nicest thing Connor had said to me in recent memory. An obvious ploy, maybe, but he wasn't wrong. These families didn't have the privilege that we did. Still, it wasn't like I ran the company. Even if I did, functional testing of genetic variants for random patients wasn't exactly in the mission statement. "It's not the best timing."

"Hear that, Connor?" Mom interjected. "Not the best timing?"

"Nothing is ever perfect timing," Connor said. "That's life."

He's not wrong about that, either. "Are they local?"

He shook his head. "All over the world."

"Could you find out the variants they have?"

He chuckled. "We share everything. I could tell you their Social Security numbers."

"Well, send them to me. The variants, not the Social Security numbers."

"You think you can help out?"

"Don't promise them anything." I sighed. "But I'll see what I can do."

CHAPTER FOUR
The Imperial

I took possession of Evelyn's old office the next morning. It felt weird to work in silence and solitude, without the whir of the biological printer and without Wong to bounce ideas off of. But speaking of ideas, it wasn't idle talk when I told Evelyn I had ideas for new mainline production models. It would take some time until dogs made their full return to the world, and there were places where dragons held advantages. The key was to find the niches with unmet needs and then design the perfect dragons to fill them.

But first, I had an already-promised dragon design on my plate to tackle. Evelyn had even sent me some notes. She rarely gave me input on specific designs. That signaled how important it was for me to get this right. I'd been doing some of my own research, too, on the cultural significance of dragons in China. I didn't have the time or the language skills to go super deep, but there was still a ton of material out there. Chinese dragons were all over the place—on their flags, on their corporate logos, on thousand-year-old pottery.

I pulled up one of our flightless models as a starting point. Most Chinese dragons were wingless; the wings had long since fallen out of fashion. The body type was long and sinuous. Serpent-like. The legs were short, too, like a snake that had hit the brakes on its own evolution. Working out the body adjustments was arguably the easiest part of the design. Not the traits themselves— length and body mass were both complex traits involving multiple genes—but the sliders built in to our design program, DragonDraft3D. It was Evelyn's baby, just like the biological simulator was mine. I used them to stretch the dragon out. Kind of like shaping clay. I compared the resulting three-dimensional creature in the simulator against the reference images of the Chinese dragons until it matched.

It was hard to gauge how the thing should move, but I had feature points to spare because of the no-flying thing. The feature points meant I could give the dragon more fast-twitch muscle response. More agility. This thing would be able to move like a mongoose. That was good, because our client would probably want to show it off to everyone he knew. There were precious few of our dragons in China. Rumor had it that the first one we'd sold belonged to the imperial family.

Then it was on to coloring. We had a wide palette of colors to choose from, but fortunately Evelyn had notes on this, too. The guy had mentioned black and red for coloring. Of course, *red* is a wide range of actual hues, so it took a bit of further research to land on the shade she felt most appropriate. The rest of the design went quickly; I kept the default values for claws and teeth and tail length. We trusted those values; they'd been precisely honed via hundreds of angry customer support calls. I ran the final design one last time in my simulator. The three-dimensional image of the red Chinese dragon materialized over my desk and rotated slowly around. It was unlike any dragon I'd designed before.

"Very nice, Noah Parker," Evelyn said from my doorway.

"You think so?"

She scurried closer and gave it a thorough inspection. "Body type looks right. Good head shape. What about agility?"

I knew it. "Nimble as a cat."

"You found the correct red, too, it seems."

"Made me work for that on purpose, didn't you?"

She smiled. "I like to keep people on their toes."

"Mission accomplished. Do you want to look it over?" With a single keystroke I could send the whole design. She liked to poke around sometimes to see what I'd done. Especially if I was on probation or something.

But this time she shook her head. "I trust my best designer."

"Your only designer, you mean."

"Press the button before I change my mind."

I sent the print command and we both hurried into the design lab proper. The biological printer's metallic arms had already swung into action, their mechanical peals and whirs a staccato contrast to the steady hum of the Switchblade servers. The odd combination of sounds brought a rising thrill to my stomach. I exhaled slowly. "I missed that."

"Me, too."

"You do?"

"Of course." She pointed at my old workstation. "I used to sit right here."

"At my workstation," I said.

"*My* workstation," she said. "I moved out the week you started."

I hadn't known that, but somehow it didn't surprise me as much as it should have. "Best seat in the house. Good view of the God Machine, and right next to Wong."

We watched together as the printer finished its work and the egg slid out on the conveyor belt. It was long and slender, its surface a mottled whorl of red, white, and black. Dragon eggs were always unique, but this one gave off a different vibe. Almost a hidden suggestion of power and prestige.

"You did well," Evelyn said.

"When do you think Wong will magically be allowed to leave?"

"It's hard to say, but he can't get here soon enough. I think we may be busy soon."

I rubbed my hands together. "You and me both. I've been kicking around some ideas for new prototypes. They're niche markets, but I think they'll bring us some new customers."

"That's good, Noah, but we have some prep work to do first. There's a potential client coming in next week."

This sounded promising, though the edge in her voice carried a hint of trepidation. "Sure thing." I grinned and nudged her with my shoulder. "Who have you roped in now?"

"The U.S. military."

"I'm sorry," I said to Evelyn. "It almost sounded like you said the US military."

"I did say it. They may be our best chance at solvency."

"Is it really that bleak?"

"I wish it was not. Our Rover sales have not been this low since the early days of the company."

The Rover was our mainstay model, the primary revenue stream for the company. Granted, it was also the model we'd developed specifically to replace dogs. Now that canines were becoming available again, it seemed that a lot of people wanted furred pets instead of scaled ones. As a person who owned several scaled pets, I didn't entirely understand it. "Yikes."

"That is why we need new clients, Noah."

I sighed, knowing I was going to regret this. "Tell me about the military thing."

"Robert and I had some conversations with them when he was still in charge."

Yet another of Greaves's secret plans that no one knew about. Except Evelyn, apparently. "Why didn't it go anywhere?"

She shrugged. "Military acquisitions take a long time. And with business booming, we didn't have the capacity to produce dragons at the scale they wanted."

"But we do now," I said.

"Yes, that is part of it. Plus, they remain interested in our dragons."

"Even with dogs coming back?"

She sighed. "Unlike the rest of the world, yes."

Well, it was . . . something. The military had deep pockets; I knew that much. Still, it was a far cry from designing hunting companions and reptilian pets. *But it's still dragons.* I mustered an enthusiasm I didn't quite feel. "It sounds promising. Lots of interesting applications."

"More than you can imagine."

"What do you need from me?"

"Take a look at this." She handed me her tablet, which was open to a list of folders on our secure server. I opened one of them at random.

"I'm seeing a lot of documents." Judging by the thumbnail images, they were very text-heavy.

"This is the statement of work, courtesy of the Department of Defense."

I opened one of the documents at random. It was a full page of text, the first of fifty-four. "It's . . . very thorough."

"They're not shy about telling us what they want," Evelyn said.

"No, I guess not. Have you been through these?"

"Some of them, yes."

That meant she hadn't had time yet, which is why this was coming to me. It made sense; she had the entire company to run now. Still, I felt a twinge of disappointment. Here I was hoping to come back to some fanfare to Build-A-Dragon, leading a team of dragon designers in finding new creative ways to put more dragons out into the world. Instead I had a pile of reading material. And apparently no designers. "What's the timetable on this?"

"They are coming for a site visit next week."

"Why are they coming *here*?"

"They asked to see some of our operations."

"And you agreed?"

"The *board* agreed, on Robert's recommendation, several months ago."

I grimaced. It wasn't my place to second-guess the board, but there were reasons we didn't let outsiders help themselves to a tour of our operations. "Seems kind of risky."

She shrugged. "We're the sole supplier of dragon technology, but not of all technology. We have to make some concessions."

"We need them more than they need us, in other words."

"That's one way to put it. Besides, the visit will be an opportunity for us to clarify our questions about the statement of work."

"We have questions?"

She pointed at the tablet and the digital mountain of documents. "We should probably come up with some."

CHAPTER FIVE
The Judgment

I spent the rest of the week absolutely buried in dense military documents. The queue of custom orders remained frustratingly empty no matter how much I willed it to fill. I didn't shy away from a design challenge, but the scope of work was intimidating. In reading the documents, I wondered if they'd simply copied an existing SOW and replaced every instance of "drone" with "dragon." Because they sure as hell were asking a lot of living reptiles.

I'd never had my own office before. The privacy was nice—or would have been, if there were many people around—but it felt too quiet. The tiniest sounds intruded, whether it was the muted noise of traffic or the strange irregular clicking of the HVAC system. I ended up moving back to my old workstation near the God Machine. I wasn't sure why, but the server fans provided an ideal sort of white noise that let me concentrate.

When Connor sent the list of VUSes from his patient

friends, it was a welcome respite. There were dozens, just like he'd promised. He'd done a pretty good job of collecting the clinical data to go with them, too. I picked one at random and started reading.

Jacob, nine-year-old male. Unable to walk until age three. Parents first noticed he had trouble climbing stairs at age six. No upper-body weakness, but his gait is getting worse.

The boy's mutation caused a single amino acid change in BICD2 near the second mutation hotspot. It had never been reported in any other patients, nor had it been observed in healthy populations. His mother didn't have it, either. The father was "not involved" and thus wasn't tested. I shook my head, muttering to myself. All of this brought it close to pathogenic status, but not quite there. Yet the boy almost certainly had spinal muscular atrophy due to his BICD2 mutation. I remember when Connor was his age, how stairs used to give him trouble. *God, it's like living our childhood over again*. With a little functional evidence behind it, this variant could be classified correctly, too. No wonder they were reaching out to Connor.

It wasn't like I could slip the mutation into a prototype. The God Machine hung still and silent, except for the steady hum of the servers. All that computing power, still going to waste. I never expected that I'd return to this job looking forward to the weekend, but that's what came to pass. In my defense, I had a good reason to be excited. And it had absolutely nothing to do with dragons.

※ ※ ※

Summer and I had breakfast before our Saturday geocache. I made damn sure I was on time. This was her busy season and I'd just taken over design, so we'd been hard-pressed to see each other for the past couple of weeks. Honestly, it was driving me crazy. We kissed in the parking lot when she arrived. It was all I could think about while we walked inside and waited for a table. So much so that I tried again when we sat down.

"We're in public," she hissed, and gently but firmly pushed me back to my side of the booth.

"I missed you," I said.

"Really? I'd never have guessed." She smiled, though, and that was her way of saying that she felt the same.

"How's work going?" I asked.

"Brutal. Our client keeps pushing back on the things we need to do to meet our specs."

"What do they want?"

"The usual energy wasters—open floor plans, wide atriums, decorative water fountains."

"I like those things. What's wrong with them?"

"Nothing at all, if you hate the planet," she said.

Summer worked for the second-largest green engineering firm in Arizona. Her company had designed, among other things, the high-efficiency condo building where I lived. I probably should have waited a year or two because she'd bought in one of their new series of buildings and her place was way, way better. I had serious condo envy. I liked to think my car was better, but the Tesla Model S somehow failed to impress her as much as I felt it should.

"Did you set the client straight?"

"My boss did, but it was ugly. Now we have to design a bunch of other features to keep them happy."

"Ooh, that sucks. Can you at least bill by the hour?"

"I wish."

"Bummer." I stirred my coffee with my free hand, as my other one remained entwined with hers on the table. I didn't mind being one-handed for the moment. Or making a statement that we were here, and we were a thing. I was in a good mood. It was Saturday, we were together, and there was nothing that could stop us from defeating the forthcoming geocache.

"How was going back?" she asked.

"Pretty good," I said. "A little weird, maybe."

She gave me a look of mock sympathy. "Does everyone hate you now?"

"No one that didn't already."

"Ha! You're funny."

Now that she'd brought it up, I was starting to worry about the whole not-liking-me thing. "I got Evelyn's office. Her old one, I mean."

"Is it nice?"

"I guess." I shrugged. "I've never really had an office." *Or a real job, for that matter.*

"What about the Venus flytraps?"

"No, she took those when she moved upstairs." I sipped my coffee, savoring the rich flavor that breakfast diners have somehow perfected. "It's too quiet in there. I've been spending most of my time at my old workstation by the God Machine."

"You have to stop calling it that."

"Why?"

"It's blasphemy, for one thing. And your company doesn't need another PR disaster after killing all those dogs."

"Hey, *we* didn't kill the dogs. There was an epidemic, and our former CEO sort of . . . delayed the cure."

"On company property, using company resources."

I sighed. "Yeah, I know." It still bothered me, just as the idea of sending dragons to the desert facility bothered me. I'd been actively avoiding the various media stories about Build-A-Dragon, at least until the next corporate scandal took some of the heat off us. "Well, the good news is we have nowhere to go but up."

The server chose that moment to bring us our bill. "And here's your carryout." She plunked it down on the table between us. "*Sixteen* breakfast burritos." She eyed us both and walked away.

"Did she seem just a little bit judgey to you?" I whispered.

"*So* judgey," Summer said.

I paid the bill and we went outside to climb in Summer's Jeep, where the ravenous menagerie awaited us: a half dozen small dragonets and one large, questionably-domesticated pig. They tore into the breakfast burritos like a school of piranhas. The food was gone in a matter of seconds. The bag, too, and nearly my hand. Then the animals sprawled in a heap on the backseat for the ride out to the desert.

We'd begun taking these trips almost every Saturday, a different geocache each time. Summer and I were trying very hard to keep our positions on the local leaderboard for geocaches. We were currently tied for third place behind *Jojo* and *Prickly Pete*, two geocachers who almost always scored together. Another couple, probably. They'd come out of nowhere while Summer and I were busy dealing with the aftermath of the showdown at the desert facility. To say it fanned the flames of our competitive sides was a major understatement. We'd met while geocaching, and we were damn sure not going to let some other couple dethrone us without answer.

Besides, the animals needed the exercise. Spending five days cooped up in a tiny condo made them all a little stir-crazy. Even Riker, Summer's porcine companion, seemed to enjoy getting outdoors. Pigs had proven surprisingly decent replacements for dogs after the canine epidemic hit. They were loyal, low maintenance, and had a phenomenal sense of smell. Of course, they didn't stand up to dragons, but not many things did.

Summer got us to South Mountain Park five minutes faster than traffic levels should have made possible, at least according to my phone. It was a large reserve of mostly hilly desert country just west of Highway 10. The cache itself was only middling difficulty; you parked in the spacious paved parking lot at Pima County Trailhead and hiked up into the hills. Various trails and paths spiderwebbed off in different directions, so it was easy to get a bit of solitude. Which we very much needed while trying to keep some sense of control over the pig and dragonets. The sky was clear, and the weather no hotter than usual. It had all the makings of a good day.

Octavius took the lead, sweeping low across the hilltops. Because of his coloring, it was hard to pick him out from the browns and yellows of the desert terrain. I could only track him by watching for Benjy, the dragon I'd inherited from Build-A-Dragon's former chief of security. He followed Octavius everywhere, and his lighter coloring made him easier to spot. Emerald-green Titus and bright orange Hadrian also made useful dragon-markers. Nero and Otho were the smallest and their earth tones helped them blend with any landscape. I could never keep tabs on them, but they usually stuck close to their more visible kin.

That only left Marcus Aurelius, who was currently trying to ride on Riker's furry back. With mixed results at best. As I watched, he lost his grip and fell off for the third or fourth time, only to flap back into position. The pig was snuffling around some rocks and didn't seem to notice.

I laughed. "How long do you think Riker will put up with this?"

"Normally, not even this long," Summer said. "He must be in a good mood."

"For a pig," I muttered. Riker would never let *me* mess with him like that.

"What was that?"

"Nothing," I said quickly. *I shouldn't be jealous of a dragonet.*

She gave me a sharp look, but let it slide. "So, it was weird going back, huh?"

"In so many ways."

"What does everyone think about Evelyn taking over?"

"I don't really have anyone to ask. Wong's in China and Korrapati's still out on leave."

"So it's just you?"

"For the moment."

"How are you not, like, completely overwhelmed with design work?"

I shrugged. "Honestly, it's a little slow. Orders have kind of dropped off." I didn't tell her by how much. Saying it out loud would make it real.

"So, what have you been doing all week?"

"A lot of reading."

"You've been reading," she said flatly, in a tone that somehow reminded me she'd probably put in sixty hours at her architecture firm.

"We got a statement of work from a possible new client. It's . . . dense."

"Who's the new client?"

"I can't say yet. It's supposed to be confidential."

"Do I need to remind you how well it went the last time you thought you could keep a bunch of secrets?"

"You do not." I remembered all too well, especially what had almost happened to us in the desert. And what *had* happened. Still, my instincts screamed at me not to tell her. Not now, at least, when we didn't know if this DOD thing was for real.

"Well?" she prompted.

A commotion among the animals rescued me from answering. The dragons had converged to a single location and circled overhead, crooning. Riker had his snout jammed under a large flat rock, digging furiously. Three or four dragons circled overhead and chirped their excitement.

"I think that's a find," I said.

"Riker's find."

"We'll see." I marched ahead, taking care to avoid the cacti flanking the narrow path. Like most geocachers, the creator of this cache didn't want anyone stumbling on it by accident. Usually that required two elements: a good concealment container and an out-of-the-way spot. Preferably an actively uncomfortable place where only half-insane geocachers would go. Such as me. I pushed my way forward through a cloud of dragonets and found Riker proudly holding the geocache container in his mouth. It was a round metal tin about the size of my fist. No rust, so it was probably aluminum.

"Told you," Summer called.

"Yeah, yeah." Riker had an uncanny ability to sniff out metal. I took hold of the case and tried to tug it free, but the stupid pig refused to let go. He shook his head and growled. "Oh, come on!"

"He only answers to one master," Summer said.

I glanced back at her. "Would you mind—?" Riker gave the cache a sharp tug and nearly yanked my arm out of the socket. "Seriously!"

"Riker, *give*," Summer said.

The pig gave me one last shake and then unclamped from the cache container. If it hadn't been aircraft-grade aluminum, the thing would've been crushed.

I needed a moment to catch my breath. "You know, maybe it's time you got a dog."

She snorted. "You first."

We logged the find, swapped out some of the trinkets inside for pewter dragon figurines, and hid it again. Then it was a matter of rounding up the animals for the trek back out.

"So, are you going to tell me who the client is?" Summer asked.

I laughed, but it sounded nervous even to me. "I was kind of hoping you forgot about that."

"I didn't," she said.

"Well, it's not a sure thing," I said, buying time. I trusted, I just didn't want to tell her.

"Noah."

Oh, what the hell. I opened my mouth to tell her, then hesitated. This was a public space. There was no one nearby, but Summer had her phone in her armband and mine was in my pocket. In other words, there were plenty of ways I could be under some kind of surveillance. So I lowered my voice to a whisper. "The government."

"Whose?"

"Um, ours, of course."

"What do they want with you?" she asked.

"Guess."

"They're going to take you to Guantánamo Bay until your war crimes trial."

"No. They want dragons."

"I'm guessing they don't want them as pets," she said flatly.

Here it comes. I should have known how poorly this would go over. Summer had had reservations about my work from the start. "It could be a big contract for us."

She stopped in her tracks and stared at me. "You're kidding, right?"

"No. It's been in the works a while, apparently."

She shook her head and stalked past me to the parking lot. "I knew this was a bad idea."

CHAPTER SIX
The Return

The rest of the weekend kind of sucked. We argued about the DOD thing through dinner. I spent the night at her condo, but things remained tense. Naturally, Summer hated everything about the idea of designing dragons for the military. I broke down and told her about the empty hatchery pods and design queues. It placated her a little, but not fully. We ended up in a too-quiet kind of truce on Sunday. Then it was back to my place and back to the grind. After an emotionally draining weekend, I was almost relieved.

I hadn't been gone from Build-A-Dragon very long, but it felt like a completely different place. Part of that was the fact that I sat in what was once Evelyn's office. It still felt weird to work in silence and solitude without Wong to bounce ideas off of. I still had ideas, of course, and I figured I'd put them to use before the SOW melted my brain. It would take some time until dogs made their full return to the world, and there were places where dragons held advantages. The key was to find the niches with unmet needs and then design the perfect dragons to fill them.

My first idea was an emotional support dragon. The concept of support animals had been exploited and then vilified by certain segments of society, but the fundamental principle remained sound: people who had been through trauma saw better mental health outcomes with a support animal.

I pulled up the Rover design to use as a starting point. If I ran it through the behavioral module of my biological simulator—my own claim to fame around here—it scored middling on most traits, but fairly low on aggression. Back in the day, we'd used the aggression score as a bellwether for domestication. The Rover still wasn't completely docile; its aggression score hovered somewhere in the low forties. We'd figured that was only fair; even a family pet might be expected to respond to something threatening its owners.

Not so for a support animal. They weren't pets; they didn't need to worry about anything but the needs of their sole owner. So I got into the neural pathways and tamped down aggression even more. While I was in there, I boosted the baseline for serotonin expression and reception. This was a bit hazardous since that particular neurotransmitter rewarded evolutionarily reinforced behaviors that tended to increase survival. Then, again, this animal would eat when its owner did and probably wouldn't have much of a sex life. The serotonin tweaks meant it could focus all of its attention on doing its job.

An odd noise from the hallway broke my concentration. It sounded like a fan that was missing a ball bearing.

Regular, but not quite. No, it wasn't a fan. I knew that sound.

I leaned back from my monitors and smiled as Wong rolled into view. The guy had just flown seven thousand miles from China, driven thirty miles from the airport, and then boarded his urban scooter for the short walk to my office. The guy hadn't changed but it was damn good to see him.

"*Hǎo jiǔ bú jiàn,*" I said. It was the Mandarin equivalent to *Long time, no see.* "*Nihao, ma?*"

"Noah Parker." He gave me his trademark crooked grin, but his eyes were inscrutable. "Or maybe I call you *lao-bahn?*"

"Oh my God, don't call me that. Evelyn is still the *lao-bahn.*"

"If you say so."

"I didn't expect we'd see you for another week. Maybe more." The egg for the imperial dragon hadn't even shipped out yet. *Was that whole thing a farce?*

"Exit ban lifted on Friday."

"Ah." So he'd known about that much, and then wasted no time hopping on a plane as soon as he was permitted. I gestured to the chairs in front of my desk. "How is your family?"

He left his scooter leaning against the doorframe, shuffled to a chair, and sat down. Somehow he made even the awkward guest chairs in here seem comfortable. "Very good, very good. No complaints."

I smiled to myself. He'd been held hostage by his own country as leverage against his employer, unsure if he'd ever be permitted to come back, and everything was still *very good*. I wondered how much he knew about what had happened. "Well, I'm glad you made it back."

"Me, too." He made a big show of looking around. "Nice office."

"Yeah, yeah. It feels as uncomfortable as it looks. How was business here while I was gone?"

His smile faded. "Slow. Too much time, not enough custom jobs." His eyes slid to my open design screen. "Unless it picked up?"

"I wish. This is just an idea I came up with for a niche model."

"What kind?"

"Emotional support dragon."

He raised his eyebrows. "Good idea. Find the right market, maybe sell ten thousand."

"Or more." I gestured at the half-finished design. "I think I have the neural circuitry stuff worked out. It's a Rover base, but I haven't touched the physical features yet."

He nodded. "You send it to me, I work on it."

I hesitated. If I sent him the prototype to finish, that meant I had to return to the drudgery of planning for the DOD visit. "You don't have to—"

He shook his head, already on his feet and moving to reclaim his scooter. "Send it."

I sighed. "All right."

He rolled off. In spite of losing the bit of design work to him, I had to admit it was good to see him back. Great, really. Our capacity for dragon design had just tripled because the guy was a true workaholic.

Now all we needed was some actual work.

% % %

I went up to see Evelyn at around ten, only to find her office empty. *Oh, right, the board meeting.* It was a fixture on Monday mornings. It occurred to me that when she'd asked me to come back, she'd implied that I would get a seat in those board meetings. She'd attended as the triple-D, so why shouldn't I? Part of me coming back was the notion that I'd help steer the company ship, so to speak. Instead it seemed like she intended to keep me in design. To churn out the work and probably not ask too many questions. It worried me that she hadn't invited me. No, it *irked* me.

I lingered outside her office and had nearly worked my anger up from simmer to boil when Evelyn hurried into view. The pained expression on her face knocked the wind right out of my bellows. "Hi, boss. What's wrong?"

"Noah." She shook her head and beckoned me to follow her. The office lights came up from dim, and her projection monitors flickered back into existence. All nine of them. That meant a heavy workload even for her. "The board is pushing very hard for us to secure a contract with the DOD."

I had an immediate and somewhat visceral reaction to the board trying to tell us what to do. *Maybe this is why she doesn't invite me.* "What for?"

"They take a dim view of our future market potential now that dogs are returning."

"It's not like everyone hates dragons all of a sudden," I said, aware of how defensive I sounded. "There will be plenty of niche markets."

"Niche markets have limited long-term revenue."

"But they can be more numerous," I said.

"They require more designer resources, which is something we don't currently have."

That was a fair point, even if it stung a little. "Well, there's good news on that front. Wong is back."

She broke into a smile. "He made it? That's very good."

I chuckled. "That's what he said."

"Knowing Wong, he came straight from the airport."

"I know, right? And great news, his little scooter seems to have made it back, too."

"He keeps it in the lab."

"Come on, you're kidding," I said.

"Right under his workstation."

I believed her, if only because he had so much crap in his workstation he could have hidden three scooters in there. "He's consistent, I'll give him that. I'm surprised we got him back so soon."

Evelyn's face went stony, so it was all but impossible to tell what she thought. Which told me she didn't want me guessing. That in itself said something. "Good luck for us."

"I thought you didn't believe in luck?"

"I believe in not asking too many questions when it comes our way," she said, with a hint of firmness to her tone.

"Understood. Now, let's talk about Korrapati."

"What about her?"

"She's on a leave of absence, right? Let's get her to come back."

"Not so fast, Noah. We need to focus on the DOD visit."

I rubbed my eyes, which suddenly carried the ache of having read all those dense government documents. "Right. Focus on the visit."

"What are you thinking for the presentation?"

"Well, we have half an hour, right?" The appointment had appeared on my calendar with the vague description of "Client meeting." One hour, in our conference room.

"Just about. Less if they have questions, which they probably will."

"How many people are coming?"

"Three or four principals, I'm told. All officers from the acquisition corps," she said.

"Do we have any idea of their level of expertise?"

"They'll be experienced at acquisitions, which is what they do. As for systems biology and genetic engineering, I don't think we can make any assumptions."

"General audience. I can handle that."

"I think it would be helpful for them to see some prototypes in your simulator. You've worked them up, right?"

Oh, shit. "I've only been tinkering. They're not production-ready or anything."

"Polish them up. Get Wong to help."

"All right." I stifled a sigh. It was going to be a long day. "We'd better get cracking." I began making my retreat out of her office.

"Noah."

I paused and looked back at her. She hesitated, and then pressed something on her desk. The hermetic seal on her doorway—instant soundproofing—made a distinct whoosh behind me.

"I want to emphasize how important this meeting is," she said.

"I know it's imp—" I began to protest, but she held up a hand.

"The board of directors represents our investors, and to them, we're a certain kind of asset at the moment. High equity, but with an uncertain revenue potential."

These were all economics terms, and even though *I* was technically a shareholder in the company as well, I still didn't grasp what she was trying to tell me. "Speak plainly, please. I'm not an economist."

"If it looks like we won't be able to generate revenue, the board may want to close us down and sell off the pieces."

A chill ran down my back. I understood what *sell off the pieces* meant. Wong was one of those pieces. So was the God Machine, the only thing that could print dragon eggs. "Can they do that?"

"If it gets serious enough, they can. However, if we secure other promising sources of revenue, it's unlikely." She put on a smile that looked forced. "So let's put our best foot forward, okay?"

"Yeah, sure," I answered. *No pressure.*

CHAPTER SEVEN
The Clients

Our meeting with the DOD was at nine A.M. the following morning. Evelyn had invited them early for coffee up in her office, which gave me enough time to get in and slug down a latte myself. Then I went to the conference room. The moment I walked in, I thought I'd gone into the wrong meeting. There stood two men and a woman, all of them in crisp uniforms of the United States armed forces. Army, Navy, and Air Force, if I had to guess. I'll be totally honest—I *would* have to guess. The military was an area where sadly I had little firsthand knowledge. Even so, there were things to glean. They all stood in front of their chairs, exhibiting excellent posture but somehow exuding a sense of comfort. Came with the territory, I supposed.

"Here he is now," Evelyn said. "Noah Parker is our Director of Design."

"Pleased to meet you," I said, almost by instinct.

Evelyn gestured to the bureaucratic-looking white guy in the dark blue uniform. "This is Lieutenant Commander

McGregor." She swept her arm to include the others. "These are Majors Johnson and Nakamura." The first was a black guy who could have been an ex-quarterback. Major Nakamura was an Asian woman who, despite being a head shorter than Johnson and a third of his size, somehow came off more intimidating.

The shock of encountering three officers in uniform hadn't quite worn off. I remembered myself enough to shake their hands and look them in the eye while doing so. McGregor had a normal handshake. Major Nakamura's was cold and hard. Johnson's hand wrapped around mine like I was a small child.

"Would you like coffee or anything else to drink?" Evelyn asked them.

They all took coffee from the silver carafe that waited. McGregor poured for the other two and took cream and sugar. Johnson took milk, and Nakamura drank it black. Hard core. They found chairs and sat without ceremony. I did the same and felt terribly awkward, but at least relieved that I'd chugged my own coffee before this.

"Thank you for coming all this way," Evelyn said.

"Part of the job," McGregor said. The others sat sipping their coffee. Clearly they expected us to run this meeting. Which I supposed made sense; they were the clients with deep pockets. We were just another technology firm hoping to supply them.

"We have been reading the statement of work," Evelyn said.

"What do you think of the specs?" McGregor asked.

Evelyn smiled at me. "Noah has been working on some prototype designs."

Noah and Wong worked until nine last night, I wanted
to say. Instead, I picked up my tablet—which was hot-
linked to my workstation and already had its display
synched with the conference room projectors. "We'll
develop at least three designs to meet your requirements.
This is the infantry model."

I'd designed it by starting with the Guardian, the
original hog-hunting reptile on which our company was
founded. I'd disabled the points system—this was only a
demo, after all—and enhanced all the features: claws,
teeth, musculature, everything. The Guardian had looked
fierce in a feral sort of way. This model, when it bloomed
into three-dimensional existence above the conference
table, resembled the dragon version of a Rottweiler. It had
a solid stance and broad shoulders balanced by a muscular
tail. Rotating slowly above the table, it looked damn
intimidating. I issued another command and the thing
began running. It moved like a lizard—sinuous, with the
head and tail moving back and forth in hypnotic rhythm—
but with the husky frame and bristling claws, it was
intimidating. And *fast*. All three of the officers were
watching.

Since I'd piqued their interest, I flipped to the aquatic
model. "This is the prototype for the marine reptile. It
won't be quite as fast on land, but it'll make up for that in
wet environments." The body reflected that—it was more
streamlined, and I'd reduced the size of the claws in favor
of webbed feet. It had a low center of gravity, too, which
would give it an advantage on both shorelines and open
water.

Reading the officers' reactions to this dragon was

harder. Nakamura said something quietly to Johnson, but neither of them offered comment to the room.

"Let's see the third design, Noah," Evelyn said.

This was a bit of planned theater on our part. We'd saved the flying model for last. Given the time crunch and the importance of wowing them, I'd gotten Evelyn's permission to revive the Condor model that had nearly gotten me fired under her predecessor. Only half a dozen of them had ever been printed, but they'd flown better than any dragon we'd designed. In my opinion, anyway.

"This is our flying model," I said, bringing the modified Condor design up in my simulator. It had a lower mass than the infantry model but the huge wingspan made an impression. Since there was no point system to worry about, I pulled out all the stops to make the prototype strong and nimble, with an extremely high metabolism. That also meant a high calorie intake, but I figured that was the military's problem, not mine. I told the simulator to show it in flight. The visual was pretty close—each movement based on a realistic simulation of the muscle movement—but nothing did justice to what my Condors could do in the air.

"Impressive," said Johnson.

"And you think these models will meet all of the requirements?" Nakamura asked.

"These are theoretical designs, but yes, I think they should be feasible," Evelyn said.

The change in demeanor was palpable. Suddenly they were frowning at us, and I felt like a kid who'd brought home a bad report card.

"With all due respect," McGregor said, "we don't need the theoretical on the battlefield."

"Hence the statement of work," Nakamura added.

"The dragons will be real enough," Evelyn said. "Drones and other technologies have their uses, I'm sure, but they're expensive. They break down. Our dragons are genetically engineered to be healthy, low-maintenance assets."

McGregor perked up a little. "Do you think it would be feasible to use the same dragon for multiple applications in the field?"

"Absolutely," I said. "A lot of our current dragons are multiuse. I've designed customs that were family pets, hunting companions, and security dragons all in one."

Evelyn jumped back in. "Take this flying model, for example. It's nimble but it has endurance, too. The same dragon can be trained to do recon, base security, aerial surveillance . . . whatever you need."

I hid my smile. With five minutes of prep time, Evelyn could talk to anyone about anything. Despite their stony appearance, the officers were nodding along.

"What about specialized applications?" Nakamura asked quietly.

Something about the way she said *specialized* held extra meaning, but I didn't know what it was.

"That's why I brought our director of dragon design," Evelyn said.

All three officers' gazes swiveled from Evelyn to me.

"What kind of specialized are we talking about?" I asked.

"Weapons," Nakamura said.

Dragons with weapons? Now there was a question I hadn't counted on. "Some of our dragons can operate basic tools, but it would have to be pretty simple weaponry," I said.

"That's not exactly what they have in mind, Noah," Evelyn said.

It dawned on me then. Dragons would *be* the weapons. "Oh, right. Of course." *I'm such a moron.*

"There is precedent," Evelyn said, and she gave me a guarded look, as if not sure how I'd take this. "Some of our custom models may be close to what you need."

She means the attack dragons. In spite of our huggable-family-pet messaging, customized attack dragons had become one of the more popular custom jobs. I'd designed many myself because they were often the most challenging orders. And sometimes I'd done a little too well. One of mine had slaughtered someone's pink-and-white pet dragon moments after they both hatched. Right in front of a little girl on her birthday, too.

But the other incident, the one that haunted me, was shortly after we'd found the dogs. Ben Fulton, Build-A-Dragon's head of security, had caught me and Summer at the desert facility that day. When Redwood and the dragons came to our rescue, there were attack models with them. Summer and I had had Octavius to vouch for us, thank God. Fulton had left his little dragon at home.

There had been so much blood. I shuddered just remembering it. "Dragons are natural predators."

McGregor was unimpressed. "It seems unlikely that something made for civilians would push the envelope enough."

"You'd be surprised," Evelyn said.

I smiled, because I'd had the same thought. "Some of our most clever designs are in response to the customization requests we've gotten from customers. Everyone wants something different."

"You got any examples?" McGregor asked.

"One customer wanted a dragon that had rainbow fur instead of scales," I said. "Because of the way the ectoderm develops, we had to make it a genetic mosaic. Seven different dragons in one. Another customer needed a dragon to guard livestock, and so we altered its metabolism to give it a vegetarian diet." Even as I shared these, I realized that they probably didn't offer the best examples to clients who wanted killing machines, but the science was still sound. Hopefully I wouldn't completely underwhelm.

"You can do that?" McGregor asked.

"Absolutely. We're tweaking the metabolism all the time."

McGregor gave me the nod, and looked to Major Johnson.

"Let's talk about implementation," Johnson said.

"What do you want to know?" Evelyn smiled, while I took the first full breath in what seemed like a while. She'd promised to handle the prep for this part. I was rather curious to hear what she had to say.

"Will these dragons follow orders?"

I nearly barked a laugh, but the guy was serious. Then I thought of Octavius and his sometimes-stubborn siblings, and felt immensely relieved I wasn't on the hook to answer *this* question.

"As well as any domesticated animal," Evelyn answered. "They're intelligent creatures and extremely trainable."

"What does that involve?" Johnson asked.

"It's a similar program to what's been developed for canines and other service animals. Obedience training as a foundation, and then layering on special skills as they develop."

"Who trains the dragons?"

"Your people," Evelyn said.

"All right. Who trains our people?"

"Our dragon wranglers."

Johnson cracked a smile. "Dragon wranglers, eh? Can't say I've heard of them."

"No one knows more about reptilian behavior. Especially the head of their division, Tom Johnson."

"The reptile guy? You're kidding."

"I spoke to Tom yesterday, and he's agreed to personally oversee the training program."

I might have uttered a soft gasp at that. Tom Johnson was part animal tamer, part television star, and part legend. He also cared deeply for dragons and other living creatures. Getting him to oversee the training was a major coup. God only knew what Evelyn had to promise him. Probably that he could hunt me for sport or something.

Now Johnson gave us the nod, and all eyes went to Nakamura.

"What you're proposing to do has promise," she said. "But for me to take this to my boss, I'll need something more tangible."

"I'm sure we could produce prototypes to accompany our proposal," Evelyn said. "To show that we can do it."

"A live demonstration would go a long way," Nakamura said.

"We have a facility outside this building where we demonstrate prototypes," Evelyn continued. She meant the amphitheater where the epic—or infamous, depending on who you asked—trials of my Condor flying prototype had taken place.

Nakamura shook her head. "We need to see real tests of the dragon prototypes. Measurable tasks in challenging environments."

Evelyn's brow furrowed, the first wrinkle in her smooth confidence. "We don't really have the experience in setting up something like that."

"Fortunately, we do," Nakamura said. "How soon can you have something ready?"

Three months, I was thinking.

"Six weeks," Evelyn said.

I managed not to groan audibly. Six weeks to produce field-ready prototypes. That was going to be tight. Hell, the incubation period would take two of those weeks.

Nakamura smiled, but it was not reassuring. "We look forward to it."

Something told me that she was going to make damn sure our dragons met their match. That pretty much settled the meeting. Evelyn walked the visitors out, and came back to find me still collecting my things in the conference room.

"Nice work, Noah," she said.

"Nice work to you. The training program is impressive," I said.

"I thought it might help sway them."

"Kind of wish we had longer to prep, though."

"So do I, but the government acquisition takes a long time. We need to set it in motion for this to help."

"We still have a lot of design work to do before these prototypes are ready."

"Yes. And they need to impress the DOD."

I rubbed my eyes; they were aching again. "I'll figure out a way to get it done. We need another designer."

"So get one," Evelyn said.

Perfect. Another thing to do. Finding genetic engineers with the right skill set was time-consuming, even in Phoenix. Training someone new took even longer. Then it hit me. We didn't need someone new, we needed someone old.

We needed Priti Korrapati.

CHAPTER EIGHT
The Recruit

I had Korrapati's number but I didn't call her out of the blue. I wasn't a psychopath who cold-calls people without a heads-up. Instead, I sent her a quick text and asked if she was free for lunch. It gave her time to think it over, not to mention the option of ignoring me outright. Evelyn had been vague about her reason for taking a leave of absence. I hoped it wasn't the same as O'Connell's.

It took less than two minutes before Korrapati replied and said she'd love to. Not that I counted or anything. I took that for a good sign.

We decided to meet down at the Cluster Truck, one of our favorite food trucks that had taken up a semi-permanent haunt close to downtown. As much as I hustled to arrive promptly, Korrapati was already there when I arrived. She hadn't ordered yet, fortunately, and I told her it was my treat. I'd invited her, after all. In spite of its name, Cluster Truck turned their orders around *fast*. In two minutes, we were juggling our hot lunches on our way to the nearest outside table. Mine was something like a rice-filled burrito on a bed of chips laden with unidentifiable cheese. But it was hot and smelled amazing. You never had a bad experience eating at CT unless you made the mistake of getting the nutrition facts.

We made small talk while we waited for the food to cool—weather, traffic, and the news about a new gene therapy breakthrough. Casual and safe topics all. Dancing around the real reason I'd asked her.

"So," Korrapati said after a while, and she looked right at me.

"So," I said, smiling. We both knew it was time to talk. To have *that* conversation. I figured I'd let her start.

"You're back at Build-A-Dragon," she said.

"You heard that, huh?"

"I saw the press release."

"Yeah. I started last week."

"How does it feel?" she asked.

"Weird."

She laughed. "I can only imagine."

"It's going to take some time to get used to sitting in Evelyn's old office. And I kind of miss being near the God Machine."

"I suppose she's moved upstairs?"

"To the C-suite, yes," I said. "She got a new plant, too."

"Ooh, what kind?"

"*Darlingtonia californica.*"

"No way, a cobra lily! They're very hard to find. How did she get one?"

"She was vague on the details."

"Ha! I'll bet."

"Her plant collection is equal parts impressive and terrifying."

"You're not wrong."

I took a bite of my burrito. It was chicken and rice and melted cheese, and out of this world. "She said you're on a leave of absence."

"Is that what she called it?"

"Why, what do you call it?"

Her eyebrows went up.

"What am I missing?" I asked, mostly in self-defense. *Maybe I somehow offended her?*

"Noah, I'm not on a leave of absence," she said. "I gave notice."

"Wait. You . . . quit?" I set my burrito down.

"Well, resigned is what I'd prefer to—"

"So Evelyn announced that I was coming back, and everyone's response was to quit? Jeez, am I really that bad?" I couldn't meet her eyes. I didn't really want to know the answer. She was the good egg, the neutral party among all of our designers. If she was against me, then I really was the problem. And it wouldn't be long before Evelyn had to accept it.

Korrapati dabbed her mouth with her napkin in a show of cool composure. "I never said I left because of you."

"I—" I lost my head of steam, and I felt a wave of shame for taking out my frustration on her. "Didn't you?"

"Of course not. What gave you that idea?"

"It's why O'Connell left and took the Frogman with him. Heck, I'm half-convinced Wong only stayed because of his visa." I took a breath, still embarrassed but also relieved that it wasn't me. Or at least, it wasn't *only* me. "Well, then why did you give notice?"

"Because of what the company did under Robert Greaves."

"Oh," I said, feeling like a complete idiot. "You know about the dogs." I wasn't sure how many people at Build-A-Dragon knew the real story rather than the public-facing one. The real story was almost harder to believe. I was still trying to wrap my own head around Greaves sabotaging his own drug trial to keep canines out of the world.

"Not *just* the dogs. He ordered his men to shoot down your Condor when it tried to escape. And he let all those dragons die out in the desert." Her voice trembled, and for a moment it seemed like she might break down. She took a breath. "Those things weighed on me."

"I feel the same way." *Especially the ones that were my fault.* "But that was all Greaves."

She laughed. "I see the PR spin has done its job on you, too."

"What does that mean?" I asked, a bit defensively.

"A company is more than its CEO. Do you really think he was the only one responsible for everything?"

I started to answer yes, but she had a point. Greaves was guilty as hell, but others could have been complicit. "I have to believe he was the driving force. We went where he pointed."

"And who told him where to point?"

"If he wasn't acting alone, I don't know."

"Then why did you go back?"

"It's hard to explain." From the outside, I supposed it

did seem incongruous for the whistleblower who'd left the company after exposing its best-kept secret to suddenly return to work there. "When I started there, I didn't even care about dragons."

"You cared about getting an answer for your brother," she said.

"Right, and finding a place where my biological simulator could have all the computing power it needed. But by the time I left, I sort of . . . started to care. About dragons."

"I know what you mean." She looked away from me and sighed. "They get to you."

"It's like Build-A-Dragon has a gravitational pull, and I can't escape."

She nodded. "Deciding to leave was really hard."

"So it really wasn't that you didn't want me leading the design group?"

"Don't be silly. You were the heir apparent even before you rescued the dogs."

Noah Parker, rescuer of dogs. I couldn't *wait* to tell Summer that one. "Tell that to O'Connell and the Frogman."

"O'Connell has had a chip on his shoulder for a long time. Did you know he interviewed for Evelyn's job?"

"He did?"

"Apparently he was one of the final candidates for triple-D in the early days."

"What happened? Did he botch an interview?"

"I think it was more that Evelyn came in from California and dazzled everyone."

"Wow. I had no idea." It was before my time, but it cast

O'Connell's bad behavior in a different light. Maybe it wasn't just me he had a problem with. "Well, he was a good designer. So was the Frogman. But you're the one that Build-A-Dragon really needs. Which is why I'm hoping you'll come back."

Nothing changed on her face, which told me she knew where this had been heading. "I don't know, Noah."

"You know that I have enormous respect for you, right?"

She smiled a little. "I do."

"If you're hesitant because you think you should be running the team instead of me, it would be fair to say." Then I swallowed my pride as best I could, and said, "Hell, maybe it *should* be you." I could talk to Evelyn. *If that's what it really takes.*

"I wasn't the one who cracked domestication," Korrapati said.

"That was Wong," I said.

"It was Wong and *you*. I saw the code, Noah. You and he have very different styles."

I opened my mouth, but then closed it again. There was no point in denying it, and she'd only be insulted if I did. *She figured it out based on our programming styles.* I knew she was smart, but sometimes I forgot *how* smart.

"You're wrong about him, too, by the way," she said, while I was struggling to find words.

"About Wong? How so?"

"I don't think he only stayed because of his visa. He likes working with you."

"It's Wong. Who can really know what goes on in that guy's head?" Even so, I really hoped it was true. "But so what? You were close behind us on domestication."

"I didn't design the best flying model we've ever seen, nor did I uncover a conspiracy that nearly deprived the world of dogs," she said.

She's got me there. "Your Laptop model flies pretty well." It didn't have the range, but to achieve flight on an animal with such a low metabolism was really an achievement.

"That's very kind of you, but all it does is make my point."

"Which is what?"

"You deserve this. And you'll be a good leader for our team."

I grinned and pointed at her. "You just said *our* team."

Her cheeks colored a little, and she looked away. "It's just an expression."

"You said it. No take backs!" I let my smile fall away and adopted a more serious tone. "Robert Greaves is gone. We can't erase what he did, but we can make sure the company doesn't do something like that again."

"I do miss the work," she said.

"And we need you. Seriously."

She cleared her throat and tilted up her chin. "I have conditions."

"Okay." *Let the negotiations begin.* Granted, I had no idea if I had the authority to agree to anything on the company's behalf, but I'd damn well try. "What would you like?"

"Your workstation, for starters."

"Wow." I felt like I'd been kicked in the teeth for reasons I couldn't easily define. "Why?"

"It's closer to the action. I hate being on the far side where no one remembers me."

"We remember you!"

"It doesn't make sense for me to be all the way over there when I could be right there talking to Wong."

She had a point. Our designers would need to talk a lot. And in fairness, now that I had an office, I didn't technically need a workstation. *It's just a place to sit*, I told myself. No matter the memories I'd made there, the scientific achievements, and the proximity to the God Machine. But it was also something I had the power to do. "Fine. Consider it yours."

"And a pay raise, naturally."

"Got to be honest, that's Evelyn's call, but I'm sure she'll give you one." Any organization worth its salt would pony up to retain a valued employee. That was Management 101. *Literally.* I'd recently bought the book.

"I'd also like to design a new prototype," she said.

"What kind?"

She waved her hand. "It doesn't matter. Something interesting and difficult."

"How about *three* new prototypes for our newest client?"

"Three?"

I held up three fingers, but otherwise let the bit of intrigue dangle. We hadn't worked on three prototypes simultaneously since the early days after domestication. It meant something was up, and we both knew it. *Come on, take the bait.*

She bit her lip for two seconds, then broke. "All right, who is it?"

"Promise me you'll come back, and I'll tell you all about them."

CHAPTER NINE
Interlude

Support Chat Log
Date: March 14th

System: Thank you for your patience. A Build-A-Dragon support operator will be with you in four minutes.

Customer1: Um, hello?

System: Thank you for your patience. A Build-A-Dragon support operator will be with you in three minutes.

Customer1: Is anyone there?

Customer1: I don't have all day.

System: Thank you for your patience. A Build-A-Dragon support operator will be with you in two minutes.

Customer1: Ugh, this is annoying.

System: Thank you for your patience. A Build-A-Dragon support operator will be with you in one minute.

Charles: Hello, and thank you for contacting Build-A-Dragon support.

Customer1: FINALLY.

Charles: How can I—

Customer1: So here's the deal. I ordered one of your Laptop models a month ago.

Charles: Oh, I see we're just jumping right in. Go on.

Customer1: My boyfriend and I ordered it together. It was our nine-week anniversary.

Charles: . . . and?

Customer1: NINE WEEKS. That's over two months!!

Charles: That's a heck of a milestone, miss. Please continue.

Customer1: Well, we were ordering this dragon to be ours. For both of us, you know? I had to convince him it was a good idea, of course. He just wanted to get me a cell phone case. A CELL PHONE CASE! After nine weeks. Can you imagine???

Charles: No more than I can imagine where this is going.

Customer1: Yes, well, we got the dragon. And I guess it turns out they're a lot of work. We have to, like, feed it. And give it water. And it keeps wanting to go outside.

Charles: It sounds like you're having a problem caring for the basic needs of a living thing. Do I understand that correctly?

Customer1: Um, that's not really my problem, though. See, it's my boyfriend.

Charles: I'm not sure that's within our purview.

Customer1: I guess I thought that when we had a dragon together, it would bring us closer. We don't live together, but I was hoping that once Plushie came here he might think about moving in.

Charles: Plushie?

Customer1: That's what we named the dragon.

Charles: Oh, poor thing. And did your plan succeed?

Customer1: Not really. He won't even stay over now, and he hasn't called in a while.

Charles: How long is a while?

Customer1: Um, three weeks.

Charles: ...

Customer1: So, I think there's something wrong.

Charles: Oh, we can agree on that.

Customer1: With the dragon.

Charles: Never mind.

Customer1: Is there anything you can do to help?

Charles: Other than point out the obvious, I'm afraid not.

Customer1: What's obvious???

Charles: What you need is a new boyfriend, and I'm afraid that's none of our business.

Customer1: But I love him!

Charles: May I suggest that you try loving Plushie for a while? He's not going anywhere.

Customer1: (indistinct sobbing)

Charles: Well, it sounds like we have resolved your issue. Thank you for contacting the Build-A-Dragon Company.

CHAPTER TEN
The Ghost

By the time Summer and I met for breakfast on Saturday, it was nearly lunchtime. We'd both worked late the night before and were a little slow to get going. I even got to the diner before her, which almost never happened. *She must be exhausted.* So was I, but I reminded myself that talking about her work was important. The more we did that, the less we talked about *my* work. That would be hard, though. The DOD contract dominated my world right now.

Summer rolled into the lot with the doors off her Jeep and her blond hair flying. It lifted my spirits just looking at her.

I met her outside the door. "Hey."

"Hey." She smiled, but didn't kiss me. Evidently we were still unofficially fighting.

"No Riker?" I opened the door for her and followed her in.

"I couldn't get him out of his crate."

We made our way to a booth in the back corner. The server approached us right away to introduce herself. "Anything to drink?"

"Coffee," Summer and I answered. We looked at each other and laughed.

"That bad, huh?" I asked.

"These clients are going to kill me," she said.

The diner had decent food, but it was the coffee that kept us coming back. It had a unique flavor that I'd tried countless times to replicate at home. It was strong, too; we split the available French vanilla creamers, three each. It reminded me of the coffee with the DOD officers, and how Nakamura had taken it straight black. Two cups even, without so much as a wince. I almost shared it but bit my tongue.

"Are you up for a geocache today?" I asked instead.

She took a gulp of hot coffee. "I don't know if I have it in me."

"What if I said that Jojo and Prickly Pete logged another cache yesterday?"

"On a weekday? Damn." She took another drink of coffee. "Fine. But let's make it a short one. I have a million things to do today."

"What about Red Rock Run?" It was one of our favorite caches, and quick to finish once you got there. A straight shot out into wild desert country. Granted, it was a bit of a drive to the parking lot, but if Summer drove we'd get there fast enough.

"Yeah, I could do that."

Yes. I didn't want this to be my only time with her.

It was almost midday by the time we reached the

trailhead for Red Rock Run. Hot like usual, and very little wind. After a few minutes on the trail, I hardly noticed because I was simultaneously trying to find the first waypoint and keep an eye on six dragons.

"The marker isn't far," Summer said, after checking her watch.

"Half a mile," we both said at the same time.

"Jinx!" she said.

"You can't jinx me out here," I protested.

"Why not?"

"Because I need to be able to yell at the dragons."

"I can do that."

"Psh." I waved her off. "They're not going to listen to you."

"Is that right?" she asked. Her voice sounded a half octave higher, and that worried me.

"It's not your fault."

"Mmm-hmm."

"They're just imprinted on me, you know? It's a domestication thing."

Summer cleared her throat. "Octavius!"

My little dragon broke off his glide and swooped down to land on her shoulder. I stared. "What the—"

"Good boy." She stroked his snout, and then gave me a sassy look. "You were saying?"

It shouldn't have been possible. Octavius had imprinted on me, and he should have been loyal. Most dragons were, unless their owners died or abandoned them. I supposed that Octavius and his siblings were unique. It still felt like a betrayal, though. "Judas," I muttered.

Octavius cocked his head to one side, then lifted his snout. His pink tongue flicked out, but not at me. He looked around wildly. Then he hissed. The primal sound raised the hair on the back of my neck. Instinctively, I moved closer to her. Gravel skittered against stone behind us. Something big moved around the corner. It was long and slender, with the scales and gray-brown coloring of a desert dweller. A dragon. It moved with a predator's grace. I hadn't made this particular one, but I knew the Guardian instantly. That was Marketing's name for the first dragon ever designed, the one that hunted feral hogs.

Another Guardian followed behind the first one. It had slightly darker coloring but was just as wild. They bared their teeth as they approached.

Octavius hissed again.

"Hold on to him!" I whispered to Summer. Octavius was fierce for his size, but I had no illusions about how he'd fare against one Guardian, let alone two. His siblings wheeled overhead, chirping and hissing; I hoped they wouldn't attack unless Octavius did. They usually followed his lead, but they were visibly disturbed. The two Guardians ignored them. They split up and made a circle around us, tasting the air all the while. I pressed myself close against Summer and tried to keep an eye on both of them.

"What are they?" she asked.

"The first prototype. The hog hunters." *Thank God Riker stayed home.*

"Dangerous?"

"Very."

A shrill whistle sounded from somewhere. The

Guardians gave us one last unblinking stare before melting away into the scree.

"Thank God," I whispered. I knew what this was now.

"Who whistled?" Summer still clung to Octavius's legs. He'd given up trying to escape and now chirped at his siblings, probably telling them to watch where the Guardians went.

"Someone who knows how to make an entrance."

She was surprised when Simon Redwood stumped around the corner. If possible, he'd become even more of a legend after his recent "death" in the fire that consumed his home. Summer and I had watched a two-hour special on him and all of his wild inventions and start-ups—most of which, admittedly, never really found success. Build-A-Dragon was the one that finally hit big, but he'd lost it to Robert Greaves. I imagine that Evelyn would welcome him back, but he'd assured me at our last meeting that death suited him.

"Hey, kids!" he called. He wore dungarees and worn hiking boots. He scrambled toward us with a spryness that belied his age. On a guy with a shock of white hair, it was downright uncanny. "Sorry to show up unannounced."

"Ghosts tend to do that, Mr. Redwood," I said, grinning in spite of the shock. Simon Redwood had been a hero of mine for as long as I could remember.

The same went for Summer, who stared at him with a starry-eyed expression. *Is that how I looked? Probably so.*

"Needed to talk to you," Redwood said, drawing my gaze back to him.

"What about?"

"I've got a warehouse where I keep some things away

from private eyes. Bits and pieces of old projects and mothballed experiments."

"Go on," I managed to say. All I could think was *I would kill to get a look inside that warehouse.*

"Thought no one knew about it, but there was a break-in the other day. They took something."

"The jetpack?" I asked.

"No. Something more valuable," Redwood said.

Summer looked at me and mouthed the word *jetpack.* Funny thing was, at least two commercial airline pilots had reported a man with a jetpack flying thousands of feet above Phoenix. Most people had written off the reports as pilot error or a simple hoax. And in my mind, Redwood had practically confirmed it just now.

"What did they take?" I asked.

"Prototype of the Codex."

"Prototype of the . . . wait, the *Redwood* Codex?"

"I don't call it that, but sounds like you know what I'm talking about."

"What's the Redwood Codex?" Summer asked.

"Part of the biological egg-printer," I told her.

"Back in my day, we used to call it the God Machine."

I opened my mouth, closed it, and raised my eyebrows at Summer. *See?* "Was anything else taken?"

"Nope," Redwood said. "And that alone is telling because of what else is in there."

"Could someone use it to build another God Machine?"

"Reckon so."

That worried me, but I also had to know something. "Why are you telling us all of this?"

Redwood shrugged. "Figured I should tell someone. Unofficially."

"You should, but that someone is Evelyn. She's running the place now." Despite my recent promotion at the company, I still felt miles below her and the board.

He shook his head. "The fewer people who know about my resurrection, the better."

So this is my *problem now.* "I'll run it up the chain, I suppose."

"Good. I don't like thinking about what he's going to do with it."

"Yeah, me neither," I said.

"You said *he,*" Summer said to Redwood.

"What?" I asked.

"What *he's* going to do with it," she said.

I'd missed that part, but she was right. I looked at Redwood. "Do you know who stole it?"

"I have my suspicions."

"Who?" I asked, but at that moment, I had a feeling I knew. "Oh, no."

"Yes. My old partner."

Robert Greaves. Former CEO, dog killer, and all-around asshole.

"Aw, what the hell? What is he planning for it?"

"Not sure, but I'll say this," Redwood said. "It's nothing good. Robert Greaves never does anything on a whim. And I'm guessing that, after how things went down at the company, he's not your biggest fan."

"No, he's not." And the feeling was mutual.

CHAPTER ELEVEN
The Rival

I spent the night at Summer's last night, partly because we were so dazzled by the impromptu Redwood visit—and concerned by what he told us—that we didn't think to do otherwise. Sunday morning, though, she gently kicked me out. She had things to do, I had dragons to feed, and there was the unvoiced risk that we might break the fragile peace between us. Besides, all I could think about was Greaves taking the prototype Redwood Codex. And the very *existence* of a Redwood Codex.

It was too tempting to think about what else Redwood had had in his secret storage warehouse. No, rather than let that distract me, I tried to chess-match out Greaves's next move. Naturally, he knew everything else necessary to construct a biological printer. He could make his own. Yet he also had a keen business sense. He had to know how our business prospects in the current consumer market looked. So what was his plan? Start a new company so he could fight us for the last scraps of revenue before all the dogs came back? It didn't make sense.

If Greaves was out for revenge, he could hit us in other ways. He knew the company inside and out. Hell, he knew its founder well enough to track down his secret storage unit, break in, and steal the Codex prototype. I'd been to Redwood's house in the desert before it burned down. He took security seriously. Not seriously enough, obviously, because Greaves got around it. And took the heart of the God Machine. The priceless, confidential, irreplaceable heart. That's when it hit me. There was no backup Codex now. Without it, we couldn't print viable dragon eggs.

Anyone who could break into a secure warehouse could break into a company headquarters. Especially if he used to run the place. He could take, or simply destroy, our Codex and we would have no recourse. As far as most of the world knew, Simon Redwood was dead. No Codex, no dragons, no Build-A-Dragon. And the worst part was, when the company inevitably went bankrupt, Greaves would get to take a goddamn victory lap. *Look how quickly it failed without me. See? I wasn't the problem.*

That made a lot more sense. It had the cleverness, the vindictiveness that Greaves had already shown. If he already had the backup, there was no reason to wait, either. Once I had that thought, I could hardly sleep. I woke up at six and forced myself out of bed. It was still dark outside for most of the drive to work. The eastern horizon had only just begun to lighten when I parked and hurried inside. Almost no one came into work this early; the place looked deserted. No one challenged me at reception. No hatchers prowled the still-dim hatchery. I rushed through into the design lab. The biological printer looked unmolested, but it also wasn't moving. I squeezed into my cubicle and leaned as far as I could into the metal-arm framework.

And there it was: the Redwood Codex. Still in place, with its old-school LED lights blinking their cheerful enigmatic rhythm. My arms shook with relief so much that I almost fell on the desk.

I thought I'd beat Evelyn to her office, but I was mistaken. She perched on her chair in the expansive suite surrounded by a flotilla of projection monitors. First thing in the morning, too. I could tell from the hunch in her shoulders that something had her stressed.

"*Nihao, Lao-bahn*," I said. *Good morning, boss*.

She looked up and smiled. "There is my Director of Dragon Design."

I had to admit, the title had a certain ring to it. I paused a moment to savor it before I ruined the good mood.

"How are you?"

"Too busy for a Monday." Her brow furrowed in my direction. "Are you all right?"

"I have something to tell you."

"Come in." She gestured to the chair, and activated the hermetic seal behind me when I entered.

I glanced over my shoulder. "Your old office has one of those, doesn't it?"

"The control is on your desk." She beckoned me over so I could see it. "This activates it, and this turns it off."

My own privacy door seal. "Thanks, I'll try it."

"What's going on?" she asked.

"I have important news, but it comes with conditions," I said. *How do I put this?* "What I know comes from a very reliable source, but I can't tell you more about the source, or why I have the source."

"Ooh, this is getting interesting." With a gesture, she minimized all of the projection monitors between us. Now I had her full attention.

I took a deep breath. "Simon Redwood built a prototype of his Codex."

Evelyn's face went stony all of a sudden. She'd met Redwood in person; she'd admitted that much a long time ago. I assumed it was in the company's early days before I joined. She was cagey whenever I asked about him. Now, as she said nothing and waited for me to elaborate, I wondered why she didn't seem more surprised. "You already knew, didn't you?"

She put her hands flat on the desk and exhaled. "I suspected there might be one. Redwood often built prototypes of his inventions."

"Well, bad news. It was stolen," I said.

"When?"

Well, crap. I hadn't thought to ask, and Redwood's sense of urgency remained hard to interpret. "I'm not completely sure, but it was recent. Three or four days ago."

"Do you know who took it?"

"Not for sure, but I have a theory it's the person who used to sit in that chair." I pointed at her executive chair, which also looked to be Nappa leather.

She nodded, but if this information surprised her, it didn't show. God, I wished I had her ability to control her expressions. Noah Parker wore his heart on his sleeve and everyone knew it.

Then she must have had another thought, and a look

of fear flashed across her face. She started to get out of her chair. "Do you think—"

I held up a placating hand. "I already checked. Our Codex is fine."

She sat down and took a breath, settling herself. "I have a feeling this may be related to *my* news."

"Okay." I braced myself against the sinking feeling that started, of its own volition, down in my gut.

"This morning I got a message from Major Nakamura. There will be changes to the statement of work."

"What kind of changes?"

"They are opening up the request to anyone. It's now a competitive bid process."

Competitive as in we have a competitor. Now the pieces clicked into place and I didn't like what I saw. "We're no longer the sole supplier of dragon technology."

"That is what she said."

"This is bull—" I caught myself, remembering whose office I was in. "Crap. Someone else can't just steal our tech and try to get the contract. Can they?"

"Is the theft going to be reported to the police?"

I wanted to answer hell yes, but now that I considered it, there was no way Redwood would want any of this official. His purpose in turning up to tell me was becoming more and more clear. "Probably not. What about patent protection?"

She shook her head. "There is no patent for the Redwood Codex."

"Because there's only supposed to be the one."

"And a patent requires disclosure of the invention, which would be like giving away the . . . the . . ."

"The secret sauce recipe?"

That made her laugh in spite of the circumstances. "Yes, Noah Parker. Secret sauce."

"What about the other parts of the egg-printing process?"

"The lawyers are already looking into it."

"That sounds . . . slow."

"It's the best we can do for now."

"So we're stuck with the competitive bidding?"

"It's the DOD's call at the moment, and they like competition," she said.

I groaned. "This sucks. You know that?"

"Yes."

"I was so sure that Greaves wanted to destroy the company by taking out our dragon-printing capability."

"He might achieve the same goal if he wins out on this contract," Evelyn said.

I was tempted to say there was no way he'd win the contract or even be serious competition. But I'd underestimated Robert Greaves a couple of times, and it always came back to bite me. "Well, that's not going to happen. He might have changed the process, but he can't beat us on a level playing field."

"He may have resources we don't know about yet," Evelyn said. "Private backing, even."

"So what? We have the home field advantage. The *design* experience."

She smiled. "Yes, we do." A look of uncertainty flickered across her face, but was gone just as quickly. She said nothing more.

"I'll get to work, then." I made to leave.

"Oh, one more thing," she said. "Guess who called me this weekend?"

I looked back at her, puzzled by the question. My first thought was Robert Greaves calling to taunt her, but judging by her little smile, it was a good kind of call. Something that made her happy. *And the fact that she wants to tell me means I should know.* So it would make me happy, too. Well, I had one educated guess. "Priti Korrapati."

"Ah!" She slapped her desk and jabbed a finger at me in mock accusation. "So this was your doing!"

I shrugged. "You said get a designer, so I got the best one I know."

"But how did you do it?" Her amusement faltered. "I didn't have the heart to tell you, but—"

"She gave notice, I know."

"I am sorry I wasn't up front about that."

"It caught me off guard a little, but I understand." I'd been plenty offended about O'Connell and the Frogman. Evelyn knew me well enough to guess what losing Korrapati might have done to my self-confidence. "Probably for the best, actually."

"How did you change her mind?"

I winked at her. "I can be very persuasive."

"Maybe Noah Parker is our other secret sauce."

"Ha! I don't think that's true. Is she coming back?"

"Assuming I can meet her many conditions, yes."

So Korrapati did ask for a raise. *Good for her.* "Please do, because we need her. How soon can she start back?"

"Tomorrow."

I pumped a fist. "Yes."

"I already sent her the DOD specs."

"Outstanding."

Greaves thought making this a competition would cause problems for us. Turned out, he didn't know me so well after all.

CHAPTER TWELVE
The Specs

The next morning, Evelyn invaded my office just minutes after I got in. And I mean that literally: I'd touched my keypad to warm up the workstation, unpacked my bag, and boom, there she was.

"Good morning, Noah!"

I jumped, and just managed not to drop my tablet. "Morning. Jeez, you startled me."

"Sorry. I thought you might be getting in."

I gave her a side-eye. "You have an uncanny knack for knowing right when I arrive." It was always possible she used the company's video surveillance to watch for me. That was another legacy of our former security chief. Yet it didn't seem like her style to sit in his cramped little booth to await my arrival. Especially because, as the caretaker for a pack of small but clever dragons, I kept wildly inconsistent hours.

"It's your tablet."

By that she meant the tablet she'd given me when I'd

been promoted, the one that was hot-linked to our servers. I glanced at it with new suspicion. "Is there tracking on this?" *I've taken the damn thing everywhere with me the past two weeks.*

"No, of course not. Unless it's stolen. But when it comes in range of the company network, your status changes. See?" She pointed to the tiny icon in the top-right corner of my tablet, which did show that I was behind the company firewall. A tiny thing, but I supposed you could use it to know if someone was on-site or off-site.

I frowned. "Well, that's intrusive."

"Relax, Noah. There are a dozen ways I could keep tabs on you if I wanted to."

"Great."

"Come on, let's get some coffee into you. You look like you could use it."

It was both an unflattering remark, and completely true. Marcus Aurelius had gotten into my coffee canister at the condo and spilled it everywhere. I couldn't make my own, and I hadn't wanted to stop anywhere before getting in. Phoenix traffic got more brutal with every minute of daylight. "You read my mind. Coffee machine?" It was a short walk down the hallway, and still state of the art. It would not only make you a latte or a cappuccino, but even 3D-printed a cup if you wanted one.

"I was thinking the Java Bean," she said.

"Ooh," I said. That was across the street, about a five-minute walk. It was a little strange that she'd made time to go off-site with me. I was certain that her CEO schedule kept her insanely busy. But hey, the coffee was better than even what our fancy machine could do, but more importantly, they had French ovens. "Sold."

We walked across the street and settled into a table by the window. I tackled a butter croissant while she nibbled on a very small pastry. I tried the coffee and sighed. This was the jolt I needed. "That's better."

"Major Nakamura has been in touch," Evelyn said.

"Okay." *This is what she wanted to talk about.*

"Since the DOD contract is now a competitive bid, there have been changes to the specifications."

"What kind of changes?"

She slid over her tablet. "Take a look."

It was a DOD document; I knew the fonts and the spacing right away. I could picture them every time I closed my eyes. I even recognized *this* document. "These are the specs for the flying model."

"Correct."

Yet even as I read it, I started to notice the differences. "Now they want it to have an eight-hour flight time, and a range of five hundred miles."

"I saw that."

I ground my teeth. "They know dragons are living creatures, right?"

"Swifts can do it," she said.

"Swifts, sure. They're all feather." She wasn't wrong, though; there were numerous avian models of long-endurance flight. Dragons had a different physiology, though; they were heavier, and there was a cost to keeping them aloft. Even so, as I scanned the rest of the updated specs, all I saw was a value with the phrase *or better* appended to it. These were all categories on which we'd be graded, and they were hard enough on their own. I shook my head and slid her tablet back. "I don't know if we can do this."

"We don't have a choice, Noah."

"Those numbers have no basis in reality."

She bit her lip. "I'm not so sure. They don't issue requests for proposals that they don't think anyone can fill."

"Sure, I guess they expect us to make the impossible possible," I said sourly. *And Greaves could have told them anything is possible.* It was very much his style to overpromise and force others to deliver.

"It's more than that. We don't simply have to meet specs. Now we have to do so better than any competitors."

I wanted to point out that we shouldn't truly have competitors, but we'd already had the argument. As far as the DOD was concerned, we weren't the sole supplier any longer. Yet the more I obsessed over the contract and the specifications for dragons, the harder it got to ignore a raw truth. "What if I have a problem with the fact that these are reptilian weapons? For use against actual people?"

"You don't seem to have that issue with the attack dragons," Evelyn said.

"It's not the same thing. With an attack dragon, I have no idea if or how the owner is going to use it. I can tell myself it's for intimidation. Or for protection, even." I gestured vaguely at the projection screens. "These are purpose-bred killing machines. If we make them, that's what they'll be used for."

"That's the job, Noah."

"I know." I squeezed my eyes shut and rubbed them

with my fingertips, but the afterimages of those phrases seemed permanently etched into my retinas. Close-quarters combat. Salvage operations. Blowing things up.

"I'm sorry about this," Evelyn said at last. "It's not what I hoped would be the new company mission. But we must survive."

"Or the world loses dragons," I said.

"Exactly."

I took a deep breath, and maybe it was just the coffee taking hold that fully brought me around, but I gave her a nod. "I can do this."

"I'm afraid that's not all I need from you, which is why I asked you here," she said.

A vague sense of foreboding started to rise in me. "What else is there?"

She stirred her coffee, almost as if to buy time. "The Director of Dragon Design duties that go beyond dragon engineering. There is *social* engineering, too."

By that she meant working with people, but I didn't take her meaning. "How so?"

"Part of your job is getting your team behind you to do what needs to be done."

Like she used to do by persuading me to do things. Come to think of it, I'd had more than a few tense conversations in her office. More than once I went marching in, all but certain that I was damn sure not going to do something she wanted, no matter how important it was. Most of the time, I came out somehow having agreed to do the thing, and even excited about it. "I think you're talking about the Evelyn Wong effect. Bringing me around on something even when I didn't like it."

She nodded. "Now it must be the Noah Parker effect. You have to lead your team to this. That's the only way it'll work."

I sagged back in my chair a little. "You know, this job is harder than I thought it would be."

"Look at the bright side. One of the hardest designers to persuade is no longer your problem."

I liked to think she meant O'Connell, but I'm pretty sure she meant me.

Evelyn and I decided to break the news in our conference room, so I hurried into the design lab to round up the troops.

Korrapati had wasted no time in settling in to my old workstation. It wasn't a large space, really, but somehow her possession of it transformed the place I once knew. She'd brought in a little Himalayan salt lamp that softened the harsh LED lights to an orange glow. Every surface was spotless. And somehow it even smelled better despite the constant outflow of metallic-scented air from the God Machine.

Luckily, Wong's workstation remained a fixture to his own personal work style. The stack of empty energy drink cans had reached three high and ran the length of the wall between our workstations. No, I reminded myself, his workstation and Korrapati's. The wheels of his chair had long ago worn tracks in the carpet from when he rolled out to talk to someone. Which he'd done this morning: I found him and Korrapati in deep conversation.

I pushed down a spike of envy and put on a big smile. "Hey, guys!"

Korrapati smiled. "Hello, Noah."

"You all settled in?" I asked.

"Yes. Wong was just catching me up on the DOD project."

"What do you think so far?"

"It's . . . intimidating."

And you only know the half of it. "Well, Evelyn wants us in the conference room. She has news."

"What kind of news?" Wong asked.

"The good kind, I think," I lied. "We have some idea what we're up against. Come on."

We made our way to the conference room. The door hissed open, and the air carried a stale quality. No one had been in here in a while, possibly since before I'd left. Normally, the tinted windows on the outside wall of the room let in a perfect amount of natural light. When I hit the button to lower the RF shield wall, however, I won curious glances from my designers and also made the room too dark. They could stare all they wanted, but if Robert Greaves was willing to steal one of Redwood's inventions, I wouldn't put it past him to train a listening device on our windows. We called it the "RF" shield but the lightweight micro-mesh blocked all manner of signals, from radio frequency to UV to heat signatures. Disrupted lasers, too. Every biotech worth its salt had curtains like these on all exterior windows.

Evelyn arrived just as we'd figured out how to turn the lights on. "Good morning, everyone." She glanced up from her tablet, saw Korrapati, and broke into an open smile. "Good to see you, Priti Korrapati."

"It's good to be seen," Korrapati said.

"You missed us too much to stay away."

Korrapati smiled, though something passed between them. "Something like that."

Evelyn's eyes went back to her tablet, and the furrows returned to her brow. "The DOD has adjusted their specs for the contract."

"Why change?" Wong asked.

"Because there may be another company putting in a competing bid."

"That shouldn't be possible," Korrapati said.

"It's possible," I said.

Korrapati and Wong looked from her to me.

"Noah," Evelyn said. A warning.

"What? They need to know." *And we need transparency, now more than ever.*

Evelyn gave me the *fine, go ahead* gesture.

"We think Greaves took dragon-printing technology and started a rival firm," I said.

Korrapati gasped.

Wong shook his head and said, "Bad business."

"As a result, the DOD no longer considers us a sole supplier," Evelyn said. "Here are the specs for the competitive bid." She made a few flicking motions on her tablet, and projection screens bloomed to life around the conference room.

Korrapati hurried to the nearest one. "This is the marine dragon." She glanced over the specs. "'Adjusted' is a bit of an understatement. These are totally changed."

"What's different?" I asked.

"They want the marine dragon to run twenty-five miles an hour on land, and swim twenty knots." She kept reading and made a little *tsk*ing noise. "Oh, and hold its breath for five minutes."

Presumably while keeping at twenty knots. Yikes. I looked over at Wong, who was looking at another screen. "What's that one?"

"Infantry dragon," Wong said, tapping at his screen. His hand went right through it, of course, but the image didn't so much as flicker. "Many new requirements."

"Are they doable?"

"Maybe." He frowned. "Hard to make so strong and fast and nimble."

If Wong didn't have brazen overconfidence, then we really did face an uphill battle. I eased over to the third screen. It was the aerial model, the one I'd already complained about to Evelyn. "This one is the flier. It'll be tough, but I think we can manage." I looked at Evelyn, who gave me a little nod.

Korrapati had gone quiet. Some of the glow of her long-awaited return seemed to have faded, too. I shuffled over to see what she was looking at. Yes, the marine dragon. Not going to be pleasant reading at any time, and God knows what they'd added.

"How bad is it?" I asked her.

"They've added a carrying load requirement. Eighty pounds."

"What could that possibly be for?"

"It doesn't specify," she said, but it was clear she knew.

After a moment, it dawned on me as well. "Ordnance."

Korrapati nodded.

"What is ordinance?" Wong asked.

"Not ordinance, that's like a township regulation," I said. "*Ordnance.*"

Evelyn said something low in Mandarin, a phrase I hadn't learned. Wong's eyebrows inched up a little, but otherwise he said nothing. Even though the meaning of a dragon carrying explosives couldn't be clearer.

We swapped screens and spent another ten minutes grumbling over the new specs. The DOD had made this task infinitely harder. Worse, they appeared to have a much more intuitive grasp of dragon biology than I'd given them credit for. They knew which things were *close* to possible, the things that we'd really have to push to achieve.

"Well, what do we all think?" Evelyn asked.

"I think this is going to be hard." Korrapati glanced at the screen with the marine dragon specs and looked away just as quickly. "Even overlooking what they intend to use these dragons for, the performance requirements are beyond anything we've ever designed."

"That doesn't mean we can't do them," I said.

"Even Wong designs are not so good," Wong said.

"The thing is, Evelyn says we need this contract for the company to stay in business." I looked at Evelyn. "That's true, right?"

"It is," Evelyn said. "I wish it weren't, but our current revenues won't keep us afloat for long." She didn't add that the board had pretty much told her they'd liquidate the company if we failed to secure the contract.

"Even so, when dragons are dangerous . . ." Wong shrugged unhappily. "Hard to go back."

"I know. I felt the same way when I learned who the

client was," I said. "But if we fail as a company, then no one gets to have dragons. I don't want to live in a world without them. So I'm willing to do what it takes to survive. But I can't do it without both of you."

I looked at Wong and didn't need to ask the question.

"Survive," he said.

"What about you?" I asked Korrapati.

She took a moment longer, the emotions warring on her face. Then she set her jaw and gave a nod.

With her and Wong, I can do anything. I faced Evelyn. "The Design team is in."

CHAPTER THIRTEEN
Desert Designs

It was tempting to dive into all of the designs simultaneously—we hadn't had this much new design work in a while—but Evelyn wanted us to take it in stages dictated by the demonstration schedule. The infantry dragon would be evaluated first, and that was going to be hard enough. Especially given the specs. She wanted us to make a good first impression with the DOD officials. I wanted us to do that, too, but also to show that I could effectively lead the Design team in crunch time.

We developed all sorts of one-off dragons for high-paying customers, but there were certain types of dragons that were ordered all the time. Mini Rovers, for example, sold well to customers in urban areas. Custom Laptop orders seemed to follow the latest color and pattern trends in the fashion world. Finally, a surprising number of customers wanted the dragon version of a Rottweiler. I didn't know why, and I didn't ask a lot of questions. But thanks to those frequent shady orders we had prototypes with a lot of the characteristics that the military wanted for their infantry dragon.

We started with a custom model that I knew too well: a jet-black slender attack dragon that, incidentally, had notched at least one kill on company property. That poor little birthday dragon.

The coloring had to change, of course. The DOD made no secret that a desert environment was likely. My personal contribution was a special modification to the pigmentation genes that changed over time. As skin cells divided during gestation, various sets of those genes would flip on and off in somewhat random fashion. The resulting pigments—a range of browns, yellows, and a few greens—gave the dragon a natural desert camouflage. *Let's see Greaves top that.*

I'd used this trick on some customs, but only ones that shipped out. Most of our orders were delivered as eggs that the customers hatched in their homes. I had yet to see an actual dragon with my genetic camouflage with my own eyes. Now, I found myself wanting to inspect one up close. But no, that wasn't yet part of Evelyn's carefully orchestrated plan. Every aspect of our approach had to mimic the eventual supply chain. We'd design and print the eggs, have the DOD hatch them, and ensure Johnson's team was in place to take up the training.

Korrapati took control of the design and increased the heat tolerance. Desert environments would be taxing, even for a reptile. Wong handled the metabolism adjustments necessary to allow it to thrive without constant access to fresh meat. We tweaked the body style as well, making it stouter and with a lower center of gravity. Unlike the custom attack dragons, which probably went after soft prey that I didn't want to think much about, these dragons would be in combat. They had to be tough.

We pored over the design numerous times, both as a team and individually. The 3D image evolved from a slender predator into a husky bruiser of a dragon. If anything, it reminded me of a Komodo dragon, one of the reptilian predators that had contributed DNA to the original dragon reference sequence. They had similar shapes, too. Yet that was where the similarities ended. A Komodo dragon looks fierce but they move slowly, only about twelve miles per hour. Our dragon model could run twice that fast and maintain the pace for half an hour.

"Well, I can't think of anything else to do," I told Evelyn. We stood at Wong's workstation, watching a three-dimensional hologram of the dragon as it rotated slowly in midair. Wong watched it, and us, with his usual crooked smile. *He wants us to make the call.* Which is probably how I'd feel. No, actually, when I was a designer I'd probably have wanted the green light, no matter what the bosses thought. God, sometimes when I looked back, it was surprising I'd maintained somewhat continual employment.

"It looks good," Evelyn said. "Fierce."

"Scary is another word for it," I said.

"How are we on performance metrics?"

"We've met the threshold for everything my simulator can model." That was strength, speed, endurance, bite pressure, and a number of other measures. "Wish I could see it in real life."

"Do you doubt the simulator?"

"Of course not." Yet it was computer code, and the

genome was biological code. There were bound to be subtle discrepancies. I wasn't going to say that, though. The team needed a show of confidence.

"So, it's ready," Evelyn said.

"Yes."

"Very ready," Wong said.

Korrapati muttered something that could have been agreement; she was still buried in the code. And probably would be until long after we'd printed the eggs.

Wong took a bite of an apple. The crunch made me wince. It was my least favorite habit of his. "Still need name," he said.

"I've been racking my brain, but I've got nothing so far," I said.

"No problem. I have one."

Of course he does. "All right, let's hear it."

"This is for army, right?"

"The DOD didn't say, but probably," I said.

"First rank in army is private. So for this one, we call it Private Wong."

I tried to contain myself. I really did, but once a bark of laughter escaped my lips, it became a roar. *Private Wong.* I doubled over, panting. Korrapati laughed, too. Even Evelyn giggled.

I put my hand on Wong's shoulder. "Someday you're going to come up with a good name for a dragon model. That day is not today."

He wrinkled his brow. "No good?"

I couldn't decide if it sounded more like a tasteless B movie or a redshirt character in *Star Trek*. Either way, it wouldn't stand a chance with the DOD clients. I tried to picture Major Nakamura saying *Private Wong*, but I couldn't. "It has to sound serious and impressive."

"We can figure out the name later," Evelyn said. "For now, we need to print the first round of eggs in order to make the schedule."

Dragon eggs had a certain incubation time, and we also had to allow for the imprinting and training exercises. Lots of places that things could go wrong, even if the design was flawless. I wanted to be there for all of it. I *should* be there for all of it, in my opinion, but not everyone agreed.

"Are we ready to call it done?" I asked.

Wong had a mouthful of apple but gave me a thumbs-up.

Korrapati glanced over her shoulder, sagged, and then turned around. "I suppose we should."

I looked back at Evelyn. "We're ready to print."

"I agree. Good work, everyone."

She walked back with me as I returned to my office. Before we got there, her tablet beeped with the approval request to print the eggs.

I grinned. "Wong doesn't waste any time."

"No, he does not."

She pressed a fingerprint to the biometric scanner on her tablet. A second later, I heard the distant whirring of the God Machine swinging into motion. *No, the egg printer*, I reminded myself. Summer really didn't care for our casual name.

"I'll start the clock," I said. Ten days to hatching, and four weeks to the field trials. The wait was going to be brutal.

% % %

When we walked into the design lab, the egg printer was still humming. However, a parade of white-clothed staffers with their egg carts nearly obscured it from view. I slipped in close enough to get a glimpse of an egg as it came out. It was larger than any of our other models' eggs, and the shell was the color of wet sand. Here and there whorls of brighter orange or pale yellow added a splash of color, but they were mostly dark, earthy colors. Serious colors for a serious egg for a serious dragon. I tried not to think about just how serious.

The hatchers team-lifted each egg and nestled it into a foam cushion atop their wheeled egg carts. I'd long since learned to stay out of their way; hatchery staffers became a bit hyper-focused when they had an egg in their care. God help you if you accidentally got in their way.

One time Wong was rolling through the hatchery on his way to work, got clipped by an egg cart, and went careening off into the side of a hatching pod. I heard it and came running in, only to find him sprawled out on the floor against the wall. The hatchers and their egg were nowhere to be seen. Later, they admitted they'd heard the crash, but their first thought was to get the egg safely into its pod.

Wong and Korrapati stayed to watch a few eggs, then left together, talking about lunch. I felt a weird flare of envy at that. Evelyn might have sensed it, as she eased up next to me as I watched them go.

"I used to be the one who people went to lunch with," I told her.

"And now you are not."

"Was it something I said?" I asked.

"You became the group leader."

"I know, but I'd still like to be included."

"Don't take it personally, Noah. You have responsibilities that they don't."

"I suppose," I said.

"Speaking of responsibility, you should get them started on the marine design as soon as possible."

Ooh, a distraction. "You know what? I'll get started right now."

"What about Korrapati and Wong?"

"They deserve a break."

Choosing to ignore the look of concern on her face, I slid into the nearest workstation to start on the design. By the time my designers returned about an hour later, I was in the zone.

"Hey," I said. "How was lunch?" I managed to keep most of the edge out of my tone of voice.

"Good," she said. "We have some ideas for the marine dragon," she said.

I gestured at the workstation. "Already started it."

"Oh." She shared a glance with Wong.

"What?"

"Well, we were thinking we might tackle the marine while you got started on the flying model."

I shook my head. "Evelyn wants us on the marine model next, so I thought I'd take a crack."

"We don't mind—" she started, but I waved her off.

"I know, and you'll get your turn, I promise you." *Once I'm confident we have what we need.* There was too much riding on this design.

"We understand," Korrapati said. "Let us know if you

need something." She slipped quietly into my old workstation.

Wong rolled himself back into his spot without saying a word.

CHAPTER FOURTEEN
The Marine

The marine dragon design quickly consumed the rest of my week. I told Korrapati and Wong to work on the backlog of custom orders that landed in our queue while we focused on the infantry model. I could tell they weren't happy, but Evelyn's words kept playing in my head. I was the team leader. I should be able to give us the head start we needed.

Most reptiles have natural abilities in the water. Snakes can swim; turtles can hold their breath for long periods. The question of how Build-A-Dragon's products would handle themselves in water had not really occurred to me in my time there, so I turned to the place most people visit for answers: the internet.

A video search of "dragon" and "water" brought back thousands of videos. Some were relevant, but not what I needed. For example, it seemed based on video evidence that our Rover models had a bit of a water addiction. Customers were supposed to limit their water intake by giving it only with food, but not all of them did. Hell, the dragon owners in Arizona probably gave them too much water on purpose. We loved to pretend that there wasn't a constant water shortage. There were dozens of videos with Rover models drinking water wherever they could find it: street puddles, rain-soaked grass, their owners' dinner glasses, and of course, toilet bowls. I made a mental note to look into the Rover drinking problem, but that could wait.

A lot of videos showed that, as far as innate swimming abilities went, our models showed a pretty clear dichotomy. The flightless models, such as Rovers and K-10s, took to the water like baby ducks. Four strong legs and a low center of gravity seemed to help. Not so much the flying models. Any video of Laptops or Pterodactyls falling into water was tagged as "funny" and it was true. They flopped about in obvious panic like a guy at a barbecue who ends up in the pool. They couldn't find balance, and their wings became an impediment when they got wet. Bottom line, any flying dragon that ended up in water had to be rescued.

And there were some that didn't get rescued, but rather were found. I tried not to watch those videos.

I'd started with a basic Rover model and then made some tweaks to help it in the water. Webbed feet would give them better purchase in the water, and an elongated, muscular tail would help them steer. I figured that beavers swam largely with their tails, so there was precedent in the animal kingdom. My biological simulator didn't have features for swimming ability, so I had to assume that these changes would make it good enough. Then it was time to figure out the O_2 problem. I didn't know for certain what these dragons would actually be doing for the military, but it was undoubtedly going to require a lot of energy.

That meant oxygen, and lots of it, but also the ability to conserve when needed. The solution of course was cloacal respiration. In layman's terms, butt breathing. By increasing the number of blood vessels in the dragon's nether regions, I made it possible for them to absorb oxygen from water passing over that surface. Many aquatic reptiles, notably water turtles, did this pretty well. So did frogs and salamanders, for that matter.

I also increased the density of red blood cells, which would make this a very oxygen-efficient animal. There were risks to that, of course. More red cells meant fewer white blood cells, which were crucial for the immune system. There was a chance the marine dragons would be more prone to infections, but I had to be honest with myself about a grim truth: an infection was not high on the list of hazards these dragons would face in the field.

And that brought me to the other set of modifications necessary for this model. Advanced musculature, sharper teeth, longer claws. I made it slightly leaner than the Rover, though not quite as wiry as some of our land-based attack models. A deep chest and stouter frame would help with stability in the water. With all of it put together, I was still within spec. Tempting as it was, I didn't remove the domestication pathway. This might not be a friendly dragon, but it would have to be trainable. At least, it would have to go wherever its commanders pointed and destroy whatever (or whoever) they wanted it to destroy.

With that unpleasant thought, I hit the button to launch my biological simulator.

The dragon bloomed into existence over my desk, between me and the projection monitors. I'd increased the muscle bulk for the legs and the tail because those were the means of propulsion. Based on the video research, most of our current models relied mostly on their legs. Alligators and crocodiles, however, swam mostly with their tails. I figured the new model might be faster if it could use both.

My simulator evaluated an animal's swimming capability using numerous factors, but strength, coordination, aerodynamics, and buoyancy really drove the performance. I felt reasonably confident that this design would set a high bar. My simulator, however, quickly disabused me of that notion. The dragon could swim, but it looked unsteady in the water, as if too high up. I made some tweaks to the body shape in case it was an aerodynamics thing, but that only made the problem worse. The dragon went belly-up in the water and couldn't right itself.

"Shit."

Of course, that was the moment Korrapati knocked on my door. "Are you busy, Noah?"

"Not really. Come on in." I beckoned her to a chair.

"Is that the current design?"

"Yeah." I reset the simulator so she could see it right-side up, but the damn thing went belly-up again.

She lifted her eyebrows. "It looks . . . very buoyant."

"And yet it would still try to drown."

"What animal were you hoping to mimic?"

"I don't know, something between a lizard and an alligator."

"Ah." She seemed ready to say something, but clamped her mouth shut.

"You disagree?"

"It's a perfectly reasonable approach."

"Stop being polite, Korrapati. Say what you will."

"Wong and I were going to use a different strategy. Less reptile, more amphibian."

"A frog?"

"More like a salamander. Their body type is similar, but they move well in water and on land."

Why didn't I think of that? Once I'd gotten alligators in my head, I hadn't really considered other species to use as inspiration. Maybe this was a sign that I shouldn't try to do everything myself. Even when the stakes were so high. Especially when the stakes were so high. Wong was a great designer. So was Korrapati. I'd fought to get them back on my team. I leaned back and rubbed my eyes. "I thought maybe I'd have some stroke of genius, but it's not working."

"That bad, huh?"

"I don't design that many dragons for aquatic environments. It's hard."

"Yes, it is."

"I think it's time you and Wong take over again."

She gave me a doe-eyed look of pure innocence. "Oh, we could never."

"Wait, what?"

"Wong and I are but simple designers. We would not *dare* to design entire dragons by ourselves."

She's giving me crap now. "I'm sorry that I took the design."

"Why shouldn't you? You are the illustrious head of our massive department."

"Yes, our massive department of three people."

"Wong and I are perfectly happy sitting around with nothing to do. It's why we came here, after all."

"All right, Korrapati, I get it!"

She broke off the innocent act and gestured vaguely at my simulated dragon, which was still flopping upside down in the water. "Would you like us to start with this model, or . . ."

"Oh, God no. Let's pretend this never happened."

"All right." She smiled. "We'll get to work."

"Great." I paused. "What did you come by to talk to me about, by the way?" It wasn't like her to show up in my office unless she needed something.

"Nothing," she said, a little too quickly.

Oh, hell. "You came up here to demand the marine design back, didn't you?"

"Of course not. It's your outstanding leadership that led to this wise decision," she purred.

I laughed. "Oh my God, stop! Go do some actual work, will you?"

"With pleasure," she said.

"I'd better be wowed by what you two come up with."

"You will be."

When Major Nakamura reached out to Evelyn to set up a call the next morning, we had no idea why. I imagined it had something to do with the field trials, but the whole thing made me nervous. I arrived in the conference room to find Evelyn already there, lowering the RF shield. I brought up the lights to compensate.

"Wish I knew what this was about," I said. "Feels like it's going to be bad news."

"It's possible she simply wants to prepare us for the trials. To make sure we're ready."

Major Nakamura didn't strike me as one who spent a lot of time worrying about whether or not would-be contractors were ready, but I didn't say as much.

Evelyn connected us to the secure video conferencing server per Nakamura's instructions. The passcode for entry was sixteen alphanumeric characters long, and then there was a two-factor authentication thing that came to Evelyn's phone. But no, we still weren't in. It prompted us for yet a *third* authentication factor.

"That's odd." Evelyn checked her phone again.

Then I noticed *my* phone buzzing in my pocket. "Um." I took it out to find a text containing six digits. The sender was a restricted number. "Try . . . 612481."

She typed it in, and the code was accepted. To my great discomfort, it needs to be said. The message disappeared from my phone's screen. I went to my message history, and there was no trace of it.

"Did you give the major my number?" I asked.

"No."

"Then how did she get it?"

She gave me a flat look. "Noah, they're the Department of Defense."

The call connected in that moment, and Major Nakamura appeared on the viewscreen. She wore fatigues and was seated, but that was all I could discern. Every other identifying feature was seamlessly scrubbed from her background. Even the chair.

Evelyn smiled. "Hello, Major Nakamura."

"Hello, how are you." This was spoken as if it was a rhetorical question, and no answer was required. Or desired, perhaps. I started to open my mouth to answer.

Underneath the table, Evelyn stepped on my foot to shut me up. "What can we do for you?"

"I'd like to speak to you about the upcoming trial of your first dragon prototype."

"We're looking forward to it."

"As are we," Nakamura said. "As you may or may not be aware, during a competitive acquisition process, all bidder activities remain confidential to each bidding party."

"So I've been made to understand," Evelyn said.

I hadn't known, but it didn't surprise me. Especially when I thought about all of the proprietary technology that defense contractors showcased to win lucrative contracts. No one wanted their competitors getting a good look at their stuff. Intellectual property offered some protection in theory, but look how well that worked for us.

"The other bidder for this contract has offered to waive confidentiality for the upcoming field trial, if you were mutually agreeable." The major paused. "Naturally, I'm not able to share anything about the identity of the bidder without such a waiver."

You don't need to tell us, we know who it is. Evelyn and I looked at each other.

"What would the practical effect of a waiver be?" Evelyn asked.

"Your trials would take place on the same day, in the same location. All parties would have equal access to the performance evaluations of all equipment."

By equipment, she meant dragons. We'd see theirs, and they'd see ours. *But why would he want that?* It seemed equally advantageous to both sides.

"Do you mind if we confer for a moment?" Evelyn asked.

"Take your time." Major Nakamura switched off her video.

Evelyn did the same, muted our microphone, and looked at me. "What do you think, Noah?"

"I don't like this."

"Why not?"

"Greaves must have an angle. He wouldn't offer this otherwise."

"It would allow us to see his dragons and how they perform," she said. "That's useful information to have."

"Maybe so, but we're the ones with deep design experience. I'm guessing that's why he wants this. He can get a look at our prototype features and try to replicate them." Especially my built-in camouflage, which I thought might help tip the scales our way.

"It won't help him in the trials," she said. "He won't have time to change anything."

That was a fair point. True, he could take our ideas for future dragon designs, but the marine dragon had drastically different performance requirements. The flying model was where I really hoped we'd shine, but

Greaves had seen my best effort there. He was the one who canceled it. Sure, we were going to improve that model, but whatever he learned from that wouldn't help him. The trials would be over. *At the very least, it'll let us see what his design capabilities are, and maybe that will tell us what he's really up to.* That last thought was what brought me around. Evelyn was right; we needed information. "All right. I'm game if you are."

Evelyn turned our microphone and camera back on. "Major?"

Nakamura blinked back into view on our screen, as if we'd summoned a no-nonsense genie. "What did you decide?"

"We'll do it," Evelyn said. "But our dragons go first."

"I think that's reasonable. We'll see you at the trials." Nakamura gave us a nod, and then ended the call.

"I like how you asked for something in return," I said.

"It'll put the pressure on Robert."

Smart. The more we kept that guy guessing, the better. "I just hope we haven't played right into his hands."

CHAPTER FIFTEEN
The Trainer

Dragons have good instincts, and our infantry model would be no exception. Yet unlike many of our production models that served as family pets, anything designed for the military would need a lot of training. Beyond that, each dragon had to imprint on humans—specifically, their human handlers—right after hatching. Per my agreement with Evelyn, I'd kept my eyes on the design process while she worried about the logistics. There were lots of those in the DOD requirements, things about training and production and delivery. I'd ignored all of it and focused on the performance specs.

So when she told me I was going with the training team to deliver the infantry model eggs, it took me by surprise.

"Me?" I asked. "Are you sure?"

"The training team wants a designer there, so yes."

We stood in a corner of the hatchery, which was busier than it had been since I'd come back. Eight active pods. The unrelenting Arizona sun—which provided an ideal incubation temperature—streamed through their windows. Two teams of hatchery staffers moved among them, rotating the eggs in their synthetic foam beds.

It was hot in here, but I didn't mind. "Can't believe I'm saying this, but it's good to see hatchery staffers in here again."

"It is. And I'd like it to remain busy," she said. "Which is why you have to go."

"How far away is it?"

"It's near Yuma. Just under three hours."

"Three hours?" That would be my whole day, probably two days. Even longer if they needed me to stay to witness the training. "You know what? Let's send Korrapati."

"Do you know who's overseeing the hatching?"

I grinned. "I know you promised them Tom Johnson."

"That's who they're getting."

No way. "How in the heck did you pull that off?"

"I can be very persuasive," she said, in a faux-baritone imitation of my voice.

"You did learn from the best."

"I think he would like Korrapati fine, but he asked for you."

Maybe it was silly, but I felt like my heart actually skipped a beat. Tom Johnson had been a celebrity in the wildlife community well before he captured many of the reptilian species that went into the Dragon Genome Project. Despite the fact that he headed our Herpetology Department, I rarely saw the guy, much less interacted with him. The trip would be like a full day in his presence. *And he asked for me.* "When do we leave?"

Evelyn smiled. "Tomorrow morning."

% % %

That's how I found myself in the cab of a box truck at the crack of dawn, driving west into the still-dim Sonoran desert. The truck was all-electric, so the noise from the engine was little more than a hum. Even at a steady eighty miles per hour, it was eerily quiet. For the last five minutes, I'd been trying to think of something intelligent to say to Tom Johnson, who was driving. Since the start of the trip, he'd said a grand total of six words to me: *Hold this. Carry that. Let's roll.* For a guy who made a name for himself in television, he really didn't talk more than he had to.

"So, Mr. Johnson," I said at last. To my ears, I sounded like an awkward teen boy.

"Call me Tom, kiddo."

"So, Tom." It felt weird addressing him by his first name.

"What's your name?"

"Oh. I'm Noah Parker."

"Good to meet you," Tom said.

"We've met before at dragon hatchings. Twice, actually." *Not that I'm counting or anything.* "I thought you asked for me."

"Who said that?"

"Evelyn." The CEO, in other words.

"Oh, yeah."

"So you asked for me?"

"Kind of." He hitched a thumb toward the back of his truck. "Asked for the egghead who knew the most about these things."

Egghead. It wasn't my first choice for a nickname, but I'd heard worse. "Well, that's me."

"Tell me about 'em."

"Are you familiar with our attack dragons?"

"That's not a production model as far as I know."

"No, they're custom jobs, but we have a standard recipe."

Tom scratched his chin. "Think I saw one of those in action once."

"Really? In the wild?" I could picture that. Tom Johnson knee-deep in swamp water, narrating as he filmed one of our sleek attack dragons stalking some hapless animal. Maybe it was dark, but I took a grim sort of pride in how well I designed those models.

"No, it was in-house. Slaughtered this ridiculous pink-and-purple dragon that hatched in the same pod."

"I see." My burgeoning confidence deflated like a popped balloon. Yes, those had been my dragons, but also my mistake.

"So that's what these are, huh?"

"That was the starting point. We're not under the points system for these, so we made the teeth and claws longer. They'll have natural camouflage skin coloring, all with earth and desert tones. The main difference is in musculature, though. They're heavier, stouter, and stronger. Kind of like a Komodo dragon."

Tom grunted. "Komodos. Nasty buggers."

"You caught one of those for the Dragon Genome Project, didn't you?" I tried to make this a casual remark, more *I heard about this bit of trivia* than *I've memorized your life in every detail*.

"I caught *three* of them for the DGP."

"Three? What, were the first two not good enough?"

"Redwood wanted a female to make sure we got a copy of each chromosome."

"Oh, right, they're on the ZW chromosome system."

"Bingo."

In humans and placental mammals, biological males had one copy of each sex chromosome, X and Y. Lizards, monitors, and most birds had the opposite system; biological females had one copy of each sex chromosome, Z and W, whereas males had two copies of Z. The names of the chromosomes were arbitrary; geneticists only used different lettering to tell them apart. "Are females harder to catch?"

"None of them are easy. Hundred and fifty pounds of teeth and claws, with bony scales that are like a suit of chain mail."

I laughed. "Sounds like fun."

"The problem with catching a female was our permit from the Indonesian government. We couldn't take one if it was tending a nest."

"How do you know that in advance?"

"You just have to stalk them for a couple days to be sure."

The notion of tracking an apex predator through a tropical rainforest frightened me to my core. I liked the outdoors well enough, but I got to come home to a soft bed in an air-conditioned condo. Maybe that explained why this guy was famous, and I was not.

We talked more about the animals he'd caught for the DGP or for zoo collections, and he peppered me with questions about the design of the infantry dragon.

"How smart are they?" he asked.

"Similar to the Rover," I said.

He nodded, as if that were good enough. "What about behavior?"

"More aggression, less impulsiveness, and theoretically a stronger comfort with risk-taking."

"Theoretically?"

"These traits are a lot more complicated than physical attributes. Lots of genes involved," I said.

"Environmental factors, too."

"Yes." I was impressed. He might not be a genetics expert, but the guy knew his biology.

"That starts with the imprinting exercise at hatching."

"How's that going to work?" I asked.

"If everyone in the hatching environment wears the same uniform, the dragons will imprint on that rather than a specific handler."

"They will?"

"Theoretically."

"Heh. Good one."

"We haven't tried anything like this before, so there's some guesswork involved."

You can say that again.

Now that we'd broken the conversational ice, the time flew by. Before I knew it, we were turning off I-95 into the Yuma Proving Ground.

We encountered the first security checkpoint not far from the highway. Checkpoint was putting it mildly; raised concrete barriers blocked the entire road. A soldier in fatigues popped out of the attached guardhouse and signaled for Tom to stop the truck right in front. More soldiers materialized all around us; I had no idea where they came from. In seconds, the back of the truck was open and soldiers swarmed up in there, too. Once they'd checked my ID, I walked back there—slowly, of course— to keep an eye on things. Dragon eggs were fragile, and this was the most crucial period of incubation.

"Be careful with that!" Tom snapped. He'd beat me back there by five feet. "They're eggs, damn it!"

If the recipient of this warning apologized, I didn't hear it as I rounded the corner of the truck. There were two soldiers searching the egg crates—a man and a woman—neither of whom looked particularly contrite. However, they did seem to open the next crate with exaggerated care. Hatchers had packed the dragon eggs with biodegradable foam peanuts. The soldiers ran their hands down deep into the foam on all four sides of the egg before putting the lid back on. I kept an eye on the digital thermometer readout on the side. If the temperature dropped more than a couple degrees, the HVAC unit in the base of the crate would kick in and apply a little heat. It could cool the crate, too, if the temperature got too hot. Neither was necessary in this instance. Movement on the side of the truck caught my eye; now there were soldiers on either side inspecting the undercarriage with mirrors.

Serious about security. Then again, since I'd once found an unwanted device hidden under my Tesla, I understood. That had been a GPS tracker, not a bomb, but thinking of it still rattled me. Luckily, these soldiers found nothing untoward. A minute later, they gave us the go-ahead to proceed. They even closed the truck back up, and one of them opened the truck door for me. I climbed back in.

Tom, naturally, seemed perfectly at ease with this turn of events. He hit the button and put the truck into drive while the concrete barriers sank slowly into holes in the ground. We glided through.

"Good security here," I said.

"About as good as I've seen, outside the Pentagon."

"Did you say the Pentagon?"

He handed me a thick sheet of paper, a map with a travel route on it traced in red marker. "Here's our route. Get us to the right place."

"Okay, sure." *I haven't used a physical map in about five years, but I'll give it a whirl.* I gave the map a hurried inspection; it appeared to have the Yuma Proving Ground and the major highways around it. I got it oriented, found I-95, and located the security checkpoint. Just inside, there were three possible roads. I hadn't seen which one he took.

"Which way did you turn when we came in?"

"Left." He glanced at me and had a little smirk on his face. "Or maybe it was right. Not sure."

The left-hand route was the one marked in red on the map; it led northeast. The other choices would have taken us due east or south-southeast. It was midmorning, so the sun would be in the east-southeast. And it was pretty much to my right when I checked. "You took the left-hand turn. Which is the marked route."

"Hope you're right, and we don't end up in a minefield."

He wasn't kidding; there was an actual minefield

according to the legend. Not anywhere near our route, but it did exist. "No, that's southeast of here." I used the distance key and my pinkie finger to estimate. "And over three miles away from our route."

"You sure?"

"I'm sure. Stay on this road another half mile, and then we'll turn right." After the turn, the red line ran perpendicular to a series of thin parallel lines. "It'll take us uphill."

"Now you're just guessing."

No, I know how to read a topographical map. "Goes up around two hundred feet, then levels out, and we'll have arrived."

Tom gave me a sidelong look. "What, were you in the Boy Scouts or something?"

"Nope. I'm a geocacher."

He nodded in a way that suggested he knew the word, and why it often came with the ability to read a topo map. Admittedly, I hadn't used a physical printout in a while. I didn't even think they still existed. I flipped this one over and found the source. Printed by the Department of Defense. Well, at least some things didn't change.

"You got any dragon experience?" Tom asked. "Direct contact, I mean."

"I own one. More like a dragonet, but very smart. Had him for just over a year."

I didn't know why I'd told him that. The fact that I personally owned an unlicensed dragon was, at the very least, a violation of city ordinance, state law, and our company's agreement with the government. Which was why I'd never told anyone at Build-A-Dragon about it.

Now I'd just spilled the beans to a department head. *Well, at least I didn't tell him about* all *of my illegal pet dragons.* Or Redwood's guardians, or the attack dragon that had killed Fulton right in front of me. Yeah, I had some direct experience, all right.

"What's his name?" Tom asked.

"Octavius."

"Does he act like an emperor?"

"More often than I'd like," I said.

Tom chuckled.

"I'm not complaining. He's a good little guy," I said.

Tom made the right-hand turn. Sure enough, the road went uphill like I'd said. "You might be useful out here in the field with us," he said.

I could have refused. I'd come on this trip to represent the Design department and address any questions about our designs. The infantry models weren't cute little pets; they were engineered killing machines.

"Sure. Happy to help." Surely it was a safe facility and I'd be perfectly fine.

I'm sure that's what the pink-and-purple birthday dragon thought, too.

CHAPTER SIXTEEN
The Hatching

One of my favorite things about our dragons was the precision of incubation timing. The moment an egg slid out of the printer, we knew exactly when it would be ready to hatch, give or take fifteen minutes. Evelyn had planned our itinerary with that in mind; by the time we got to the designated parking area, we had about two hours to go. Several of Tom's staff had driven up early to prep the hatching area. I almost didn't notice them at first, because the dragon wranglers tended to keep to themselves at the company. Plus, they were all wearing the green-brown-tan pattern of camouflage that the soldiers were; they just didn't have names or rank insignia. Of course, it also helped that they were lounging in the shade of the squat stone building at the end of the parking lot. No one knew how to lounge better than our dragon wranglers. I supposed they were saving their strength for the wrangling of the dragons. Tom called them over and set them to unloading the eggs while he and I went inside.

The building turned out to be an old bunker with a single room. Large metal lockers lined the far wall. Closer to us, just inside the door, were stacks of large white coolers. These contained the raw meat we'd use to entice the hatchlings into bonding with humans. The only other thing in the room was a long metal table, around which six soldiers—three men, three women—stood together, all reading from stacks of crisp white paper.

"What is that?" I whispered to Tom.

"The training manual for the infantry dragons," he said. "Covers everything from hatching to discipline training."

They're actually reading it, too. That was the really impressive part. On the consumer side of our business, we had a manual that covered ninety percent of the issues customers called our support line about. The fact that they still called suggested that very few read it.

The soldiers kept reading, but straightened when another man walked in. Must have been an officer of some kind. He and Tom knew each other already; they shook hands. Then they were coming at me, and I was suddenly very conscious of how straight I was standing.

"This is Noah Parker," Tom said. "He'll assist with the hatching."

"Captain Santoro." He crushed my hand in a friendly sort of way.

"Good to meet you, sir," I said.

"You don't need to call me sir. You're a civilian."

"Right. Sorry about that."

"Let's get you suited up."

We followed him to the equipment lockers, where he

produced camouflage shirts and pants like the soldiers were wearing and gave us each a set. "Try these on."

We changed right there in the bunker. Normally, I'd have been a little self-conscious, but the thrill of getting to borrow a legit Army uniform more than compensated. The shirt didn't have a name or rank, just like the dragon-wranglers were wearing. It ended up a little big on me, but I didn't mind that, either.

Outside the bunker, the dragon wranglers had removed the eggs from their crates and placed them in a wide semicircle facing the bunker. Soldiers carried out the coolers and got them arranged in the middle of it, within easy reach. It looked like there was going to be one soldier in place for each dragon, which made things easy.

"How are we looking on time?" Tom asked.

I checked my watch. "Any minute now."

He set off and made a quick pass of the eggs, then came back to egg number four and pointed. "This one will be first, Captain."

I swear, the egg trembled as if obeying his command.

"Feldman," the captain said.

One of the young women ran forward and took up station in front of the egg, which had begun to crackle. She had a pile of raw meat in each hand. It might have been the heat, but I thought maybe her hands were shaking, too. *Rightly so.* I remembered my first hatching, back when we were trying to crack domestication. Pretty sure I shook a lot more than that.

Tom appeared at her shoulder and spoke to her in low tones. Another crack came from the egg and a snout emerged. Tom snapped his fingers and pointed to egg number three. The captain called a name, and another soldier jogged into place, fresh meat in hand. One of the dragon wranglers moved over to coach if needed. This happened three more times in quick succession. When there was one egg left, the remaining soldier moved in front of it without being told. I thought Tom might go over, but he was occupied helping the first dragon emerge from its shell while the soldier fed it. He caught my eye and jerked his head in that direction.

Guess he means me. The egg was already shaking by the time I joined the soldier, a clean-shaven guy whose name tape said his last name was Kim. He was about my age, Asian American, and his face was set with sheer determination. We watched the first crack appear, and the snout emerge. The dragon made fast work of the egg. Once it was two-thirds out, it shook itself and sent eggshell fragments flying. I jumped. Kim didn't so much as blink.

The dragon uncurled itself in a single sinuous motion. Its body was long, almost six feet snout to tail. The musculature rippled as it moved. Compared to the Rover or dragons like Octavius, it had a far more dangerous air. The spikes along the dorsal ridge—which were Wong's idea—added to the effect. It was thirty seconds old and already looked like a deadly predator. Its eyes fixed on us. The tongue flicked out, tasting the air. Kim reached out one of his hands, offering the meat. Which the thing had to smell, and if it was anything like other dragons I'd seen hatch, it was hungry.

"Come on," Kim said, his voice surprisingly soft. He turned his hand to give the dragon a better look at the meat.

I'll be damned, he did *read the manual.* This was the imprinting exercise right out of the Tom Johnson textbook. The only problem was, the dragon didn't budge. It lifted its head back and forth, watching us, but it stayed in the comfort of its little nest. Kim's determination flickered and he glanced at me. Oddly enough, it reminded me of when Octavius had hatched. He hadn't wanted to come near me, either.

"Try throwing him a little piece. Halfway between you."

Kim did that, keeping his motions calm and slow. The dragon fixated on the little piece of meat as it flew and landed wetly on the ground. It looked up at us, back at the meat, and lunged at it. The thing was *fast*. It scooped up the meat and chewed, watching us.

"Again," I whispered.

Kim threw another piece, which the dragon caught in midair. Now it was only a few feet away, watching with a bit more of an inviting expression. Kim took a knee and offered the rest of the meat in one of his hands.

The dragon came. I let out a breath I didn't realize I was holding. *It worked.* It had worked on Octavius, too, the only difference being that if I'd failed back then my life wouldn't have been in immediate peril.

"Nice work," I told Kim.

He smiled and gave me a nod. He and the dragon were almost touching now, and it didn't seem to bother the dragon at all. *Imprinting for the win.*

While he fed it, I took stock around the rest of the half circle. All of the soldiers had the dragons eating out of their hands. The things were ravenous, too. Most of the meat was already gone. But the tension was, too. The dragons now associated the humans in camouflage as a source of food and protection. The bond was in place.

Tom Johnson ambled over a few minutes later. He'd worked his way up the line, chatting with each soldier and admiring the dragons. He got to ours and congratulated Kim, pausing to pet the dragon along its back. I marveled at his instant rapport. The guy got along with every dragon as well as its owner.

Tom stepped over to stand next to me. "That went well."

"What do you think of the dragons?"

"They're well-built. I like the body shape, sort of a Komodo dragon who's been going to the gym."

I laughed. "Yeah, that's what we were going for."

"They're agile right out of the egg, too. The Army's going to love 'em."

"I hope so," I said. "So, what's next?"

"The risky part's over. The dragons get a nap, their handlers get a briefing from the captain."

"What do we get?"

"Lunch is what I'm thinking," he said.

Twenty minutes later, we were back on the highway headed home. Tom stopped at a taco shack on the side of the road. Good Taco, this one was called. It was the kind of place that had a handwritten menu and only accepted cash. By the time I extricated myself from the passenger seat, he'd already ordered. For both of us. In fluent Spanish. I kept an eye on the truck, mainly because he'd left it running. He came back a minute later with two bags of tacos and chips and two non-brand colas on ice. The delicious aroma made my stomach growl. *Hatching dragons is hungry work.* I was going to smell like the taco shack when this was done, but I didn't care.

"You speak Spanish like a native," I told him.

"I picked it up when I lived in South America."

"Man, you really have been all over the place."

"I go where the animals are. Often as not, that's somewhere they don't speak English." He put the truck in drive.

"We can eat here if you want."

"Nah, I'd just as soon get home to the family."

Your wife of fifteen years and your two kids. I elected not to volunteer that I had this information. "Works for me."

He turned out to be an especially adept driver-while-eating. Of course, it helped that the truck had an auto-drive feature. The hand on the wheel was mostly for show. "You married?" he asked.

"No."

"Girlfriend?"

I sighed. "Kind of."

He laughed. "What kind of answer is that?"

"She's mad at me."

"What did you do?"

His casual lob of that question took me aback. "Why do you think *I* did something?"

"Oh, come on."

"Well, basically, I agreed to do this. The whole developing-dragons-for-weapons thing. She doesn't like it."

"Why not?"

"She thinks it's wrong to subvert nature into killing machines."

"Nature does a pretty good job of that on her own, if you ask me."

I couldn't help but smile. "You'd know."

"Yeah, I would."

It reminded me of something I really wanted to ask him, and I figured now was my best chance. "How did Evelyn get you to do this, anyway? You've always been really protective of dragons."

"And?"

"Training them for the DOD seems out of character."

"I don't agree." He took a slug from his soda, but never took his eyes from the road. "Let's say I wasn't here. Would the company still be trying to win this contract?"

I didn't know how much he knew about the company's financial problems, and it occurred to me that maybe I shouldn't say. But ultimately it didn't matter, because the answer was the same. "Probably so."

"Someone was going to have to hatch the dragons and train the people. If it's me, then I know it's done right," he said. "That gives them the best chance of survival. Seems pretty protective to me."

"Fair point. Still a lot of responsibility to take on, though."

"I figure I owe it to them to try."

He owes it to the dragons. Now that I thought about it, maybe I did, too.

CHAPTER SEVENTEEN
The Deal

Director-level systems permissions gave me some new privileges at Build-A-Dragon that I hadn't yet explored. First on the list, and something I was very excited about, was access to some of Build-A-Dragon's internal camera feeds. It was possible that they'd granted this to Evelyn's office workstation, not realizing she moved upstairs. I didn't know, and I wasn't going to ask. Build-A-Dragon, like many high-tech companies, was careful about where they placed their cameras and sensors. Hardware and the systems that controlled it could be hacked, so it was risky to point a camera at anything that might be proprietary.

Even so, there were plenty of cameras in public spaces—I'd catalogued most of these back when I was working as a sometimes-rogue employee with a hidden agenda—and my workstation had access to most of those. I opened separate projection monitors with the feeds from the main entrance, the design lab, and the hatchery.

I didn't turn up the sound—that felt creepy and invasive—but the visual feed was plenty entertaining. The hatchery was quiet, but the building's main entrance had plenty of people coming and going. Most of them worked in sales or customer service, but there was the occasional exception—Wong and Korrapati going out to lunch, Evelyn entertaining some visitors in suits, even the occasional group of dragon wranglers sauntering out the front door. It was always easy to spot the dragon wranglers. I thought I recognized a couple of them from the dragon hatching sessions, but I couldn't be sure.

By the end of the week, the workplace voyeurism lost its cachet. I went back into my workstation and spent some time running the list of VUSes from Connor's patient-friends through my biological simulator. Sure enough, they all seemed disruptive enough to cause BICD2-associated syndrome. Some were more severe than Connor's variant; some were predicted to have milder consequences. Any of them, in the right model system, should disrupt muscle fiber development enough to have a demonstrable effect on a tissue biopsy.

All I needed was a dragon to put them in.

Of course, that was a problem right now. We weren't designing new prototypes for the wider market, and because I'd tasked Korrapati and Wong to work on custom orders while I fiddled with the marine design, that queue was empty as well. We weren't even printing eggs for the DOD designs; Evelyn wanted to wait and see how the first trials went. I had a feeling resources were stretched thin at the moment; whatever capital we currently had was committed to winning the contract. It sucked, but there was nothing I could do about it right now.

Friday after lunch, I finally had to take a break from the modeling. It was almost the weekend, and for the first time in a while I wasn't expecting to come into work on Saturday or Sunday. Which meant maybe I could see Summer, and try to follow Tom's unspoken advice.

She and I had remained at an unspoken truce for the past couple of weeks, and we'd both been so busy we hadn't even fit in a geocache. I usually called her Friday nights anyway. Maybe I could talk her into doing a geocache tomorrow. It would have to be special, though. Something that really drew out her competitive side. I brought up the geocaching app on my phone to start a search. That's when I saw the notification.

New geocache near you.

"Oh, let it be." We didn't get new geocaches often. You had to get a permit from the city to install them, and promise to do annual maintenance. It was a whole thing. Any cache we hadn't claimed already was worth more points. As long as it was close.

It was close, all right. Even better, the cache had only gone up this morning. That was incredibly lucky timing. New geocaches went live after a two-step process. First, the cache owner registered the coordinates of the cache, ideally with two independent devices. The cache got submitted, but didn't become public knowledge until a team of volunteer moderators approved it. Someone had probably established this nano cache over the weekend, submitted it, and just now gotten approval. I held my breath and scrolled down to the cache log.

0 entries.

"Oh, hell yes." I flipped out of the app and called Summer.

"Hi," she answered, with a twinge of concern. She knew what a crazy week it had been. "I'm still at work."

"Yeah, I figured," I said. "Did you get the notification?"

"About what?"

"There's a new geocache."

She sucked in a sharp breath. "Where?"

"Glendale," I said.

"Are you serious?"

"In Lawrence Park. It's a nano."

Nano caches were usually tiny, usually an inch long and half as wide. They contained no toys or trinkets; there was only room for the microchip and a tiny rolled-up paper log. You had to bring your own pen to sign it. They were so small that many were hidden virtually in plain sight in public areas—screwed into a signpost, tucked in an alcove, or attached to a handrail via magnet.

"I love those," she said.

"I know. And here's the best part. It went up this morning, and no one's logged it yet."

"Shut up!"

"We can get the FTF." That meant *first to find*, and it was a distinct honor for a new geocache. In the ranking system, it was as good as finding five caches in a single day. Because Phoenix was so crowded, I'd never gotten one myself. Neither had she.

"Damn," she said. "Someone's bound to get it this weekend."

"Which is why I think we should go now," I said. "Do you think you can get away?"

"I don't know."

"Come on, it's Friday afternoon. You've put in, what, sixty hours this week already?"

"I guess no one will care if I leave a little early."

That's my girl. "Want me to pick you up?" Lawrence Park was closer to her than it was to me. In fact, I'd pass her firm on the way. It made sense. Plus, it meant more time with her. A win-win.

"Good idea. I'll grab my boots from my Jeep."

"I'll be there in fifteen."

"See you." She hung up.

I made some frenetic flicking gestures on my touchpad to shut down all of my projection monitors. I saved the video feed for last, though, and cycled away from the hatchery cams to the parking garage. Yes, there was my Tesla in center frame. On the first floor, too—yet another perk of director-level ranking within the company. I found my key fob and pressed the button for remote start. The brake lights flashed. *Yes.* My old workstation wasn't in range of the parking garage, but Evelyn's former office certainly was.

I logged out of my system, grabbed my bag, and walked out. The lights were motion-activated, so they'd shut off automatically in fifteen minutes. Until then, if someone stopped by and it seemed like I'd just stepped out, so much the better. I caught a quick elevator down to the parking structure and had my Tesla back out the moment I could lay eyes on it.

I hopped in.

"Hello, Noah," the car said.

"Hello, gorgeous."

"You're leaving work early today."

I laughed. "Don't you start."

"Where would you like to go?"

"Summer's work."

"Summer's work," she repeated. "I can get you there in ten minutes."

"Okay. Remind me when we're one minute away." I double-checked the nano cache's page. Still no finds logged, thank goodness. I pulled up a map of Lawrence Park and decided which of the two modest parking lots would put us closest to the cache. I grabbed its coordinates and beamed them to the car's navigation system as a secondary destination.

"One minute to destination," said the car.

"Wow, that was fast." I put my hands on the wheel and my foot on the gas. "Disengage auto drive."

"Disengaging."

I swung into the long circle drive for Summer's firm and approached the main building. There she was. She stood in the shade of the building's entrance portico wearing shorts, a tank top, dark sunglasses, and an air of visible impatience. The whole ensemble looked pretty good. Maybe there was a better use of our time than this geocache, no matter the allure of the FTF honors.

She pulled my door open almost the moment I'd stopped moving. "Right on time!"

I patted the Tesla's dashboard. "Wish I could take credit."

"Hi." She closed the door, leaned over, and kissed me hello.

This only brought about certain stirrings and even

further doubts that geocaches were the best use of our time. Yet before I could voice an alternative, she'd pulled back to buckle her seat belt. "Let's go."

I suppressed a sigh. "Resume navigation."

"Do you want to go to the next waypoint?" the car asked.

"Yes," I answered.

"Twelve minutes to destination."

"Thank you, gorgeous."

Summer snorted. "You know it's only a car, right?"

"Hey, don't be jealous."

"I'm more disturbed than jealous."

"You're disturbed, all right."

She punched me, but it was playful. "Are you planning to do the cache in those?" She pointed at my shoes.

"Crap, you're right." I flipped on the autopilot and fumbled to extract my hiking boots out of the backseat.

"Um, hands on the wheel, please!" Summer said.

"It's on autopilot." I gestured to the wheel, which made a minute adjustment to keep us between the lines on the highway.

"So the machine's driving us now?"

"Just for a minute."

"You know how I feel about that."

I found my boots and kicked off my loafers as I fumbled the laces clear. "It's perfectly safe. I don't know why it worries you."

She gripped her door handle so hard that her knuckles turned white. "I just . . ."

"What?" I prompted.

She lowered her voice. "I don't trust her."

"Why? It's only a car, right?"

"I'd rather not discuss it here."

I finished lacing my boots. "It's a useful feature. Keeps my hands free for more important things." I reached out and brushed a strand of hair behind her ear, and let my hand linger on her cheek. "You really *are* gorgeous."

"All right, keep focused, will you? We have a cache to find." She pulled my hand down from her cheek, but she held on to it.

"Arriving at destination," the car said.

Both of us eyed the other cars in the lot while we pulled in. There was a gray coupe plastered with dog-themed bumper stickers in one corner, and a dented electric minivan in the other. Dog walker and family outing, by my guess.

"Good, no competition," Summer said.

"You have the coordinates?"

"Already loaded."

"Me too."

"Let's go." She threw open her door almost before the car parked itself in an open spot.

I climbed out, locked it, and checked my watch. "Zero-point . . ."

"Three-six miles," Summer finished.

That's what my watch said, too. "Well, that's a good sign," I said.

A distant rumble sounded then, almost like thunder. Yet the skies were clear. It grew louder, eventually announcing the arrival of an oversized silver pickup with off-road tires. It rolled past us on its way to parking across two spaces. The rear bumper had a sticker that read CACHERS FIND THE SPOT EVERY TIME.

"Shit," Summer said.

"You saw it?"

"Yeah. Come on." She grabbed my hand and pulled me down the gravel trail that began just past the parking lot.

"Okay, then." By instinct, I went to check my watch, but she held my hand tightly and kept my arm pinned downward.

"Don't look," she said. "*Listen.*"

"I *am* listening." I heard a heavy truck door open, then boots crunching gravel, then the door slamming shut. He or she was alone. If we were lucky, he was just now turning on his GPS device, which meant we had a ninety-second lead on him. At most. But now I heard what she wanted me to hear, the series of soft but regular beeps that came from her watch. She'd activated homing mode, which caused the watch to emit audible tones as we approached the target. "Oh."

"We're out for a walk, got it?"

I barely heard her; I was too focused on the sounds her watch was making. Based on the geocache coordinates overlaid with satellite imagery, the cache was in a little copse of trees. There was only one of those in view at the right distance. I steered us toward it, trying to act casual. Sure enough, the beeps gradually increased in frequency. It was like a faint version of the sonar from *Jaws*. I hazarded a glance behind us. There was a guy in jean shorts, a tank top, and combat boots walking the same direction as us, maybe seventy-five yards back. He was gaining, though.

"It can't be far," Summer whispered.

We followed the path into the copse of trees, grateful

for the bit of shade. I pulled us to a halt soon after, that, though.

"What?" she asked.

"We just went off course."

We moved left off the trail and the beeps slowed even more. So, we backtracked and went right. *Yes.* More beeps, and then a soft chime that signaled arrival.

"It's here," Summer said. "Give or take five yards."

"Oh good, 'cause it's only a nano cache." And looking around, there were far too many places a nano could hide.

Summer squeezed my hand. "Less talking, more looking."

"I'm trying. But he's going to be here any second."

"Maybe I could go, you know, stall him."

I knew that by *stall* she meant *flirt with* and I didn't like that idea. Nor did I think it would work. "He had to see us walk in here holding hands. I think he'd know what you were doing."

"Do you, or do you just not want me talking to other guys?"

"Oh, I definitely don't want you talking to other guys."

She laughed. "You're adorable."

Under the edge of the foliage, I saw the heavy boots approaching our position. "You know what? That gives me an idea."

She was still looking for the cache and didn't catch my meaning until I pulled her into me.

"Oh—" she had time to say, and then we were kissing.

I'd meant it as a strategy. Moments later when Tank Top ambled into the trees, spotted us, and then hastily retreated out of sight, it seemed like a good one. The part of it I didn't plan for was how nice it was to be kissing Summer again. Or the softness of her lips, or the feel of her body against mine when I held her so close. As a result, I completely forgot what the purpose of the strategy was. When she put a hand on my chest and pushed me back, I started to voice a protest.

She put a finger on my lips and whispered, "I think I see it."

"Huh?" My brain had a little trouble reacquainting itself. *Oh, right.* I released her and she took two steps to the nearest tree. There was a small gray protuberance on its trunk wedged into a natural opening in the bark.

Summer pried it out; it was only about an inch long, but clearly man-made. There was a seam in the middle, so she held it on top and bottom and twisted. The top half came free, revealing a tiny, tight-rolled length of paper.

"The cache log," I breathed.

She plucked it out of the tube, and then appeared to have a moment's panic. "I didn't bring a pen."

I fished in my pocket and came out with two pens. "Do you prefer black or blue?"

"I knew you'd prove yourself useful."

"All right, let's check it." This was the moment of truth.

She unfurled the log, which was a single sheet of lined paper about an inch wide and over a foot long. Nano logs were specialized print jobs, so we had to inspect the front and the back. She let out a breath she'd been holding. "No entries!"

I handed her the blue pen. "Put us down for the win, and don't be afraid to go John Hancock."

I held the log flat across the back of my phone while

she signed our handles along with the date and time. Then we each took a turn plugging the tiny chip drive—embedded into the cache tube's lid—into our phones to make it official. Summer rolled up the log while I verified our credit. Then we reassembled the nano cache, jammed it back into the tree, and hurried out of the copse.

Tank Top guy had lingered nearby, and seeing us depart, walked right in with his eyes glued to a handheld GPS.

"Too late," Summer whispered.

"Shh. Two more incoming." I'd spotted two older women on the path coming toward us. They walked arm in arm, looking at a watch one of them wore. I took Summer's hand and resumed the out-for-a-stroll routine. They smiled at us as they passed.

"Jeez, if I hadn't left right away to pick you up, this would have all been for nothing," I said, once we were out of earshot.

"For nothing?" Summer's tone carried a hint of danger.

"I meant, no FTF credit," I said quickly, squeezing her hand. "Obviously I loved knocking off early and getting to see you."

"Good save."

"Mostly I'm relieved you came at all. So, you're not mad about the DOD thing?"

She sighed and let go of my hand. "I still don't like it."

"Because it seems wrong to make dragons for war."

"It's wrong to make dragons at all, but especially for war."

"I get it," I said. "But when I was talking to Tom, he made a really good point."

"You're calling him Tom, now?"

"He told me to! Anyway, I asked him why he's doing it."

"What did he say?"

"He said he realized it was going to happen whether he wanted it to or not, and he wants to make sure we do it right."

She was silent for a moment. "That's . . . noble of him."

"And he's a tree hugger like you."

"Hey!" She jabbed me with an elbow.

I caught her arm, though, and slid my hand into hers again. "That's why I have to do it, too. The dragons will get made either way. At least if I involve myself, I know we'll do right by them."

She let me keep holding her hand. I took that for a good sign.

"I have conditions," she said.

"Go on." I'd agree to almost anything if it meant having her support.

"Condition one, full disclosure. You have to tell me everything you're allowed to. The good and the bad."

"Sounds reasonable," I said.

"Condition two, you balance the work on this project with other things, like the mutations Connor asked you about for his group, and new prototypes that aren't made for killing."

"I can do that."

"It won't be easy, Noah. You have obsessive tendencies."

"Ouch."

"It's true and you know it. I don't want to be with

someone who spends all day every day thinking about maximizing destruction."

She wasn't wrong. Even working on the infantry prototype had consumed me for days at a time. I'd gone to bed trying to think over every feature, and woken up thinking about it, too. I preferred to think about my tendencies as *hyper-focused* rather than *obsessive*, but I didn't want to bicker about semantics. "Fair enough. I will balance."

She nodded. "Condition three—"

"How many conditions are there?"

"This is my last one." She fell silent as we neared the parking lot, where another couple had just started down the trail. They were probably about our age, but wearing all dark clothing despite the heat. The girl had a pixie cut and tattoos of roses on both arms. The guy was tall and lanky, with spiky dyed-black hair. He had so many visible piercings that I nearly winced. I offered a half smile as we passed them, but otherwise tried not to make eye contact. The two motorcycles in the lot parked side by side had to be theirs. One of them had a name bedazzled in cursive on the side. Jojo.

I squeezed Summer's hand and nodded at the bike so she'd see it.

"It's them," she hissed.

Jojo and Prickly Pete. Our rivals on the local leaderboard.

"They're too late."

"Barely."

We climbed into my car. I started it so that the A/C would start cooling us off.

"Ahh . . ." I sighed and closed my eyes. It was a relief to have bagged the FTF, but this also meant our little jaunt was over. Now I had to take her back to work, and she might decide to call it a night. "How about we go to your place and have dinner? I can take you to get your Jeep tomorrow." *Or Sunday, or even Monday.* A whole weekend together without any work would be pretty fantastic.

"Condition three," she said.

"I was hoping you'd forgotten."

"Nope." She put on her seatbelt and fussed with it, probably stalling to figure out how to say it. "I want you to promise me that if this DOD contract goes south or Evelyn breaks her promises, you'll walk away."

"From the contract?"

"From the job."

"I see." This was serious. Leaving Build-A-Dragon would mean starting over. I really hoped it wouldn't come to that, but it wasn't entirely in my control. She was right, though. Once I put my mind to a scientific challenge, it was hard to stop. I needed someone to tell me when it was time to pull the plug. I wanted it to be her. I put my hand on top of hers and looked her in the eyes. "I accept your conditions."

She exhaled, as if she'd been holding her breath. She smiled. "You can take me home now."

I grinned like an idiot and put the car into drive.

CHAPTER EIGHTEEN
The Mentor

The desert trials took place in southeast Arizona, about halfway between Phoenix and Tucson. Evelyn had lobbied hard to make this the first trial, to give us a boost of confidence. Our dragons did well in the desert; hell, the original prototype had been created to hunt hogs in the southwest. The Guardian, as it was later named, had proven the most effective population control measure invented. Invasive wild hog populations were down ninety percent. That was good for ranchers and wildlife preserves, though not as good for us. Orders for the Guardian were also down ninety percent from their peak levels.

Yet another reason we needed the contract.

We met in the desert in the high, dry heat of early summer. I thought the heat a good thing. Dragons liked the hotter days in Arizona. Some weeks, we could almost hatch the eggs outside rather than in their incubators. Korrapati and Wong were going to hold down the fort at

Build-A-Dragon while Evelyn and I drove up to watch the trials. I'd offered to take us in my Tesla, but she insisted on driving herself.

She knocked on my door at nine thirty, dressed and ready to go. "Are you ready, Noah Parker?"

I checked my watch to be sure I had the time right. "Uh, sure. Let me grab my things." Truth be told, I'd only just gotten into work and figured we wouldn't leave until ten, maybe ten fifteen. *Why is she here so early?*

Ten minutes later, as I sat in the passenger seat of her silver SUV and watched the needle on the speedometer hover one below the speed limit, I understood.

"So, what happened to the car service?" The last time I'd seen her out and about, she had a black sedan with a uniformed driver.

"I still use it sometimes, but I missed driving too much." She pressed the button to wash her windshield for the third time, then quickly returned her hands to the ten-and-two position. "It helps me think."

It made me think, too, that it might have been faster for me to walk. "Fair warning, I might fall asleep."

"Are you tired?"

"It's been a rough month." We'd started tackling the next design while we waited for this trial, and meeting the requirements was proving even harder. "These DOD specs are ridiculous. It's like they make everything hard on purpose."

"The specs ensure that whatever the contractor supplies will do what they need it to," Evelyn said.

"I guess. It took a lot longer than I expected, that's all." We'd had more than our fair share of overdemanding customers over the years. It wasn't like this was a completely foreign experience for me. Still, with a Build-A-Dragon retail customer we always had the option of saying no. What were they going to do, find a different dragon manufacturer? Most clients, faced with that choice, found a way to be reasonable. Not so with the DOD, apparently.

"The DOD wants a level playing field. If their bid were a perfect match to what we can already do, it would unjustly favor us."

"Wouldn't be the worst thing," I muttered.

Evelyn checked her mirrors, put on her signal, checked her mirrors *again*, and eased into the right lane. There were no other vehicles in sight. On one hand, she'd pass a driving test with flying colors. Whereas I probably wouldn't. On the other hand, we might never actually get there.

"I know some people who work in the defense industry," she said.

"Oh, I'm sure you do."

Her mouth fell open. "What are you implying, Noah Parker?"

"You have contacts *everywhere*."

"Is that such a bad thing?"

I considered it for a moment. She'd built a reputation in academia, moved to big pharma, made the jump to biotech, and then worked her way up to CEO at biotech. While I enjoyed giving her trouble about knowing everyone in tech, it hadn't exactly harmed her career. "I guess it's good to network."

"Network." She repeated it with disdain. "I never liked

that term. I build relationships with good people. Competent people. They can come in handy."

"How? Our industry is so small and specific."

"There is more crossover than you realize. We got early access to Switchblades because Robert knew some of the people there."

"Oh, I remember." Back in grad school when I was desperate for more computational resources, I'd read a magazine article about Greaves. There was this photo of him in front of his Switchblade servers. There was a microchip shortage at the time and nobody could get Switchblades. The waiting list was a year and a half. Somehow Greaves had gotten *stacks* of them. "They were one of the reasons I came."

"And one of the reasons we recruited you, because we actually had the resources to run your simulator on a complex genome."

"Very true." Granted, there were other companies that had good setups, but none of them were producing synthetic organisms close enough to human that it could help Connor. I nearly told her about his support group and the other BICD2 patients who were desperate for their own answers. But I bit my lip, because I knew how that would go. Right now it was all-hands-on-deck for the DOD bid.

"And now, my relationships with people in the defense industry may be just as valuable."

"What have they told you?"

She shrugged. "Apparently, this is similar to every acquisitions process."

"Yikes."

"Also, we've operated under the assumption that either we will win the DOD contract, or Robert Greaves will. In past acquisitions, there have been multiple winners. Competitors can receive joint awards."

"Well, that would be a nightmare." There was no way in hell I'd work with Robert Greaves again.

"There have also been contracts that no one wins. It's possible they will decide not to acquire dragon technology from either of us."

"So there are two ways to lose." I sighed and shook my head. "It's a wonder anyone gets into defense contracting voluntarily."

"The money is good."

"Yeah, sure. But how good can it really be?"

"Hundreds of billions."

I don't think I heard that right. "I think you mean hundreds of millions."

She laughed. "Noah, a single fighter jet costs more than fifty million."

"Hundreds of *billions*, huh?" It was hard to even put a figure like that into perspective. It was the entire revenue Build-A-Dragon had ever made since its founding, many times over.

"That's only the procurement budget," Evelyn said. "Less than a quarter of the DOD's funding."

"Jeez." Well, we'd said we wanted deep pockets. They could sure afford dragons if they wanted them. "So, what's it going to take to really capture a piece of that?"

"Prove that we can deliver what they need, and that we can do so better than our competitors."

"How are they going to decide?"

"They'll look at how well we meet the performance metrics. If it's still close, then I don't know. It's up to the acquisition corps."

"How much do we know about them?"

"Little. I hadn't met any of them before their visit."

"Not even Major Nakamura?" Somehow I doubted that. Nakamura was a Japanese surname. Evelyn was Chinese, but they were both smart, ambitious women who intimidated me. There had to be a club.

"I'd heard of her."

"Big surprise." I cleared my throat. "So, any insights you can offer?"

"She's the one we have to win over."

I was afraid of that.

Her GPS, which she'd muted after its constant barrage of "insufficient speed" warnings, finally flashed a message that we were approaching our destination. The lot itself was a flat rectangle of hard-packed gravel with no painted spaces. Maybe thirty yards across, bounded by the road on one side and a ten-foot chain-link fence on the other. Two weatherworn signs adorned the fence. One just said KEEP OUT. The other promised that vehicles parked without a permit displayed would be confiscated. Not towed, not booted until you paid a fine. *Confiscated.*

"I hope you have a permit," I said.

She tapped the dashboard, where a two-inch square piece of paper that I hadn't noticed sat unobtrusively beneath the glass. It bore a large two-dimensional barcode.

"That's it?"

"That's what the majors sent me."

"Hmm." As barcodes went, it was almost comically oversized. "Oh, don't tell me." I leaned forward and craned my neck upward. Yes, there it was, a black speck against the otherwise clear sky.

"What is it?"

"A drone."

As if on cue, a red horizontal line appeared on the barcode, centered itself, and rotated. It flickered to green for two seconds, then disappeared.

"Good security," Evelyn said.

"You know what? I'm glad you drove us."

She laughed, but broke off as the crunch of gravel announced another vehicle arriving. It was a big SUV with dark-tinted windows. The sight of it brought a cold feeling to my stomach.

"I hope that's our host," Evelyn said.

"No," I said. "It's him."

I didn't have to say his name. The driver's door opened, and there he was. Robert Greaves. A man somehow still fawned over by the business media despite his inglorious departure from Build-A-Dragon. To my great irritation, he looked the same as ever. Same black fitted shirt and sunglasses as always. Same air of easy confidence.

A wave of self-doubt swept over me. It froze me in place. But I'd be damned if I let the guy think he had such an effect on me. I forced myself to open the door, walk around the front of the car, and look him right in the eye.

"Hello, Parker," Greaves said. He made it sound pleasant, like we were old friends.

I didn't answer him. To my credit, I also didn't reply with a rude gesture.

"Evelyn," he said, with a nod to his former protégé.

"Hello, Robert."

"You look well."

"As do you."

These seemed like polite words, though they were exchanged like the early jabs in a sword fight.

"No driver?" Greaves asked.

"I felt like driving."

"And you still got here. You must have left at what, eight A.M.?"

Normally I'd have chuckled, but I wasn't in the goddamn mood. Evelyn didn't rise to the bait, either.

Our silence seemed to disappoint him. "I wasn't sure you guys were going to show."

"Why not?" I asked. Maybe a bit louder than necessary, because he snapped his tinted gaze from her to me.

"Because you don't really have a chance at this contract," he said.

I scoffed. We were the company with the reputation and the proven tech. It had to be a bluff. *But why does he sound so certain?* It irked me. "Last time I checked, it was Build-A-Dragon one, Robert Greaves zero."

He stared at me for a moment, his face unreadable. "Not sure that's where the score stands, actually."

I glanced at Evelyn. Her face, too, was neutral, but she'd clenched her jaw.

Further niceties were interrupted by the arrival of three Army Humvees. They roared up the road and just stopped, effectively blocking both lanes, rather than pull into the lot itself. A soldier in fatigues jumped out and opened the back door of SUV number two. "Dr. Chang!"

"Come on, Noah." Evelyn shut her car door, activated the alarm, and marched up to the road to the waiting SUV. I followed her, hoping that was what I was supposed to do.

Robert Greaves. Man, I'd forgotten how much I hated the guy.

CHAPTER NINETEEN
The Trial

We convened in a large, utility concrete structure near another ten-foot chain-link fence, this one plastered with signs reading WEAPONS RANGE—KEEP OUT. Beyond these lay a rugged landscape of scree and cacti, most of it too dense to see anything useful. The building itself was at least two stories tall, and the concrete glistened as if recently poured. Still, I couldn't help but feel a little disappointed. Even if we stood on the roof of the structure, we probably wouldn't have much of a view.

A man and a woman in Army fatigues led us down a long flight of stairs into the semidarkness. There, we encountered a security checkpoint that made Build-A-Dragon's procedures look like Mickey Mouse. Our escorts keyed us in through two steel doors that led to a small kind of anteroom. There, two more soldiers, both dudes, both of them huge, asked to see our IDs—mine and Evelyn's—which they passed under a scanner interface discreetly tucked into an alcove in the wall. Meanwhile, yet another pair of soldiers—both women, and both cradling automatic weapons—watched the proceedings with impassive expressions.

We stood there in silence for at least ten or fifteen awkward seconds. I couldn't decide where to look, and settled on my hands, which I held carefully in front of me. Then a buzzer sounded, everyone relaxed, and I started breathing again. Our escorts pulled open the inner doors. We passed through and entered a large, well-lit room. A few more personnel with a decidedly tech-savvy vibe occupied the workstations along both walls—some typing on keyboards, others speaking softly into headsets. I registered their presence for a brief moment before my eyes were drawn to the far wall, which was lined with high-definition flatscreens. Not projection monitors, but next-gen display mesh that even we couldn't get out hands on yet. Of course the military had it, and they put it to good use. The definition was *incredible*. It was like using your own eyes to look at something with a pair of binoculars. There were four rows of four panels each, each one rotating through a few video feeds. Some showed areas inside the bunker, like our security checkpoint, but most were exterior views showing rocky desert terrain or sun-drenched buildings.

For a brief moment, I remembered the first time I'd been inside Ben Fulton's office at Build-A-Dragon. It was called Reptilian Corporation then, and I'd been getting ready to start my first day. The guy would have loved it here. The cameras shifted and pivoted views so quickly, it had to be controlled by some sort of AI. In harmony, they all shifted to show the same dilapidated stone building. It was two or three stories high, with several windows and a single door out front. I thought I saw a flicker of movement inside, but it was hard to tell. Then all the views pivoted away, and it was gone.

I leaned in to Evelyn. "Do you have any idea what's happening?"

"No."

"Got to admire the tech, though. When can we get some of these monitors?"

"When we get the contract. Maybe."

The soldiers who'd escorted us stood up straighter—which I hadn't believed possible—as Major Johnson swept into the room. He waved the tech operators back to their chairs before they'd finished standing, and turned to greet us. "Dr. Chang, Dr. Parker. Good to see you again."

"Good to see you, Major," Evelyn said smoothly. "And please, call me Evelyn."

I shook his hand. "You can call me Parker, if you'd like." Fulton had done that. I kind of missed it.

"I like your style, Parker," Johnson said.

"Is this a new facility?" Evelyn asked.

"Some of it, including this bunker. The range has been mothballed for a while."

"What was it used for?" I asked.

Johnson gave me a flat look, and then looked back at the monitors. "Something else."

"Right. Sorry." I kept forgetting who these people were and how little they were allowed to talk about their jobs.

Evelyn swept in to my rescue. "Will Major Nakamura be joining us?"

"She's watching from the other building."

The other building, where our competitors are, I

thought grimly. Evelyn pursed her lips, and I gathered she'd had the same suspicion. We all knew Nakamura was the shot caller. The fact that Greaves had her at his elbow wasn't a good sign. Nor was it an accident, most likely. Our former boss was good at worming his way close to influential people.

Evelyn started to ask a follow-up, but one of the operators cleared her throat and said, "Major?"

Johnson acknowledged this with a nod, and drew our attention to the monitors. "It's starting."

The camera angles shifted again to the run-down building. Holes pockmarked the worn stone surface, and there was no front door. Without warning, gunfire erupted from two of the windows. The staccato bursts caught me off guard, and I nearly stumbled into Evelyn.

"Those are simulators," Johnson said, pointing to each of the windows where the guns had gone off. "Not live rounds, but made to look and sound like them."

I'd let my eyes drift to some of the other monitors, the ones that showed the boulders and crags of the surrounding landscape. There was a flicker of motion, and then the loping, almost elegant movement I'd come to recognize in our attack dragons.

I nudged Evelyn. "Here they come."

The dragons flowed across the broken landscape with almost preternatural grace. Their camouflage hid them well, but not so well that we couldn't watch their progress toward the bunker. When they reached open ground, I could count them. Five dragons, with one out front, two behind it, and two behind those on the outside.

"Look at that," Evelyn said softly.

"That's a wedge formation," Johnson told us. "Infantry tactic. Looks like your dragons took to their training."

We'd kept the prototype eggs in the hatchery for most of their incubation period, but allowed the military to take possession before they hatched. The idea was that they'd imprint on the soldiers who did their training. They were domesticated animals, and theoretically as trainable as dogs or cats. Still, it was reassuring that this held true for some of the most intense training in the world.

Evelyn was telling the major the story of how we'd finally cracked domestication, but I listened with half an ear. The dragons were approaching their target. The first two moved to flank the door and held their position. The ones behind them charged through the doorway, colliding with one another and getting stuck for a moment as they did. The flanking dragons waited a beat and then followed them, disappearing into the darkness with a flick of their long, desert-colored tails.

The enemy "combatants" were lifelike dummies holding replica weapons. So the major told us at least; if there were cameras inside the target building, we didn't get a feed. Instead, we had to rely on the play-by-play from the operators.

"Target one is down."

"Targets three and four are down."

A few more seconds passed, and then came the word. "Target two is down. All targets neutralized."

"Time?" Major Johnson asked.

"Fifty-five seconds from breach."

The major looked at me and Evelyn, smiled, and gave us a nod. I wasn't an expert in these things, but it seemed like we'd done well. *Take that, Robert Greaves.* The best news was that it had happened so fast, he wouldn't have had time to take many notes on our dragons.

"Ten minutes to reset," said one of the operators.

"Are they going to do it again?" I whispered to Evelyn.

"Yes, but not for us. It's Robert's turn," Evelyn said.

"Oh. Right." In the excitement of our dragon's success, I'd nearly forgotten about our competition.

I excused myself from the operations center and managed to find a restroom. I couldn't bring myself to go, even though my bladder felt like it wanted to burst. My whole body felt clenched. I compromised by washing my hands twice, and drying them four times. The routine motions helped. Greaves was Greaves, and it wouldn't help me to hide in the bathroom while his dragons undertook their field trials. We didn't know anything about his operation or plans, and we needed to. So I forced myself to get out there.

Of course, the moment I walked back in the command center, the simulated gunfire started up again. I nearly wet myself in what would have been a moment of humiliating irony. But I clenched my teeth and went up to stand beside Evelyn. She scanned all of the screens, frowning, her brow furrowed in confusion.

"What's wrong?" I asked.

"I don't see them."

The AI that controlled the video feeds seemed to be having the same problem. The cameras panned left and right, zoomed in and out, and swiveled. When nothing appeared, we all inched closer to the monitors for a better look.

"Front of the building," Major Johnson said suddenly.

Several screens blurred as their cameras pivoted that way. I didn't see anything at first. Then a shadow appeared on the wall beside the door. A gray-brown dragon's physique appeared for a heartbeat, then disappeared just as quickly. *What the hell?*

"Where did it go?" asked one of the operators.

"It's still there," Johnson said. "Look." He traced the outline of a dragon-like shape on the monitor. The edge shimmered against the backdrop whenever the thing moved. "Looks like some kind of active camouflage."

Evelyn caught my eye, and the explanation came to me.

"It's a chameleon," I said. *And here I thought my degeneration pigments were so damn impressive.*

"Very clever," Evelyn said, in the tone of a grudging compliment. Greaves had clearly found someone who knew what they were doing.

Judging by the way Johnson was glued to the screen in front of him, he agreed. And it only got worse form there. The dragons' long and slender bodies served them well in the urban terrain. They had no trouble negotiating the entry—one of them even scaled the wall like a creature from an old sci-fi movie.

"All targets neutralized," said the operator.

We didn't even get a play-by-play. It had been fast, too. Major Johnson asked for the time again.

"Thirty-three seconds from breach."

They'd nearly cut our time in half. Not only that, but they did it with flair. Hell, even the operators had had trouble spotting the dragons before they approached the doorway.

Johnson's phone rang. He glanced at the screen and answered before it got to a second ring. "Major." He listened for a few seconds. "Copy that." He hung up and looked at us. "So far, so good. Your dragons met all performance objectives."

Evelyn and I looked at each other. *But so did Greaves.* And his times had been faster. Unfortunately, it only got worse from there. Our dragons did well on the next exercise—which tested their speed and agility—but again, the other team's were faster. On the one after that, a strength evaluation, they had the edge yet again. The final test combined stealth and endurance: a long run along the bottom of a rock-strewn ravine, then over the top of a ridge, and through another ravine. Our dragons had a slight edge on time—that told me a little bit about how the other team had made theirs so fast—but the bigger part of the evaluation centered on stealth. Camouflage was well and good, but the opposition's chameleon-like dragons were practically invisible. I grew more and more dejected as the competition wrapped up.

When it was over, Evelyn and I walked out in silence, shadowed by our wordless guards. Maybe it was my imagination, but they seemed a bit more stiff and a shade less courteous than they'd been on the way in. Evelyn waited until we were outside in the baking-hot sunlight before she turned at me and pressed her lips together.

"I know." I put up my hands to keep her from saying what I already knew to be true. "We lost."

She frowned and stared back at the test facility. "I'd hoped that he put in a competing bid just to make our lives difficult. But based on what those dragons did . . ."

"He came to play," I finished. *Greaves one, Build-A-Dragon one.* No wonder he'd seemed so confident. Like a fool, I'd written it off as alpha-male bravado. Yet if he really wanted to beat us, this was going to be a lot harder than I'd thought.

CHAPTER TWENTY
The Aerial

Evelyn and I got back to Build-A-Dragon in late afternoon after a supremely uncomfortable car ride.

I was sorely tempted to make a beeline for my car and go home. She wouldn't fault me for that; she was doing the same thing. But Wong and Korrapati would probably be hanging around, waiting to hear about the results. I'd assured them that we had this field demonstration in the bag.

How in the hell am I going to tell them?

I didn't know, and I really didn't feel like ruining someone else's day. Still, it was my duty to report back on how the trials had gone. How we'd underestimated Greaves and watched their dragons beat ours. So I sucked it up and walked through the hatchery to the Design lab.

Wong and Korrapati weren't even pretending to work; they stood by her desk watching the God Machine do its thing. They looked relaxed and happy. This was going to suck.

"Hey, guys!" I forced a smile that I truly didn't feel. "What's printing?"

"A custom order. Nothing special."

"Little bit special," Wong said.

"Yeah, how so?"

"From China, special request for another imperial dragon."

"Really?" It perked me up to hear that. Not enough to forget how my day had gone, but a little.

"We . . . found the design in DragonDraft 3D, so we printed another egg," Korrapati said. "They wanted it to be identical."

They found *my* design, which meant they'd poked around my personal workspace. It should have bothered me more, but they'd been here when I wasn't, and they'd handled the situation. I shrugged it off. "That's good. They must have liked it."

"Who got the first egg?" Wong asked.

Uh-oh. It hadn't occurred to me that Wong didn't know what Evelyn and I had done to boost him from his unofficial exit ban. Well, there was no reason he couldn't know about it now. "When you were stuck over there, we sent a gift to someone in the Chinese government. A little *dragon diplomacy*, if you will."

"Very clever."

"If they want another one, maybe it's a good sign," I said. China was a huge market, and largely untapped because of their import restrictions.

"Yes, wonderful, we sold a dragon and maybe we'll sell more," Korrapati said impatiently. "How were the trials?"

"The good news is that the dragons did well. They took

to the training, and they reached the objective in under a minute."

"Oh, that's *fantastic*," she said.

Wong didn't share her enthusiasm. "What is bad news?"

"Well, Robert Greaves is running the other team, as we pretty much knew. I thought he wanted a joint demonstration in order to copy our design ideas, but he didn't need them. Their infantry dragon was really good."

"Better than ours?"

I sighed. "I'm afraid so. It's not official yet, but they beat us on most performance metrics."

"What does this mean?" Korrapati asked.

"It means they're ahead, but they haven't won yet."

I turned my attention to the flying model, which I'd already started calling Air Force One in my head. The aerial trial would come quickly after the marine demonstration. Designing flying dragons was tough, and I told myself it was to get myself extra time. It definitely was not due to the concern that a third trial might not happen.

Besides, even Korrapati couldn't argue with the idea of me taking first crack at the flying design. The live demonstration of my Condor model would live long in the institutional memory of Build-A-Dragon. That was the day I'd simultaneously showed everyone at the company the near-limitless potential of our creations and landed myself on the CEO's private shit list.

Let no one say that Noah Parker did things half-assed.

Build-A-Dragon's computational infrastructure archived

everything. Especially the code produced in the Design department. Any code changes saved by Thursday got mirrored overnight, and then saved to a backup server over the weekend.

With that knowledge, back when I was a designer I'd taken steps to ensure that my two ignominious failures—the Condor flying model and the tiny, supersmart dragon that became Octavius—never got saved to the company backups. I'm not sure why I did it, really. Maybe I'd sensed what was coming for the Octavius design. With the Condor design I wanted to make sure that no one stumbled upon its secret purpose—a mutation in a gene only seen in one other organism: my brother, Connor. Of the human species, or so he claimed. Never mind that the hidden genetic change and the dragons that carried it were the reason Connor got into his gene therapy trial. It still could've gotten me into a lot of trouble.

Ironically, the rest of the Condor design—the super flying machine sans the urge of progressive muscular atrophy—offered the perfect starting point for the AF-1. So I smuggled in my biometric-encrypted thumb drive and uploaded the model into DragonDraft 3D. Then I couldn't resist the urge to pull it up in the three-dimensional simulator, if only to remind myself of what I could do when I designed outside the box.

The simulator's rendering of my Condor bloomed into life in midair above my desk. It was lean and lithe in this prediction, the wings generous, the legs and tail hinting at the strength. Its scales were the color of weathered sandstone. The simulation didn't really capture the eyes, though. When I'd seen those dragons in person, there was a depth to their gaze that made my breath catch just remembering. Maybe it was intelligence, or understanding, or something even deeper. The Condor had looked at me and just known me, inside and out.

I hadn't seen them since the day they'd turned up unannounced in my mom's backyard, drawn to the person with whom they had something in common. Connor and I still talked about it sometimes. Neither of us could figure out how they'd found him, or more importantly, why they'd decided to come.

Beneath the simulated dragon, various performance stats scrolled up in orderly fashion on a projection monitor. My simulator quantified *everything*. It scored the dragon high across the board: strength, intelligence, agility, flight time. Even the metabolism performed above average, though their caloric intake was necessarily high. Build-A-Dragon sold high-energy foods specifically designed for our flying models, but the stuff was expensive. A lot of customers quit buying it after the novelty of a flying dragon wore off. Then they called us to complain when the dragon started preying on songbirds or neighborhood pets.

Yes, the Condor model was a thing of beauty, but it would still need a lot of work to meet the DOD specs. Aerial combat was no joke. These dragons would have to fly in the worst conditions—gale-force winds, torrential rain, heavy snow—when ordinary drones couldn't function. Agility would be key, too. So would speed. The DOD wanted a horizontal flight speed of sixty miles per hour, and diving speed of twice that. Only swifts, golden eagles, and some falcons could match that in the natural world.

Diving speed wouldn't be a problem. Dragons were heavy as flying creatures went, and their scaly bodies had some key advantages when it came to aerodynamics. The real challenge would be to optimize this dragon for horizontal speed. It would need strength, which meant muscle. But muscle was heavy. There were metabolic issues, too. Few forms of physical movement bring a higher energy demand than flying. An extremely efficient metabolism would be required, but this also meant that the dragon's diet must be strictly managed. I'm sure the military was going to love that.

Those were complicated issues and would require complex answers, probably with input from others. So instead I started with the fun part: wing design. Although most people think of the peregrine falcon as the fastest bird in the world, a lot of them don't realize that the falcon's top speed is maximized by plummeting toward the earth from high altitude. Peregrine falcons preyed mainly on other birds, caught in flight, so a high diving speed was necessary. The AF-1 had different needs entirely. It would have to fly fast without the aid of gravity as well as in a dive, while still maintaining the agility to do what it needed to do.

The best model for that was a different type of bird, the swift. There were over a hundred different species of swifts. The family is aptly named, as many swifts have been clocked at over a hundred miles per hour. In horizontal flight. That's because swifts, unlike falcons, generally prey on flying insects. Swifts also spend most of their lives in flight; in essence, they're evolution's best solution for an agile flying bird.

The wings of a swift have two special features. The first is the long, curved, elegant shape that most people associate with swifts (or swallows, a distant relative that achieved similar looks through convergent evolution). DragonDraft 3D had built-in sliders for wings, but these only adjusted the size. The shape was pretty much the same. To alter the fundamental shape of a dragon's wing, I had to take a deep dive into the genetic code itself.

Limb formation is a tightly controlled process in animals, and it happens much earlier in development than you might think. Many of the genes for development processes have a common sequence called the *homeobox*. It's just 180 base pairs long. The encoded protein, which is sixty amino acids long, forms a triple helix that bound DNA. This allows homeobox genes, or HOX genes, to control the activity of other genes in the genome.

For a genetic engineer like myself, the homeobox was useful because it told us which genes play key roles in forming a dragon embryo. I isolated the genes that were most active where the dragon's wing began to form, and I began tinkering. With each step, I ran the code through my simulator to visualize the effect on the resulting dragon. It was trial-and-error stuff, really, because the effects of even a single homeobox gene can be wide reaching. Some of my early efforts produced square wings, or eight wings, or wings that grew inward instead of out. Eventually, though, I found the right HOX genes that guided the shape of the wing itself. Like a conductor guides a symphony, I eased them into a crescendo. The wings grew longer and more slender, almost like those of a hummingbird.

And speaking of hummingbirds, the second feature of the swift wing had to do with the joints. Swifts could rotate them, enabling them to change the angle of their wings during upstrokes and downstrokes to maximize efficiency. Supposedly it increased efficiency by something like sixty percent, and this dragon would need every edge it could get.

With the wing design done, I focused next on musculature. Unlike the infantry model, we didn't have the luxury of not caring about weight. This was all about balancing different types of muscle fiber. Animals basically have two kinds: fast-twitch fibers, which are best for quick movement at a high energy cost, and slow-twitch fibers, which have better efficiency and endurance. The balance between them, in humans at least, is what separates world-class sprinters from marathon runners.

It was hard to know what the right answer should be for the AF-1. Flight required some fast-twitch response, no debate there. Especially takeoff. Yet the DOD wanted endurance, too. Otherwise they wouldn't tell us that the flight duration was a performance metric. I waffled back and forth but couldn't reach a decision on my own. So, I went in search of my favorite sounding board.

Wong wasn't in his cubicle, though—I spotted him next door, in my old workstation. Korrapati's, I mean. They laughed at something on her projection monitor, then continued on in pleasant conversational tones. The sight caused a weird twist in my stomach. Not sure what it was. Envy, perhaps, though I really had no reason to be envious. Except that being a designer—at least when you weren't secretly trying to help cure your brother's disease—meant all of the scientific fun without the stresses of leadership. I missed it a little. Seeing them carefree, in the thick of it, I didn't want to interrupt.

But Korrapati glanced over her shoulder at the sound of my footfalls. "Hello, Noah."

"Hey, guys. How's the design looking?"

"Very good. Good design," Wong said, with his usual easy confidence.

"It's . . . progressing," Korrapati said. "The performance requirements are—"

"Ridiculous, I know." I waved off her obvious concern. "How close are you?"

"We have the swimming speed achieved, the diving depth, and all of the payload minimums."

"Also have name," Wong interjected.

"We do *not* have a name," Korrapati said.

I looked at Wong. "All right, what do you want to call it?"

"Think of this," Wong said. "Team in trouble. Hard underwater operation. What do you need?" He swept his hand across in an arc between us, as if painting a sign. "AquaWong."

Korrapati shook her head in a way that said she'd heard this before.

I laughed. "You don't lack for creativity."

"Now all we need to do is meet the specifications," Korrapati said.

"You'll get there."

Wong grunted in agreement.

"I hope so," Korrapati said.

"You're already much further along than I was."

"Have you been able to work on the flying model at all?"

Am I that predictable? "How did you know?"

"Noah Parker loves flying dragons," Wong offered.

Korrapati nodded. "Besides that, you and Greaves have history. It's fitting somehow."

"I hope you're right."

I left the Design lab with just a hint more optimism. The Wong-Korrapati dynamic seemed to be working, and if Wong was ready to name the model, it meant they were close. Which is a lot more than I could say for my own model. Then again, it might not matter. If Greaves beat us at the second field trials, we might not have a chance to compete with the flying models.

CHAPTER TWENTY-ONE
Interlude

Support Chat Log
Date: June 29th

System: Thank you for your patience. A Build-A-Dragon support operator will be with you in three minutes.

Customer1: HELLO, MY NAME IS GLORIA JEAN ADAMS.

System: Thank you for your patience. A Build-A-Dragon support operator will be with you in three minutes.

Customer1: I'M CALLING YOU ABOUT A LOST DRAGON.

System: Thank you for your patience. A Build-A-Dragon support operator will be with you in two minutes.

Customer1: HE'S A GOOD BOY AND HE'S NEVER BEEN GONE.

System: Thank you for your patience. A Build-A-Dragon support operator will be with you in one minute.

Customer1: FOR THIS LONG!

Charles: Hello, and thank you for contacting Build-A-Dragon support. My name is Charles. How may I help you today?

Customer1: ...

Customer1: ...

Customer1: HELLO, MY NAME IS GLORIA JEAN ADAMS.

Charles: Hello, Mrs. Adams. Is it possible that you have the Caps Lock key turned on?

Customer1: ...

Customer1: Oh, I sure did. Thank you, young man.

Charles: It's my pleasure. So, how can we assist you today?

Customer1: Well, Charlie Rose didn't come home last night and I'm worried about him.

Charles: Charlie Rose?

Customer1: He's my pet dragon. One of those whatchamacallits. The kind that go fetch and such.

Charles: A Rover model?

Customer1: Yes, that's it.

Charles: I'm pulling up your account now. How long has Charlie been missing?

Customer1: Haven't seen hide nor scale of him since yesterday.

Charles: One moment, please. I have your account up, but I think something must be incorrect.

Customer1: Why? What's it say?

Charles: Nothing to be concerned about, Mrs. Adams. It's trying to tell me you own eleven dragons.

Customer1: That must be a typo.

Charles: I thought as much. Let me just update the record—

Customer1: Counting Charlie, I've got twelve.

Charles: ...

Charles: I'm sorry, Mrs. Adams. Did you say you have TWELVE of our dragons?

Customer1: I think so. Let's see. There's Charlie Rose, Jimmy Kimmel, Jimmy Fallon, Anderson Cooper, Anderson Cooper 2—

Charles: There's no need to—

Customer1: Lester Holt, Bryant Gumbel, Seth Myers, Jimmy Kimmel Junior, and Fluffy McFlufftail.

Charles: Fluffy McFlufftail?

Customer1: My granddaughter named him.

Charles: I wondered.

Customer1: Now, if you'll just tell me how to locate my missing baby, I'll be on my way.

Charles: Of course. Do you know if Charlie Rose had a GPS chip implanted?

Customer1: A what?

Charles: A GPS chip. It would have been done by your veterinarian.

Customer1: I don't know anything about a GPB or whatzit. And we don't need a veterinarian, either.

Charles: May I ask if Charlie Rose has done this before?

Customer1: No, never. He usually sticks close by me, as he doesn't always get along with his brothers.

Charles: Really? Why is that?

Customer1: They're different, that's all. He's my sweet cuddly boy. The rest of them are downright mean.

Charles: Oh, that's really too bad. They're Rovers as well, I assume?

Customer1: No, they're something else.

Charles: Ah yes, I have it here. They're K-10 models? How in God's name did you get law enforcement—

Customer1: Watch your mouth, young man.

Charles: I sincerely apologize for that. What I meant was, how did you manage to end up with the dragons that we sell exclusively to law enforcement bodies?

Customer1: My husband was the chief of police, that's how.

Charles: Oh, this is too much. I take it that your husband is . . . no longer with us?

Customer1: He died last year, God rest his soul. Job got him at last.

Charles: I'm so sorry. He died on the job?

Customer1: No. Heart attack. But he left me this lot to look after me. Bless him.

Charles: That certainly was kind. Unfortunately, our K-10 models are not really designed to be household pets.

Customer1: Says who?

Charles: It's clearly stated in our dragon care manual that these are not for civilian use.

Customer1: You leave my good boys out of this. Let's keep our mind on the task at hand, which is finding Charlie Rose.

[System Log: Operator Charles opened incident report with security flag, immediate routing to Director of Security.]

Charles: Of course. Have we discussed the possibility that he ran away?

Customer1: What?

Charles: You have the equivalent of a Golden Retriever living with a pack of Rottweilers. Maybe he saved himself.

Customer1: He wouldn't do that. He wouldn't leave me.

Charles: Well, there is another possibility. May I ask you if you've fed your dragons in the last day?

Customer1: Well, that's a good question. Come to think of it, I can't remember. I'm as bad about that sometimes as I am at taking my pills.

Charles: Is it possible you forgot?

Customer1: Now that you mention it, yes. I think it's been a couple of days. Darn! I keep meaning to get that new bag of food out of the garage.

Charles: What are your K-10 dragons doing at the moment, if I may ask?

Customer1: Laying around. I've got two on the couch with me, a few others on the floor. Anderson Cooper 2 is probably upstairs on one of the vents.

Charles: How is their mood?

Customer1: The ones in here look pretty pleased.

Charles: Contented?

Customer1: Like foxes who found the henhouse open.

Charles: Oh, no.

Customer1: What's wrong with that?

Charles: Nothing. Nothing at all, Mrs. Adams.

Customer1: What about Charlie Rose?

Charles: Well, I'm afraid he's . . . gone.

Customer1: Gone where? Don't break my heart, now, you hear?

Charles: Oh. I'm sure he went to a nice farm with lots of fields to run in. And chickens to chase around.

Customer1: Do you really think so?

Charles: Of course, Mrs. Adams.

Customer1: It does sound like something he would do. Charlie Rose always was a clever one.

Charles: Well, it sounds like we've resolved the reason for your inquiry today. Thank you for contacting the Build-A-Dragon Company.

CHAPTER TWENTY-TWO
The Ramp-Up

To my immense disappointment, we didn't get to attend the trials of the water dragons in person. Apparently, this had something to do with a nuclear submarine that was necessary for the demonstration, but whose precise whereabouts we weren't allowed to know. The majors sent cars for us this time. Evelyn and I headed out the front door two minutes before our agreed-upon pickup time to find a large SUV waiting for us. No, not an SUV. A *Humvee*.

"Yes!" I hissed. I'd always wanted to ride in a Humvee.

Evelyn glanced up from her tablet. "They're here already?"

"I guess in the military, early is on time."

Two men in fatigues climbed out. They were young guys, maybe early twenties. Clean shaven and fit.

"Evelyn Chang and Noah Parker?" The guy from the passenger side reached us first. "I'm Sergeant Delgado." He jerked his head over his shoulder. "That's Corporal McGuire. He'll be driving us."

I really wanted to ask if Corporal McGuire was old enough to drive, but I also didn't want to spend the trip in the trunk. If Humvees even had them.

"Thanks for the ride, Corporal," Evelyn said.

"Our pleasure, ma'am." Delgado opened the door for her.

I got a terse nod from McGuire as I jogged around the far side to let myself in, but that was about it. The door was so heavy, it barely moved on my first pull. I'd been spoiled with the Tesla's power-assist doors. I put my back into it and got it open, then had to climb up to get onto the seat. This was made of sturdy polyester, and dull green in color like the rest of the sparse interior. The actual space inside was massive, though. Evelyn and I were separated by a steel table that had to be three feet wide.

Delgado produced a heavy metal container about the size of a shoebox and set it onto the console between us with a heavy *thunk*. He unlocked this with a key on his key ring and flipped the lid open. I was hoping for some sort of refreshments, but no, the thing was empty. "Please put your phones in the box."

"Tablets, too?" Evelyn asked.

"Yes, ma'am."

So what am I supposed to do while we drive? I didn't ask. I put my tablet in first, and my phone second. *At least I get to keep my—*

"Is that a GPS watch?" Delgado asked me.

I suppressed a sigh, unstrapped my watch, and set it on top of my phone. "Good eye."

"It's in good hands, I promise." He locked the box,

lifted it back into the front, and set it down in the middle of the center console.

Evelyn looked a little bit frazzled to be without her tablet. She'd had that thing in hand pretty much since I'd met her, and I imagined that becoming CEO made it even more essential.

I gave her a smile. "Whose idea was this again?"

The ride was uneventful. I had to crane my neck down to get a good look out the window, but I tried not to do that too often. That was just asking to be blindfolded. Or tranquilized. Not that we should have bothered. Once we were on the highway, Delgado flipped a switch in the center console and suddenly the window glass went opaque.

I caught Evelyn's attention and rolled my eyes at the glass. It was like staring at a plain white wall. Instinctively, I touched the glass, but it felt normal. Whatever caused the opaqueness wasn't on this side.

It might even be a variant of the privacy mesh that protected Build-A-Dragon's exterior windows from eavesdropping. Only this type could be turned on or off, whereas the RF shield had to be lowered into place.

Man, we really need this contract. Not just to save the company, but because the military had the coolest tech.

The drive lasted fifty-five minutes. I only noticed when the vehicle came to a full stop. McGuire, who hadn't uttered a word since we'd started the journey, shut off the engine. I'd been lost in trying to visualize the marine dragon design and remember all the changes Wong and Korrapati had made to it. Which was hard to do; I'd gotten too used to our design programs and the biological simulator, all reachable through my hot-linked tablet. I used to make fun of Evelyn for keeping hers with her all the time, but now I understood. Without it I felt disconnected, and not in a good way.

Delgado climbed out and pulled open my door. Hot desert air washed over me as I climbed out. We were in an unmarked parking area completely enclosed in ten-foot fences. A three-story, glass-and-steel building occupied most of the fenced area. Similar in design to Build-A-Dragon's headquarters, but something about the architecture gave it a utilitarian feel. Plus, there were several other Humvees and a tan transport truck parked in precise fashion along the near wall.

We followed our hosts along the edge of the structure to the southwest corner, where two panels slid apart at our approach. Behind them waited a steel door, a biometric access panel, and two not-so-subtle surveillance cameras that swiveled to follow our progress. Delgado used the panel while McGuire discreetly blocked our view with his body. There came a soft beep, and then the steel door swung inward.

We were in.

Five minutes later, we sat in comfortable chairs beside Major Johnson in a large conference room. A huge projection monitor occupied the far wall. Overhead lights illuminated the table and the chairs around it, but kept the periphery of the room in darkness. Unlike the bunker near the weapons testing range, this whole place had the feel of a planned, permanent installation. We'd passed a tidy mess hall on the way in, as well as several smaller conference rooms that were similarly equipped.

"What can you tell us about the testing location?" Evelyn asked.

"It's a training site for Navy divers," Major Johnson said. "Two hundred feet deep with a sandy bottom. Visibility in the water is only about thirty feet today, so that'll make things interesting."

"How so?"

"We have fixed cameras on the bottom in certain locations, but we'll have to send in some drone cameras during the trials to make sure we can see everything." He frowned. "Will that be a problem for the units you're testing?"

Evelyn looked at me, and I shrugged. We certainly hoped not, but the possibility of distraction by surveillance cameras wasn't a scenario we'd planned for. "I suppose we'll find out," she said.

The projection monitor flickered into life, and suddenly we were under water. Or so it seemed, at least. The monitor wall became six panels, all with live feeds from the training site. Four underwater cameras, two on the surface. It was calm on the surface; the gunmetal gray ships in the background barely moved with the ocean swells. And it *was* ocean. The color, the surface texture, all of that spoke to a very large body of water.

"Where are they?" I muttered, half to myself. It had been the usual waiting game since we sent off the eggs to be hatched and trained for these trials. My simulator, as much as I loved to tout its benefits, was never designed to predict performance in an ocean environment. The salinity and the limited visibility could affect things. So could the waves. Quite honestly, I had no idea how they were going to do.

"Patience, Noah."

"You know that's not my strong suit."

"The other team is going first," she said, without a trace of surprise.

"You knew about this, huh?"

"Since the end of the last trial."

"I kind of figured we wouldn't always get first-run advantage. You didn't want to tell me?"

"We've found it's best not to give you too many things to obsess over at a time."

I cleared my throat. "We?"

"You know." Evelyn gestured broadly with one arm. "Society."

"Oh my God. Evelyn Chang made a joke!"

She opened her mouth in mock offense. "I make jokes."

"Sure, all the time. Now seriously: Are you going to call the Associated Press, or should I?"

"If I asked the major to throw you out of here, do you think he would do it himself?"

"Nah, he'd order someone to do it." I nearly made a joke about the major not wanting to wrinkle his uniform, but I bit my tongue. He was a big dude and all jokes aside, he *could* throw me out if he wanted.

The man materialized right beside us, which made me very grateful I'd kept my mouth shut. "It's starting," he said.

CHAPTER TWENTY-THREE
The Deep

I watched one of the gray ships move out from its picket and take up position right in the middle of the surface camera frame. Two sailors moved to the starboard rail and threw several bright orange objects over the side. These hit the water and sank fast, plummeting past two of the underwater cameras. Down on the ocean floor, they hit the bottom with a little cloud of sand.

I glanced at Evelyn. "Those look heavy."

"The water will add buoyancy."

"I suppose." Still, I felt a twinge of relief that Korrapati and Wong had taken ownership of this design. I'd been flailing anyway. Airborne dragons spoke to me. The wing layouts, the body lines . . . I got those. A reptile in water felt different. We rarely got customized requests for water-friendly dragons, either. Maybe that explained why I was bad at it.

"Think they accounted for that in the specs?" I asked.

Evelyn laughed quietly. "I'm certain of it."

Another ship maneuvered into position, this one smaller. Six steel cages sat on the deck. Dark shapes moved behind the bars with the pacing, predatory grace of dragons. They were olive in color, with long necks and slender bodies. That design had worked well on the previous test, so I wasn't terribly surprised.

"Four dragons will do the retrieval exercise," Major Johnson said.

The cage doors slid open simultaneously. Two of the dragons dove straight in. The other two seemed to hesitate—or perhaps were held by their trainers—and then followed suit. We started picking them up on the underwater cameras within seconds. They swam mostly with their strong back legs, both of them kicking in unison. Like a frog kick, and so they plunged into the ocean depths with a thrusting motion.

It was effective, though. They reached the bottom and took hold of the bright orange diving targets. Evelyn was right—the water buoyancy did help—but it was still slow going. A couple of the dragons really struggled with the weights. I was torn between grim satisfaction that it wasn't a perfect performance, and a rising sense of dread at how tough this challenge might be for our own dragons.

"Payload delivery is up next," Major Johnson said.

The top-right camera switched to a surface view of a lone ship. This one wasn't a spotless gray or white Navy vessel, but the rusted hulk of what looked like an old container ship.

"That's the target," Johnson said. "It's anchored about a mile out in slightly deeper water."

The dragons had been lifted back on deck using a hydraulic arm device with a cargo net on its end. Now, with some encouragement from their handlers, they lined up on the deck facing the rail. Still more handlers appeared carrying small, dumbbell-shaped objects about a foot long. I recognized them from the set of DOD specs. They weighed just under three pounds. One served as a loop handle that the dragons gripped in their jaws. The other end held a plastic-encased cylinder about the size of a soda can. The edge farthest from the handle had a powerful magnetic ring, ideal for attaching to flat metal objects. Like tanks, or the steel hull of a ship. Inside the cylinder was an inverted copper cone—a void that would be packed with C-4. The safety ring for the explosive shock was a hundred yards. Once a payload was delivered, the dragon had thirty seconds to get outside of blast range.

Each dragon took a dumbbell in its jaws and then leapt back into the water. The last one fumbled its dumbbell to the deck. As it fell, all of the handlers dove to the floor and covered their heads with their hands. Evelyn gasped. Nothing happened, though, and after a moment they found their feet again. The dragon plucked up the dumbbell and jumped in after its littermates.

I looked at Johnson. "They're acting like they're live rounds."

"That's what they're trained to do."

"They, um, aren't live rounds, are they?"

"We removed the detonators, but munitions specialists don't like taking chances."

"How much C4 does one hold?"

Johnson gave me a flat look, the one that I was starting to learn meant *you shouldn't ask that, son.* Whoops. But this time he decided to answer. "Two pounds."

"Is that a lot, or a little?"

"Enough to blow a serious hole in steel plate."

I shared a wide-eyed look with Evelyn. In that moment, the reality of what we were doing caught up with me. This contract, if we won it, required us to build weapons. And the military planned to use them as such. The country wasn't at war currently, but that could change at any time. Like reservists being called into active duty, our dragons would be deployed whenever and wherever the military needed them.

I'd managed to ignore that fact when the specs came in. When it was just a scientific and intellectual challenge that needed solving. Now, with dragons carrying real explosives to a real ship, I found it harder to ignore the implications of weaponized dragons. It bothered me, and these weren't even my dragons. This wasn't what I'd joined the company for. Then again, if I failed to win this competition and the funding that came with it, no one would be able to have dragons. Not even our customers, dwindling as their base might be. It was a tough spot and a shitty position to be in. I glanced at Evelyn, wondering if perhaps she'd had the same line of thought as me. Yet she only had eyes for the monitors.

"They're approaching the target," Johnson said.

"How's the time looking?" Evelyn asked.

"A little slow."

More screens switched over their views, and now we had a camera feed from the target hulk itself. A dark undulating spot in the seawater appeared off in the distance, followed by two others. The first two dragons approached the target. Honestly, even the lead animal looked like it was flagging. But they still had their "payloads" and attached them to the steel hull with a series of dull thumps. *Well, at least the magnets work.*

Then they were supposed to swim away quickly to reach the safety zone. Despite being relieved of their burden, they did seem to be moving a bit sluggishly. That wasn't my professional jealousy talking, either. Evelyn noticed it, too.

"They're tiring," she said quietly.

"Yeah, they look drained."

"It doesn't make sense. They had good muscle tone."

I let my eyes wander to the numbers in the bottom left quadrant of the nearest screen. I'd tried to ignore them thus far because two of the numbers were clearly GPS coordinates. The Navy might not expect it out of a civilian, but because of my hobby I could compute decimals to minutes and seconds, and convert those to distances, without even trying. Which is how I knew that these drills were happening in the Pacific Ocean a couple hundred miles northwest of San Diego. Yet there were other numbers, too, like surface temperature. And more importantly, water temperature.

"The water's fifty-eight degrees," I said.

"Cold," Evelyn said.

"Especially for reptiles, if they're not fully endothermic." Most vertebrate animals—including humans and birds—maintained body temperature via their internal metabolism, hence the name *endotherm*. In contrast, ectotherms like lizards and frogs relied on the environment to help maintain body temperature. When they got cold, they sometimes entered a state of torpor to conserve energy.

"They did seem to swim like frogs," Evelyn said. "But how would they inadvertently produce a dragon that's ectothermic?"

"Might not have been intentional. If they were tweaking the metabolic systems and only tested the dragons in stable temperatures."

"It's strange that they'd risk altering the metabolic system," Evelyn said.

"You saw the DOD specs," I muttered. Greaves knew he had to tick every box for a shot at the contract. More than that, he had to produce dragons that were better than ours. He must have taken some chances with the metabolism to reach the energy requirements. So had we, actually. It occurred to me then that *we* had not thought to compute the effects of our dragons in cold-water environments. Or at least, I hadn't. I prayed that Korrapati and Wong had thought of it.

As usual, Evelyn seemed to guess what I was thinking. "Did you alter our dragons' metabolisms?"

"We'll be fine," I said, with a confidence I didn't feel.

Major Johnson was checking his watch. "Mark."

"Was that thirty seconds?" I asked.

"Yes."

According to the monitors, only one of the test dragons had reached the safety zone by then. The other three still moved in almost slow motion, their frog-kicks coming at a notably reduced frequency. I did my best not to imagine them being caught in the shock wave from the explosion, but the images popped uninvited into my head anyway. The flailing when the blast hit them, then the limbs folding. Then the view from above as their bodies sank slowly into the blue abyss.

"They'll be scored for a seventy-five percent casualty rate," Major Johnson said.

"That's bad, isn't it?" I asked.

"Casualties are never good, Parker."

That wasn't what I meant. But I'd irritated Johnson enough today, so I kept my mouth shut.

Some weird instinct made me want to offer an excuse for the other team, and point out that the reason their dragons didn't perform probably had to do with the Navy's choice of running this trial in the cold Pacific waters. Where, let's be honest, most military confrontations didn't seem likely to take place in the near future given the state of global politics. Granted, saying so would reveal that I'd figured out the secret location, which probably wouldn't win me any points with the Navy.

Evelyn gave me a pointed look at that moment, and offered the tiniest shake of her head. This was a competition, and there was a lot riding on it. Especially for us, as the current underdog in the field trials. I bit my lip and kept silent.

"They're going to reset for the trial of your dragons, so we have some time. Feel free to visit the mess," Johnson said.

I stood up, eager for an excuse to stretch my legs. "Want anything?" I asked Evelyn.

"No, thanks. But you go."

I cleared my throat. "Can I bring you back anything, Major?"

He smiled in a kindly way. "That's nice of you, son, but I'm good."

I rather liked the way he called me *son*, and on that glowing note I made my retreat.

CHAPTER TWENTY-FOUR
The Mess

I felt far too nervous to eat, but I figured I could stand to have coffee. Besides, I wanted a closer look at the mess hall of this facility. If it was anything like the conference rooms, there might be a robotic cook. Hell, with their early access to technology they probably had their own food replicators.

Tea. Earl Grey. Hot.

Some guy had beat me to the mess, though. He looked to be a fellow civilian. Husky frame but bad posture, nondescript hoodie, and headphones around his neck. Come to think of it, I knew those hunched shoulders and headphones. "Frogman?"

He flinched at the sound of my voice. He turned around, and it *was* him. "Oh. Hey."

"What are you doing here?"

It was completely unexpected, and my mind raced with the implications. Frogman, here, as a civilian. What would the DOD want with a genetic engineer, anyway? Maybe they'd hired him to independently assess the animals. He had developmental expertise.

"Looking for coffee, same as you, I'm guessing," he said.

What's with the attitude? Maybe it was my imagination, but he didn't seem surprised to see me, either. I stood there with my mouth open for a second, and then I put it together. "You're *working* for Greaves?"

"Guess you could say that."

"Why?"

He shrugged. "Not many places you can take our kind of skills."

That was a total dodge of my question. Then again, I hadn't asked it in full, like *Why would you go work for that total asshole after what he did?*

"Oh, here you are," said another voice, this time from behind me. And I recognized him, too.

"O'Connell," I said.

Brian O'Connell had a slight build and the same dirty-blond goatee that I remembered on him. As usual, he wore faded jeans and a flannel shirt that looked at least twenty years old. He gave me a heavy-lidded stare. "Parker."

"I guess I shouldn't be surprised, you both working for Greaves. You two were always a package deal." Everything fit. With O'Connell to run the biological printer and Frogman to design the dragons, all Greaves needed was a place to work and the prototype Redwood Codex. He'd essentially duplicated the dragon manufacturing process on which the Build-A-Dragon Company was founded.

"Someone had to do it," O'Connell said.

"You didn't *have* to do anything."

Frogman half turned back toward the back wall of the mess, looking like he wished he could be somewhere else. He never was one for confrontation.

"Better to join a winning team than stay on a sinking ship," O'Connell said.

I made an indignant noise, but comebacks were never my strong suit. And honestly, I was still thrown with the realization that they were part of the competition. Part of the enemy.

"Come on, Frogman," O'Connell said. "They're starting."

Frogman shuffled past me and mumbled something I couldn't hear to O'Connell. The latter snickered. "The contract is practically ours anyway."

The encounter soured me on the idea of futuristic coffee. And I wasn't sure how long it would take them to reset before our dragons got their turn. I hurried back to the conference room so I wouldn't miss anything.

"You're just in time," Evelyn said. "Almost late."

"Sorry. I ran into some old friends."

"How is Frogman?"

I gave her a double take. "You knew?"

"I surmised."

"From what?"

"Robert needed someone to design dragons. And that last one had Frogman's fingerprints all over it."

I should have seen it. Frogman loved his developmental model organisms and *Xenopus* most of all. Hence his nickname. This model did seem his style. "Not the first model, though. He's not the type to build attack dragons."

"No. That seems more like Brian O'Connell."

"Jeez." I shook my head. "How do you do it?"

"It's the logical conclusion. They worked together a long time and were close."

"Doesn't explain how Greaves got to them, though."

A shadow passed across her face. "He has ways."

I wanted to follow that up, but Major Johnson interrupted us.

"Here we go."

First up were the diving retrievals. Just as before, the sailors hauled their bright orange dive targets to the side and threw them overboard. The cages slid open. Four dragons—our dragons—dove in after them. They were bicolored, iridescent blue on the top and pale on their bellies. Korrapati and Wong had insisted that this coloring offered advantages, and besides, they just looked *cool*. Almost like a bluefin tuna.

I scanned the underwater cams, eager to see them in action. At first, I thought maybe the cameras weren't working.

I leaned closer, fighting the urge to jump out of my chair. "Where are they?"

"There." Evelyn pointed. Motion flickered on one monitor, then the other. It hit me then about the coloring. From above, they blended almost perfectly with the ocean's depths, and from below, their pale bellies blended in with the sky. A coloring system perfected by nature in pelagic species.

Then Camera Four zoomed out for a better view, and

we saw our dragons swimming for the first time. It reminded me of the contrast between seals on land and seals underwater. Or an ungainly bird on land that suddenly takes flight. Our dragons didn't just swim. They *undulated* through the water, their entire bodies swaying in elegant motion.

"Look at them go," Evelyn breathed.

"Way to go, Wong and Korrapati," I said.

The dragons were fast, too. I hadn't even thought to time them when they swept down on the diving targets, clamping them in strong jaws. No hesitation, no struggle. One moment they were undulating down, and the next, back up toward the surface. I had the presence of mind to glance over at Major Johnson. He stared at the monitors, transfixed. So did the operators. The curving, sweeping rhythm of their bodies was hypnotic.

Only when they broke the surface, targets held high, did the spell break. And the best part, the craziest part, was that they were still in formation. A perfect diamond of dragons, equidistant from one another, the targets at precise angles.

"Outstanding," Johnson said.

I couldn't agree more.

Then it was on to task two, the package delivery. If the cold water had started to bother our dragons, they didn't show it. All four of them raced to the target. As far as I could tell, they held their pace. The endurance was impressive. Then, as they approached the hull of the target ship, they fanned out. One dragon went to the bow, one to the stern, two amidships beneath the mast. Johnson started his watch. Then the dragons reformed and peeled away, still bending like sinus waves through the dark blue water.

Still in formation. I shook my head, marveling at the performance. It wasn't that the other team's dragons had done too poorly. These weren't easy tasks. Yet our dragons did it faster and behaved like a cohesive group, rather than four individuals each making their own struggle.

"The speed trials should be next," Major Johnson said. "We're going to test the remaining dragons simultaneously."

"What's the format?" Evelyn asked.

"Straight run, Point A to point B."

"Winner takes all?"

"No, the times will be averaged."

That made sense. A good team was only as fast as its slowest member. Besides, whoever won this contract would go into production and make *lots* of these dragons for the military. The mean performance was the key metric.

There was a setup period, of course, but I didn't dare leave the room again and risk missing the action. So I fiddled anxiously while they got the ships and dragons into position. Not having my phone or my tablet was slowly killing me, especially in the downtime. Then again, I doubted I'd have a signal on either device anyway. *This whole building must have shielding.* Or even active jamming for all signals except their own.

Evelyn was making conversation with Major Johnson, trying to get to know him a little better. This proved rather entertaining to watch, because the major seemed either reluctant or unaccustomed to giving up information about himself.

"So, Major," Evelyn said. "You're a married man."

Johnson was still reading his tablet—the link for which still worked, lending support to my theory—but he made eye contact when responding. "I am." Then he looked down again, clearly unaware that he was the object of a burgeoning interrogation.

"Any kids?"

"Two."

"And they're . . ."

Johnson smiled for the first time that I'd seen that day. "Girls."

"Aww. How old?"

"Six."

No second number was forthcoming, and Evelyn's eyes lit up. "Twins?"

The major nodded.

"Genetic engineers love twins. Don't we, Noah?"

"Sure." I grinned. "Built-in experiments on nature versus nurture."

Evelyn was poised to ask another follow-up question, but the major's tablet beeped.

Must be nice to still have your tablet.

Johnson grabbed it with a hint of relief. "Here we go."

It was midday at the testing site but the winds had calmed, and the sea was almost flat. The "lure" for the dragons was a bright orange buoy attached to a winch cable on the destination ship. It all happened so suddenly. The winch started turning, a buzzer sounded, and the dragons' cage doors flew open. All of them dove into the water, fast as lightning. As if they knew what this was.

The race was chaos. A single mile, and it was hard to

really tell what was going on. We could tell the dragons apart individually because of the swimming styles—frog versus snake was a useful shorthand—but I had no idea how to tell which ones were in front. Right until our dragons began leaping out of the water like a pod of dolphins. Evelyn and I laughed in astonishment. It was clear then that they had the lead. Both of them. The other team's dragons had lagged behind by a good distance, clearly struggling with the cold water. *What made ours think to jump?* It was like they knew this was a competition and took the chance to dunk on the other team. And oh, it was *sweet*. I hoped Greaves was watching.

"Not much of a race," I said to Evelyn.

She smiled but made hushing motions at me. "It's not over yet."

But it was over in less than two minutes. For our dragons, at least. That's how fast they were in the water at top speed.

I could tell Johnson was impressed. His voice seemed louder, and his handshake felt extra bone-crushingly firm. By the time Evelyn and I had taken our victory lap with him, Greaves and his team had already left. I guessed they saw the writing on the wall, at least with this exercise.

It still rankled me that Frogman and O'Connell had not only refused to work for me as Director of Dragon Design, but thought they'd be happier under Robert Greaves. The guy who'd imposed a debilitating points system for dragon designs, thoughtlessly killed dragons to save costs, and even hid a cure for the canine epidemic from the world so that his company could reap huge profits. I mean, what a *dick*.

Surely Frogman and O'Connell knew the truth about what he'd done—everyone else in Design did—but they still went with the guy. I didn't get it.

But that didn't matter for the moment. My small-but-scrappy team had clearly won the marine trials, which put us back into real contention. Only the air trials remained, and I intended to win them.

CHAPTER TWENTY-FIVE
The Dry Run

We won the water dragon trial. Major Johnson only waited a day before giving Evelyn the official word. That made it one-to-one, which meant that everything rode on the performance of the flying dragons. Yet compared to how the infantry dragon trial had gone, things looked much better. I tried not to think about the fact that it was mainly because I'd let someone *else* do the design.

We held a little celebration in the Design lab, of course. Wong and Korrapati deserved their victory lap. They were both curious about my encounter with Frogman and O'Connell, too.

"I had no idea Greaves was recruiting genetic engineers out from under us," I said. "Did you?"

Wong shook his head.

Korrapati blushed and looked away. "A little."

"What?" I thought maybe she was kidding, but not the way it showed in her face.

"After he left, O'Connell contacted me and asked if I was looking to find a new job."

Oh my God. I'd had *no* idea they tried to poach Korrapati, too. If we'd lost her this would have been a very different competition. "What did you tell him?"

"I told him I was going to stay and give Noah a chance."

Well, that flabbergasted me too much to say anything. Of course, Evelyn chose that moment to swoop in. "Do you regret it, Priti?"

Korrapati shrugged. "Not so far."

Everyone laughed, and I did, too, though I'm sure my cheeks were bright red. "Well, I'm glad you stayed. The dragon you and Wong made—"

"AquaWong," Wong interjected.

"—will definitely not be named AquaWong," I continued. "And it was a thing of beauty. I wish you could have seen how they swam."

"Like salamanders," Wong said.

"Yes, I suppose that's true. But seeing a group of them, trained to act in concert, all swimming like that . . . it was . . ."

"Hard to look away," Evelyn said.

"Exactly. I'd have taken video on my phone, but Major Johnson would probably have confiscated it."

"Yes, he would have," Evelyn said.

"Not Evelyn's, of course," I said casually. "She could have live streamed the whole day on her phone and he wouldn't say a word."

"Noah Parker!" Evelyn's mouth fell open with mock offense. "What are you saying?"

"You're up here." I held my left hand up as far as I could reach. "And I'm down here." I held out my right hand down near the floor.

"It is your imagination."

"I think he's kind of sweet on you, too, after your little conversation."

"I was asking him about his family," Evelyn said.

As much as I wanted to give her more trouble about it, she was being honest. We should get to know these people a bit if we were going to be working with them. *Hell, maybe I should chat up Major Nakamura if she ever decides to meet with us again.* I had nothing against Major Johnson, but it still bothered me that she spent her time with the other team.

So yes, we had a mini celebration to recognize the achievements of the never-to-be-named-AquaWong. Then all of our attentions focused on the crucial third trial. The aerial dragon. I'd taken to working on it at one of the workstations adjacent to the God Machine. My office was nice and all, but it felt too removed from the process. I chose Korrapati's old spot because it was out of the way, but if I'd hoped that would let me avoid the scrutiny of my fellow designers, I was mistaken. Wong and Korrapati both wanted to see the design in my simulator before we hit the print button. For some reason, this made me nervous. I suppose I considered myself the expert in flier designs and didn't want that particular bubble bursted at such a critical time. But they both had only compliments for me as we admired the three-dimensional dragon conjured by the simulator.

"You've put a lot of work into this," Korrapati said. "It looks good."

"Very good. Very strong flier," Wong agreed.

The *click-clack* of approaching high heels announced Evelyn's arrival. "Is that the flier?"

"Yes, what do you think?"

She peered at the model as it spun in the air in front of her. She even took the liberty of controlling my projection keyboard to tilt it back and forth. "The wing design is very interesting."

"It's a design from nature. The swift," I said.

"It looks more like a swallow."

"They're pretty similar, actually. Convergent evolution," I said. That happened sometimes, when Mother Nature worked out the optimum solution in two different groups of organisms and got the same answer. The most famous example in humans was lactose tolerance, which had arisen independently at least twice in hunter-gatherer groups.

"Did you give it the wing joints to . . . Oh, I see you did. Nicely done. It should be very efficient in the air."

She knows about the wing joints. Sometimes I forgot that Evelyn had a broader knowledge of biology than all of us put together. Sure, she was the CEO now and rarely got time to enjoy it, but for years before that, she was a scientist in the trenches. Just like I was.

"I hope so. For the horizontal flight speed, it should make a difference."

"There is one way to find out," Evelyn said. "Let's print a couple of eggs and put them through their paces."

The warm, lifting feeling in the pit of my stomach felt strange. It had been a while since I'd printed a dragon egg. Too long, really. Korrapati and Wong handled the day-to-day workload, which occupied less then twenty percent of their time. Even Marketing seemed to be holding its breath to learn how the DOD trials turned out.

I took a deep breath and hit the print button. The God Machine purred into motion, its robotic arms moving back and forth like knitting needles. Then the conveyor belt started up.

The egg came out the color of sky and clouds. Pale blues, soft white, and a touch of yellow. All three colors whorled together in intricate curving patterns. We admired it while a second one was printed. They were taller and skinnier than most eggs I'd seen so far.

"They're very slender," Evelyn said.

"What's wrong with that?" I demanded.

"Nothing, nothing. Different is good."

I stared at the eggs and hoped she was right. Their shape reminded me, somewhat ironically, of the huge caches of pterosaur eggs that paleontologists had discovered in China in the mid-2010s. Hundreds of fossilized eggs—presumably swept into a lake when a roosting area flooded a hundred million years ago—were encased in slabs of rock that had once been muddy lake-bottom. Some with the tiny, fossilized embryos still inside. They resembled turtle eggs in some ways, but were taller and more slender, too.

Fossilized pterosaur eggs didn't have this coloring, though. Our admirations were cut short when two white-garbed hatchery staffers whisked both eggs away to our on-site incubators.

We haven't printed an egg in days, but they're ready to answer the call. I wondered what the hatchery staff did in their increasing amounts of downtime. These two eggs would give them something to do. The distraction would be short-lived, however, because we'd already implemented the shorter incubation periods. Still, at least they had a couple of eggs to fuss over. I couldn't do much else until we knew how close these dragons were to spec.

"Another aerial demonstration," Evelyn murmured. She looked at me, probably curious about how I felt.

I put on as big a smile as I could manage. "I hope it goes better than the last one."

CHAPTER TWENTY-SIX
The Demo

We met in the coliseum-style arena outside the building for the first trials of the AF-1 dragons. The waiting was tough. Day after day I made small tweaks to my design and ran them through the simulator, all while knowing I'd have to revert to the original printed egg if we needed significant changes.

There was a good turnout on demonstration day. Obviously, Evelyn and the Design team were all there, but we also drew some of the support staff. Tom Johnson also showed up in a broad-brimmed hat with several of his dragon wranglers in tow. They settled down a little way away from us, but Tom wandered over a minute later.

He greeted Evelyn with a friendly nod and sprawled down next to me. "Good hatching weather."

"Good flying weather," I said.

"That, too."

Jim and Allie, the most recognizable of our hatchery staffers, arrived on the scene, each pushing a cart with an egg and a bowl of raw meat. They team-lifted each egg into the nest-like enclosures in the center of the arena. They left the bowls and carts and retreated back inside without so much as a backward glance. It surprised me a little that they didn't want to stay for the hatching, but I tried not to take it personally.

"Want to help with the hatching?" I asked Tom.

He chuckled. "Try and stop me."

"Heh. I should have known." I checked my watch. "Should be any minute now."

It came to my attention that Evelyn, Wong, and Korrapati were all staring at us with a mixture of envy and admiration.

"Let's have a look," Tom said.

We walked over together. He moved with his usual swagger, the very image of confidence. I felt like a nervous intern beside him, conscious of all the eyes on me. By the time we reached the eggs, one was already trembling.

"Oh, yeah. These are ready," Tom said.

The left egg shook and crackled. A minute later, the other one did the same. The noise of the cracking eggshell seemed to echo in the coliseum. Tom scooped up a fistful of meat and handed it to me, then took one of his own. He moved up next to the left-side egg as a snout broke through. The egg split down the middle and fell open, revealing a perfect dragon with wings and tail coiled around itself. It was the color of pale sand, speckled with darker brown.

"You're an eager fellow," Tom said, offering it a piece of meat. The dragonet ate right out of his hand.

Tom snapped his fingers and pointed at the other egg right before it, too, split down the middle.

I shook my head and took up position beside it. "How do you *do* that?"

"Years of practice, kiddo."

My dragon emerged in the same way. Even sticky and shell-covered, it looked more impressive than most of my previous designs. Maybe all of them. The body was slender, almost to the point of snakelike. It unfurled and turned toward me, slit-like eyes narrowing. I offered a piece of the raw meat. The pink tongue flicked out; it had the scent. I tossed it gently and the dragon snapped it from the air like a robin catching a worm. Then it flipped the meat up and caught it again in a better grip. It watched me as it chewed.

Tom's dragonet had eaten three handfuls of meat but refused the fourth. Instead it stood and stretched out its wings to dry them. They were elegant, sweeping things. Quite unlike anything I'd designed before.

"Not our usual dragon designs," Tom said.

"No, they're not."

"Did you design these?"

"It's a team effort." I felt odd about taking more credit than that, even though I could have. "I did the wings, though."

Tom gently took hold of the tip of his dragonet's wing. I gasped softly. Hatchlings didn't usually like to be touched. Especially on their wings, which came out wet and fragile. For a flier to allow this was extraordinary. The chatter in the viewing gallery died down. I could feel the sudden attention, even though it wasn't on me. I stared so hard that my own dragonet almost took off my hand.

"Whoa, easy, little guy." I fed it a big clump of meat and looked back at Tom.

"Almost looks like a swift wing," he said.

"You've got a good eye."

"So that was an intentional choice, then?"

I shrugged, suppressing a tinge of nerves at his attention. "Fastest bird in the world."

He harrumphed. "For horizontal flight."

Damn, he knew his birds. "We put in the wing joints, too. I hope they'll know how to use them."

My dragonet stood and stretched out its wings. Tom gave it a once-over, then an encouraging nod. "Can't wait to see what it can do." He sauntered back toward the dragon wranglers.

I could feel the eyes on me again; for once, I was savoring it. Of course, this could all crash and burn around my ears. If the dragons failed to fly, or the new wing design proved disastrous, this would be a fairly epic embarrassment. Then again, last time I'd come to this arena, my flying dragons had dazzled everyone.

Both dragons now crouched in the sunlight with their wings outstretched. In this heat and sunlight it wouldn't take long. I hurried out of the field and back to where Evelyn, Wong, and Korrapati waited.

"What did Tom think?" Evelyn asked.

"He liked the wings." I tried to keep my face neutral, as if it were totally normal to be chatting with one of my childhood idols. "Knew where I got the idea, too. Man, that guy knows everything about the natural world, doesn't he?" I had the vague sense that I was talking a bit fast. My nerves were getting to me.

"What is Noah saying?" Wong quietly asked Korrapati.

She shrugged. "Something-something, he loves Tom Johnson."

"I do not." I could feel my cheeks heating, though. "I think he's really impressive."

"We should get this moving, Noah." Evelyn handed me a tablet.

"Right." I brought up the command module for the release cages. These were strategically positioned in a grid facing the hatching area. The wranglers had stocked them for us. First up was one of the most popular game birds in the world, a bird whose pear-shaped body and explosive flight patterns triggered a predatory response. The birds' cooing from their cages had already caught the two dragons' attention as they dried their wings. It was now or never. I hit the release button for the first cage.

The mourning dove shot out of it in a flurry of gray, white, and black. Its flight path took it right over the dragons in their nests. If it spotted them and recognized the threat, it made no change to its trajectory. The dragons both crouched. *Here we go.*

The dove flew right over them. The dragons stayed on the ground.

"Shit." I glanced over at Evelyn. "Sorry."

"Try another one," she said.

I hit the button to open another cage. The dove flew out on a similar trajectory, and why not? The first one had escaped unscathed. The dragons watched its approach, their heads tracking its movement. *Come on, go for it.*

But it was déjà vu. The dragons stayed on the ground, and a second dove found its freedom. *Damn it to hell.*

"Why aren't they flying?" Korrapati asked.

"I don't know. Maybe we fed them too much." I'd already wasted a third of our mourning dove inventory and neither dragon had so much as blinked. With a rising desperation, I looked around at everyone who'd come to watch. The sales and marketing folks were fanning themselves in a disgruntled sort of way. They didn't handle the heat well on a good day. I bit my lip and looked at the wranglers, who seemed comfortable and patient by comparison. Then again, they understood dragons better than most.

Tom waved to get my attention. When I looked at him, he held up two fingers. *What the hell does that mean? Two strikes?* It dawned on me then that he was talking about the doves. Two at once. It was half of what we had left, but I figured, why the hell not.

I chose two dove pens and jabbed the open command before I could think about it too much. The birds shot out in tandem, wings flapping madly. It was only two doves, but together they seemed like three or four. They'd not yet reached the center of the field when suddenly both dragons launched themselves into the air. I only saw it out of the corner of my eye; I was watching the birds. The doves sensed the looming danger and scattered. One dragon took off in pursuit of each.

I'd like to say it was a close contest. That one-on-one, the birds had a reasonable chance of escape. Yet there were several reasons we chose mourning doves for these exercises. They couldn't fly particularly fast, and when they did it tended to be in a straight line. In about twenty seconds, each dragon had caught its quarry. By then I was already hitting the release on the last two dove cages. The birds flew out, but were no fools. They made a hard left out of the gate and fled for the desert.

The dragons, though, had banked their wings at the sound of the cages opening. Sharp, controlled turns with good speed. It gave me a boost of confidence in the wing design, because the dragons seemed quite agile. As they bore down on the hapless doves from opposite sides of the arena, I could appreciate their speed as well.

"How fast, Wong?" I asked.

He was clocking them with a small portable radar gun that he'd acquired from one of his many nameless friends in the Phoenix area. Strictly speaking, civilians weren't supposed to have speed guns like that, so Evelyn and I both pretended not to notice.

"Forty-five," he said. "Very fast dragon."

So far, so good. We'd met the performance minimum for flying speed and turn radius. No one could argue with agility, either. Once they caught these last two doves, we might even have a successful demo, just the boost of confidence we needed going into the last trials.

The dragons closed fast, coming at the doves from opposite sides. The birds flew for all they were worth, but their fate had been sealed the moment their cage doors opened. I almost felt bad that we had to sacrifice them in the name of a preliminary test.

The doves never made it to the desert. The two dragons intercepted them at high speed, catching and killing them in a flash. I started to raise my hands to celebrate when it happened. The two beasts collided in midair, right after catching the doves. The *thwap* of the impact echoed in the coliseum grounds. A hard, gut-wrenching sound. It thundered inside of me. *Oh, no.* All I could do was watch as both dragons fell together in a tangle.

The wranglers were on their feet almost the moment it happened. They ran to where the dragons had fallen, with Tom out in front. I should have gone, too, but I couldn't move.

It was like the air had turned solid around me. The wranglers reached the dragons and knelt. Gently disentangled them from each other. But the dragons didn't move, and in the resigned droop of Tom's shoulders, I could read the truth.

They were gone.

CHAPTER TWENTY-SEVEN
The Side Quest

I went through the rest of the workday in a daze. Partly there, partly not there. Tom tried to offer me some assurance, and Evelyn tried to talk to me, but all I could produce were muttered half responses. Summer texted me not long after.

HOW DID IT GO?

I didn't want to tell her, but I'd promised to hold nothing back. I found a terse way to respond.

COMPLETE DISASTER.

When I got back to my office, I still had the flying design open on my workstation. I loaded the simulator and watched the three-dimensional dragon rotate slowly in midair. It was utter torture, but I felt like I deserved it. One minute Tom and I were helping hatch those dragons, joking while we fed the ravenous little things their first meal. The next minute they were dead and gone. I couldn't think, I couldn't work. Eventually I gave up and headed home.

An eerie and unexpected silence greeted me at my condo. That meant one of two things. First, the dragons could be hiding on purpose. They liked to make me come and search to find each of them. They were pretty good at it, but I'd started to learn some of their quirks and it helped a lot. Hadrian, the emerald green, inevitably chose my cactus collection to conceal himself. Nero and Otho sought out earth tones. Titus usually tagged along; his orange scales gave them away. Marcus Aurelius would only hide somewhere warm, which almost always meant the top of the fridge. I had a distinct feeling the proximity to food played a role in that as well.

Octavius and Benjy, the two cleverest dragons, were usually the hardest to find. Octavius gave me plenty of trouble on his own. Both of them working together took it to a whole new level. A month ago, I'd given up searching for them after half an hour and had to bribe the others to sniff them out. Octavius and Benjy had fallen asleep in my chest of drawers on a stack of T-shirts.

A week before that, I found them in the HVAC system. I still don't know how they got in there.

So when I got home after the terrible day of the field trial, I was kind of looking forward to finding all of them. Yet there was not a dragon to be found. It was too quiet. No scurrying sounds, no whisper of scales on ceramic as one of my dragons tried to hide. Not only that, but all of my motion-activated lights were off, which meant that nothing had moved inside for the last ten minutes. None of it made sense.

"Octavius?" I called.

No response.

I checked the top of the fridge. No Marcus Aurelius. That's when I really knew something was wrong. *Maybe they finally got out.*

The idea had always terrified me. The dragonets were too clever for their own good, and I don't think they appreciated the danger of the outside world. Octavius knew better, but he could also open doors. If his siblings put him up to it . . . well, no. He wouldn't be that foolish. At least, that's what I told myself as I searched the condo with a rising sense of panic. That's when I spotted the bright orange piece of paper in the middle of my dining room table. An unfamiliar piece of paper. Maybe I should have seen it when I came in, but I didn't. There were no words on the paper, just numbers. In Summer's handwriting.

GPS coordinates.

I cursed, even as a twinge of relief broke through. I didn't have any idea what was happening, but if Summer was involved it might not be all bad. I thought about changing out of my work clothes, but I'd wasted enough time already. I grabbed my hiking boots from the closet and punched in the coordinates on the way to the car.

"Good afternoon, Noah Parker," said the car over its speakers.

"Hello, gorgeous."

"Where would you like to go today?"

"I'm not sure yet, but you can back us out." And while she did that, I strapped on my hiking boots. I beamed the coordinates to the Tesla's nav computer, which confirmed an inkling suspicion that had just started forming in my mind. I knew that place. Red Rock Run, one of my first geocaches. The route from the parking lot to the cache itself was a straight shot with several intermediate stops on the way. Based on the satellite image of the nav computer, however, the coordinates wouldn't take me to the usual cache. It showed a rough swath of unimproved terrain. Reddish boulders, brown earth, and blots of green that were probably saguaros. No structure was visible, and based on my GPS history, I'd never set foot there, either. Which either meant that something unusual was happening, or she'd made a mistake. The latter seemed unlikely.

I suppose I could have texted Summer to be sure, but it seemed like I should just show up in person. She'd gone to some trouble to make this a game.

"Unable to find route to destination," the car said.

I wasn't sure I heard correctly. "What?"

"Unable to find route to destination."

She couldn't drive across boulders and scrub brush, in other words. "Oh, right. Sorry." I changed the coordinates to the parking lot, which she accepted with far less of a fuss. I kept the controls, though, because I needed the distraction. Otherwise I'd start wallowing in what had happened, and that wouldn't be productive.

We had to win the flying trial to have a chance at securing the DOD contract. The thing was, I believed in our fliers, right up until they'd collided in midair. Now I found myself second-guessing the whole design. Maybe I hadn't engaged my designers as much as I should have. Wong and Korrapati together possessed more experience than I did at genetic engineering, even if I'd been the one who managed to pull off some key breakthroughs. She designed models methodically, one system at a time, split-testing different changes. Wong took a completely different approach, sort of chaotic genius, but he put in the time to make it work. They'd done a hell of a job with the AquaWong. Even though we weren't calling it that.

"Now arriving at your destination," said the car, jolting me back to reality. I eased gingerly into a spot on the gravel lot beside Summer's Jeep. Judging by the angle at which she'd parked, she'd driven straight across the drainage ditch and then parked wherever she wanted. The gravel lots in places like this didn't have painted lines, but somehow she made a statement anyway.

I armed my car's first-tier alarm and plunged down the trail, glancing at my watch for guidance. At the first waypoint in the official geocache, the destination I'd put in required a sharp left turn. I hesitated, if only because this meant I'd step off the well-worn trail and down something that looked like an old ATV path.

"Stick to the trail" is generally good advice for the Arizona desert. ATV paths didn't count. But I hadn't come this far to chicken out, especially with my girlfriend involved. So I took a breath and stomped down along the sunbaked tread marks. It felt strange to be out alone in the hot sunlight without a cloud of flying reptiles to guide me. Or a domesticated pig to lead the way. I had to admit, I didn't care for it very much.

The sun beat down on me, and the scrub brush on either side of the narrow trail kept pulling at my clothes. *I knew I should have changed.* My watch encouraged me to keep going, though, as I was less than half a mile from the waypoint. It beeped again at a quarter mile, which told me I was zeroing in. That's around the same time I noticed the clever scaled creatures concealed atop boulders or behind scrub brush. Then, at last, a glimpse of blond hair and there she was, in the shade of a jagged pillar of rock almost two stories tall. She had her water bottle—another thing I'd forgotten in my rush out the door—and a casual hand on Riker's collar.

"Hey," I said.

"Hey." She overtly checked her watch. "An hour and five minutes. You are slow."

Everything about her posture and the way she spoke was relaxed, but I still had to be sure. "Everything kosher?" That was one of our code words, the one that meant *Tell me if you're under duress*.

Her brow furrowed. "What?"

"Is everything *kosher*?" I asked, hitting the word more this time, and reaching casually for my phone in case this was really a bad situation. Not that I had an elaborate plan or anything if that turned out to be true. More like I'd call Connor and hope for the best.

"Oh right, that." It was hard to tell since she was wearing sunglasses, but she seemed to half-roll her eyes. "Everything's fine."

"That's not the response!" I hissed.

"We're *five by five*." She definitely rolled her eyes this time.

"Good."

"Not everything is a life-or-death situation, you know."

Sure, she said that now, but when it really *had* been a life-or-death situation, I didn't remember any complaints about my secret phrases. "So, what's this about?"

"You need a distraction," she said.

She wasn't wrong, and it made me smile to think that she'd picked up on that from a few texts. "You know, this was my first successful geocache."

"I know. You finally figured out how the comments worked so you wouldn't chase nonexistent caches, and you picked the one that everyone described as easy."

"Hey now, this is the cache that put NPdesign on the leaderboard."

"And who was at the top of that leaderboard?"

"I think it was someone named SumNerdOne."

"Sum*Number*One."

I grinned. "Oh, right. That's quite different."

"*Anyway*, I thought we'd create a side-cache for Red Rock Run."

"Hey, cool idea." We'd created a geocache of our own once before, but that had been a surprising amount of work. You had to establish the cache, of course, but also map out waypoints and little challenge questions to make it difficult. Side-caches were different—they weren't required to log the main cache, so most competitive geocachers ignored them. Summer and I usually put ourselves in that category, but we took on the occasional side-quest from time to time. By unwritten rule, they took you to spectacular, sometimes overlooked areas of the outdoors.

"I knew you'd like it." She looked past me and raised her voice. "Octavius?"

My dragon zoomed into view, swooped right past me, and landed on her shoulder.

"Um, hello!" I threw up my arms. *You're supposed to be* my *dragon*.

Summer was heaping praise on him, then held out her phone and set the timer. "All right, Octavius, sky shot!"

Octavius flapped his wings like mad, circling upward. I reluctantly jogged over to make sure I was in frame. I looked up and reminded myself to smile, even though inside I fought a twinge of jealousy. The sky shot was our thing. I taught it to him. He didn't even drop her phone until he was coming back down. If I hadn't caught it, the thing would have landed on my head.

"You two are getting thick as thieves." I admired the photo while Summer uploaded it to the cache's drive.

"Well, we've been spending a lot of time together because *some people* have been super busy."

"Where are the other dragonets?"

"Hiding. I told them they had to stay until you find them."

I turned around and took stock of the field. First I pointed to the old saguaro I'd passed on my way over. Hadrian blended in rather well. Unfortunately for him, bright orange Titus did not. "Hadrian and Titus!" I called. Obediently, they gave up their perches and took to the air. I pivoted to the high, rocky ridge to the west. "Nero and Otho, I see you!" They chittered and took off, probably surprised. They matched the color of the rocks perfectly, but probably didn't realize they were silhouetted against a bright blue sky. Benjy would have hidden by Octavius, so I drew a line from how he'd flown in and spotted him in a jumbled pile of rocks. "And last of all, Benjy!" I turned back to Summer. "I think that about wraps it up."

"Um, you didn't find Marcus Aurelius."

"He's on the boulder behind you."

She turned and made an exasperated sound. "You little bum! You were there the whole time, weren't you?"

Marcus Aurelius made a big show of waking up from where he'd stretched out in the sun. It made us both laugh.

I moved closer and hugged Summer. "Thanks for this. I needed to get away."

"Was it really that bad?"

"The two dragons collided in midair."

"Oh." She grimaced. "Were they all right?"

"No." I took a deep breath and exhaled slowly. "They died instantly, Tom said, but it was still hard to watch."

"I'm sorry. That sucks."

"Yeah."

"Wow, you just don't have good luck at that coliseum."

I laughed without humor. "You know what? I really don't."

We placed the cache right on the boulder where she'd waited for me, then we both took GPS measurements.

"Ready to walk back?" I asked.

"Always." She held my hand, and we let Riker find the way for us. He was good at sniffing out the easiest route. The dragonets formed an aerial escort overhead, gliding back and forth, chasing one another, and generally burning off the energy from having kept still for so long. Watching them reminded me of the mini field trial, and I shuddered.

"Speaking of seeing people, I was talking to my dad last night," Summer said, in a not-so-subtle attempt to distract me.

"Yeah?"

"He's all worked up about the latest pipeline."

"That doesn't surprise me." Her dad was a bit of an environmentalist nut. It was probably where Summer got it. I wasn't following the latest pipeline debate too closely, but it had sounded like run-of-the-mill stuff: fossil fuel company wants to build a pipeline through protected land, bribes the right people, and gets the approval despite vociferous protests.

"He asked about you," Summer said.

I nearly missed a step, and half-stumbled. "Really?"

She laughed at my reaction. "Yes, really."

"I wasn't sure you'd even told him about me."

"Well, I didn't at first."

"Um, ouch."

She shrugged. "I didn't know if you were serious, and he's . . . kind of overprotective."

"I would be, too."

"You're sweet." She hesitated. "You should meet him."

She wants me to meet her dad? This was unprecedented. I knew they were close, but she hadn't shared a lot about him. Maybe he wasn't the only overprotective one. "I would like that," I said carefully.

"Good," she said.

"Do you think he will? Like me, I mean."

She smiled, but there was a hint of nervousness behind it. "For your sake, I really hope so."

CHAPTER TWENTY-EIGHT
Interlude

Support Chat Log
Date: September 6th

System: Thank you for your patience. A Build-A-Dragon support operator will be with you in three minutes.

Customer1: Hi.

System: Thank you for your patience. A Build-A-Dragon support operator will be with you in two minutes.

Customer1: I'm Billy!

System: Thank you for your patience. A Build-A-Dragon support operator will be with you in one minute.

Customer1: System is a weird name. Do your parents hate you or something?

Charles: Hello, and thank you for contacting Build-A-Dragon support. My name is Charles.

Customer1: Hi, I'm Billy!

Charles: Hello, Billy. Do you have a last name?

Customer1: Um, yeah. Everybody does.

Charles: Can you tell me it?

Customer1: I'm not supposed to give it to people.

Charles: That's perfectly fine. We can get to it later.

Customer1: Where did that System guy go? Did he get fired?

Charles: Uh, no. I'm happy to talk to you, though. How can I help you today?

Customer1: Well, my mom said I should talk to you if Boomer ever got into trouble while she was at work.

Charles: I see. I take it your mom is at work right now?

Customer1: Yep! I'm in charge.

Charles: And Boomer is?

Customer1: My dog, DUH!

Charles: Your . . . dog?

Customer1: He's the best dog in the world.

Charles: What is he like?

Customer1: Well, he's a great friend. He let me pet him, like, right away. And he only likes people in our family. NOT strangers.

Charles: I was hoping you could tell me what he looks like.

Customer1: Oh! Well, he's about three feet long, and kind of gray in color, with no fur.

Charles: No fur?

Customer1: He has this soft skin, kind of like a snake. Mom said it's what makes him safe for our house, because I'm allergic to regular dogs.

Charles: Is it possible that he's not really a dog at all?

Customer1: OH MY GOD you sound like my friends. He IS a dog. He's just the special kind for kids with allergies.

Charles: I think I understand. You said Boomer got into trouble, right? Tell me about that.

Customer1: Well, we were playing in the backyard and he did something bad.

Charles: What did he do?

Customer1: It wasn't his fault!

Charles: I'm sure that's true. Just tell me what happened.

Customer1: We have this stupid bird in our oak tree. It's gray and white and black. I can never remember its name.

Charles: Sparrow?

Customer1: No, not a sparrow. Why would anyone care about a tiny bird like that, dummy?

Charles: I had that one coming.

Customer1: It's that bird that they wrote a book about being all innocent. But really they're a pain in the butt. You know the one?

Charles: I believe you're describing a mockingbird.

Customer1: Yes! Mockingbird. Well, it has a nest or something so it always flies at us and makes all kinds of noise when we play outside. It was doing that today and it was super annoying. I had to go inside just for a second to get a drink.

Charles: Did you leave Boomer outside?

Customer1: Yes. Just for a minute! Anyway, when I came back, the bird was gone. But Boomer had all of these feathers he kept coughing up.

Charles: Did anyone see what happened?

Customer1: No.

Charles: Then I don't think you have anything to worry about, Billy.

Customer1: Oh, good. I feel MUCH better!

Charles: If that's all—

Customer1: The same thing happened to Frisco.

Charles: Who's Frisco?

Customer1: Our neighbor's hairless cat. It's ugly. It was in the yard trying to catch the bird.

Charles: Okay.

Customer1: It went on a long time. But then, I started to get a little hungry.

Charles: Oh, no.

Customer1: So I went in for a snack. SUPER fast.

Charles: Please tell me you brought Boomer in, too.

Customer1: Nope. But when I came back, Frisco was gone!

Charles: Well... maybe the cat left after the bird disappeared.

Customer1: But he left his collar behind. And a foot!

Charles: What did you do with those?

Customer1: Nothing. My neighbor, Mr. Jenkins, came and got them.

Charles: Did he say anything?

Customer1: He said bad words. He was holding the collar and the foot, and yelling at Boomer. And Boomer was hissing at him.

Charles: What happened next?

Customer1: I don't know. I came inside and talked to you.

Charles: Billy, can I have your mom's name and phone number?

Customer1: Sorry, that's a secret.

Charles: Billy, it's important!

Customer1: Nope, those are Mom's Rules. And like you said, I have nothing to worry about. So I won't worry! Thanks for your help. And tell System I said thanks, too.

Charles: Please stay on the line.

[System message: user disconnected]

Charles: They really don't pay me enough for this.

CHAPTER TWENTY-NINE
The Unknowns

Evelyn summoned me to her office the following morning. I had a feeling I knew what this was about. In the wake of the AF-1 demonstration, she probably wanted me to step aside on the flier design. That's what had happened after the Condor demonstration, when Greaves had scrapped my design: She pulled me from the project and told me to keep my head down. I could sense a similar conversation looming as I got off the elevator and made my way to her office.

For the first time ever, Evelyn wasn't behind her desk when I found her. She stood over by the windowsill that held many of her carnivorous plants. Even these failed to capture her attention; she was looking out across the desert through her tinted glass.

"Hello, boss," I said.

"Noah." She didn't have her usual smile for me, but she didn't look angry, either. More concerned. And this was me trying to read a person whose face showed little emotion. It was a guess at best. "How are you doing?"

"I've been better." I walked and stood by her, wondering what she was staring at. The view of downtown Scottsdale still amazed me, but to her it should have been old news. That was assuming she ever took a moment to enjoy it. Most of the time she never got out from behind her projection monitors. "Yesterday was bad. I really don't know what to say other than sorry."

"Don't be so hard on yourself," she said. "The dragons flew well."

Right up until they crashed. "That's not the part of the demonstration I was talking about."

"I understand, but you need to remember the big picture. The goal yesterday was to verify that we've reached the minimum performance specs, especially the difficult ones to measure, like horizontal flight speed."

"We didn't get to test them on endurance," I said.

"Are you really worried about that?"

"Not as much as some of the other categories."

"Then the exercises were worthwhile."

"I've been thinking about the way I tackled the design," I said. "Especially the strength, dexterity, and sensory trade-offs."

"And?"

"I know we're short on time, but I think we could get a better result if we started the design over. I'll let Korrapati and Wong work more of their magic."

She shook her head. "That's too drastic, and we really don't have time for it."

"I know, but it's hard not to want to change something after what happened."

"It was an accident, Noah."

"An avoidable accident." A memory that would probably haunt me whenever I watched my pet dragons flying around. How many times had they played their silly flying games out in the desert, never realizing the risk? It had been hard enough losing two dragons I barely knew.

"It only seems that way in hindsight," she said.

"What if it happens again?"

"You are forgetting a key element of this contract."

"Which is what?"

"The training program designed by your new best friend, Tom Johnson. Have you read the training manual?"

"I haven't gotten to it yet." Not for lack of interest, but I'd been too busy.

"Noah, you are as bad as our customers that you always complain about."

Touché. "Have you read it?"

"Of course," she said. "There are many drills aimed specifically at spatial awareness and collision avoidance."

"Oh." I wished I'd known that; maybe I'd have let Tom put the dragons through their paces before a live demo. Yet deep down, I knew that probably wasn't true. I'd wanted to see them fly as badly as anyone else. "Do you think that will help?"

"I think that with the right training and precautions, dragons will be able to avoid midair collisions."

"God, I hope so."

"The military doesn't send soldiers into combat until they're well-trained. This is similar. So don't worry so much, Noah."

"I'll try not to," I said.

"Good." She did smile then, because we both knew I'd remain paranoid until the final field trials happened, and then probably a while afterward.

But her tone had a finality, suggesting we were done talking about the AF-1. Which meant she'd asked me here to discuss something else.

"How are things going?" I asked.

"About the same." She glanced at the projection monitors that hovered over her desk, but seemed to find no comfort in them.

"Anything up?"

"I just got off the phone with our lawyers. It seems as though we're close to getting an injunction against Greaves and his operations."

Deep inside me, a glimmer of hope started to form in the darkness. "That's *great* news."

"I'm not so sure."

"Why?"

She shrugged. "I'm not a lawyer."

"Wait a minute. You aren't?" I deadpanned. "This has all been a big scam."

"Our real lawyers made it sound like Robert is not putting up much of a legal fight."

"Doesn't that make it easier for us to win?"

"Any lawyer worth their fee has countless ways to make litigation like this difficult. They can ask for delays and extensions that push things back for months."

"Maybe he's out of money."

"Don't count on it," she said.

Yeah, that's too much to wish for. The guy had been loaded even before he landed the lucrative CEO job and the stock options that came with it. "All right, so let's chess-match this out. What happens if we win the injunction?"

"Then Robert and his team would not be allowed to produce dragons using the protected part of the technology."

"Aren't they already not supposed to be using our tech?"

"At this point, all we have is a claim against them. Until the court makes a ruling, they are not breaking any laws."

"What happens if we win the court case?"

"They'd have to cease operations, at least until they negotiated a license or reengineered the process. We would petition the DOD to get back sole supplier status. They're very careful with IP stuff, so we'd have a good chance of getting it."

"So we'd probably win the contract, and Greaves would be out of business."

"At least as far as the U.S. military and U.S. jurisdiction goes."

Something about the way she said that gave me a sudden chill. "What about outside the U.S.?"

"It's a gray area. He could, in theory, move his operation outside U.S. jurisdiction and resume operations."

"Still, it doesn't make sense. It takes time and resources to compete for the DOD grant." It was damn near killing me and my team, frankly. Between that and the dragonets and seeing Summer, I was low on sleep. The stresses of the home stretch in this competition were running us ragged.

"This is what I'm thinking, Noah. Robert does not care about winning the DOD contract. Or at least, that's not his ultimate goal."

"Then what is?"

She looked back out at the cityscape beyond her window. "I wish I knew."

CHAPTER THIRTY
The Father

Somehow in the middle of all of this came my opportunity to meet Summer's dad. The timing wasn't her fault; it was the only night he was in town and was free. I held no illusions about how the words *No, I'm too busy with work right now* would be received, so I agreed. Besides, I did need something to keep my mind off Greaves and the DOD contract for a bit.

Summer rolled up the circle drive in front of my condo to pick me up. She had the actual doors on her Jeep, which was unusual. I opened the passenger side and climbed in. "Hey."

She leaned over to kiss me. "Hey."

"You look cute," I told her. I was being honest—the black-and-white summer dress looked good on her—but the outfit represented a deviation from the Summer Bryn fashion playbook of shorts, tank top, and strappy sandals. This seemed more formal, like something she might wear to a wedding.

Or a funeral, came the unbidden thought.

"Thanks." She couldn't entirely hide the nerves from her voice. "Are you ready for this?"

"I can't wait," I said. *For this to be over.*

I didn't have the best record when it came to the whole meet-the-parents ritual. The only other time I'd experienced it was a couple of years ago when I was with Jane, my last serious girlfriend and Summer's former roommate.

Jane's family was from Bullhead City in northwest Arizona. Obviously my mom and brother lived in town, but she was completely preoccupied with Connor's worsening condition. Connor had met Jane once or twice, of course, but that was as far as family introductions went. Things changed over the summer; Jane went home to Bullhead City. Two and a half months was a long time to be apart, and sure, we were fairly serious, so we decided that I'd come for a visit.

Her family lived out in the sticks. There's no other way to put it. I knew that about her from pretty much the moment we met; the small-town kids came to school with a bit of a twang and a bit of that bright-eyed *so this is a real city* look on their faces. Jane had told me stories, but having grown up in the suburbs I truly had no idea what I was in for when I drove to her parents' house. Single-lane gravel roads. Miles of wind and solar farms. And worst of all, spotty cell phone coverage. Still, she was my girlfriend so I did my best to show up and be polite.

Her parents were perfectly nice, too. They invited me in—I'd be staying with them for two days—and gave off nothing but relaxed, welcoming vibes. I was still nervous as hell, though. Maybe because of the arduous drive in my jalopy of a car, or maybe because I had no experience on how to interact with a girlfriend's parents.

So I talked.

I talked *a lot*.

In the back of my mind I was slightly aware that no one else had gotten a word in edgewise since I'd come inside, but still. I kept telling stories and remarking on what I'd seen on my drive to their place. Telling them all about the jalopy and its quirks. Giving a far-too-detailed summary of my research.

Jane said that after I'd left to return to suburbia, her parents had looked at each other, then at her, and said *Well, he sure is a talker!* Needless to say, my relationship with Jane did not withstand the test of time. That wasn't purely because of my failure to impress her parents. Even so, the idea of that first impression with the parents holding significance for the future of a relationship stuck with me ever since. The irony of it all was that Summer and I hated each other back then. It still amazed me how much that had changed.

"How much have you told your dad about me?" I asked.

"Nothing. He has no idea you exist, or that you're coming to this dinner."

"What?"

"I'm kidding, Noah."

This had to go well. Summer and her dad were really close. In fact, part of me wondered if she'd waited this long to make introductions because she wasn't sure we had staying power as a couple. Even so, if her dad hated me for some reason, it did put our relationship in jeopardy. Sure, she only saw him once every few months, but they talked all the time. Come to think of it, I had no idea how much she'd told him so far. "He doesn't know about the whole me-being-a-jerk-to-you when I was with Jane, right?"

"No, I told him that was a different Noah who died."

"Oh." I wasn't sure how I felt about that. "How did he die?"

"Horrifically," she said.

We pulled in to the parking lot of Smokey Joe's—a barbecue place, which Summer said was her dad's favorite—and found the lot reasonably crowded for a weeknight. We smelled the mesquite smoke before we turned off the road. It smelled good and my stomach rumbled; I hadn't eaten much all day.

For the first time that I could remember, Summer followed the directional flow of traffic into the lot and parked in a legitimate, marked spot. And looking at the clock, I noticed that we'd only barely arrived on time. In fact, we might even be a minute late. I looked at her sidelong.

"What?" she asked.

"Nothing." *You're just a totally different person right now, that's all.*

We held hands on the walk to the restaurant door. That's all I could focus on: the door. Summer squeezed my hand tight, almost to the point of uncomfortable. At least I wasn't the only one who was nervous.

We walked in to find a small, rustic waiting room. It was barbecue-joint classic decor inside: pinewood flooring and dark wood panels plastered with years-old cookout posters. The man waiting in the corner matched the environment well. He wore a denim jacket, jeans, and leather boots like a cowboy on his day off. And maybe it was the lighting or my imagination, but his beard was the exact same color as Summer's hair.

"Hi, Daddy!" Summer hugged him and then turned toward me. "This is Noah."

I smiled in what I hoped was a friendly way. "Nice to meet you."

"Same." He offered his hand, and we shook. Firm handshake. His hand was rough—no surprise there—and I'm sure mine felt soft by comparison. "Heard a lot about you."

"Oh." I raised my eyebrows and looked at Summer, but learned nothing from her face. "All good things, I hope."

"Mostly."

Uh-oh. I didn't really know what to say to that.

The hostess rescued me. "Your table's ready."

"Lead on." Her dad followed, his boots clicking audibly on the floor.

I looked at Summer and mouthed *Mostly?* She took my hand and dragged me after him.

The hostess took us to a booth because it seemed the universe really wanted to torment me. Summer's dad slid into one side, I slid into the other, and that left her to choose between sitting next to her dad or her boyfriend. After an almost-imperceptible hesitation, she slid in next to me. *Small victories.* This brought a momentary frown to her dad's face, and it looked like I'd be starting even deeper in the hole, points-wise.

Don't talk too much, I reminded myself. It seemed like asking some questions was a good start in that regard. "So, what brings you to town?"

"There's a hearing about opening up new leases for copper mining."

"Whereabouts?"

"In Gila County, which is already home to some of the biggest copper mines in the country."

"I see. And, uh, which side are you on?"

Her dad's eyes widened, but Summer laughed, and I held up my hands. "I'm joking. I know what side you're on. So, what do they want?"

"The usual: an open pit mine, no restrictions, no third-party environmental studies."

"I'm sure they did *some* environmental studies," I said tentatively.

Summer snorted in her way that said *You're so naive*.

"Yeah, they did their own," her dad said. "A sponsored study by a research group that has no independent funding."

"Which found, of course, that the environmental impact would be minimal," Summer added.

"Hey now, independent grant funding is virtually impossible to get," I said. I'd experienced some of that when I was in Dr. Sato's lab during graduate school. The NIH was funding grants at the four percent level back then, and it had only gone down. "Maybe the independent group is legit, but they need the sponsor funds to survive."

"That's a fair point," her dad conceded.

One point for me.

"Then again, they've done thirteen environmental

impact studies in the past four years," he said. "Every single one of them came up with minimal impact."

"Oh." I was all for defending researchers because I considered myself one, but that figure was pretty damning if it was true. "Yikes."

"Yeah. Yikes."

"So, you said they wanted open pit mining," I said. "Is that as bad as it sounds for the environment?"

"More."

"Why can't they make it a closed mine?"

"Oh, they can."

"But it's a lot cheaper to run an open-pit mine," Summer said.

Jeez. The thing was, copper was super valuable and always in high demand—I knew that because we needed it for components of both the God Machine and our computing servers. I hated to admit it, but the crunchy tag team of Summer and her dad was starting to get to me.

The server came to take our order. Summer, of course, found some kind of a braised salmon dish and ordered that with fresh-steamed vegetables. She had a habit of making me feel bad about my meal choices. Hell, I didn't even know they served any seafood dishes at Smokey Joe's. But I rarely got to come here and I wasn't going to waste the opportunity to eat real meat.

"Do you have burnt ends?" I asked. These were pork tenderloin tips charred to perfection—a specialty of the restaurant but they often ran out.

"I'll check with the kitchen, but I think so," the server said.

"I'll have that with..." I trailed off as I noticed Summer's side-glare, which told me that if I ordered the cheese-bacon fries, I was a dead man. "Loaded baked potato, and green beans."

Summer looked a tad less murder-y. "I thought we were trying to get away from meat." Her tone was chiding, not angry, so it seemed I'd get away with this one.

"It's too good to pass up," I said.

"You know what, that sounds good," her dad said. "I'll have the same."

"Dad!" Summer looked aghast.

What a baller move. Surprising, sure, from the devoted environmental activist, but a baller move.

"Noah says it's good. Seems like I should put that to the test."

Oh, fantastic. Now my reputation was on the line for a food order that I had no idea he'd duplicate. The thing about burnt ends was that they were kind of an acquired taste. If you liked seasoned meat with a charred flavor, then you were in heaven. On the other hand, if you didn't go for that savory combination, burnt ends were pretty much inedible to you. "Well, this should be interesting," I muttered.

"So, Summer tells me you work in biotech," her dad said.

"Yes, I work at..." I hesitated. "Just, uh, a company in Scottsdale."

Summer rolled her eyes.

"This company have a name?" her dad asked.

"If I tell you, are there going to be protesters out front next week?"

"That depends. Your company doing anything wrong?"

"Well, we're not strip-mining anything if that's what you're asking."

"I hope not," he said. All serious.

I swallowed. "The company is Build-A-Dragon. I work for Evelyn Chang, who just became the CEO. She's as ethical as they come."

"What happened to the old CEO?"

"He, um, left." *After the board fired him.*

"Dad, I told you that, remember?" Summer lowered her voice. "The dog thing?"

I gasped softly and hissed, "You told him?"

"Of course." She shrugged, like it wasn't a bit deal. Like we hadn't signed mountains of nondisclosure agreements explicitly forbidding us from telling anyone what really happened.

Her dad cleared his throat. "There's one part about that incident that I don't understand."

"Okay . . ."

"Why'd you let the animals out?"

"What do you mean?"

"Your whole company existed to fill the roles that dogs couldn't. So why bring them back?"

It was a fair question, and not the first time I'd been asked it, either. Or asked it of myself. But the fact was, in the moment when it happened, I hadn't even considered helping Robert Greaves keep his dirty secret. "It was the right thing to do."

He nodded, whether in agreement or understanding, I couldn't be sure.

"Also, that guy was a total ass," Summer said.

"Summer." Stern dad brought the tone.

"Yeah, Summer, watch the language," I deadpanned. It earned me a kick in the shins but was worth the color that rose to her cheeks.

"I don't know where she gets the swearing from," her dad told me, almost in apology.

I shrugged. "I actually think she's toning it down a bit because you're here. Ow!"

"What?"

"Sorry, I just hit my shin on something."

The food arrived soon after that. The burnt ends announced their arrival with their unique aroma, somehow savory and mesquite at the same time. They looked good. So did Summer's salmon dish, in fairness.

"I can't believe you ordered fish in a barbecue place, but that looks pretty amazing," I told her. *Hell, maybe I should try it sometime.* But my real focus was on the burnt ends, my plate and her dad's. Smokey Joe's had never let me down before, but this was a finicky preparation, and the fact that they hadn't run out of them already had me worried. I couldn't make myself eat first.

"So the name *burnt ends* is not an exaggeration," her dad said.

"I know they don't look like much, but give them a try."

He stabbed a big chunk of meat with the tip of his steak knife and popped it into his mouth.

"Now who's got bad manners?" Summer mumbled. But I was watching her dad's reaction to the food. It seemed strange to think that our whole meeting hinged on that single moment. His forehead smoothed out a bit, and his eyebrows shot up in an expression so like Summer that it threw me a little. But I knew the meaning of it and felt a surge of hope.

"What do you think, Mr. Bryn?" I asked.

He chewed for a moment, then stabbed another piece. With the fork this time. "Not bad, Noah. And you can call me Paul."

After that, the rest of the evening cruised by. Her dad—Paul, as I was supposed to call him—refused my offer to pay and took the bill himself. He was a generous tipper, too. He shook my hand when we said goodbye and said it was good to meet me. Also, not for nothing, but he let me actually leave the restaurant in his daughter's Jeep, which said something.

A couple of hours later, her phone beeped. We were lying in bed at my condo, speculating about what the dragonets were doing based on the noises that filtered through my closed bedroom door. Summer's phone buzzed. Over my protests she wiggled over to pick it up from the nightstand.

"Oh, I missed a call from my dad," she said.

"That's strange. What would you have been doing to miss a call from him?" I slid my hand up her side.

She swatted it away. "Hush, you. He left a voice mail."

She played it, and even though her phone wasn't on speakerphone, I could make out most of the words.

"I really liked Noah . . . seems like a good guy."

"What did he say?" I asked.

"I'm not allowed to see you anymore," she said, as if I couldn't see the big smile on her face.

"Well, I guess this makes it our last night together." I grabbed her and tickled her.

"Stop!" She laughed and grabbed my hands. "He said you're a big corporate sellout."

I tickled her with renewed effort. "Are you sure?"

She squealed. "Stop it! All right, he liked you, okay?"

I relented finally and pulled her close to me. "I'm glad. I like him, too."

CHAPTER THIRTY-ONE
The Air Trials

We convened in the desert for the third and final dragon field trial. At least, I hoped it was the third trial. The military could really decide to do whatever they wanted. If none of our dragons made spec, they could scrap the idea entirely. And then we might find ourselves back at square one, with lots of incredible designs for dragons that no one seemed to want. I supposed it was possible that we could shop them around to other buyers, like the militaries of U.S. allies. I didn't know anything about the laws surrounding that, but selling technology that our own military had rejected seemed like an uphill battle. New customers would want their own modifications. All of that would take time that Build-A-Dragon didn't have.

But that was a problem that had to wait. The Humvee that had picked us up at Build-A-Dragon's headquarters brought us to yet another location, this one an outdoor facility deep in the desert. Tall scree-topped dunes enclosed the area where we parked, which was about the size of four football fields. The central field held what appeared to be a spread-out obstacle course. One section held tall narrow towers painted in bright colors with various hoops at the top. Another featured short concrete pipes with various diameters. Some were only two feet in diameter. Others I could have walked through with my arms outstretched. The dominant feature, though, was a ramshackle three-story concrete building with cut-out doors and windows.

On the far side of the obstacle course were two long parallel stretches of pavement; they ran beside the course and had to be half a mile long. I could see the heat mirage shimmering above them. It must be asphalt. How that factored in to this setup, I couldn't determine.

The soldier in the front passenger seat opened my door for me. That was new. Then he said, "Right this way, Dr. Parker."

So now I'm "Dr. Parker" and I do exist. Amazing how winning the second field trial in such dramatic fashion changed opinions. That wasn't the only change, either. We approached a small bunker on the edge of the obstacle-course field, and out front waiting for us was Major Nakamura.

"Hello again," she said.

"Hello, Major," Evelyn said.

"Where's Major Johnson?" I blurted out, because I'm that gauche. His constant presence had been, perhaps, more of a comfort than I realized.

"With the other team. I thought I should get to know you a bit better."

"Will he—" I began, when Evelyn stepped on my foot.

"Oh, sorry, Noah." She gave me a look that said *shut up* and then turned to Nakamura. "That is a lovely idea. Shall we?"

Now I see. Nakamura was the shot caller and her presence here signaled that we were the new front-runners. Deservedly so, though I'd rather been looking forward to seeing Major Johnson. Being around the guy made me feel instantly calm. With Nakamura, I felt like I should be standing at attention at all times.

Nakamura gestured to the shadowed interior of the bunker. Evelyn entered, she followed, and I was an afterthought once more. I understood—and deeply appreciated—the Army's forethought in building these stone bunkers. The short walk from the Humvee to the building door already had me smudging sweat onto the inside of my sunglasses.

The inside of the bunker was a series of contrasts between old construction and new tech. Anything physically connected to the structure itself was plain and utilitarian: the narrow rectangular hallways, the low ceilings, the wide viewing window. Spliced into that in almost awkward fashion was the modern tech—electrical wiring, comm stations, and what appeared to be a large radar screen.

"The place we're standing does not technically exist," Major Nakamura said. "You won't find it on any maps or satellite images."

I kept my amusement to myself because Build-A-Dragon knew all-too-well about paid exclusion from satellite imagery. Then again, when it was the U.S. military, they probably didn't have to pay for the privilege.

I considered asking about property maps, which were often an indirect means to identify the owner of a property. But this was the military and they knew what they were doing. Besides, I didn't need Evelyn to step on my foot again.

"Why so much security?" Evelyn asked. A more sensible question.

"We normally use this facility to test some of our other high-performance aircraft. The kind of thing best kept hidden from curious eyes."

She means drones. It had to be the unspoken explanation, because the military, as far as I knew, had little other reason for aerial obstacle courses. And in fact it explained why the large building in the center of the course bothered me. Its architecture was decidedly non-American. More like Middle Eastern. There were old shipping containers stacked into blocky semblances of outbuildings. It looked like a fortified military compound. That realization had me seeing each obstacle in a new light. The big blocks of concrete represented a convoy. The building was a terrorist cell or enemy headquarters. The long tubes could represent indoor hallways, or even sewers. The rings atop tall poles might represent… something else. Gun ports on aircraft, maybe.

Everything here was a test of the flying dragons' performance requirements. Come to think of it, those long stretches of pavement on the far side of the field were probably twin runways. Man, it'd be sweet to see a Gray Eagle or a Predator land on one of those strips of asphalt. I'd never seen a military drone in person outside of a museum. Connor, naturally, claimed that he'd encountered them multiple times while flying his own little drones out in the desert.

"Will we see any of those things?" I asked, in what I hoped was a casual tone.

"No. We've cleared the airspace for today's demonstrations."

"Ah." Well, at least our dragons wouldn't inadvertently get blown out of the sky by air-to-air missiles. I supposed that was good.

"Major," said the operator of the radar screen, and then he gave her a nod.

"They're starting," Nakamura said.

We're going first again. I liked seeing my dragons before the competition, but I also hated how much it left unknown. The first field trials had taught a memorable lesson in humility. We moved closer to the viewing window.

"Contact," said the guy watching the radar screen.

I hurried over, enticed by the lure of the radar tech. Sure enough, six blips had appeared, approaching the radar position from the north and flying in a V-formation.

"Those are the dragons?" I asked.

"They should be. Altitude and bearing are on spec. We'll have visual in thirty seconds."

I shook my head in wonder. "I can't believe you can pick up something so small."

"Normally our software would filter these out as anomalies. Now, we have the sensitivity set so high it'll pick up anything bigger than a mourning dove."

I started to laugh but reined it in when I realized he was serious. He was a young guy, probably about my age, and probably had the slightest build of anyone we'd encountered in the military thus far. But he stared at the radar screen and spoke with an air of intensity. Like a hatcher handling an egg. This guy was committed to the tech. I could appreciate that. "That's awesome. But our dragons eat mourning doves."

"Here they come!" Evelyn had borrowed a pair of field optics and was looking north. "Oh, are those . . ."

"Munitions," said the major, who'd taken the other pair of binoculars and stepped up beside her.

"They're bigger than I expected."

"Twenty-five pounds. They're the same weight as the live rounds we designed for them," Nakamura said.

"Oh, so not real, then." Evelyn sounded as relieved as I felt. Despite our self-assurances that the past weeks of training would prevent these dragons from flying into one another, that wasn't something I wanted to test with live explosives. At least while I was on-site.

"They have only half of the normal explosives, and we left out the incendiary and antipersonnel effects."

"Oh," Evelyn said after a minute.

We were probably thinking the same thing. *Antipersonnel effects.*

I was kicking myself for not thinking to bring my own binoculars, but now I could see the dragons without assistance. I knew what Evelyn had meant about the weight—the dragons flew well despite their burdens, but lacked that flair that had taken everyone's breath away at the Build-A-Dragon arena.

Nakamura produced a two-way radio and hit the transmit button. "Start the targets."

Seconds later, half a dozen vehicles that I'd mistaken for stationary targets shuddered into motion. They were all in a line and moving in the same direction, away from the dragons, at something like twenty miles an hour. Instantly, this seemed to trigger some recognition among the flying reptiles. They altered their flight path to intercept.

Nakamura leaned over to ask something of my buddy at the radar screen.

"Forty-six knots," he said.

I smiled to myself, because that was well above the required airspeed while burdened. *Just wait until you see them not carrying anything.*

The dragons had shifted their positions and now flew in a diagonal line approaching the simulated convoy. The first dragon released its ordnance. The bomb tilted downward as it fell, and I knew it would be a direct hit. Nakamura put a hand on Evelyn's binoculars to lower them. *Thump.* A yellow-orange flash, then the sound, and then a wave of displaced air washed over us. All I could think was *That's a half-power munition?* The second dragon had released. Its bomb flew true, detonating on the second vehicle in the convoy.

"Yes!" I shouted, but the sound of the explosion drowned it out. That was two for two. In short order, the next two bombs found their targets. I stood there on the verge of celebration. The explosion looked different, though. Less bright orange flame, more brown dust.

"What happened?" Evelyn asked.

"That's a miss," Nakamura said.

Damn. Five for six made the spec, but I'd wanted a

perfect score so there could be no debate as to the dragons' performance. But I soon forgot that, because the dragons had shifted into the next phase of their trials, obstacle flying. They swept down into the gauntlet of tunnels and hoops and moving pendulums. You'd think that, as somewhat-intelligent animals flying through a dangerous course, they might slow down a little.

Instead, freed of their burdens, they pushed themselves to the limits of speed. They dove, pivoted, and danced their way through every danger. I held my breath, waiting for a collision like the one we'd seen in the coliseum. But this group of dragons seemed aware of one another. They kept an almost perfect distance apart even as they dodged among concrete pillars and over sharp embankments that meant certain death with one small mistake. They were fearless.

And fast, too, it went without saying. My buddy at the radar station wasn't about to let it go unsaid, though. "Sixty-five knots. Not bad."

Nakamura shot him a stern look; evidently she wasn't seeking editorials. But we couldn't deny how well the dragons were flying. How effortlessly they handled themselves despite the dangers. Then, when they passed through the course, it was an all-out sprint to the finish line on the far end of the field. The dragons seemed to sense it, too. They pumped their wings faster and faster, low to the ground, jostling with one another for the lead position.

Radar guy whistled. "Seventy-six knots."

Evelyn smiled and nudged my hand like *Way to go*.

The dragons passed the finish line, a fifty-foot pole

topped with a white streamer. Whether it was their own recognition or a response to some signal, they stopped flapping and glided, wings fully outstretched, turning in unison to make a circle around the entire field. It was at least as good as watching the Blue Angels. Maybe better. And I definitely let out a whoop as their shadows passed over our bunker.

Meanwhile, an Army truck had trundled into view from the north alongside the runway. It was a flatbed loaded with empty dragon cages. This, too, seemed to convey some signal. The dragons turned and winged toward it, cutting short their victory lap around the field. Which alone spoke to their training, because it took real discipline not to want to finish a victory lap.

They landed on the rims of their cages and then swung in, almost bat-like, closing the cage doors after them. That whole trick—entering the cage and shutting it afterward—was something we'd written into the Build-A-Dragon training manual for our customers who bought retail dragons. The key was to reward the dragon whenever it did so. Sure enough, the driver of the truck emerged from the cab, climbed up, and began dropping meat into every cage.

I'll be damned. Someone actually did *read the manual.*

"That was a good performance," Major Nakamura said. "Your competition has their work cut out for them."

I tried, unsuccessfully, not to bask in the first bit of praise I'd heard from the sternest of the majors. Meanwhile, a squad of soldiers had swarmed onto the field to reset the obstacles and clear the vehicles in the simulated convoy. A whistle sounded, and then the vehicles trundled slowly back into position.

"Contact," said the radar operator.

Here we go. It was time to see what Greaves and his team had come up with. As much as I wanted to pretend that the stakes weren't high, it was hard to deny that a lot was riding on this. The next five minutes would decide the fate of the DOD contract, the company, and possibly my future as a dragon designer.

Evelyn and Nakamura both had their binoculars again, leaving me feeling like the third wheel.

"I have them," Nakamura said, and pointed for Evelyn's benefit.

Both of them watched without speaking. The silence seemed to stretch until it was heavy and awkward.

"Interesting wing design," Evelyn said finally. Then she handed her field glasses to me.

The binoculars were, hands down, the best quality optics I'd ever handled. The field of view was wide enough that I found the incoming dragons almost instantly. The magnification made it up close and personal. Which is how, despite the energetic flapping as they struggled to fly with heavy ordnance in tow, I recognized the long and slender wings with pointed tips that were reminiscent of a certain migratory bird. *Son of a bitch.* "That's our wing design!"

"It does look remarkably similar," Evelyn said.

Remarkably similar, my ass. "It's a carbon copy."

"Maybe they reached the same answer we did by going about it the same way," Evelyn said.

"Convergent evolution in dragon design?" I asked.

Evelyn shrugged. "It's possible."

"Maybe," I said, and I tried not to let all of my disbelief

seep into my tone. She could be right; anyone with half a scientific brain might look to the fastest modern birds for design inspiration. Then again, corporate espionage was right out of the Robert Greaves playbook. I fumed about it but there was nothing I could do. We watched their dragons approach the convoy. One, two, three direct hits. Then a fourth. Then a fifth. *Oh, hell. They're going to beat us again.* But the sixth dragon's release looked awkward somehow, as if the creature let slip the ordnance before it was ready to. The bomb fell way short and detonated in the ground, throwing up a cloud of dust. I celebrated quietly out of respect for Major Nakamura.

The other dragons were fast, but not as fast as ours had been. They cleared the obstacles without too many issues, though at least one of them clipped a hoop while passing through. I found myself wincing each time it happened, quietly hoping the dragon was okay, even though an injury would probably bring me success. Dragons were dragons, and I didn't wish any of them harm.

As they neared the final stage of the flight test, Nakamura asked radar guy for the speed and was told sixty-eight. Above spec, but not nearly as fast as ours. Before too long, another truck arrived to collect the dragons. On another day, I'd have admired their design. They had slimmer body profiles than our dragons, and a more triangular head. The eye position seemed a little different—more to the side of the head, which would reduce depth perception but give superior peripheral vision.

Major Nakamura's phone rang—undoubtedly a call from Major Johnson to discuss the trials—and she stepped out to answer.

"They stole our wing design," I said to Evelyn. I didn't care if radar guy heard this part.

"We don't know that for certain."

"Come on, Evelyn."

She lifted her eyebrows at my tone.

I held up my hands. "Sorry. But you know what I mean."

"Even if they did, it would be difficult to prove."

"It's not just personal offense here. What really worries me is *how* they got our design." If they compromised our flier design, they might have access to other things. Every custom design, every mainline model.

"That's a valid concern."

"Could they have hacked our servers?" I asked. Network security wasn't really my forte; when I'd been interested in hiding from security measures at Build-A-Dragon, I was on the inside.

"Doubtful. The design network is on a closed system, and the rest of our network has state-of-the-art encryption." She frowned. "I'll still have everything audited tomorrow, but that seems an unlikely route in."

"Do you think someone inside the company helped him?"

She frowned. "I don't want to think that. It would have to be someone close to Design."

Yeah, I didn't want to think that either. I trusted Korrapati and Wong implicitly. The other employees closest to us were the hatchery staff. They were a bit odd, but I couldn't see them helping Greaves. "I wonder if they actually got the full design," I said. "To me, it looked like they didn't incorporate the wing joints that maximize the aerodynamics."

"Are you sure?"

"It didn't look like it. And their dragons weren't as fast as ours." The other dragons had other differences, but the wings were what really mattered. If they'd watched our dragons flying today, they'd most likely realized how critical the wing joints were, and would incorporate that in their next design. The theft of the shape, though, still bothered me. Maybe they'd seen the simulator results when one of us ran it during the design phase. But no, Build-A-Dragon's buildings were shielded against intrusions.

Outside intrusions.

Damn. "I just figured it out."

"What did you figure?"

"The field trials." I'd suppressed the memory of those trials because of how they ended, but we didn't enjoy nearly the same protections in the arena as we did inside the building. "We flew the dragons outside. Anyone could have gotten a good look." *And maybe even eavesdropped when I was trying to impress Tom Johnson.* I felt a pang of guilt.

Evelyn let out a long breath. "I'm sorry, Noah. That was my fault."

"What? No it wasn't."

"Robert knows me too well. He knew I'd want a field demonstration to make sure the aerial dragons had met spec."

"We had no reason to think he'd spy on us."

She bit her lip. "We'll have to be more careful in the future."

"This is the final trial, isn't it?"

She glanced at the radar guy, then looked back at me. "We'll talk later."

Major Nakamura reentered with her usual brisk manner. "The field demonstrations are over, so let's get you back. You'll have our decision within a week."

"Really? So long?" Evelyn asked.

I shared her disappointment. It seemed like we'd won two out of three trials hands down. Even if we hadn't, I wanted to know sooner rather than later.

"There's a lot to consider. We don't award defense contracts lightly," Nakamura said.

"Of course," Evelyn said. "Take all the time you need."

Her voice echoed with quiet confidence.

I wished I felt the same.

CHAPTER THIRTY-TWO
The Mother

We didn't hear anything about the DOD contract the next day. Not that I expected to or anything; Nakamura had said it might take up to a week. The waiting was torture. A few custom orders had trickled in overnight—that was when our East Asian customers were awake—but I let Korrapati and Wong have them. I reviewed the DOD specs and compared them to my hasty notes about our dragons' performance, trying in vain to guess what was coming.

The evening after, Summer had come over to my place for dinner. For reasons not entirely clear, she'd decided that the dragonets needed to be eating more vegetables, so she brought a huge tray of carrots, celery, broccoli, cauliflower, and cucumbers over for them to try. We figured we'd start with Octavius, since all of the other dragonets tended to follow his example. Granted, I'd never known him to eat a single vegetable in his life, but Summer wanted to try. So we were trying and thus far had had zero success.

When Connor called me out of the blue, it was almost a relief.

"C-monkey," I answered.

"N-circlement."

"Really?"

"Been reading about Genghis Khan."

"Ugh, you're such a nerd," I said, though I'd been slowly reading a long book about the battles of the Hundred Years War. I was more into the longbow than pincer movements.

"Yeah, that's why my girlfriend named her dog after a *Star Trek* character," Connor said. "Oh wait, that was you."

I grinned. "I knew it was a lie when you said that first part, about having a girlfriend."

"I date plenty of girls."

"It has to last more than a week to count as dating, dude."

He chuckled. "That's kind of why I'm calling, actually. You know how you met Summer's dad and he inexplicably didn't hate you?"

"Yeah . . ." I said. That wasn't exactly how I'd have put it, but I hadn't forgotten.

"Well, it's come to the attention of our parental unit—"

"Connor," I said warningly. *He'd better not have.*

". . . that if you and Summer are at the meeting-of-parents stage, then maybe it should be a two-way street."

My mouth worked for a moment until I remembered some useful words. "What— I mean, how did this happen?"

"Well, Mom and I were talking today over lunch."

"You went home for lunch?" I asked.

"No, we talked on the phone. Stop interrupting me. Anyway, I didn't realize that this meeting Summer's dad thing was confidential information, and it sort of came up."

"It *came up*?"

"Yeah, you know. Conversation drifted your way and it was out before I even knew what was happening."

Oh hell. This was bad. Mom was a believer of parity, especially for herself. Now I was two offenses deep: not offering parity, and not telling her. "This is what happens when you go and talk to Mom on the phone voluntarily."

"We talk most days. She knows when I take a lunch break."

I groaned. "Why can't you be a normal person who dodges his mother's calls?"

"Why can't you be a better son who doesn't?"

I suppressed a sigh, because there was no putting the cat in the bag once it was out. It wasn't entirely Connor's fault that he was a mama's boy. He lived at home as an adult, and before the gene therapy it looked like that might be a permanent scenario. "Well, thanks for the heads-up."

My phone beeped. I didn't even have to look to know who it was. "And now she's calling. Talk to you later."

"Nice knowing you." He hung up.

I flipped over to the new call. "Hello?"

"Noah, it's your mother," she said, with that immediately chastising tone of voice that moms have perfected: the perfect mix of hurt and accusation.

"Hi, Mom. I'm on the other line," I lied. "Hang on a second." I put her on hold before she could raise a protest and ran to the door of the balcony, where Summer was playing with Riker. Apparently she'd given up on the vegetable-feeding the moment I took the call from Connor.

"Hey," I whispered.

She must have seen something on my face that caused concern. "What's wrong?"

I took a deep breath. "Is there any chance you'd like to meet my mom?"

"Um, sure. When were you thinking?"

"I don't know, kind of soon."

She wrenched a rope toy away from Riker and held it up so that he'd have to rear up on his legs to reach it. "We have a lot going on right now."

"I know, but I really want you to meet her."

That won me a look and a lovely smile. "Then set it up."

"Bless you." I shut the door and took my mom off hold. "Hey, Mom, what's shaking?"

"Who was on the other line?"

"Wrong number," I said.

"How are you doing? We haven't seen you in a while."

"It's been crazy busy, but the aerial dragons did well."

"Did they reach a decision yet?"

"Nope. Still waiting." As long as we were talking, I figured that the best defense was a good offense. "Why don't we get together this week. Maybe for dinner?"

"That would be wonderful."

"What about El Poblano?" It was a Mexican place on the super-busy road near her house; as a kid I'd eaten there too many times to count. "I haven't been there in a while. I assume it's still good."

"Oh, it's fantastic. Great margaritas, too."

Uh-oh. "You know, maybe we should go somewhere else."

"No, El Poblano sounds good. How about tomorrow?"

When it rains, it pours. "Sure. Why not?" There was no sense putting it off anyway. "Do you mind if I invite someone?"

"Boy or girl?"

Oh my God. "Jeez, Mom. Does that have a bearing on your answer?"

"Of course not."

"You know quite well that Summer is a girl."

"Summer or Sumner, it makes no difference to me."

This was exactly why no one should call their mother every day. "Will you stop it?"

She laughed. "All right. I can't wait to meet her."

"She can't wait to meet you. How about seven?"

"I'll be there with bells on."

"I'm sure you will."

"*Wedding* bells."

I laughed in spite of myself. "Stop it. I'll see you tomorrow."

The next day at work, all I could do was obsess over the coming meeting of the two most important women in my life. It felt a little different from when I'd met her dad; when that happened, I was the one who had hoped to impress. If her dad had hated me, given their relationship and how close they were, I'd have faced a long uphill road to stay in a relationship with her. In contrast, I generally kept my mom at arm's length. I was worried about two possible bad outcomes here. First, that they wouldn't get along and I'd spend the rest of my days scrambling to maintain healthy relationships while keeping them mostly apart. Which, if I was honest with myself, I didn't have the organizational skills to pull off.

The second outcome, the one I didn't want to admit worried me, was that Summer would get a good look at my gene pool and decide to cut me loose. Mom had a bit of a drinking problem. It was hardly a secret; Connor and I had been dealing with it our whole lives. She never hurt anyone other than herself, but it was still embarrassing. And it was something I hadn't told Summer much about.

Maybe it was silly, but moms are permanent and for all I knew, she was worried about what she might have to live with long-term. All this was a long way of saying that the stakes felt high and I'd been somewhat rushed into this at the worst possible time.

I convinced Summer to let me drive to El Poblano, which helped. I was glad to have an excuse to take the Tesla somewhere other than work. It seemed like every other time Summer and I went somewhere recently, we had reason to take her Jeep. Which was fine I guess, but I felt like arm candy most of the time when I wasn't busy hanging on to the *oh shit* bar. Driving my bright red coupe with a pretty girl in the front, that was the American dream.

Naturally I kept these thoughts to myself.

"Thanks for doing this," I told her.

"Why are you thanking me?"

"You thanked me for meeting your dad." I cleared my throat. "Multiple times, if I recall."

"That's different. My dad is intimidating."

"Hey, my mom is not exactly a picnic."

"We're meeting her at a Mexican restaurant during happy hour. I'll take my chances."

I bit back an unpleasant word. "It's happy hour?" *This is going to be fun.*

We parked in the lot, which was crowded—always a good sign—and walked in the front door. The interior was cramped and dimly lit, but the smell of delicious things fried in hot oil pervaded everything. I inhaled deeply. "Oh, that's the stuff."

"Oh my God, I can already tell it's going to be good," Summer said.

I took her hand and pulled her close to me. "You know the best part?"

"What?"

"We're going to smell like this for the rest of the night."

"Ooh. Tell me more," she whispered.

I pulled her deeper into the interior. There were diners crowding every table. The waitstaff wove their way between them, depositing baskets of chips with salsa, taking orders, ferrying sizzling platters of fajitas past groups that were just getting ready to order. They really pulled out all the stops when it came to getting fajita orders. In fairness, the food lived up to the hype. I was rather hoping my mom would do the same.

We squeezed our way down the main aisle past a short divider wall to the only not-full table, and there *he* was.

"Connor!" I said.

"Hey, bro. Hey, Summer."

"I didn't know you were going to be here." Seeing him was actually a pleasant surprise. He already knew Summer and they got along. I felt like some of the pressure had shifted off of me. "Glad you came, though."

He leaned back, dipping a chip casually in the salsa. "Not sure you will be for long." A nearly full beer in a frosted glass sat in front of him. In front of the other booth seat were two empty margarita glasses.

"What have you done?"

"So, Mom called me and said that she got here an hour early."

"Oh, delightful," I said. "Where is she?"

"Getting another drink from the bar."

"Do you not have a waiter?"

"He was making them too weak."

I rolled my eyes. "Of course she'd say that."

"Oh, it was true. I bribed him while she was in the restroom."

"Clever."

Summer watched this exchange with obvious amusement. "God, you two are so much alike."

"Don't you start," I told her.

"Well, I managed to get some food into her," Connor said. "Even so, I apologize for what's about to happen!"

"There he is!" My mom skirted around a server, nearly dislodging his tray full of chips and salsa. She had a full margarita glass in one hand but threw the other arm around my neck. I managed to avoid a direct kiss on the mouth, but just barely.

"Uh, hi, Mom," I disentangled myself from her grip and held out my arm. "This is Summer."

"It's nice to meet you," Summer said, with a smile that made my heart melt even though it wasn't for me.

"And you. Oh, aren't you just a doll!" My mom threw her hugging arm around Summer, whose eyes widened as she got a firsthand taste of the strong family tradition of boundary violation.

"Please have a seat, guys," Connor said. "There's a huge tray coming through."

From my peripheral vision, I could tell this was more of a ploy than an imminent concern, but I wasn't about to challenge the authenticity. Letting Mom swing her arms around with a full margarita in hand was just asking for trouble. We squeezed into the booth and chairs. In the course of this, Mom settled her margarita on the table and Summer pounced.

"Aw, you bought me a drink? You're so sweet!" She plucked it up from the table, took a drink, *and* managed to squeeze my leg, all in the span of two seconds.

"Oh, sure. It's your first time here, after all," Mom said. "You shouldn't have to drink alone, though."

Connor kicked me under the table.

I winced and hopped up. "Next round is on me. Margaritas?"

"Good boy," Mom said.

"I'm good," Connor said.

"Two it is." I dodged two servers on my way to the bar and got the bartender's attention. *"Buenas tardes."*

He was Latino, of course, almost certainly a member of the large family that owned El Poblano. I didn't recognize him but he was younger, probably just old enough to serve. He looked at me, recognized I was already at the limits of my Spanish, and politely said, "What can I get you?"

"Two margaritas, and I'd like them weak. But they can't taste weak. Know what I mean?"

"No."

Oy. "Okay, two margaritas, half power. Does that make sense?"

He nodded and got to work, whisking out two salt-rimmed glasses.

"That's my table over there, with the pretty girl and the guy who's not as good-looking as me." I pointed, made sure he clocked the table. Then I slid a few tightly folded bills across the bar. "Everything that goes to that table is half power, *comprende?*"

"*Comprende.*"

So it turns out I did know another word in Spanish. But not as many as Summer. When I got back to the table, she was *ordering* in it. Like, flawlessly. First it was Tom Johnson, now it was her. Summer even ordered for me, correctly guessing that I wanted my go-to dish, chilaquiles mexicanos. Sure it was a little emasculating but the impression it left was worth it.

"Oh, you speak Spanish so beautifully," my mom said, with a little sigh.

"I'm glad to have a chance to use it," Summer said. "This place is amazing."

I took a long pull from my margarita, enjoying the tang and the mild flavor of the tequila. Even with half strength, this was the only one I'd allow myself. The Tesla had a Breathalyzer built into the steering wheel.

"The same family has owned it for almost twenty-five years," Mom said.

"Hey, that makes it older than Connor," I said. "Not to mention more important."

Connor snorted. "Since I'm considered the newer and

better-looking version of you, all you're doing is putting yourself down."

"Have they always been like this?" Summer asked my mom.

"Unfortunately, yes."

The food came soon after that. Summer volunteered to get up mid-meal and get the next round of tequilas—just for her and my mom—which didn't worry me as much as it might have, mostly because the bartender saw her coming, met my eyes, and winked. I looked back at the table and found Mom staring at me with a stern look.

"What?"

"Don't screw it up, that's what," she said.

My mouth worked for an appropriate thing to say while Connor found it necessary to wipe his mouth with his napkin for an extra long time.

"Two margaritas," Summer announced, sliding one in front of my mom.

Mom looked at me, and raised an eyebrow in her way of saying *See?*

Connor gave me the pursed-lips nod, like he agreed that everything was golden.

I grinned and basked in that moment.

"In other news, I'm pretty sure the bartender has a crush on Noah," Summer said without preamble.

I choked on my drink. "Excuse me?"

"This doesn't surprise me at all," Connor said. "The only question is, will his be an unrequited love, or not?"

There was a good laugh at my expense, and I joined in.

"All right, eat your tacos, people. I've got a busy day tomorrow." Either a day of self-confidence or my last day of gainful employment. I still didn't know which.

CHAPTER THIRTY-THREE
The Good News

The next morning was rough. I got up ten minutes later than usual and had to drag myself into work. I'd gone easy last night, but even one margarita before dinner did not mix well with weeknights. Naturally, Evelyn summoned the entire Design team to the conference room first thing in the morning.

Something about her summons seemed ominous. I mean, there were only three of us and her office was huge. We could have met up there and been quite comfortable. As we walked down the hallway to the door, I tried to remember, historically speaking, whether meetings in the conference room meant good news or bad news.

She'd announced the domestication challenge in her office when the Design team was twice as large. That was arguably good news. We'd watched the auction of the first domesticated dragons—the funds from which kept the company afloat in the early days—in the conference room. That, too, had counted as good news, though we hadn't known how it would go. We hadn't been certain that the world truly wanted dragons. Looking back, it still boggled my mind. Who wouldn't want a dragon?

The world was a better place with dragons in it. Most people took it for granted. Most people didn't realize how fragile the whole system was. Only Build-A-Dragon had the assets and infrastructure to produce dragons at scale. If the company failed, all of it would be sold off piecemeal. Maybe that's what Greaves wanted to happen. Of course, it was unlike him to have selfless ulterior motives. This was a guy who deprived the world of dogs for years to keep his company profitable.

Then again, given how Build-A-Dragon's financials looked now that dogs had returned, it was hard to question Greaves's business acumen.

Wong and Korrapati were already waiting in the conference room. She sat in a chair, notepad and pen square in front of her, perfect posture and somehow appearing patient. He slouched two chairs over, looking like he could be half asleep. The handlebars of his mini scooter said that he'd rolled here to save himself the walk, even though it was all of two hundred feet down the hall.

"Hey, guys," I said. "Good morning?"

"Not enough work," Wong said.

"Really? What about the customs for China?"

He shrugged. "We finish Tuesday."

"Sorry. Not much we can do about that for the moment." I'd already briefed them on how the third field trials went, so there was no point in rehashing it. I even told them about the wing design and our suspicion on how Greaves had gotten the intel. Beyond that, all we could do was wait.

High-heeled shoes clacked down the hallway toward us, and the door slid open. Evelyn bustled in looking frazzled and high-energy, but there was a positive vibe to her manner. "Oh good, you're all here."

"Waiting on tenterhooks," I said.

"Tenter hooks, Noah Parker?"

I grinned, enjoying the rare event of an American idiom that Evelyn hadn't yet encountered. "Waiting for something to happen, like cloth hung up to dry."

"Well, you can get off your tenterhooks now. I've been talking to the DOD all morning."

Wong, Korrapati, and I looked at one another. I'm sure I had the same look of excitement and alarm on my face.

"And?" I asked.

"The good news first. We have been awarded a DOD contract."

"Yes!" I pounded the table a little too hard in my excitement. Luckily it didn't break.

"Good news. Very good," Wong said.

"That's fantastic!" Korrapati said.

"Congratulations, all of you," Evelyn said.

"So, it's all three models, right?" I asked. "Aerial, marine, and infantry?"

Evelyn's smile flickered. "It is for aerial and marine only."

"What about the third model?"

"The DOD elected not to contract us for it."

"Is it going to Greaves?"

"I don't know yet."

I ground my teeth to keep from saying more. This was a victory, even if it wasn't a complete one. It rankled me that part of the contract might go to Greaves, but I had to put on a brave front for the team. "That's still fantastic news."

"We're going to be very busy to meet these specs. The DOD wants some adjustments to the field-tested dragons, and based on their confidence in them, they would like prototypes for seven additional models."

"*Seven* models?" I shook my head. We wanted work to do, of course, and seven run-of-the-mill custom jobs ordinarily wouldn't make us break a sweat. But the DOD was no ordinary customer. No doubt they had performance specs for each and every model.

Evelyn seemed to read my mind. "And they'll have to meet a variety of minimum performance thresholds."

I sighed. "Remind me, why did we want this contract again?"

"To keep the company going," Evelyn said.

Oh. Right. "Well, Wong *was* just telling me he needed more work." I grinned at him. "You're going to be busy. Both of you."

"Bring it on," Korrapati said.

Wong grinned back at me. "Busy is good."

"Any word on the legal front?" I asked Evelyn.

"Nothing yet."

"If Greaves gets a contract, what do you think is going to happen on that front?"

"If there's money on the line, he'll put new resources toward fighting us in court. To stall things so that he can keep the contract."

That's exactly what I'm worried about. Maybe Greaves hadn't fought us yet because he didn't think he had a chance at landing DOD money. If his resources were limited, he probably gambled everything on the flier trials. Which we won fair and square. However, if the DOD decided to give him a contract for even the infantry model, that would be a huge influx of financial security. Not to mention prestige and experience, which would enable him to fight us for future DOD contracts. Hell, he might even decide to compete with us for the last scraps of the open market. Bottom line, this meant that the Greaves problem wasn't going away. He could harass and hound us at every turn. And he would, too. This was a guy who confined healthy dogs to living in cages for years, simply because of something a dog had done when he was a child.

"What if he . . . no longer had a Redwood Codex?" I asked.

Evelyn frowned at me. "What do you mean?"

"If he doesn't have the Codex, he can't print viable eggs. And with Redwood gone, that effectively restores our monopoly on dragons."

"Robert knows that. He's not going to give up his Codex."

"Oh, I wasn't planning to *ask* him."

Evelyn frowned at me. "Noah, I want to be clear. You should not do anything to interfere with Robert's operations. Corporate sabotage is off the table."

"I know."

"Promise me you won't try anything foolish."

"All right, I promise."

But in my head, the wheels had already begun to turn.

% % %

Korrapati and Wong ambushed me even before I'd left Build-A-Dragon's property. It was the end of the day, I was walking toward my car in the underground parking garage, and both of them materialized in front of me.

"Noah," Korrapati said.

I nearly jumped out of my skin. "God, Korrapati, you scared the crap out of me!"

"Oh. Sorry," she said.

"What are you doing here?"

"Want to talk," Wong said.

In a dark parking garage, after work. Yeah, this isn't good. "About what?"

"You're going to try to go for the other Redwood Codex," Korrapati said.

I stopped myself from blurting out something incriminating, but only just. I took a deep breath and made sure my voice was steady. "I don't know what you're talking about."

Korrapati tilted her head as if speaking to a child. "We *know* you, Noah."

"You don't know everything I do."

"We do. You go rogue, do the crazy thing," Wong said.

That, coming from him, miffed me a little. *I like to think of it as the brave and selfless thing, but whatever.*

"So listen. We want in," Korrapati said.

"In on what?"

"Whatever you're planning." She gestured at herself and Wong. "We can help."

"Guys, I'm not planning anything." More accurately, I hadn't had the time or mental energy to plan anything.

"Good, then we can help you plan."

I glanced up at the corner near the stairs where the red light of a security camera glowed steadily. That was the camera, I was pretty sure, where Ben Fulton had caught me tagging the dragon wranglers' trucks with GPS trackers. It felt like a lifetime ago. I remembered what it had felt like to be so isolated. Just me against the big corporate machine. They were dark times to say the least. The idea of having good, smart people on my side this time held a lot of appeal. I knew I should refuse them, especially since I was technically the group leader, but I really didn't want to go it alone. Nor did I have any real idea what to do.

Still, the red light was watching and we were standing on company property, no matter the hour.

"Have you guys ever gone on a geocache before?" I asked.

"No . . ." said Korrapati, looking nervous.

Wong just furrowed his brow. "Yes. Why?"

"Because we're going to do one Saturday," I said. *And while we're out in the desert, we can talk.*

CHAPTER THIRTY-FOUR
The Pressure

You'd think that after we won the DOD contract, the pressure would be off. We'd designed the best dragons, won the head-to-head competition against Greaves. Hell, there was even a daydream I had where the majors called us up to thank us for doing such a fantastic job. But no, there was no congratulatory note, no bouquet of flowers. Instead, we got several *multipage* documents outlining the specs of what they wanted in their dragon soldiers.

And the thing was, no matter the bombshell that Evelyn had dropped, we still had to get the work done. The DOD's laundry list of specs came with a delivery timetable and it was *tight*. Korrapati, Wong, and I spent the next hour going over them in the design lab. First, we looked at the specs for the existing models.

"They have our actual scores in here. All of the performance metrics they reached in the trials," Korrapati said.

"Really?" I appreciated that, even though it still felt like we were being graded. The marine and flying dragons had received decent enough marks, but our first model had a ways to go.

"Was it not obvious when you were there?" Korrapati asked.

"Maybe it was, but I was mainly there to watch whether or not we won." If we hadn't, all of this would have been a moot conversation.

Wong was focused on the specs document. "Marine dragon is already close."

"I'm sure. That thing was badass." I frowned at the rest of our official report cards. "Why don't you guys start with that one?"

Wong nodded.

"You'll take the aerial?" Korrapati said.

"Yes. It's close on most of the performance metrics, but needs some tweaks. I think I can get it there." Especially if I persuaded Evelyn to let me bend some guidelines. Granted, I'd been burned by that before, but the company's contract was now officially on the line.

"What about new models?" Wong asked.

"Let's take a look," I said, spreading the folders out on an empty workstation. They each grabbed a folder, betraying some of the eagerness that I felt. It had been a long time since we got to design something new, and even these prototypes carried that allure of *novel designs*.

I flipped open the folder on top of my pile; it contained specifications for an aquatic model codenamed *Marine Scout*. I hadn't realized that the military was assigning codenames to their desired prototypes. I kind of loved it. "This one is called Marine Scout. A lighter version of the aquatic model with more endurance, no payload requirements." I reread one of the bullet points just to make sure I had it correct. "Oh, and they'd like night vision."

"I'm guessing this one will need it as well," Korrapati said. "It has the codename *Night Flier.*"

"These codenames are no good," Wong said.

"What?" I protested. "I kind of like them."

"DOD should consult me before naming things."

"What's that one?" I pointed to the folder in his hand, the one that had gotten him riled up.

"Aquatic model, needs to go underwater a long time. Lighter payload, though. They call it *Deep Diver.*"

"That's not so bad," Korrapati said.

"I have better name. DeepWong."

I snorted. "That sounds like some kind of illegal massage device."

Wong shook his head. "We must tell the DOD."

"I'll be sure to bring it up the next time Major Nakamura drops by." I handed him the folder for the Infantry Scout. "Take this one, won't you?"

He took it and offered his own to Korrapati. "You take DeepWong?"

"Oh, you mean PritiDeep?"

"Not bad," I said.

She handed me her own folder. "The Night Flier is all you."

"All right." I took a deep breath and exhaled. "Let's get to work."

I shuffled around the God Machine to the far side of the design lab and sat down in Korrapati's old workstation space. She'd taken over my desk, so it was only fair. If she or Wong thought it odd that I wanted to work here rather than the big office I'd inherited from Evelyn, they didn't say so. In truth, I missed the looming presence of the God Machine and the steady hum of the Switchblade servers that made it possible for us to create and model ever-more-complex reptiles.

The Night Flier specs outline from the DOD demanded similar performance metrics to those they'd required for the AF-1 model, namely horizontal flying speed and the ability to carry cargo of a certain weight. They wanted a smaller overall body size, though, as well as extreme agility. Those wouldn't be easy, but they were the kind of improvements best reached through a cycle of small adjustments and simulation. Mundane work, in other words. I'd get to it later. For the moment, the creative part of my brain needed to tackle the hardest scientific challenge of this model.

Night vision.

The eye is an incredible organ, and the parts of the genome that code for its various components are under immense selective pressure. It's why prey animals have good peripheral vision and predators have great perceptive vision. When it comes to seeing at night, however, it's all about light perception. And when it comes to light perception, it's all about the retina.

Most animals have retinas with two types of photoreceptors, rods and cones. They're highly specialized cells, but they're also fragile. The wrong mutation in a lot of different genes can cause photoreceptors to die. When that happens in humans, it causes an inherited disorder called retinitis pigmentosa. When I'd been in grad school at ASU, my advisor Dr. Sato had worked with a group in Texas who studied the genetics of the disease. Identifying all the genes that could cause it was super important because if you knew the problem, sometimes you could correct it with gene therapy. Not unlike what we'd done for Connor. RP was a tough nut to crack, though; when I last counted, our friends in Texas had identified more than a hundred RP genes. And they still didn't know all of them. All this was to say that messing with the components of photoreceptors themselves was risky, even for a genetic engineer. There were just too many ways for something to go wrong. It was arguably safer to manipulate their distribution across the retina itself. Cones are good for distinguishing colors and seeing things at a distance. Rods, though, are the more light-sensitive receptors. So I got into the code of the dragon flier and altered the developmental pathways to favor cones over rods. I did it everywhere on the retina except the very central portion, also called the macula, that they needed for perceptive vision.

When I ran the new model through my simulator, its retina looked like that of a white-tailed deer or another nocturnal mammal. Lots of rods, excellent light response. The only drawback, of course, was that it wouldn't exactly have binocular vision in daytime. I estimated its visual acuity would be around 20/40, maybe 20/60. That would have been fine for a terrestrial animal, but this thing needed to fly. It would be able to see reasonably well in the dark, but when flying at high speed . . . well, our own Pterodactyl mainline model had shown us how it went when flying dragons couldn't avoid solid objects.

The trouble was, I couldn't have it both ways. Once the layout of rods and cones was established, it was set for the life of the animal. And the DOD document made it very, very clear that night vision was a required trait. This was the point where I usually rolled out to bounce ideas off of Wong. I had to trek out of Korrapati's old spot and around the God Machine and found him already chatting with Korrapati over the wall that divided their workstations. I suppressed a weird flare of envy. "This design is killing me."

Wong, who was somehow eating a comically large sandwich on a French loaf, barely interrupted his chewing to shake his head. "Night Flier is easy. Take regular flier, give good dark vision, keep rest the same."

Typical Wong, just do everything perfectly by hand, it's easy. I'd have been more amused if I wasn't so frustrated with the actual work. My biological simulator's predictions of the thing's flight abilities had not been kind. "I've got the vision part handled. And I made the adjustments to body size that should get us flight."

"What, you've already got the *night vision* part handled?" Korrapati asked.

"Yeah. It's just rods over cones."

Wong nodded emphatically, but had taken too large of a sandwich bite to weigh in.

Korrapati turned back to me. "So what's the problem?"

"It's going to be flying fast in the dark, probably through obstacles. I don't think seeing in the dark is enough."

"Not to mention daytime, or artificial lights."

Crap. I hadn't even thought about those complications,

but she was right. "Without decent perceptive vision, it could be . . ."

"The Pterodactyl all over again?"

"Exactly."

"If you've pushed the limits of vision, you'll have to rely on other senses."

"To help it fly? I don't see how," I said.

Korrapati turned to Wong and they shared a look. "We have to give it to him."

Wong shrugged.

"Give me what?"

"Something we wanted to use for the aquatic model, but couldn't afford to keep." She ducked back into my old workstation. Her fingers tapped the desk in a delicate flutter. Then I heard the whoosh of an outgoing message. "I just sent you a patch."

"Want to tell me what it does, first?"

Korrapati started to answer, but Wong held up a hand to stop her. He was in the middle of a swig of his energy drink, so we had to wait until he finished gulping it down.

"Make it surprise," he told her.

"I like that idea," Korrapati said.

I wanted to grumble something about who was the triple-D, but I also wasn't afraid of a challenge. It was the sort of thing Evelyn used to do to me before she got too busy as CEO. And besides, I was deeply curious to learn about something they'd worked on together. "Bring it on." I hurried back to my borrowed workstation.

Patches were like updates that you download for computer software, except they had changes to genetic code. I applied Korrapati's to my current Night Flier design and instinctively brought it up in the simulator. There were no obvious physical changes, though the head shape looked a little different. Broader and more squared off, especially near the base. There was something different about the mouth, too, though I couldn't quite put my finger on it. So I ran a comparison of my model's code before and after the Korrapati-Wong patch.

"Holy crap," I whispered. There were *hundreds* of changes, and most of them to systems that we didn't ordinarily touch in dragon designs. I pulled the list of genes and ran it through PathFinder, an analysis tool that identifies significant biological pathways controlled by sets of genes. The results were always noisy because many genes in complex organisms played multiple roles. Even so, some of the pathways that ranked near the top of the list were unusual. Auditory processing, neuronal connectivity, and some developmental processes for the inner ear. There were a lot of genes that were active in specialized neurons. Especially auditory neurons for very high-frequency bands.

The different head shape suggested some change to the brain physiology. Sure enough, the inferior colliculus, which was part of the midbrain, was much larger than usual. I admit, I had to look that up, but when I did I learned that it, too, played a key role in auditory processing.

On a whim, I ran the design through the simulator again and paid special attention to the head. There were actual ear ridges behind the usual featureless auditory canals. *What a killer idea. And they had to scrap it.* I still admired the scientific audacity of it, though. Much like the swift wing, it was a concept already perfected by nature. I moseyed back to their side of the design lab.

"Well, this is interesting," I said.

"Any guesses?"

"Almost all of your changes have to do with hearing, so I'm guessing that this is intended to give the dragon echolocation abilities."

Korrapati's mouth fell open in legitimate surprise. Wong gave her his half smile and said, "Told you."

"It's a clever idea. Do you think the dragon can make those vocalizations, though?"

"They already make noises. Adjust palate to make higher frequency," Wong said.

"So *that's* why the mouth looked different. I couldn't quite put my finger on it."

"How in the world did you figure out the bio sonar so quickly?" Korrapati asked. "It took forever to code, but the physical changes are subtle."

I nearly blurted out that I'd done a simple code diff that got me most of the way there, but I held back. *No need to give everything away.* The more they thought I deserved this position, the better. Especially now that we might actually get to stay in business thanks to the DOD contract. I winked at her. "Even a blind pig finds an acorn every once in a while."

"Pigs eat acorns?" Wong asked.

I laughed. "Pigs eat everything. Trust me, I know."

If the bio sonar worked, the DOD was going to be pleased. I only wished I'd thought of it before the aerial trials.

CHAPTER THIRTY-FIVE
The Heat

Saturday morning, Summer and I rumbled into the parking lot just before nine A.M. We'd taken her Jeep, partly because the rough gravel parking lot was a threat to my Tesla's undercoating, and partly because I wanted some time to think without having to focus on driving. We'd even left all of our various pets at home, which was saying something. Summer claimed that Riker behaved himself while he was alone in her condo. I wished I could say the same for my little dragons. The last time I'd left them alone on a Saturday, two of my neighbor's cats had suddenly gone missing. I never saw any evidence, but I doubted it had been a coincidence.

Summer glanced at the parking lot. "Are you sure they're going to find this place?"

"They'll be here. We're just early due to *someone's* lead foot."

"Hey, I'm efficient."

"Well, Wong is not. So don't be surprised if he's late."

"Is *she* efficient?" Summer asked. Her tone was casual enough, but I sensed the danger there.

"Yes, but they said they'd come together, so it probably balances out," I said.

"Don't know why she needs to come anyway."

"They both offered, and they didn't have to. We're going to need help."

Summer muttered something under her breath that I imagined I didn't want to be repeated, so I'd let it slide. With the trials and everything occupying nearly every waking moment of my consciousness, I'd been leaning on her a lot lately. Her business at the firm had slowed down a fraction since their big project wrapped up, and she'd offered to take all of my dragons for a couple of weeks. Judging by the scratch marks on her arms, it hadn't gone very smoothly.

A soundless flash of sunlight on muted steel marked the arrival of another car, Korrapati's little white electric coupe. I should have known she'd be the one to drive; Wong was a firm believer in bumming rides whenever and wherever he could. In fact, I wasn't even sure if he owned a car.

"Now, be nice," I said. "They didn't have to come."

"I'll try," Summer said dryly.

Korrapati parked on the far side of the little gravel lot, probably a wise move on her part. She climbed out, already biting her lip. Wong managed to saunter out of the passenger seat. Both of them wore dark sunglasses. For a moment, the pure comedy of the situation made we want to laugh. Here we were, meeting in an all-but-abandoned parking lot.

"Hey, guys, thanks for coming," I said as they walked up. "This is my girlfriend Summer." I still got a little thrill at introducing her as *my girlfriend*.

"Hello, I'm Priti," Korrapati said.

Summer blinked, undoubtedly having the same reaction that I did when I first heard her name.

"It's P-R-I-T-I," I said.

"Ohhhh," Summer said. "Sorry."

"It's perfectly all right. I get that a lot."

"Well, it's fitting. You *are* pretty."

Korrapati blushed. "Oh, stop. You're the pretty one."

They were being incredibly nice to each other, and yet alarm bells were ringing all over my head. I took the opportunity to jump in. "And this, of course, is Wong."

"Nice to meet you," Wong said. He looked from her to me, and his eyebrows lifted over his sunglasses. "*Zuò dé hǎo.*"

Good job. I chuckled. "*Xiè xiè.*" *Thank you.*

Summer elbowed me in the ribs. "Stop that."

"So, we're here," Korrapati said. "What now?"

"Now, we're going to find a geocache."

"What?" Korrapati asked.

Summer gave me a side-eye. "You were serious about that?"

"Of course. We're here, aren't we?"

"I've not done one before," Korrapati said.

"They don't get any easier than this one," Summer said. "It's so easy, even a complete noob could do it."

I was fairly certain that was a jab at me, but I let it slide. Summer and I both had the destination waypoint saved in our watches, so we set that as a destination.

Wong brandished his own watch. "Send me coordinates."

I beamed the coordinates over, and couldn't help but notice that he had the same model watch as I did—only a much newer model. "Whoa, let me see the hardware."

He obliged, holding out his wrist so I could have a look. Sure enough, it was my watch—and Summer's watch— but his was even cleaner than hers, and had some display items I hadn't seen. "Is this a gen-three?"

"Think so."

"They're not even out yet! How did you get your hands on this, Wong?"

"Borrow it from a friend."

"You have a lot of friends. I wonder why I've never met any of these people."

"Maybe you meet them already."

I laughed. "Yeah, maybe."

He fell back to walk beside Summer, who wanted to compare watches.

0.34 MILES TO TARGET. Well, not the most ambitious start to our geocache, but I supposed that was a secondary goal anyway. Korrapati's shadow fell into step beside mine.

"So, have you figured out a plan yet?" she asked.

"I was hoping you had one."

"You're the planner, remember?"

"I know what we need to do, but I have no idea how we're going to accomplish it," I said.

"And what is that?"

"Take the Redwood Codex back from Greaves."

"How did you find out he has one? Did he tell you?"

I wanted to share it with her, but I'd promised

Redwood to keep his secrets. Summer had, too. And somehow I knew that if I betrayed his confidence, he'd find out about it. Not to mention the fact that she probably wouldn't believe me anyway.

"He must. How else is he printing living, breathing dragons?"

"I thought there was only one."

"Evelyn told me there was a prototype. Redwood had it." Only part of that was a lie, and it was more of a matter of perspective. "I'm guessing Greaves somehow got his hands on it." *Nothing false about that.*

"That sounds, um, highly illegal."

"I'm sure it was."

"Can we do anything about that?"

I nodded. "Evelyn's trying, but it's a slow process."

"Plus, legal procedures are not what Noah Parker is known for," she said.

"Hey, now. What is it that you think I *am* known for?"

"I plead the fifth."

We skirted around an old saguaro that split the trail. 0.27 MILES TO TARGET.

"So, you think we should take Robert's Codex."

"Take it *back*, yes. It's the only part of the process that he can't reverse engineer on his own. If he doesn't have it, he's out of the game."

She sighed. "I suppose it's better than arson."

What I didn't tell her—what I didn't want to tell any of them—was that if we couldn't retrieve the Codex, I wanted to destroy it.

0.19 MILES TO TARGET. I nearly yelled for Octavius to glide ahead and start looking for the cache when I remembered that I hadn't brought him. I guessed we had good reasons—there was no need to reveal all of my secrets to my designers in one sitting. As far as I knew, all of my unlicensed dragons were technically illegal.

We crested a ridge then, and we could see the area where I knew the cache to be. "All right, you two are on your own. It's straight ahead, not far from the trail."

"You aren't coming with us?" Korrapati asked.

"It's not allowed. Summer and I both found this one already."

"Oh, that's right," Summer said, as if suddenly remembering. "And... who was it that found it first?"

"Come on, this was my first successful geocache."

"It wasn't *my* first."

I smiled at her, because I liked flirty Summer. "Little did I know the capable and experienced woman who'd been here before me."

To their credit, Wong and Korrapati trekked down the slope and began making a "search" for the cache. They tackled it with about as much vigor and enthusiasm as Connor cleaning his room. Which is to say, not much.

"Did you explain to them what the word *cache* means?" Summer asked, as Wong nudged around a few rocks with the toe of his boot.

"Nah. You know how it is with kids these days. They have to learn it for themselves."

The weather heated up in predictable fashion. Finally, in a surprise twist, Wong nudged the correct log with his boot, and actually got down on his knees to look inside.

"Isn't he the guy who rides a scooter everywhere?" Summer asked.

"I think this is the most I've seen him move under his own power."

Wong reached into the log tentatively. Then he went elbow deep and still didn't come up with it.

"That's odd," I said.

"Not really." Summer stretched and yawned. "I came here yesterday. Shoved it really far in there."

I laughed. "You are *evil*. You know that, don't you?"

"Gotta haze the rookies."

With some encouragement from Korrapati, Wong committed the full arm and came up with the cache container. He held it up in the sky like he'd just won a trophy.

I sighed. "I remember that feeling."

They opened up the container so that Korrapati could sign the log inside. Wong dug into his pockets and found something small to exchange for one of the trinkets inside. Since he and Korrapati had legitimately found the cache, I logged it for them under the account I'd created and named "KoraWong."

"Well, you're on the board," I said, once they'd returned the container and come back. "Congratulations, Team KoraWong."

"That was fun," Korrapati said. She had a sheen of sweat on her face but was smiling.

"Lot of work," Wong said.

I didn't have the heart to tell them that, as far as geocaches went, this was a pretty easy one. Instead, I made sure no other geocachers were coming down the path, and scanned the sky for drones. Nothing. We stood in a shallow basin of sorts, with rocky, unforgiving slopes on three sides. The path we'd taken was the only way in. Anyone following us had nowhere to park except the small gravel lot, and no way to approach us without being seen. Maybe I was being a touch paranoid, but when you went up against Robert Greaves, you didn't want to take chances.

"Well, here we are, so let's talk," I said.

Everyone seemed to register the tone; they moved closer until we were all within arm's reach. Which might not have been the optimal scenario given how much we were all sweating, but oh well.

"Greaves has to be operating somewhere around Phoenix. We need to figure out where before we do something to stop him."

"And by *something* you mean take his Codex," Korrapati said.

"Right. The problem is finding his facility. I checked property tax records and corporation filings, but if Greaves filed anything, it's not under his own name."

"He doesn't have a corporate lease on file, either," Summer said. "I checked."

My mouth fell open. "You did what now?"

"I looked while I was at work."

"Oh. Thanks." Her autonomy on my risky project threw me a little. *What if she got caught?* I'd never really planned for Summer to face any consequences. The idea sat uncomfortably in my gut, but I plunged forward. "My best idea right now is to try to track down Greaves himself. He's not exactly hiding from the public."

"I don't like that idea," Summer said. "What if he catches you?"

"I'll be careful."

"Blending in and being cautious are not your strong suits."

"Maybe we follow O'Connell or Frogman," Wong said.

I bit back a sharp retort aimed at Summer. "That's actually not a bad idea. I bet we can track down one of their home addresses."

"Or ask me. I know where both live," Wong said.

I clapped him on the shoulder. "I knew there was a good reason to bring you in on this." A dark thought intruded. "You don't know where I live, too, do you?"

"You offer me carpool, maybe I find out."

"Ha! You are too much." A little plan had started to formulate in my head. "So here's what I'm thinking. We get eyes on one of them and see if they lead us to their lab."

"Which one?" Summer asked.

"Both of them. It doubles our odds." I pointed at Korrapati and Wong. "You two take O'Connell. Summer and I will try to follow the Frogman." These assignments weren't arbitrary; O'Connell and I had never really gotten along very well, so if he spotted me it could go really badly. In contrast, I could walk five feet behind the Frogman wearing a clown suit and he might not notice me.

"So if one of them leads us to their lab, then what?" Korrapati asked.

"Then we find out what we're really up against," I said. *And hope that we're equal to the task.*

CHAPTER THIRTY-SIX
The Stakeout

Monday morning, Summer and I staked out the address Wong had provided, a row building of duplex housing in downtown Scottsdale. A surprisingly trendy area, though I imagined Frogman had probably picked it for the proximity to Build-A-Dragon's headquarters. A drive less than twenty minutes at rush hour, and you could probably bike it in half an hour. We'd arrived at seven A.M. in Summer's Jeep, which probably woke half of the duplex residents with its rumbling engine. Still, I didn't want to risk getting recognized in my car and the Jeep had other advantages. Including one Summer had only recently told me about.

"So it's this knob here, right?" I asked, even though I knew quite well which knob she'd used to tint all of the Jeep's windows when we'd parked. Evidently it was an electric field tint, not unlike some of the privacy glass at work, and she could adjust it anywhere from transparent to solid black.

She slapped my hand. "It's dark enough."

"It's the coolest feature. Aside from driving over things, that is. Why didn't you tell me about it before now?"

"Because I knew it would give you *ideas*," she said.

"Hmm, ideas, you say." I darted my hand out, turned the tint to very dark, and moved closer to her.

She put her hand on my chest to hold me off. "See? I was right."

"What? I'm just testing the system out." I slid past her arm and landed a kiss on her neck.

She laughed and pushed me away. "I'm serious. We're supposed to be paying attention."

"No one has come out of these buildings since we got here." And in staring at them, I'd not seen a sign of life past the faded exterior and overgrown hedges. "I'm kind of wondering if the place might be abandoned."

"So much for your intel."

"Hey, my intel comes from Wong. Take it up with him."

My phone rang and I glanced at the screen. *Speak of the devil.* "Hey," I answered. "What's going on?"

"We have O'Connell."

"What's he doing?"

"Going to work, we think."

I motioned at Summer to start her engine, which she did. Right after adjusting the window tints and giving me a saucy look. "Where are you?"

"Getting onto freeway, going west."

"Ten west," I whispered to Summer, before getting back on the phone. "Ping me your GPS tag, will you?" Immediately after I asked it, I cringed. Technically, Wong reported to me, and it would let me track his phone's GPS with my own. In his shoes, I'm not sure I'd want my supervisor having that kind of power over me.

He didn't answer for a few seconds, and I wondered if he'd had the same thought. "Sent."

I glanced at my phone, which showed the ping location Wong had sent overlaid on a traffic map. "Got it. Don't let him see you. I'll call you when we're closer." I hung up.

"How far up are they?" Summer asked. She was already getting onto the freeway.

"Not much." I extrapolated our location relative to Wong's, and the traffic speed. "Less than a mile ahead."

She hit the gas pedal hard enough that I was jolted back against my seat.

"Assuming we survive," I grumbled.

"You want to catch up, don't you?"

In a few minutes we'd woven our way through the moderate traffic and were approaching Wong's tiny dot on my phone's map.

"*Wey?*" he answered, the Mandarin phone greeting.

"*Wey*. We're coming up behind you. Where's O'Connell?"

"Right lane, four cars up. Black sedan."

Of course it was a black sedan. Only O'Connell would buy a black car in a city where the average temperature in summer was a hundred and six degrees. Sure enough, a dark sedan cruised in the right hand lane. Summer eased up behind Korrapati's SUV, which happened to be hovering in his blind spot. *Clever girl.*

I pointed. "It's that sedan."

"Are we sure it's him?" Summer asked.

"We saw him get in," Wong told me.

"They saw him get in," I told Summer. "Be cool."

Judging by the side-eye that comment won me, I was going to pay for it later. I tried to surreptitiously use my binoculars to get a closer look at the car. The window tinting was just too dark. That was the problem with Arizona: dark glass was always in the way.

"Hey, 007," Summer said. "We're trying not to attract attention, remember?"

I had that coming. I put down the binoculars. "Touché."

O'Connell drove steadily west through the outskirts of Phoenix. Traffic thinned out enough that we could drop back and follow him from a quarter mile. We took turns being the lead car with Korrapati. They had the front position when Wong called me.

"He's getting off."

"Really?" I glanced at the map but there was nothing marked on it, not even a road.

"We follow?"

"No, it would be too obvious. Go past and tell me what you can see. Then we can take the lead."

Wong relayed this to Korrapati. "We're passing. Plain road on right. Maybe gravel."

"Copy. Find a place to turn around." I covered the mouthpiece and said to Summer. "Get ready to turn right."

Wong had the forethought to ping me with GPS coordinates where O'Connell had turned, so we had a tiny bit of advance notice. I pointed. "Right there. Might be gravel."

"I can handle it." Summer barely slowed before she swung us onto the side road. I grabbed the *oh shit* bar to keep myself upright. We fishtailed once but Summer had it under control before I could really panic. Wisps of dust still hung in the air from O'Connell's passing, though his car was no longer in sight.

"We made the turn. It's gravel like you thought," I told Wong.

"Do you see him?"

"No, but he can't have gone far."

"Where the hell are we, anyway?" Summer shouted over the rumble of the gravel road, which was jouncing us pretty good.

"It's not an established road."

"You're kidding."

I ignored the jab and flipped my phone's mapping display to GPS mode. Gravel roads often weren't official on maps, but satellite imagery told another story. The gravel road wound through a few winding S-curves and ended up in a wide basin where, as of the year-old satellite imagery showed, there was recent construction. And not far from the road, either. "Shit," I said. "Find a place to pull over if you can."

Summer didn't so much find a place as create one: a somewhat level piece of terrain beside the road simply became her parking spot.

"Well, that's one way to do it."

"You said to pull over."

She has a point. "It can't be far. We need to be careful," I said. "In fact, I think it's time to play the wild card."

"Really? Already?"

"Come on, he lives for this."

Summer sighed. "If you think it's absolutely necessary."

I grinned. "I do." I jumped out of the Jeep before she changed her mind and jogged around back to unload the camera drone. On the way I popped in my earbud and summoned my virtual assistant. "Call Connor."

The phone barely rang once before Connor picked up, which told me he'd been waiting for us even though I told him I didn't know how our day would go. He was supposed to be working on his senior thesis for engineering school.

"N-game," he answered.

"C-horse. Are you busy?"

"Just killing Nazis, but they'll keep." He spent more time playing video games than anyone I knew.

"We're looking at a blind corner and we need the B team."

He snorted. "I think you mean the A-Team. Version 2.0, if you will."

"I will not. But fire up your controls, man, because we need aerial recon."

"What about your reptiles?"

"Didn't want to risk them," I said.

"But my drone—"

"Is just a thing."

"Well, put that *thing* on the ground so I can get busy saving your asses," Connor said.

Ten seconds after I'd done that and woken the drone, Connor had it hovering at head level and was getting his bearings. It was a more compact model than the one we usually took geocaching. Four rotors, just enough to hold the high-def camera and the satellite transmitter. All of it the color of desert camouflage. If he lost this thing out in the terrain, we'd never find it.

"Is your video feed up yet?" I asked.

"Oh my God, all I'm getting is some sort of pale monster!"

I glanced up and predictably he had the camera trained on my face. "You're hilarious."

"I know. Be a doll and tell me which way."

I pointed. "The road is over there. Do you think you can follow it?"

"Please."

The drone swept off, and I had to duck so it wouldn't clip me. Connor had become a pretty good drone pilot, not that I'd ever tell him so. My phone buzzed with an incoming notification; he'd forwarded me the drone's video feed. I pulled it up as Korrapati parked behind Summer's Jeep, almost timidly. We stood in the shade of it and watched the dry landscape zip past on the tiny screen. Wisps of sand dust still drifted in the air from O'Connell's passing. The drone crested a steep ridge, after which the land sloped downward. Then came one, two, three thin black lines.

"Hold up a sec," I told Connor. The drone held still and hovered almost as I said it; he must have seen them, too.

"Power lines," he said.

"Kind of like the idea of following those, in case they're watching the road. If you can manage not to hit one."

"I can give you a haircut if I want to."

"All right, all right. Just get going." I had that itch between my shoulder blades like we were being watched.

I tore my eyes from the screen and looked around. There was traffic on the highway, of course, but nobody seemed to pay us any mind. Still, I couldn't shake the feeling.

"Well, that's interesting," Connor said, drawing me back to the video feed. The power lines snaked downhill from the drone's position into a shallow basin and into a huge stainless-steel building. Well, technically into a massive transformer *connected* to a massive steel building. It was at least three stories tall, with dark glass all around. It resembled a medical building and looked completely out of place in the raw desert. Yet there were also large, round skylights along one edge. Two rows of six. *Hatching pods.*

"This is it," I said.

"Looks like our building," Wong said.

"You want me to make a flyover?" Connor asked.

I considered it because I really did want to know how many pods had eggs in them. But desert camouflage wouldn't hide a drone flying over a steel structure, and we didn't want to alert anyone to our presence. "No, better keep your distance."

Connor sent the drone sideways on a slow circle around the facility. "This place is huge. How was it not on any satellite maps?"

"It's either brand new or paid exclusion."

"That's uncanny."

"It's his style, though." Build-A-Dragon's desert facility, which was called the Farm, had also enjoyed satellite anonymity. "Circle around the back, would you?"

Connor obliged my request, but had to pivot the drone away from the building so that he didn't run into something. When he got around back and panned over, things got more interesting. There was O'Connell's car, parked beside the black SUV I'd seen Greaves in at one of the trials. And there was O'Connell, walking in the front entrance with another man. I recognized the doughy frame, slumped posture, and ever-present hoodie.

"Well, that explains why we never saw Frogman. Apparently they're carpool buddies."

"Very eco-conscious," Summer said.

"Yeah, it's something all right."

O'Connell used his keys to unlock the front door, and they both disappeared into the shadowy interior. My brother zoomed in the camera and snapped some still images before the door swung closed.

A long balcony ran across the front of the building above the entranceway. It was hard to tell on my little phone-screen, but I thought I saw movement on the balcony.

"Hey, Connor, pan up a little bit."

He did so, and did something with the camera to widen the view. I saw it then, a sinuous creature pacing back and forth. We'd been so focused on O'Connell and Frogman, we hadn't noticed it until they went in.

"What is that?" Korrapati asked.

"An attack dragon," I said grimly.

"There's another one," Connor said, panning over and zooming in. It was still hard to make them out in the shade. He flipped to the infrared mode, and their bodies bloomed bright red and orange. They moved with a predatory grace, one at each end of the building.

"Can you get closer?"

"I don't know, man."

"Come on, you're still way out of range."

He sighed with obvious reluctance. I almost called him a chicken, but it was his drone and therefore his call. Still, I wanted a closer look and we might not have a better opportunity. The drone crept forward across the desert landscape, keeping the entrance and guard dragons in frame. I had a suspicion, and the closer view confirmed it. The lean, muscular frames and powerful jaws gave it away. The image of the dragon that had outshone our infantry prototype, the one that had attacked the compound with such brutal efficiency, was forever burned into my brain.

"They look mean," Korrapati said.

I shuddered. "You should see them in action."

The dragons were alert, too. They started tracking the drone when it was still seventy-five yards out. Maybe they saw it in spite of the desert camouflage, or maybe they heard the rotors. Hell, it could have been the vibration the little craft made. First the dragons went absolutely still. Then they hissed at one another.

"I think they've spotted the drone, Con. Keep your distance."

"I will."

The drone broke off its approach and drifted sideways, giving us a better view of the attack dragons. Their heads moved slowly as they followed it. Then one of them lifted its snout and made a guttural, grunting cry. Three staccato notes.

"Shit," I said.

"What was that?" Korrapati asked.

"I don't know. Connor, better get out of there."

"You don't have to tell me twice." He'd just started to turn the drone when two reptilian shapes shot out of the building, heading right for it. At first I'd thought the guard dragons had jumped, but no, these were different models. Flying models.

"Connor!" I shouted into my headset.

"Shit, I see them!"

The little drone sped away from the compound, but the dragons were coming fast. Suddenly the drone just dropped.

"What are you—" I started.

The drone sank, and right when I was sure it would crash, Connor brought up the thrust and leveled out. The drone skimmed over the terrain, making a break for it. We couldn't tell where the flying dragons were, but his little drop maneuver seemed to have evaded them.

"Back to the cars!" I shouted, moving while refusing to look away from the screen. Summer didn't need telling twice; she was in the driver's seat and roaring the Jeep to life in seconds. She hardly waited for me to hop in my seat before making a sharp U-turn. Connor's drone was not yet in sight, but couldn't be more than seventy-five yards out. Korrapati was turning more timidly behind us in her little SUV. I gestured madly at her to speed things up. I looked back at my phone just in time to see a triangular, scaly head loom in the video feed. Connor shouted, and then the drone feed went black.

"Shit!" I looked at Summer. "We lost the drone."

"Are you sure?"

"Yeah."

She cursed, but floored it out into the lane. Korrapati and Wong followed us back to the highway.

"Sorry, man. I'll call you later," I told Connor, and hung up.

"This is the place you want to break into? It's crawling with dragons," Summer said.

"Apparently."

"I think that changes the plan, doesn't it?"

"In a manner of speaking. We're going to need some dragons of our own."

CHAPTER THIRTY-SEVEN
The Brother

The only saving grace from our interrupted scouting expedition was that Connor had streamed his drone's video into the cloud, so we still had most of it. I drove over the next day so we could review the footage. Also, I felt bad about his lost drone. He'd been reluctant to lend it out in the first place.

I parked my Tesla out in front of Mom's house in the same spot under the same tree where I'd parked the jalopy as a teenager. It felt right somehow to reclaim possession of an otherwise unmarked stretch of curb by the house where I grew up.

"Hi, honey," Mom called from the porch. She sat on the swing in the hot, still air, somehow looking quite comfortable. She had a reading tablet in hand—I strongly suspected it was loaded with trashy romance novels, though she'd never let me confirm this theory—and the box of wine on the table beside her.

"Look at you, living the American dream." I bent down

and hugged her, tolerating a wine-laced kiss on the cheek. "Jeez, it's two in the afternoon."

"What do you think retirement is for?"

"I thought it was mostly taking naps and eating dinner at four P.M."

"Did you come here just to harass your mother?"

"Of course not. I came to harass Connor, too."

She grabbed my wrist. "I really like Summer."

Her sincerity threw me for a bit. "Uh, good. She liked you, too."

"She's good for you, I think."

I smiled, and for some reason I felt like I might be blushing. "You think right."

"How's work?"

"It's fine. We're getting busy again," I said, and forced myself to clam up after that. Connor and I had both taken the vow of silence when it came to telling Mom the full scoop behind what was happening with Build-A-Dragon and the company's former CEO. She was a smart lady but a loud talker, and had blown more than her fair share of secrets wide open over wine at bridge night.

"When are you going to bring one of those dragons by for me to see, anyway?"

I'd brought Octavius over once when she wasn't home, and she still held that against me. Yet I had the feeling that the whole pack might be a little much. "Uh, sometime. I don't know. I should get inside. Connor's waiting for me."

She made an exasperated sound, but went back to her reading tablet. I took that for permission to proceed.

It's always a strange feeling walking into a house where

you grew up. No matter the inevitable decor and furniture changes over time, the *feel* was always the same. The dim foyer still took an extra minute to let the eyes adjust. The carpet was new—Mom wanted to replace it once Connor no longer needed his wheelchair—and the lamps were different, but I knew the distance to every wall by heart.

A dutiful younger brother with access to modern technology like the doorbell camera would have been inside to receive me. Instead, of course, my only greeting was the distant rumble of a first-person shooter on surround sound. There was machine-gun fire, and then a loud explosion that shook the floor.

"Connor!" I shouted.

No response.

I stalked down the hall to his room. Well, *my old* room. He'd taken it over the moment I left for college—over my vociferous objections, it needs to be said—all because it was slightly larger than his. Now I think he kind of enjoyed having erased any trace of my presence from the room, if not the house entirely. The newest evidence of this was an actual keypad lock on the door.

"Oh, what the hell is this?" I muttered. *As if he has anything in there that someone would want to steal.* Come to think of it, he'd probably just wanted to keep Mom from snooping around while he wasn't home under the guise of doing laundry.

I knew the keypad model; it was a six-digit code, all numeric. And I knew Connor. He was, first and foremost, a nerd who thought he was smarter than everyone else. This was a ridiculous notion when you thought about it; he wasn't even the smartest person in our immediate family. So, what number would he have chosen? Well, he had memorized pi out to around twenty-five digits, so I tried that first.

3-1-4-1-5-9

Red lights flashed; that wasn't it. Maybe he'd gone with prime numbers instead. I punched in the first six prime numbers.

2-3-5-7-11

Still no sale. The sounds of electronic warfare continued unabated on the other side of the door. I had one more shot, but if this one missed it would sound an audible alarm and freeze out for two minutes.

What other dorky numeric sequence would give Connor a tiny satisfying hit of intellectual superiority when he punched it in? Then it hit me: the smug satisfaction would appeal most if he used it to take a shot at his older brother. He'd probably pick something I *should* know, which meant closer to biology than pure mathematics. There were a few possibilities, but the one that seemed most likely was a seemingly random number sequence named for an Italian mathematician. The Fibonacci sequence—in which each ensuing number equals the sum of the two that precede it—was a pattern that turned up all over the place in nature. It described the distribution of seeds on a sunflower and the growth of a nautilus spiral shell. The reason why has to do with spirals and the golden ratio. That ratio was often described as six digits, but something told me that the sequence itself was the sort of thing Connor would most enjoy. I punched it in.

1-1-2-3-5-8

Green lights flashed, and the lock gave a soft click. *So predictable.* I grinned, shoved the door open, and barged in. "Is Mr. Fibonacci home?"

Connor sprawled at his mess of a desk, which held three huge curved monitors behind a wall of empty chip bags and soda cans. He sat in an ordinary chair, which was an improvement. Only months ago, before the gene therapy, he'd spent most of his time in a wheelchair. He didn't even need the cane anymore. Mom had told me they'd donated both and weren't looking back. *Incredible what gene therapy can do.* Connor was just one patient. There were thousands of patients like him who might benefit from similar therapies.

"Took you long enough," he said.

I scoffed. "You mean to break the code on your little door lock? Child's play."

"What did you try first?"

I guess I hadn't been as subtle as I thought. "Something nerdier."

"Six digits of pi?"

"Yep."

"It used to be that. But Mom knows them."

"Ooh." I winced. "That's no good. I assume that's who you're trying to keep out."

"Mom, the cleaning lady, government agents, and whoever else might want to steal my assets."

I scanned the snack food wasteland that lined the top of his desk. "I'm not sure we agree on the meaning of the word *asset*."

"Yeah well, I think you're going to find some value in my drone's footage." He executed a quick few commands, minimizing his game to one monitor while the other two brought up a list of video files. Judging by the annotations, he'd already reviewed them manually and put the raw videos through some AI-based enhancements. That was all the rage with surveillance video footage—machine processing of a basic two-dimensional video to help identify things that a computer could recognize.

The trick, of course, was a rich source of video to train your algorithms on. And for us, that meant dragons. One of the folders on display held dozens of videos of Build-A-Dragon's products. The first one I noticed was a Rover playing with two children in a grassy, fenced backyard. Next to that was a video of a woman with a Laptop model perched beside her at a kitchen table; she was feeding it meat from a long wooden skewer. After that, was a video that looked like drone footage of a dense swampland as a lean predator dragon stalked through the undergrowth. *A Guardian searching for wild hogs.* They were the first dragons, and arguably the most dangerous.

"Where did you get all of these videos?" I asked.

"ChewTube, mostly."

"Are you serious?"

He nodded. "People love filming their dragons."

"How many did you—"

"Thousands. And I had to cut myself off, because most of them are just Rovers getting stuck in doggie doors."

"Hey, man, that's my livelihood."

"I'm just telling you what's out there."

He wasn't wrong, either, because the Rover obesity thing was a pretty well-known issue. Evelyn and I had worked on a microbiome application that helped the animals stay leaner, but even so. The Western diet did not do wonders for reptilian physiques.

"Did you get enough training footage for all of our known models?"

"And then some." Connor zoomed down to a file he'd marked with several annotations. "I was wondering if you could explain this."

The dragon in the video was a custom job, a flightless model somewhere between a Rover and a Laptop in size. It was cuddled on a bed with a little girl who was reading a picture book. *Goodnight Moon*. The dragon, though, was pink. Bright, eye-jarring, unforgiving pink. The girl didn't seem to mind; guessing by the similar color palette on her bedspread, pillows, and walls, it was her favorite color. Worst of all, I'd designed the dragon myself. I remembered most of my customs. *I'll die before I tell him that, though.*

"The customer's always right," I said.

He gave me a mock-serious stare. "How far you've fallen."

I could have stayed there for hours perusing those videos, but the clock was ticking. "So, what have you got for me?"

"Some things we knew, and some things we didn't." He pulled up a new screen that showed the now-familiar drone video from our scouting expedition. First it was flying down the country road, then veering along the rocks toward the compound itself.

Just as before, I was fixated on the newly constructed building and whatever secrets it held behind tinted glass. Yet before the drone started to move closer, lighted circles superimposed on the images drew my attention to the bottom of the video. There, along the floor of shallow basin where the facility was built, and nearly hidden by some scraggly bushes, was a dragon's head and torso.

"See it?" Connor asked. In case I hadn't, the annotation software pulled up a separate frame with six composite images of similar dragons. They were rangy predator-type custom models, all of them, though one had the stockier build of a Guardian prototype. Connor resumed the video playback. As the video grew larger, the AI picked up another reptilian form hidden in the landscape. This one was just a tail as the dragon ducked from view. Almost imperceptible as a light brown against a backdrop of brown and yellow desert.

"If we picked up these two, there are probably another four we didn't even see," I said. Even with the help from AI, dragons were made to blend with desert environments. "No wonder we lost your drone."

"That's what I was thinking," Connor said.

"It reminds me a little of Redwood's place before it burned down. The land around it was crawling with dragons, too."

"Those were ferals, though, weren't they?"

"I think so. And Redwood claimed they showed up on their own. But these dragons?" I gestured at the screen. "I doubt they're hanging out voluntarily."

I did some quick calculations. "Figure the ones we saw, plus these two, and two more we didn't see. Could be six or eight all told."

"That's a lot of dragons. And they're mean."

"Oh, you don't even know. If these are anything like the dragons Greaves used in the field trials, they'd tear a human to pieces." I sighed. "Unfortunately, I don't see a way around it."

"What are you talking about?"

"I mean, he wouldn't have security if his means of production isn't there."

"You're not still serious about doing this, are you?"

"Well, yeah."

"What for? It's not really your problem," he said.

He wasn't wrong about that. I hadn't stolen the prototype of the Redwood Codex, and it belonged to Build-A-Dragon, not to me. But somehow everyone else passed the buck and it ended up with me anyway. "Anything concerning dragons is my business."

"You're crazy."

I bit my lip. "Maybe. But I promised Redwood I'd try."

"I hate it when you invoke him." He stared at me, sighed, and shook his head. "What about other promises you made, though? Like the ones to all my friends in the BICD2 support group?"

"Oh, that." I'd been so consumed with the Greaves thing, I'd nearly forgotten. "The variants you sent me tick most of the boxes. They're leaning pathogenic, and they're even supported by my biological simulator."

"I know that, bro. But it's not enough to change the classification."

"They need experimental evidence," I said.

"Which is what we're counting on you for."

"I know. I've got a lot of promises to keep these days, but I'm holding to that one." I had no idea how I'd accomplish it, but I'd figure something out. I owed it to him. "But I want to tackle the Redwood situation first."

CHAPTER THIRTY-EIGHT
The Misdirect

There was no question that some parts of our planned raid on the Greaves facility were illegal. It was private property, first and foremost, and we had no justifiable reason for trespassing. Then there was the question of theft. I had no hard proof that the Codex had been stolen. My only evidence was the word of a dead man, against the word of a polished corporate executive with near-limitless guile and resources. I'd swallowed that reality pill already, though. What truly worried me was the part about the dragons themselves.

Having seen the sort of military-grade dragons Greaves and his team could design— not to mention what they were capable of when properly trained—I didn't dare risk trespassing on his property without some way to handle them. Tech was a possible angle. Ever since the advent of the hog-hunting Guardian model, third-party companies had been developing all manner of unsanctioned products for "dragon security." We tended to find out about them when something went wrong and a customer called the support hotline. That's how Evelyn learned that there were such things as sedatives, tranquilizer guns, and snout muzzles for our products. Supposedly there were ultrasonic devices, too—strictly black-market items—that delivered incapacitating audio pulses designed for reptiles.

Yet I hesitated to rely on something unproven like that against dangerous attack dragons. The more reliable course of action was to bring dragons of our own to neutralize the threat. The good news was that we knew how to design the type of dragons that would work best. The downside was that Greaves and his team did, too. The other downside was that if we were going to do this, it had to be totally off the books. No matter the gray legal area of ownership of the Redwood Codex, trespassing and breaking and entering were crimes. I wasn't sure, but I thought it possible that releasing weapons-grade reptiles into an unsecured area was a crime all by itself. And whatever happened, however it came out, there could be nothing that linked Build-A-Dragon to our raid.

That meant Evelyn couldn't know, and any dragons we designed to help us had to be produced without creating any documentation in the company's records. The trouble, as I'd discovered during my rogue employee days, was that our systems for printing dragon eggs were tightly linked to all kinds of tracking and billing systems.

"How did you get around this before?" Korrapati asked. We sat on the curb in the shade of a food truck, waiting for our orders. We'd taken to walking a couple of blocks during lunch, which afforded us a bit of privacy.

And took us off company property, too. Evelyn hadn't replaced Ben Fulton with a new security chief, so maybe I was being overcautious. Then again, this was biotech. There was no expectation of privacy anywhere, anytime.

"I tampered with the scale in my workstation so that it read light," I said. Maybe it was a managerial mistake to tell them this, but I figured it counted as ancient history. "Then I printed the eggs really small."

Korrapati looked shocked. "Oh, you are so bad!"

"Clever," Wong said, with a hint of his crooked smile.

"That won't work this time around, though," I said. "Four or five pounds and a printing error are not going to cut it for the sort of dragons we need."

"Five pounds not enough," Wong agreed.

"What if we just purchased them?" Korrapati asked. "Custom jobs, with specs close to what we'll need."

"Well, sure, if you're independently wealthy I suppose you could do that," I said dryly.

Something flickered across her face that told me maybe my offhand remark wasn't so far from the truth.

"Wait, *are* you?" I asked.

"Of course not."

"Oh." I could have sworn there was something to it.

"Not me, personally," she said.

"Okay."

"My family is another story."

She comes from money. Korrapati almost never spoke about her family, which was unusual. I knew she and her parents spoke often—they lived somewhere on the East Coast—but I didn't have much more information than that. Tempted as I was to delve into this new twist, I could tell it was making her uncomfortable. "That's very kind of you, but I don't think it would be fair. Besides, we're inside the walls here. We should be able to come up with a solution."

"Maybe we can find a loophole in the payment system," Korrapati said.

"Maybe." I was dubious, though. If there was one thing our company paid attention to, it was money coming in.

"I know where the code is. I can poke around."

"Do it, but be careful. We don't want to trigger an internal audit or something." The last thing I wanted was extra scrutiny of our team and its recent past. Evelyn and I had swept a lot of irregularities under the rug after Greaves left.

"I will tamper with scale," Wong said.

I barked a laugh. "You think you can get it to ignore a twenty-pound egg?"

"Worth a try, maybe."

"All right, knock yourself out."

"Knock myself?" Wong asked.

"Try it if you want." I managed not to grin, Sometimes I forgot how strange my casual slang must seem to anyone from somewhere else.

Unfortunately, by our next outing it was clear that both of these were dead ends. Wong had only managed to get his scale off by six pounds—better than I'd achieved on my own, but still far too small to be used for our purposes—and Korrapati had not found a weakness we could exploit in the payment system. She began hinting again about buying the dragons outright. I objected to that idea for so many reasons.

And on top of it all, Evelyn summoned me to her office to talk about our official work.

"How are the designs looking for the DOD?" she asked, once I'd settled into a chair opposite her desk.

"They're coming along." I was hedging a little because, truthfully, we'd spent the past couple of days tinkering with scales and poring through the code for our accounting and inventory systems.

"Coming along as in almost done?"

"The aquatic model is close."

"The aquatic model *started* close."

She had a point. Wong and Korrapati had designed an outstanding first prototype, and even the DOD's revised specs didn't hold them back for long. It occurred to me that I hadn't asked them what they did to get the aquatic dragon to swim like it had. Seemed like something I should know.

"What about the others?" Evelyn asked.

"We'll make the deadline," I promised.

"And all the specs?"

Of course all the specs. But I managed not to say it out loud—not only because I was speaking to my boss, but because an idea had struck. "I'm *pretty sure* we're going to meet the requirements."

"Pretty sure?" she asked.

"Well, the simulator only gets us so far." I hated to say it, because I'd written the damn thing. "There's no substitute for seeing the dragons in action."

"You want a field test?"

"Just the flying and infantry models." The aquatic models would be hard to test, especially in the desert. On the bright side, those had done so well that the DOD could hardly give us more to accomplish with them. Technically, we weren't under contract to develop the infantry models, but we were still hoping the DOD would come to us for them. When they did, we wanted to have a design that was just as good as the other team's dragons during the first field trials.

She wrinkled her brow. "I don't know, Noah."

There was a lot to be nervous about. We'd field-tested plenty of dragons, but they were generally the safer models designed to be placed with families. Hatching and testing a purpose-built killing machine was another matter entirely. I knew she was thinking about the risk, so I tried a different tack. "You want the models to hit all the specs when we deliver them, don't you?"

"Yes."

"This is the only way we can know for sure."

"It makes me nervous just thinking about it."

"We can take precautions. Tom will help with the hatching and the obedience training so that we can test them safely." I'd already visited him in Herpetology to get his sign-on. It had come easy, in the sense that he was always willing to hatch and train new dragon prototypes. Granted, he'd extracted a promise from me to come on his next desert hike to catch some kind of venomous lizard, but I was hoping he wouldn't hold me to it.

"And what happens to these dragons when the trials are done?" Evelyn asked. "The military won't take them if they haven't overseen the hatching. It's in the contract."

I sighed. "I guess they can go to the Farm."

"I can't believe you are saying this."

Neither can I. The idea of sentencing any of our products to live out their lives in a cage bothered me more than a little. "Hey, I don't like it either. But failure is not an option if we want to keep producing dragons."

She chewed her lip, which meant she was thinking about something and not liking where the thought led. At last she said, "You are right, Noah Parker. It's worth the cost. And they may not have a worse life at the Farm."

"Thanks, boss. I'll let you know when the designs are ready." I ducked out of her office before she could change her mind.

CHAPTER THIRTY-NINE
The Disappeared

The field trials went well. There's no point in dwelling on the details. The flying dragons had already met most of the DOD's specs the first time around. A few tweaks here and there, and they met the new horizontal flying speed requirements. Soared past the high-altitude test. They even demolished the cargo requirements, which I'd had some doubts about.

As for the infantry model, Korrapati and Wong had worked wonders on the design. It was five kilograms lighter but longer overall, with a whiplike tail to balance out the heavier front end. They hadn't seen the infantry dragons that O'Connell and the Frogman produced firsthand, but they'd inadvertently created something very similar. We kept the desert camouflage in place for the moment; the military wanted the chameleonlike skin patterns, but we hadn't yet cracked the code. Luckily, that wasn't in the required specs, but something they hoped we'd provide down the road.

We came away from the field trials feeling encouraged.

Not only did our models seem to meet the stringent requirements, but the demonstration had proven that Tom Johnson and his team really could train dragons to perform basic actions. The dragon wranglers used a series of voice commands and gestures to tell the dragons what to do. The dragons complied, while I made careful notes and Wong took a video on his phone. We hadn't asked Herpetology for the command instructions for the dragons—that might have made them suspicious—we'd simply laid out what we needed to make them do.

Now it was the morning after the field trials, and if they followed the standard practice, the dragon wranglers would be taking all of the prototypes to the Farm. I'd casually asked Evelyn if my team could have the day off, under the guise of rewarding them for the incredible effort Wong and Korrapati had put into the designs. She'd agreed, of course, imagining that both of our designers and I would be taking advantage of some well-earned R&R.

Instead, we were sweating together under a pop-up canopy shelter out in the Sonoran desert. Boulders ensconced us from either side; behind us it was a half-mile hike over raw desert terrain to our cars. In front was the shallow valley I'd stumbled on all those months ago that was home to Build-A-Dragon's desert facility. Better known as the Farm, this was where the company sent dragons that were returned, defective, or no-longer-useful prototypes. And, somewhat infamously, it's where we found the dogs from the Canizumab trial, the ones that proved that the medicine could effectively stop the canine pandemic.

"How long does this usually take?" Korrapati asked, with just a touch of impatience.

I didn't blame her too much; it was a hot and windless afternoon. The three of us were crammed into a ground blind that allegedly had a capacity of six. Somehow, lying prone shoulder to shoulder between Korrapati and Wong, I doubted that figure very much. "Shouldn't be too much longer."

"You said that already. Two times," Wong said.

"I know, I know. But I mean it this time." I'd done the math on a dragon wrangler leaving more or less first thing in the morning and driving out here at normal speed. Of course, that assumed the wrangler left right away, that there were no unexpected delays in traffic ... *Maybe I miscalculated.*

I'd no sooner had that thought than a plume of dust rose over the far end of the valley where the road let in. A *large* plume. "Here we go."

Three pickup trucks trundled into view along the unpaved road that led in through the cliffs. They'd have triggered the road alarms on their way, of course, but this was official Build-A-Dragon business so the security team probably wouldn't need to respond. That was assuming there was a security team. They'd worked for Fulton, and it still wasn't clear whether or not the big man's role had been filled since his death. To me, at least. *Evelyn probably replaced him, and just didn't tell me.* She knew the full story of what went down between me and the security chief. Beyond that, she was an ardent follower of avoiding topics that might upset Noah Parker when he was on a design deadline. So yeah, it was best to assume our security department was fully staffed again.

The trucks proceeded single file to the far corner of

the complex—conveniently, the corner nearest to our vantage point—and jet-parked next to one another in the open space, their tailgates pointed at the building. We could already see the cages. Four to a truck, and the dragons inside looked *lively*. Having seen them in action, I could understand why the wranglers seemed to be exercising more than the usual level of care. They shoved wooden poles through the cages to lift them from the truck beds, and pressed each cage against the gate of the holding pen. Two men held it there while the third operated the controls to slide open the gate. On the bright side, the dragons didn't thrash or knock their cages around. In fact, it looked like they followed a command to enter the holding pen as soon as the gates were open. As they closed, and the wranglers walked back to get another cage, Korrapati noted the location of the new resident on the grid. She and Wong hadn't thought this step was necessary; like most good designers, they believed they'd know their own dragons on sight. But having been to this place before, I knew better.

"So many cages," Wong said.

"Yes. I never imagined we had this many returns and defective models," Korrapati said.

I closed my eyes, remembering the moment I'd first stood in the sand and stared at this building. Not only that, but the piles of sun-bleached skeletons piled all around. Dragons didn't live forever—the song was wrong about that part—and I guess the dragon wranglers hadn't known what to do with them when they died. They seemed to have figured something out, though, because the bones were no longer visible. It was probably Tom Johnson's doing. The guy knew his way around animals. That was for damn sure.

"I know it's a lot to take in, but stay focused," I said. "We don't want to have to do this twice."

"God no," Korrapati said. "But if we do, could you at least get a two-person tent?"

"Hey, come on, it said capacity six."

Wong snorted.

"Just keep your eyes on the dragons."

"That's it. That's twelve," Korrapati said.

She was right—the dragon wranglers had finished their unloading work and now were climbing back into their trucks, eager to escape the heat. I envied them that. Seconds later, they'd fired up their engines and trundled out of sight down the dirt road that led out of the valley.

"Let's move." I wiggled back out of the ground blind and started breaking it down.

"How are we looking on transportation?" I called to Wong as we climbed down the boulder-strewn slope into the vale. He was ten yards behind and above me, with Korrapati trailing him. Both of them had proved better than average climbers, Wong especially. For a guy whose preferred mode of transportation was a personal scooter, he seemed oddly comfortable scrambling down the rocky slope.

He paused long enough to tap his bluetooth earbud. I heard one side of a muttered conversation. Then Wong called, "Five minutes."

"They know where to meet us, right?"

"They know."

We needed a truck to make this work. Wong, for reasons still not clear to me, said he could get us one, no problem. Sure enough, by the time we reached the base of the boulder pile and hiked over to the road, an unmarked white box truck waited. A youngish Asian dude leaned against the cab on the shady side. I didn't recognize him on sight, but with his big dark sunglasses it was hard to say for sure. He handed Wong a key fob, and they had a brief conversation in Mandarin. I listened, of course, but only caught the occasional word. Yet another reminder that when Evelyn and Wong spoke the language with me, they were doing so slowly out of courtesy. Then the dude just turned and jogged off down the dirt road in the direction of the highway.

I edged closer to Wong. "Who is that?"

"Good friend. Very good."

"He doesn't work for—"

"No," Wong said, almost as quickly as I'd begun to ask.

I sagged a bit in relief, because I really hadn't wanted him bringing anyone close to this, much less someone who worked for Build-A-Dragon. "Where's he going?"

"The highway, for friend to pick him up."

"How many friends do you have, anyway?"

"Are we interrogating Wong, or are we doing this?" Korrapati's tone carried a good dose of impatience.

Note to self, Korrapati does not *do well in the heat.*

First things first, disabling the road alarm. This was a wire sensor attached to a metal control box with a satellite transmitter on top. Old-school technology in many ways, but still effective. It had busted Summer and me the first time we came out here. And it made a certain kind of sense: the only real trouble Build-A-Dragon had to worry about for its farm tended to arrive in a vehicle. Still, any security system had weak points. I'd considered a few possibilities. Cutting the wire would probably just trigger an alert from the control box, and that would bring security out here even faster than a routine perimeter breach. I imagined that most triggers of the alarm were accidental, but an act of sabotage signaled some intent.

I dragged my eyes away from the still-tempting stubby antenna on top of the control box, and joined Wong at the back of the truck. We heaved a long two-by-four—real wood, not that cheap composite stuff—out of the back of the truck and laid it down on the road alongside the alarm cable. Then it was back to the truck for a second identical two-by-four to lay on the far side of the cable. The wood pieces were low enough to drive over, but gave the tires an inch of clearance over the cable. I hoped that would be enough; I hadn't really accounted for how heavy a full-on box truck would be on the way out. Still, it was a convenient but low-tech method for circumventing the alarm.

It still surprised me that this cable—and the regular patrols who responded to it—represented the full extent of security Robert Greaves had thought to put in place. He'd learned this lesson, though, and wouldn't make the same mistake with his shiny new dragon factory. Which is why this raid had to work.

Korrapati, who'd already climbed into the driver's seat of the truck, leaned out the open window. "Is it ready yet?"

Yeah, she absolutely didn't care for the heat.

"Go ahead, try it!" I called up to her. "Nice and slow."

I crouched down at the end of the boards so I could watch the gap as the truck went over. If this didn't work—if the alarm got triggered—we had to scrap the entire mission.

Korrapati eased the truck forward. It must have been an electric engine; the thing was absolutely noiseless beyond the crunch of its tires on the dry roadbed. To me, it looked like the boards worked and kept the tires off the road trigger. It was close, though, especially when they shifted as the rear wheels hit. I looked at Wong after it had passed. "What do you think?"

He'd moved from the far side of the road where I *thought* he'd be waiting, and stood by the transmission box instead. He also had out some kind of handheld electronic device a bit smaller than a phone. "No signal."

I knew better than to ask him what the device was or where he got it. "So, we're good?"

"We are good."

We climbed into the cab of the truck from the passenger side. Korrapati already had it in gear by the time we were settled. I'd hopped in first, vainly hoping for air-conditioning. Not only did the electric truck let me down on that account, but it also meant I got to ride bitch between the two of them. Which got interesting when she yanked the massive gearshift into second. That was for damn sure.

I pressed myself far back into the threadbare seat as we trundled down the lane toward the complex. "Where did you learn to drive a stick shift, anyway?"

"When I was growing up, most cars in India were still manual transmission."

She made a wide turn as we approached the complex

and threw it in reverse—nearly sterilizing me in the process—and backed up to the side of the massive complex. At least, that's what I assumed she was doing. I couldn't see anything past her on one side, and Wong's massive squarish head on the other side. Then she threw it in park and the three of us climbed out.

Wong threw up the truck's hatch door and vaulted inside, again showing rather remarkable agility for a guy who liked to hail a rideshare rather than walk two blocks. A large blocky pile hidden by moving blankets occupied most of the cargo space. He tugged the blanket aside to reveal a dozen cages similar in size to the ones that had just brought the dragons here. Most of them weren't even dragon cages, but used dog crates I'd been slowly buying at the flea market or through buy-sell-trade sites. I was glad to get them out of my condo. Did they meet spec to transport military-grade dragons? Hell no. But they were the best I could do on short notice without drawing attention. Wong shoved the first cage to the rear of the truck, then hopped out to help me lift it down.

"Where's the first cage?" I panted.

Korrapati consulted her notes. "Fourth from the edge of the building. Infantry model."

Wong and I carried the cage to the spot and set it down. The first cage held a Laptop model with vivid aquamarine colors; it looked like a cartoon. The second had a K-10, probably one returned when German shepherds came back. Both were mercifully asleep in the heat of the day. Not so with the third cage, which held a Rover-sized model. It ran to the front of its cage, panting and wagging its tail the way my childhood dog had done when Connor and I got home from school. It was so eager to be petted that it tried to squeeze its head through the bars. Rovers were friendly but not to this extreme. Unfortunately, I knew the reason why. This was the dragon I'd given a dopamine receptor feedback loop, an intentional defect that doomed it to life in quarantine. I'd done it because I'd been desperate to locate the Farm that held my canceled Condor models, the ones I'd secretly given my brother's mutation. It seemed a small sacrifice at the time, but seeing it here all but crushed me with shame.

"Friendly Rover," Wong grunted.

"Yeah," I said. *Don't remind me.*

The fourth cage held our infantry model as promised. It had curled up in the far corner but lifted its head as we approached. The moment we set down the cage against its cell, it came to its feet and stood facing the door.

"Hold the cage here, will you?" I jogged down the road toward the large control panel at the far corner of the building. Dragons dozed in almost every cage but I kept my eyes forward. I felt guilty enough as it was. Maybe that's why I didn't notice the changes at the control panel until I was right on top of it. I turned to double-check the count. *Fourth from the end.* Then I looked at the control panel and it was completely dark except for a steady red light above a numeric keypad. "What the hell?"

I counted four switches in and tried the one for the cage at which Wong waited, with no result. I was completely locked out. With no way to open the cages, we'd never get any dragons out. This mission was blown. Hell, the whole plan was blown. Evelyn wouldn't let me print more military-grade dragons under the guise of a field trial. I stood there, wondering how I was going to explain this all to Wong and Korrapati.

"Noah, what's wrong?" Korrapati asked.

The panel emitted a soft chime, and the red light turned green. I swear I wasn't touching it when this happened.

"I'm not sure. Maybe nothing." I reached out tentatively for the switch I'd tried only a moment earlier, and was rewarded with a buzzer followed by distant mechanical whirring. *Thank God.*

Wong looked a bit panicked as the infantry dragon slinked into the cage he was holding all by himself. I jogged back to help him steady it as we slid the door into place and latched it tight.

"Was there problem?" Wong asked, as we carried the much-heavier cage to the truck.

"They added a security keypad to the controls."

"How did you get around it?"

"I have no idea."

Wong frowned at this, but said nothing more. I knew what he was thinking. *This is too easy.*

We threw the cage in and went for the next one, a flying model three cages down. The control panel didn't offer any further challenges. One by one, we liberated military dragons from their cages and loaded them into the truck. It was hot, heavy work in the afternoon sun. Even with two of us, even with the box truck parked as close to the structure as we could get it. Finally, we got the last of them thrown into the truck.

"Go tell Korrapati we're loaded up," I told Wong. "I'll make sure the cages are secure."

He disappeared from view, and I found my satchel and dug out the long, cold cylinders that I'd brought for this moment. It had been a while since I used a field biopsy pen, but I had a little bit of experience. I made my way up to the front of the truck. The dragons watched me silently. The two front cages were an infantry model and a flier. I started with the ground dragon.

"Down," I told it.

The dragon lay down on its belly facing me. *Well trained*, I couldn't help but thinking. *Well done, Tom.*

"Stay." I crouched low enough to reach through the cage with the biopsy pen. It was a single mechanism—a shot of anesthetic, extraction of a tissue sample, then an antibiotic spray followed by a wound sealer. All in less than a second. The soft *click* or the sensation of the needle made the dragon flinch slightly, but otherwise it held still. "Good boy," I whispered. "At ease."

The dragon shifted, curling up in one corner of the cage, while I turned to the flier. It let me do the biopsy thing, too, and it stared at me with those knowing eyes. I found myself talking to the dragons, little bits of praise here and there as I worked my way down the line. One biopsy per dragon. It did take a few minutes to work my way back through.

I finished the last of them and placed it carefully in my satchel. Then I looked up and saw Wong watching me.

"What was that?"

Crap. I hadn't meant to read him in to this part of the plan, this most-unofficial use of our borrowed dragon resources. "A needle biopsy pen."

"You took samples?"

"Yes. It's for something else. I'll explain later."

He nodded, accepting this for the moment. I climbed down and we closed the back of the truck. I paused then, and held him by the shoulder. "Don't tell Korrapati, all right?"

He didn't answer, but led the way to the passenger side of the cab.

I was drenched in sweat and every part of my body ached. Wong, too, looked spent. His entire body language said *This is why I don't like strenuous activity*. We could barely heave the door open and climb in.

"I have a bit of good news," Korrapati said.

She'd figured out how to turn on the air-conditioning. *God bless her.*

CHAPTER FORTY
The Ambush

We met in the desert at five A.M., so early it was still dark outside. No moon, no clouds. I'd forgotten how many stars you could see outside the city at night. The air still held warmth, though, and a promise of a brutally hot day. Wong and Korrapati beat us to the rendezvous point by a good ten minutes. Driving a big truck, as it turned out, was no match for wrangling half a dozen small flying dragons into a standard-size Jeep.

"Sorry we're late," I said. "How are the dragons?"

"Hungry," Wong said.

"Yes, we fed them," Korrapati smiled. "I've never fed a dragon by hand before."

"Really?"

"Me neither," Wong said.

"You guys haven't done any hatchings?"

"Not everyone is the golden child who gets to imprint the dragons alongside Tom Johnson during field tests," Korrapati said.

"I guess I just assumed..." I said.

"You are very special," Wong said.

"All right, that's enough out of you." I gestured back to the Jeep where Summer was in the middle of a tug-of-war to reclaim her hoodie from Marcus Aurelius. "Besides, the charm of feeding dragons wears off. Trust me."

"It hasn't yet, at least for me," Korrapati said. "I almost hate to do this to them."

I did, too, if I was honest with myself. Even knowing that they were purpose-made for things like this didn't make it much easier. Dragons were living, breathing things. "With luck, they won't come to any harm."

She nodded, but looked as though she didn't entirely believe me. I wouldn't have, either.

Summer joined us, looking frazzled but wearing a mostly undamaged dark hoodie. All of us pretended not to notice the delay or the tooth marks.

"Are you ready for this?" she asked.

"Yeah. Are you?"

She brandished a leather tool-bag. "My part's easy."

I hoped that was true. Summer was going to disable the Frogman's vehicle outside his place, and then guard the entrance to the road that led to the facility. Well, *guard* was a bit of an overstatement. She'd park her Jeep on the side of the road—which wouldn't attract too much undue attention in this area—and let us know if any vehicles started heading this way. It was Saturday; I didn't expect anyone to be working, but you never knew. The Frogman had always kept odd hours, and for all I knew Greaves was demanding a seven-day workweek.

"Be careful, all right?" I hugged her.

"You too." She waved to Wong and Korrapati. "Good luck!" Then she opened her hatch.

Benjy flew out first with Octavius right at his tail. Hadrian and Titus made streaks of green and orange after them. Then came Nero and Otho; I quickly lost them in the dull brown landscape behind the Jeep. I eased off my backpack and extracted my tablet. We'd fitted each of the little dragons with a pinpoint camera and GPS tracker—the kind that extreme athletes used—and all of them were hot-linked to my tablet. The video feeds scrolled with rugged desert terrain, alternating with glimpses of the gold-streaked horizon. All but one feed, that is. The bottom right corner of my grid showed an unmoving view of Summer's backseat. *We've got a straggler, and guess who.*

"Marcus Aurelius!" I called.

The last dragon took wing in a manner that could only be described as grudging.

I called Octavius to me and winced as he landed on my shoulder. He'd gained almost a pound in the past week—they all had—as I'd let them eat as much as they wanted. "Listen, buddy. Just liked we talked about. Stay high, spread out, and watch for other dragons."

He started to take off, but I grabbed his legs. "Hey. Look after your brothers, all right?" I released him and he launched himself into the air, chirping to his mates. They all wheeled around to form up in something resembling a line. I watched them until they disappeared over the high ridge that separated us from the shallow valley where the facility was.

"All right, we're ready," I told Wong.

He jogged to the back of the truck and hauled the

doors open. Korrapati came over to look at the video feed. Dawn was breaking as we got our first glimpse of the target facility. It looked bigger somehow than the drone footage. Darker, too, and more intimidating. I was fairly sure that was just an effect of the light.

"It looks like our building," Korrapati said.

"I know. It's weird, huh?"

"Very."

Nero and Otho were coming up on the building at a good angle. I pointed out the balconies where we'd seen the flying dragons. Nothing moved as far as we could see, though I hoped Octavius and his siblings maintained a high altitude.

Wong had the cages open by that time. "We are ready," he said.

I took a deep breath and let it out slowly. Up until this moment, we hadn't committed any serious crimes. "Are we sure about this?"

Korrapati laughed nervously. "It's a little late for that."

"What about you, Wong?"

"We go," he said, without hesitation.

Their confidence got me over the hump. "All right, let's get this over with."

They called out the dragons, which had waited patiently in their cages. They already showed far more discipline than my lot, though that wasn't saying much. The infantry models flowed down the ramp onto the sand, tongues flicking out to taste the air. Wong ordered them forward. I tore my eyes from their sinuous movement to watch the flying dragons emerge from the truck. They took to wing straight out of their cages. They swept low to gain momentum, and then shot up into the sky.

Korrapati set them sweeping over the dunes, air cover for the ground troops.

The three of us jogged after them; they were fast. We crested the ridge together, trying to keep them in sight. It was fully light out now, and a trill from Octavius—the only dragonet with duplex audio linked to my tablet—told me he'd spotted something. I brought up his feed to full screen, and there it was. One of Greaves's infantry models. It prowled the shallow vale in our direction. I could barely see the thing, it blended so well.

"Contact," I said. "About halfway between us and the building."

Korrapati and Wong both issued the same command, an order I'd never imagined I'd hear someone speak to a dragon.

Kill.

The flying dragons swept forward, climbing to gain altitude. Two broke off left and another two right. The dragon on the ground had marked them now, and craned its neck to follow the central pair. They dove, swooping down at him like falcons. The dragon hunched low to the ground, watching them approach. They plummeted toward him. They were maybe fifteen feet up when it crouched and leaped upward, slashing. Only the flying dragons broke off right then. They banked away, out of reach. That's when the infantry dragons arrived, catching the thing in midair. They were quick about it. Brutally so. Korrapati looked away. Wong and I stared, but said nothing. It wasn't the first time I'd watched dragon-on-dragon violence, but seeing it again was no easier.

Nero and Otho, meanwhile, had located another

dragon slinking its way among the dunes. Two of our infantry units ran to intercept it. The dragon saw them coming, and they didn't have the luxury of an airborne distraction. Nero's camera view showed only a blur of scales, claws, and teeth. When the dust settled, two dragons were down: one of theirs, and one of ours.

"Shit!" I said. "We lost an infantry unit."

Then another pair of Greaves's ground dragons appeared and we were too busy to lament the loss. Which might have been for the best, because there were others: another infantry unit that reached them first, and a flying model that strayed too close to the ground. *Damn, they're dropping like flies.*

"Any more ground dragons?" Wong asked.

The dragonets were searching, their video feeds all scrolling different directions across the vale. While that happened, I fed all of the video they'd recorded so far through Connor's dragon-detection algorithm. It picked up the enemy dragons as well as our own infantry units, but no others. "I think we're clear."

We pressed forward, climbing down from the ridge into the protected vale beyond. Into the battleground. *I hope I'm right.* The remaining infantry dragons formed up and quested across the ground in front of us. It offered some reassurance. But our activities had not gone unnoticed. No sooner than we'd walked fifteen steps, dark wings unfurled on the balconies of the steel building. Greaves's flying dragons leapt into the cloudless sky. They didn't come for us, nor did they engage the aerial units that had taken up formation just ahead. No, they shot up into the sky and went straight for my dragonets.

Oh hell. "Korrapati!"

"I see them." She sent the aerial units skyward but they had a ways to go. And Greaves's flying dragons were *fast*. It seemed that they'd figured out the missing piece about the wing joints. I don't know whether it was his bright orange coloring or the fact that he was the smallest of the pack, but they closed on Hadrian. He sensed them approaching and swerved just in time to avoid slashing claws. They swept past him, already banking to make another pass. I opened my duplex audio to Octavius. "Octavius! Hadrian's in trouble."

Octavius folded his wings and dove toward Hadrian, with Benjy close behind him. The other dragonets continued providing air support. At least, I think they did; all I could watch was Hadrian dodging the bigger flying dragons while Octavius and Benjy streaked toward him. They had to see the size of the enemy dragons. They had to know it was practically suicide to challenge creatures purpose-bred to kill. In the same way, I didn't want to watch but I had to. They slammed into the lead dragon simultaneously. It broke off its pursuit of Hadrian, snapping back at them. They kept away from its head, harassing it about the midriff. Which would have been fine if there weren't another aerial dragon right behind it.

I saw it coming. "Octavius, watch behind you!"

But the big dragon had already swept forward at them, claws extended. I winced as they disappeared under it.

Then they both broke off to either side. The rear dragon tried to backpedal but instead flew right into the other one. *Clever, boys.* Their wings and tails tangled together and then they were falling.

I pumped a fist. "All—"

The lead dragon whipped its tail up and wrapped it around Octavius's leg. He squirmed but couldn't get free. I watched, helpless, as they plummeted in a tangle of scales, teeth, and claws. *Come on, buddy, get free!*

He tried his best. I'm sure of that. But they were too low already. Falling too fast. They slammed into the hard, unforgiving earth. A plume of dust marked where they'd struck. In my heart, I knew nothing could survive that. I looked in desperation but nothing moved. Octavius's video feed winked out.

He was gone.

I stood there, numb and unable to move. A dull roar in my ears blocked out every other sound. It wasn't supposed to happen this way. He wasn't a soldier, born and raised for fighting. He should have been home asleep, dreaming about breakfast. I hadn't even fed him anything on the way here. I'd wanted him light and alert. The thought that he'd gone hungry...it was too much. *This was all a mistake.*

I became aware of a tug at my arm. There was a sound, too, intruding on the dull roar.

"Noah!"

Korrapati's face loomed into my field of view. "Noah!"

My mind was running on autopilot. I tried to brush her aside, but my arms had no strength.

"We have to go," Korrapati said.

She was right. We had a small window of opportunity to infiltrate the main building. As much as I wanted to run out into the scree to find Octavius, we had no time. I stumbled after her up to the front door of the building.

Wong was already there, hunched over a small tablet that he'd wired to a port beside the double glass doors. We reached the threshold in time to see them hiss open. Wong pulled his wire free, wrapped it around the tablet, and tucked it into a large pocket of his cargo shorts.

Cool air and the smell of fresh paint rushed out to envelop us.

Korrapati and I hurried inside and paused to take off our sunglasses. The plan was for Wong to stay outside and maintain a perimeter with our dragons.

My eyes adjusted as the ambient light came up; it must have been motion-activated. It was like we'd stepped out of the elevator onto the seventh floor of our building. Frosted glass walls on either side bordered the lobby. Assuming the layout was the same, the design lab would be to the right on the far side of the hatchery. "Well, this looks familiar."

"You're right, it's the same," Korrapati said. "How peculiar."

"Did he design our building, too?"

"I think so."

"Well, he's done us a favor. Come on."

We had to pass through the hatchery first, of course. Between the two sets of heavy doors were twelve hatching pods, six to either side. Same design as ours. Out here in the desert with no air pollution to contend with, they probably maintained perfect hatching temperature with very little effort. All of them were active, too. It was tempting to peer into the windows for a glimpse at their dragon eggs. Yet another luxury of time we couldn't afford. The design lab was up ahead. We pushed through the heavy door back into the coolness of the dark space. Oddly enough, the sense of being in a seemingly familiar place was comforting.

Here we encountered the first aberration from the Build-A-Dragon corporate schematic. Instead of six workstations arranged honeycomb-style around the biological printer, there were just three. Two of them showed signs of use—scuffs and Post-it notes covered part of the work surface, and the floor was crisscrossed with wheel marks from the chairs. I told myself that was a good thing; it meant that Greaves hadn't managed to recruit another genetic engineer beyond O'Connell and the Frogman.

Beyond the workstations was another piece of déjà vu: a large instrument the size of a minivan, bristling with metallic arms and wiring. Three conveyor belts connected it to the workstations; that was where the eggs came out. I squeezed between the center workstation and its conveyor belt to get at the heart of the machine. Beneath all the high-tech machine wizardry was a laptop-sized piece of silicon wrapped in plastic wires, lit by the steady flashes of old-school LED lights. *The Redwood Codex.* I had no idea what it truly did—only some educated guesses—but without it, Greaves couldn't print viable dragon eggs. This was the prototype, which looked even more janky and cobbled-together than the one in Build-A-Dragon's biological printer.

Hot air blew in my face as I pushed closer to it. There were two wires to disconnect. The first came unplugged easily, but the second wouldn't budge. Crammed as I was up under the machine, I couldn't get any leverage to pull it free. "Damn it!"

"What's wrong?" Korrapati asked. She stood over by O'Connell's workstation, rearranging his Post-it notes. He'd always hated that.

"I can't get it loose."

"Let me try."

I yanked at the plug again, with no result. *Might as well.* I wriggled out and let Korrapati have a go. While she did, I took the liberty of lowering the Frogman's desk chair to the lowest setting, and then removing the adjustment knob. I pocketed it and came back to check on Korrapati, who was backing out of the machine with the Codex in hand.

"You got it? How?"

"Strong fingers." She handed me the Codex and scooted out from under the machine. "Careful, it's hot."

I took it eagerly and nearly singed my fingers as a result. "Jeez, you weren't kidding. I always knew this thing was a fire hazard." I tucked it into my knapsack and then helped her up. She managed to be graceful even crawling out from all the metal arms. "Remind me again why you're single."

She straightened, stretching in what was almost certainly an unnecessary display. "Who says I'm single?"

I held up my hands in mock surrender. It was the first time I'd borderline-flirted with Korrapati and it was *weird.* "Fair enough."

My phone rang. Summer was calling. Either that was the universe reminding me that I had a pretty good thing already, or she had news. I touched my earpiece to answer. "Hey."

"You've got company. Dark SUV."

"Shit. How long do we have?"

"It just passed. Maybe three or four minutes."

"All right. We're coming out. You can jet."

"On it. Be careful!" Her Jeep engine rumbled to life so loud I could hear it over the phone.

I hung up and turned to Korrapati. "We have to hurry."

CHAPTER FORTY-ONE
The Army

Korrapati and I hustled to the door that led to the hatching pod. I pulled the door open, straining at its weight but glad to see no one waiting on the other side. Greaves would have hired hatchers, and the people who took that job tended to obsess over it. We ran out of the building into the heat and bright sunlight. Wong must have heard us coming and assembled our remaining dragons to cover our departure. I checked my watch; it had been ninety seconds since Summer saw the SUV pass.

On my left was the route back into the desert and the truck, the planned egress. Even with the vehicle approaching, we were within our timetable. A short jog to the boulder cliffs and we'd be under cover, bound for freedom. Instead, my legs carried me to the right, into the scree and scrub brush. The dragonets were all flying there in tight circles, chattering to one another. With Octavius down, I had no way to talk to them. There was an urgency to the way they were flying.

"Noah?" Korrapati asked.

"I need a minute."

"Do we have a minute?"

Not really, no. I didn't answer her, though. I didn't have a good explanation for what pulled me the wrong way with the weight of the Codex prototype heavy around my shoulder. I heard a quiet conversation between Wong and Korrapati behind me. Moments later, half of the surviving infantry units fanned out in the brush to either side of me, while two aerial units winged forward.

The brush was thicker here in the deepest part of the vale. Boulders, too, were piled almost on top of one another. It was like every hard or uncomfortable obstacle had drifted down here just to be in my way. I pushed through it all, ignoring the scratches on my arms. There was no wind here, and the heat pressed in. It was hard to breathe. It got harder when I saw the glint of scales through the brambles. The bodies of Greaves's flying dragons lay in a lifeless tangle on a jumble of sharp rocks. The adaptive camouflage that once made them so striking was gone now, leaving only a dull gray behind.

Even after what they'd done, seeing the enemy dragons so grotesque in death bothered me. They had been elegant creatures in the air. Dangerous, too. It infuriated me to think that they'd gone for the weakest aerial targets rather than picking a fair fight. There was a brutal caginess to that.

Octavius was clever, too. The smartest little dragon I'd ever met. It was so like him to take on dragons four times his size. What had he been thinking? Maybe he hadn't been thinking. Like me, he saw Hadrian in trouble and just acted. And yet I couldn't find him. As much as it would break me to find him crumpled over the rocks like these, I couldn't leave him out here alone with them. I couldn't see him anywhere, though. Then I heard it, a soft noise.

"Noah!" Korrapati called.

I shushed her. *Maybe I imagined it.* No, there it was again. I grabbed the top dragon by the limb that was not broken at a horrifying angle and pulled. It barely moved; the thing was heavier than I'd expected. I heaved, throwing my body into it and stumbling back into the cactus behind me. "Ow!" The flying dragon's body slid free at last.

There was a small gap between the dragons, a pocket protected by the lower one's crumpled wing. And there he was, tucked into it. "Octavius!"

He was alive. That was all I could tell as I gently plucked him out of the carnage and tucked him under my arm. His wings looked torn and I was pretty sure one was broken, but his eyes were still open. He made another little croon, so faint I could barely hear it. "Hang on, buddy."

I jogged back to the building, not daring to check my watch. I knew it had taken too long. Korrapati and Wong called the dragons back and led the way to our escape route. My dragonets wheeled after them. Maybe they sensed the urgency. I hazarded a look at Octavius. His eyes were closed, and his breathing seemed labored. Between carrying him and the now-awkward satchel holding the Codex, I was struggling to keep up.

By the time we reached the boulder pile, they were a good distance ahead. They turned as if to wait, and have the dragons wait with me. "Keep going!" I shouted. Getting all of the surviving dragons back was almost as important as keeping control of the Codex prototype.

I kept checking on Octavius, but he wasn't responding any longer. He felt warm, but I was worried even so. Between checking on him and lugging the bulky, uncomfortable Codex in my satchel—like the One Ring, it felt like it was getting heavier with each step—by the time I reached the top of the boulder pile, they were far behind. And then I heard it.

"Parker!"

Robert Greaves stood in the basin behind me. It could only be him. No one else wore a dark turtleneck and pants in this heat. His dark SUV was parked haphazardly in the clearing behind him, not close to the building. That meant he'd seen us running out. Or maybe seen our dragons. It didn't matter which; both were bad.

I shouldn't have stopped, but I turned and looked at him.

"What the hell are you doing?" he demanded.

"Just reclaiming some stolen property."

"Take all the dragons you want. We can make more."

I snorted. "That's what you think."

His eyes flickered to my satchel, which until that moment he might not have seen. "Well, we can add larceny to your list of crimes today."

I said nothing. Benjy had winged back and now circled overhead, listening in to our conversation. Nero and Otho joined him a moment later. In another minute, my entire cadre of dragonets would be here eavesdropping. I wished I had a way to tell them to keep out of sight.

"Looks like you brought some friends along," Greaves said, glancing up at the dragonets. "But those aren't production models."

"They're not your business."

"Too small to be customs, though," he continued. "You have permits for these animals, son? Or should we add harboring illegal animals to your growing rap sheet?"

That hit a little close to the mark, because I legitimately did not have any sort of paperwork for my dragons, including Octavius. And that could get me in trouble; as genetically created organisms they were supposed to be entered in a registry when they left our building. He was onto something, in other words, and I really didn't care to pursue that line of discussion. "Sounds a lot better than espionage," I said.

He shook his head. "Every time we talk, you're in over your head."

"You have no right to this." I shook my satchel. "Just as you had no right to set fire to Redwood's place."

"Don't talk about things you don't understand. And that you can't prove."

This was getting old. I was hot and tired, Octavius hadn't moved in a long time, and worse, the dragons were coming back. I could sense the infantry dragons creeping back up the rocks. Korrapati and Wong must have seen that I'd stopped and sent them back to cover me. Out of the corner of one eye, I saw the flicker of dust-colored wings. The aerials were back, too, gliding low across the cacti toward the rocks where I stood.

"We both know what these kinds of dragons can do. I don't trust you with them. I barely trust myself."

He stared at me for a moment, but with his dark sunglasses I couldn't get a read on his face. "Competition in a free market is good for everyone."

"It's not always good."

"Can you honestly say you'd have designed dragons as cleverly if we didn't go for the contract?"

I opened my mouth to reply, but didn't have the words. I hated it when he did that, when he said something that I couldn't refute. Competing to build the best thing seemed very different from offering it to whoever could pay the most.

"Yeah, that's what I thought," Greaves said. "So how about you worry about selling your dragons, and we'll worry about selling ours."

"Sorry, but you don't have the right to sell dragons. You lost that right when, as you'll recall, they fired you." I started to walk off.

"Don't be stupid, Parker. I've got a security team already on the way. Give me the Codex and I'll forget I ever saw you and your unauthorized dragons."

He's bluffing. But I couldn't resist the urge to look out across the valley for the sign of more approaching vehicles. I saw nothing, though that didn't mean there weren't some on the way. I'd told our lookout to leave, after all. I held Octavius and my satchel close against me. I shifted away again, toward escape. Which is how I saw that our dragons were close, just below the precipice where Greaves wouldn't see them. I didn't fear them. Even knowing how dangerous they were. What they could do. These were my dragons, in one of those moments of rare bravado inspired by Robert Greaves.

"You're not leaving with my Codex," he said.

"Your army's not here yet." I pointed behind him. "But mine is." The infantry dragons prowled over the rocks and into view at that moment. Flying models soared up behind me like fighter jets at an air show. They circled him once, no more than an arm's reach away. They must have sensed the threat he offered, and that made him a hostile.

With one shouted word, I could have told them to attack. I could have put an end to the thorn in my side that was Robert Greaves.

"Stand down," I called instead.

Greaves relaxed a shade when the dragons left him and followed me.

I climbed down toward Wong and Korrapati. It was painfully slow going with the weight of the bag and only one free arm. The infantry models climbed down much faster, spreading out to either side of me like a security escort. They could go almost vertical on the rocks. They made practically no noise. Their light-adaptive skin rendered them almost invisible, especially when they paused to let me catch up.

"Show-offs," I muttered.

Within minutes we had the animals back at the truck. Korrapati and Wong helped me load them in silence, and then we climbed into the cab.

"What was that about?" Korrapati asked, as she started the truck. She must have heard.

"Nothing. Let's get the hell out of here."

CHAPTER FORTY-TWO
The Handoff

When we met Summer at the rendezvous point, Octavius still hadn't woken. His breathing was light and shallow. The A/C in the cab of the truck seemed to bring a bit of color back to his scales, but I was still worried. I handed him off to Summer.

"Oh, God, what happened?" she asked.

"He got tangled up with some other dragons and fell."

She cradled him gently and carried him to the front seat, concern etched in her face. Then I had to turn my attention to the cloud of keyed-up, concerned dragonets. It took two minutes to settle them into the backseat of her Jeep.

"Calm down, guys," I said. "I'm sure he'll be okay." Then I turned to her. "If he wakes, see if you can get him to drink something."

"I thought I was supposed to follow you to the Farm," she said.

"Change of plans. We can handle going to the Farm if you can get the dragonets home."

"Are you sure?"

Hell yeah, I'm sure. Too many dragons had already died today. If I lost Octavius on top of that, I wasn't sure I could bear it. "It'll make me feel better to know he's safe with you."

"All right." She hugged me. "Be careful."

Korrapati, Wong, and I took the rest of the dragons back to the Farm and got them into their holding pens. We were three short, but I was hoping no one would notice. I did feel bad leaving our casualties out in the fields where they had fallen. I started to wonder what the military would do with the dragons that fell in the field. It wasn't clear if the credo of *no one left behind* applied to animals. Probably not, by my guess. Best not explore that line of thought.

The drive with Wong and Korrapati brought little relief. We were hot, we were tired, and I imagined that we were all more than a little bit worried that Robert Greaves had caught us in the act.

"How is Octavius?" Korrapati asked.

I sighed. "I'm not sure. I hope it's just heatstroke or something."

"Me, too." She paused, and cast a nervous glance at me. "Do you think he'll say anything?"

"He's not really a talker. The only word he knows is *medicine*. Long story."

"I meant Robert Greaves."

"Oh, him. I honestly don't know." He couldn't really gripe about taking back the Codex, but we'd technically broken into his building. Worse, he knew we'd deployed our weapons-grade dragons in the field. There hadn't

been much legislation in the area of aggressive reptiles—
mostly thanks to the devoted efforts of Build-A-Dragon's
high-priced lobbying firm—but it didn't seem very
different from aggressive dogs. Which were making quite
the comeback now that the canine pandemic had ended.

"Our dragons did well," Wong said, in characteristic
oblivion to the mood of the truck.

"Wong! How can you say that?" Korrapati said.

"It's true, no matter what."

He wasn't wrong about that part. The dragons had
done well, as had their handlers. This was a victory no
matter how you did the math. It just didn't feel like one
because of goddamn Robert Greaves. "Both of you did,
too. You were lifesavers out there today."

"So were *your* dragons." Korrapati gave me a little
smile. Then she shifted into fourth, which threw the
gearshift very close to my sensitive parts.

"We got the Codex. Most important thing," Wong said.

"No, we didn't," I said.

"What?"

"We got to the Codex and managed to destroy it so that
Greaves won't be able to print more illicit dragons."

"I don't understand," Korrapati said, looking down at
the bundle on my lap.

"Me, too," Wong said. "No understanding."

"First of all, we didn't do anything today. Korrapati, you
were across town eating at the Endless Pitabilities food
truck. There's a receipt on your desk. You had the chicken
Parmesan."

"How is there a receipt from today already on my—"

"The date on their printer is a day ahead. I went there

yesterday." I left out the part where I loitered for half an hour until an Indian woman of similar build walked up, just in case Korrapati's alibi needed backup from security camera footage. Cameras were everywhere, after all.

"Uh, thanks," Korrapati said.

"Wong, you're not here either."

He put on his little smile. "Where am I?"

"You're at work, of course. Server logs show you were running simulations from your workstation all day. We really should give you a raise."

"Yes, you should."

I chuckled. "I don't actually have the authority to give you one."

"This is disappointing," he said.

"On the bright side, you have a good alibi." I paused. "You know that word, right?"

"Of course. American television."

"Good."

"You have another problem."

I'd love to have just one problem. "What?"

"*Lao-bahn.*"

"Don't worry. I'll talk to the boss."

I meant to arrive nice and early at work Monday morning, maybe even catch Evelyn before she started her grueling daily meeting schedule.

Sadly, that was not to be—Sunday night, I noticed a trickle of blood on Octavius's snout. Cue all kinds of panic and a very expensive visit to an animal hospital that treated exotic pets without asking too many questions. Cash only. They could not find a precise cause of the bleeding, but we ruled out the scary stuff like pulmonary edema. That was some comfort, though it cost me my Sunday evening respite. Summer, too, did not enjoy this period; apparently after I ran out with Octavius tucked under my arm, his siblings feared the worst and took a long time to calm down. I was up another hour after getting home, because I insisted she go to bed while I cleaned up. She had a job, too, and she didn't do well on too little sleep.

I overslept by almost an hour before I dragged myself in to work. So I came late, post–board meeting, to deliver the unofficial good news about our dragon-building competitor. This brought me face-to-face with Roger, the assistant we'd all insisted Evelyn hire when we were pulling crazy hours working on the DOD contract. She was plenty effective with her ever-present tablet but she was also gone so often that I could never find her.

Enter Roger. I don't know where Evelyn found him—rumor had it, he grew up in Hong Kong—but he brought an almost insane level of efficiency to her office. Suddenly you could get face time with Evelyn if you really needed it and if her day wasn't too crazy. The guy had her schedule memorized. He was always appearing at her shoulder to quietly tell her to go to the next thing.

Oh, and he was obnoxiously good-looking.

I mean next-level Korean soap opera star good-looking.

I approached his desk outside Evelyn's office, which appeared to be dark. She had motion-detecting light switches, so that meant either that she hadn't returned or was sitting very, very still.

"*Nihao*, Roger."

"Good morning," he said, with a perfectly polite smile. Any indication that I'd attempted to speak Mandarin to him was soundly ignored per usual. For all I knew, he didn't speak it, though I was hell-bent on finding out.

"Evelyn's not back yet?"

"She'll be here in two minutes." He didn't have to check his watch or computer or anything. He just *knew*.

"All right."

"Would you like to wait in her office?"

With the carnivorous plants was the unspoken end of that sentence.

"Sure, I guess. Thanks." I walked past him, for some reason acutely aware of the fact that there was not a single wrinkle on his tight-fitting slacks and silky dress shirt. Meanwhile, I'd apparently worn my old shoes that were gradually separating from their treads, toe-first. I'd been in a hurry and couldn't find my good ones. If I didn't consciously lift my toes, each step was announced with a *ker-clop*. Mercifully, I made it to a chair by Evelyn's desk without tripping over my own feet.

And then there were the carnivorous plants to contend with.

I took inventory of the Venus flytraps, pitcher plants, and other green monstrosities while I waited. The cobra plant was doing well. To my surprise, there were a couple of new additions: a waterwheel plant growing in a glass tank and a lovely little cape sundew on the sill. This last one was hard to get; they were native to South Africa but classified as invasive species in most of North America and Europe.

The clicking of heels announced Evelyn's approach. I heard a murmured conversation outside, and then she bustled in. "Noah Parker."

"Morning, boss."

"You are looking comfortable."

"Yeah, the Asian Ryan Gosling let me in. I hope it's all right."

"Ryan Gosling?"

"Good-looking actor."

"I wish you'd stop saying that!" she whispered, a little too fiercely.

"Do you really not watch movies?"

"I am busy," she said, with a touch of primness.

"I can see that." I gestured to the new carnivorous plants. "Is that actually a cape sundew?"

"It is."

"I'm impressed," I said.

"Why?" She shrugged. "They practically grow themselves."

"Yeah, sure, if you can get them. They're illegal, you know."

"It's a grafted hybrid."

"Hmm." If that was true, then the plant was classified as a genetically modified plant, putting it neatly outside the import bans. *Not to mention, bonus points for doing it with science.* "Congratulations."

"I feel like I should be the one saying congratulations."

I did my best to put on a neutral face. "I don't know what you mean."

"Do you know the first thing I did when I took over as CEO, after the whole canine debacle?" She activated her keyboard and brought up a new projection monitor in the air between us.

"Yeah." I pointed to her cobra lilies, which had almost doubled in size. "You got those."

"That was the second thing I did. The first thing was to improve security at the Farm." She beckoned me to her side of the desk.

Uh-oh. I moved around and got a look at the screen. Yep, she had me on video at the control panel of the holding pens, flipping switches. *Whoops.* The last thing I'd been looking for was a camera.

"Care to explain?" She asked.

"It was only me."

She brought up another video from a camera that must have been pointing down the row of cages. Wong and I were clearly visible, carrying a cage with an aerial dragon out of frame. "You were saying?"

"I hadn't finished. I was saying, it was only me and Wong."

In response, she brought up yet a third video with Korrapati and the truck.

I grimaced. *This is bad.* "And Korrapati."

"I'm trying to remember when I gave you permission to remove dragons from their holding pens. Or even to go to the desert facility in the first place."

"That's because you didn't give me permission." There was no point in denying any of it now, not when she had me on video. I watched myself jog back to the control panel and flip another switch. *Man, I look sweaty.* It reminded me of an oddity I'd nearly forgotten. "Funny thing, though. That control panel had a security keypad on it. I didn't know the code, but it decided to unlock itself right when I needed it to."

Evelyn put on her stony face, but the corner of her mouth flickered upward. "Strange."

"It's almost like we had help from an unseen benefactor with security override permissions, which I certainly don't have."

She leaned forward, her eyes sparkling. "So, where is it?"

"What?"

"The Codex prototype."

"Oh, that. It was destroyed."

She frowned. "That's unfortunate."

I paused, because now I was going off script from what I'd planned. "I didn't really have a choice. Greaves showed up out of nowhere."

She frowned. "He caught you?"

"Kind of, yeah. I wasn't expecting anyone to show up on a Saturday."

She sighed. "Robert works on Saturdays."

"Ah." *That information would've been useful a week ago*, I didn't say. This was the disadvantage of keeping Evelyn out of the loop so that her hands were clean. She knew things I didn't.

"So what happened? Did he talk to you?" She asked this rather casually, but I sensed she was keen to hear the answer.

"A little bit."

"What did he say, exactly?"

"The usual Robert Greaves crap. I wasn't really listening." That was only half a lie. It *had* been crap. I was pretty sure of that.

"He is not trustworthy."

"You don't have to tell me that. But he's out of the game, for now at least."

"I suppose that's true." Her brow furrowed with concern. "Was everyone all right?"

"The humans were." I didn't tell her the rest. If she had security footage and could count, she already knew.

"That is what matters," she said.

"Yeah." I looked away from her, trying unsuccessfully not to think about the dragons. "I should get back to work."

She put her hand on my arm. "You did well, Noah Parker."

"Thanks."

I left her office, not quite on the cloud nine I'd been expecting. I passed Roger on my way out.

"Thank you for coming by," he said.

"*Zài jiàn,*" I said. *See you later.*

Still nothing.

"Worth a shot," I muttered to myself, and headed back down to design.

CHAPTER FORTY-THREE
The Ghost

Tracking down a ghost is not as easy as you'd think. Especially a capricious spirit that tends to show up on a whim. That night while we were trying to get Octavius to eat a carrot, I'd told Summer about my meeting with Evelyn and its many surprises. We still couldn't wrap our heads around how it had played out.

"Why didn't you give her the Codex?" she asked.

"It didn't feel like the right thing to do. Besides, it doesn't belong to Build-A-Dragon. Ow!" I jerked my hand back. Octavius had lost his patience and nipped my forefinger. *Someone is getting his spirits back.*

"Is this really about property rights, or do you just want to see Simon Redwood again?" Summer grabbed my dragonet by the snout and jammed a carrot in his mouth. "*Chew.*" They stared at each other for a few seconds, and then my dragonet complied.

I grinned at her. "Can't it be both?"

Unfortunately, since Simon Redwood was legally

deceased, there was no way to reach the guy electronically. Not that I'd had any luck with that before, but recent crackdowns by technology companies ensured that all of someone's verified accounts got deactivated when they passed away. He might not even be in the country. Still, I had to try. My best idea was to return to the place I last saw him and put the word out. So Summer and I strapped on our hiking boots, herded the dragonets into the Jeep's backseat, and drove out to Big Mesa. This was the name of a geocache in a huge natural area, a bit farther out into the desert than our usual jaunts. I couldn't say why, but I had a feeling it was somehow closer to what we needed.

We brought the dragonets, which were key to my plan. While Summer drove, and after the required breakfast burritos had been consumed, I gave them the briefing.

"Listen up, guys."

They were sprawled in a heap in the backseat, many of them still licking crumbs from their lips. Except for one, who was pretending to doze.

"Marcus Aurelius," I said firmly.

He perked up and blinked as if waking from a deep slumber.

"We're going out to the desert. I'm going to let you fly free for a while. I want you to look for other dragons, and tell them that I need to talk to Simon Redwood."

"This is crazy," Summer said.

"Ignore her," I told the dragons. "Find the crazy white-haired guy, okay? Or find one of his dragons. It's important."

The dragons chirped—or in one case, snored—what

sounded like agreement. Only Octavius was quiet. *He's going to be a problem.*

Summer got us to the lot, drove basically over the culvert, and parked in something that might have been a parking space, or might not. More importantly, it put us into a narrow band of shade cast by one of the rock formations.

I climbed out and called Octavius to me. Once he'd hopped onto my shoulder, I threw the door open more widely and pushed my seat forward. "Out you go!"

The dragons took off in a flurry of wings. I held Octavius fast to my shoulder. "Not you, buddy."

He fought me, straining against my hold. When that didn't work, he dug his claws into my shoulder.

"Ow!" I swatted him. "Stop that. You're not healed enough yet to fly."

He stopped struggling and resorted to pouting instead. It was the equivalent of having a large wet rag drooping on my shoulder.

"Perk up, little buddy. It's for your own good."

He turned his head deliberately so he wouldn't have to look at me, and acted as if he hadn't heard.

"Would it make you feel better if I told you I still had half of my burrito?"

His hearing miraculously returned, and he snatched the burrito from me almost before I got it unwrapped.

Summer was tracking the dragons on a tablet; we'd kept their GPS units just in case there was a problem. This was the desert, after all, and they weren't necessarily at the top of the food chain.

"How are they doing?" I asked.

"Well, they're spread out. Nero and Otho went south. Hadrian and Titus are flying northeast. Benjy is heading due west; he's the farthest out. And Marcus Aurelius is . . ." Her brows furrowed. She leaned over the side of the Jeep. "Still in the backseat."

"Of course he is." I threw up my hands. Sometimes his stubbornness was endearing, and other times it irritated me. "Why don't *you* try managing him?"

"Marcus Aurelius?" Summer called sweetly.

The dragonet lifted his little head over the edge of the door. Summer put out her hand and he flopped into it. He *did* look a little drowsy; maybe the sleep wasn't an act. I made a mental note to review my security camera feeds from the condo. If he was this tired, he must've been up late.

"We need a big, strong, clever dragon to fly east of here," Summer purred. "None of the other dragons were brave enough. Do you think you could?"

It was such an obvious play to his ego. There was no way he'd go for it. He marched to the beat of his own drummer, but he was no fool. None of them were.

I'd no sooner had that thought when Marcus Aurelius puffed up his chest, chirped, and took off across the rocky landscape. Life just wasn't fair, sometimes.

"See? It's not so hard," Summer said.

I shaded my eyes to follow his progress. "He's flying west."

"Crap. Marcus Aurelius!" She waved at him and then pointed. "That way, please."

The dragonet backpedaled and took off in the opposite direction, chirping contentedly. Only Marcus Aurelius—or maybe Octavius in his younger days—could do so much wrong and look happy about it.

Summer sat down against her Jeep on the shady side, and I slid down next to her to help watch the tablet. The dragonets had scattered—enjoying freedom not only from me, but from their watchful and injured older brother—and they were covering lots of ground.

Summer sighed. "It's hot."

"Must be that global warming you kept ranting about when we were in college," I said.

"Global warming is real, Noah."

I knew it was, but I also enjoyed getting a rise out of her. "Climate fluctuates over time. Isn't global warming just a scam that the progressives use to stunt corporate growth?"

She nudged me with her shoulder. "Stop trying to rile me up."

I smiled and nudged her back. "Hey, I'm just trying to pass the time."

"Oh, are you bored? Here's something we can talk about."

I laughed, because I knew that tone. "Uh-oh."

"So, now that you've met my dad, and I've met your mom, what's next?"

Yikes. Caught totally unprepared, I went with humor to buy myself a moment. "I say we start having kids. I'm thinking, like, five."

"That isn't what I meant."

"Well, we can't do that yet anyway, because my mom hated you."

She laughed. "That's just mean. But I know it's also a lie."

I sighed overdramatically. "Yeah, she loved you. And bonus, now you know what my mom is like."

"You're too hard on her. She's a sweet lady."

"She's mostly harmless, I'll give her that."

"Anyone who raised you and Connor while keeping their sanity deserves a Nobel prize."

I chuckled. "Fair enough."

"Against all odds, my dad finds you tolerable."

"Good enough for his little girl?" I asked.

"Oh, hell no. Nobody's going to hit that bar because it's impossible. But he hasn't ordered me not to see you."

"Well, that's . . . good," I finished lamely.

"And now we come back to my original question."

"What do you want to be next?" I asked her.

"I need to know that this is real."

"I know it seems rather haphazard on my side, and my life has been a little complicated recently."

"A *little*?"

"Okay, *a lot* complicated." I'd been stalling for time, but now that I had to answer, it was easy. I didn't have to think about it. "What's next is, I'm in love with you. If it wasn't clear, I'll have to double my efforts."

She watched me silently for a moment. "Don't you mean *redouble* your efforts?"

Oh my God. "Are you really attacking my grammar right now?"

She giggled. I scowled at her.

She squeezed my hand and said, "I'm in love with you, too."

She leaned closer to me and I kissed her. That's when Octavius chirped from his perch on the Jeep.

Every damn time. I forced myself to pull away from her and glared at him. "What?"

He was staring at the horizon. I followed his gaze and saw two dragons were returning. "Nero and Otho are coming back."

Summer looked at the tablet. "Benjy's heading this way, too."

"Bring them all back."

She used the tablet to activate the beacon, which sent a ping to the GPS units via satellite that told the dragons to return. We watched the remaining dots on the map slow in their trajectories and start heading this way. Even Marcus Aurelius, who'd decided to do as he was told for once. As the dragonets returned, I corralled them all in the back of the Jeep. If I was right about this, we didn't want a bunch of little dragons flying around unsupervised.

"Look," Summer said.

A dusky-colored flying *thing* had appeared on the horizon to the southwest, sweeping across the tops of the dunes. It was still far away, but approaching fast. And too large to be a bird of prey. I knew it from the coloring and the way it flew, somehow graceful and efficient at once.

"Is that—" Summer started to ask.

"A Condor," I said. It came out a whisper, as if some part of me feared that saying it out loud would make the thing disappear. This was one of the flying dragons I'd designed to replace the Pterodactyl. I'd gone well outside the points system to the displeasure of Robert Greaves, who canceled the design. Thus there were only a handful of these dragons in the world, and here was one. It glided in a wide circle around us and overhead, looking down. Shortly after hatching, my Condors flew better than any dragon ever printed in our lab.

This one seemed to be struggling to maintain altitude. It flapped more than it should, its entire body quivering with the effort. Still an impressive animal, but slowly succumbing to the genetic fate I'd given it all those months ago.

"It doesn't look too good," Summer said.

"That's my fault." This was the fate of any animal with BICD2 disease that couldn't get gene therapy. It would happen to the surviving field trial dragons we'd brought back to the Farm, too. Dr. Sato told me that their muscle biopsy specimens had all shown the characteristic signs. He'd gotten in touch with the clinical laboratories that did their testing, and we expected their variant classifications to change pretty soon. Connor was ecstatic when I told him the news. In the next breath, he asked me how soon I could do the same for some other patients. We were building a bunch of new prototypes, not just for the military but also for the rapidly growing Chinese market. It wasn't hard to slip more of those mutations in.

Now, as the Condor approached us and I felt the weight of its gaze, I experienced a pang of something. Guilt, maybe. There was too much knowledge in those eyes. *I wonder if it understands what I did, and why.*

I forced myself not to look away and hoped it understood.

If it recognized me, it made no sign, but it broke off its circle and flew back to the southeast. The little dragonets watched it with starry-eyed gazes, like people encountering a celebrity on the street. I knew exactly how they felt.

It was not long—maybe a minute, maybe two, before more dragons came. These were ground-based predators, a Guardian and a K-10. They blended well with the landscape but their shadows made them a bit easier to track. They came fast, and even though the rational part of my brain knew that we expected dragons like this, the primal survival instincts made me want to jump into our vehicle and lock the doors.

"Noah . . ." Summer said, her voice rising.

"It's fine." My voice shook a little. She heard it, and squeezed my hand tight.

The two dragons slowed as they approached us. They prowled close, tongues flicking in and out, and then skirted around us. The K-10 stopped ten feet away and stared at us. We stared back. The Guardian leaped onto the Jeep so it could look inside. This brought a cacophony of alarmed flapping and hissing from the dragonets. None of this seemed to perturb the Guardian, which snorted and leaped back to the ground. It rejoined the K-10 and both of them bounded off into the brush. Summer and I each let out a long breath.

Then we heard something new: a low rumble like the sound of a distant lawn mower, but somehow deeper in tone. A cloud of dust rose southeast of us and the rumble grew to a roar. Over the dust cloud, a dark figure resolved itself against the blue sky.

It was a man on a jetpack.

"No frickin' *way*!" I shouted, because otherwise Summer wouldn't have been able to hear.

The pilot wore aviator's glasses and a breathing apparatus that obscured most of his face, but the mop of chalk-white hair was unmistakable.

"Is he serious?" Summer shouted.

"I told you, he likes to make an entrance!"

The jetpack itself was a metal frame strapped to Redwood's back, with two L-shaped arms that stretched out near his hands. Those must be the controls. I watched him fiddle with right-side control, and the roar of the engine faded to a loud purr. He lurched downward, landing heavily on the far side of the parking area. The angle gave me a quick glance at the jetpack; it had three tarnished metal tubes mounted vertically on a battered steel chamber. Forget futuristic, this looked like a low-budget steampunk costume from Comic-Con. Still, I couldn't argue with the results. Like a lot of Redwood's inventions, it didn't look like much but still managed to work as promised.

"I hear you want to talk to me," Redwood said, without preamble.

"You got here quick," I said. "I'm impressed."

Redwood waved me off. "I was in the neighborhood. Spend a lot of time in the desert these days."

"Yeah, me too. And I have good news." I took a breath and smiled. "Robert Greaves is out of the dragon-printing business."

"Really? Good for you, kid."

Summer nudged me. "He keeps calling you *kid*."

"I know, I'm right here," I whispered back. I shouldn't blame her for being a little starstruck; I'd had more time to adjust to being in the presence of a legend than she had. I lifted my satchel out of the Jeep and handed it to him. "I believe this belongs to you."

"Thanks." Redwood threw the satchel over his shoulder and gave us a big, toothy grin. His teeth were perfectly white. "I'll try to hang onto it this time."

"Greaves saw it happen."

"Did he?" Redwood laughed. "Good."

"He told me some things." My mouth felt dry, but I pressed on. "He said I didn't know what I was doing."

"Of course he said that. It's what he does. Back in the day, he got me thinking that I was the problem. That the dragons would be better off with him in charge."

"He gaslighted you," Summer said.

"Gaslights would be a thing of the past if more people bought into my solar LED idea."

What a classically Redwood thing to say. "It worried me a little, that's all. That he was trying to look out for me or something."

"The only person old Rob looks out for is himself. Trust me on that."

I had to believe him. He knew Greaves better than anyone. And believing him meant letting go of the doubts that he'd started to sow in my mind. "Do you think Evelyn is going to do right by the dragons?"

He gave me a side look. "You're asking me?"

"Well, yeah. It's your company."

"Dead people don't have companies. Besides, I'm not the reigning expert on Evelyn Chang."

I shrugged. "Well, who is?"

"Someone who studied under her. Spent time problem-solving with her and learning how she operates,"

Redwood said. "Someone who helped remove her predecessor so that she landed in the big chair."

"I don't know anyone like that."

Summer giggled. "He means you, dummy."

"I don't— I can't . . ." I stammered.

"Everything he said is true. You've worked with her as long as anyone. More importantly, she trusts you."

"She can see it, kid, so why can't you?" Redwood asked.

"I wanted to be sure."

"You've got to trust your instincts." He pressed a switch on his controls and the jetpack's engine rumbled to life.

"Thank you!" I shouted.

"I'll tell you one last thing." He pointed at Summer with his free hand. "Whatever you do, don't let that one get away."

The jetpack revved up, dispelling a swirl of dust around his feet. Then he was climbing steadily ten, twenty, thirty feet in the air. He pivoted in place until he was facing southeast, banked forward, and flew away over the ridge to the southeast. He was still visible at a quarter mile away when two winged dragons joined him in the sky, forming up around him like a fighter escort. They were Condors as well, but too far away for me to tell if they included the one that came up close.

"Not bad for an old guy," Summer said.

"He's got style, doesn't he?"

She climbed into her Jeep. "Let's go get some lunch. I'm thinking Mexican."

"Again?"

"Your mom's got me hooked on the mahi-mahi tacos."

I climbed into the passenger seat. By the time Summer

fired up the Jeep's engine, Simon Redwood was only a speck in the distance. He could have been a bird. Or even a dragon.

Author's Note

Thank you for reading my book! This is the second installment of a series that I began working on almost a decade ago. If you liked it, I hope you'll leave a review somewhere, or maybe tell a friend about it. Word of mouth matters! I appreciate the help.

To learn more about me and hear about my upcoming books, please join my mailing list at http://dankoboldt. com/subscribe. Sign up and you'll get at least one free story to read. You can also find me on Twitter at @DanKoboldt.

As usual, many people helped shape this book and bring it to the world. I'm grateful to Mike Mammay and Tim Akers for insightful critiques. I should also thank my agent, Paul Stevens, for convincing Baen Books to let me write it on spec. Speaking of Baen Books, I'm grateful to the entire team, especially Toni Weisskopf, Jim Minz, Corinda Carfora, Sean Korsgaard, and David Afsharirad. Thanks also to Steven Roman for outstanding copy edits, and to Dave Seeley for the incredible cover.

Finally, I'm grateful to my family for continuing to believe that there should be dragons in the world.

LOOKING FOR A NEW SPACE OPERA ADVENTURE?

Praise for
CATHERINE ASARO

"Asaro plants herself firmly into that grand SF tradition of future history franchises favored by luminaries like Heinlein, Asimov, Herbert, Anderson, Dickson, Niven, Cherryh, and Baxter . . . They don't write 'em like that anymore! Except Asaro does, with . . . up-to-the-minute savvy!"
—*Locus*

"[Bhaajan], who starts out keeping an emotional distance from the people in the Undercity soon grows to think of them as her community once more. Asaro . . . returns to the Skolian empire's early history to tell Bhajaan's story."
—*Booklist*

"Asaro delivers a tale rich with the embedded history of her world and bright with technical marvels. Her characters are engaging and intriguing, and there is even a bit of romance. What really touched my heart was Bhaaj's interaction with the children of the aqueducts. I spent the last fifty pages of the book sniffling into a tissue."
—*SFcrowsnest*

"I'm hooked, both on her writing and her Skolian universe. This book had everything I wanted: strong characters, a new and unique world, and a plot that isn't as simple as it first appears." —*TerryTalk*

About Catherine Asaro's Skolian Empire saga:
"Entertaining mix of hard SF and romance."
—*Publishers Weekly*

"Asaro's Skolian saga is now nearly as long, and in many ways as compelling, as *Dune*, if not more so, featuring a multitude of stronger female characters." —*Booklist*

"Rapid pacing and gripping suspense."
—*Publishers Weekly*